The

MW00327204

Will O'Brien was a successful advertising executive who retired at the age of fifty-nine with no financial worries. He was looking forward to a retirement filled with fishing, family adventures, and community service in his neighborhood on the Southside of Chicago. He and his wife, Deirdre, had a loving and supportive relationship. They were surrounded by family and good friends and had interests that made their lives fulfilling, satisfying, and happy.

One fateful evening, after a tempting encounter with a beautiful young woman, Will has an accident that propels his future into unknown and potentially disastrous territory. A mother of three is killed and others are injured. Will suffers a concussion and a broken wrist. Crushing civil suits are filed. Criminal actions are contemplated. Everything Will and Deirdre had worked and longed for is suddenly in jeopardy and in a whirlwind of fear, doubt and unknown consequences. Deirdre, especially, is devastated and withdraws into herself and harbors great anger and resentment.

An unexpected phone call and an unusual meeting with a mysterious person give Will hope that he can leave all of his troubles behind and resurrect his nearly perfect life.

The story, as told by Will and his son Owen, takes the reader on the greatest odyssey any human has ever experienced. It is filled with mystery, awe-inspiring adventures, psychological twists, cutting-edge science, and reshaped reality. The ending is unexpected but emotionally and intellectually satisfying.

LEAVE IT ALL BEHIND

Michael J. Sise

This is a work of fiction. All characters and incidents are products of the author's imagination and any resemblance to actual people or events is coincidental or fictionalized.

Copyright 2020, Michael J. Sise, all rights reserved. This work may not be reproduced or copied in any form without the author's written consent. Short passages may be reproduced by those writing reviews or commentaries about this novel. The author may be contacted at mjsise@cs.com.

Printed by Kindle Direct Publishing, an affiliate of Amazon. Order additional copies on Amazon.com.

ISBN: 978-0-578-78939-2

V4

"There are more things in heaven and earth, Horatio, than are dreamt of in your philosophy."

Hamlet, Act 1, Scene 5

"We believe in one God, the Father Almighty, maker of heaven and earth, and all that is, seen and unseen."

Nicene Creed

"Then what to do?
Stay or go through?
Sustaining Matter,
reality shatter, tatter,
or chasing the Mad Hatter?

Will O'Brien

Chapter 1

The Hard Part

My name is Owen O'Brien, and this story is about my father, Will O'Brien. Being an only child, I was very close to my mother and father and care deeply about them. It is going to be hard for me to relive some parts of this story, but I want my family and friends to know the whole truth about what happened to my father and how it affected my family, especially my mother.

Since I can no longer hurt my mother's feelings, I'm free to tell this story about my father honestly and without reservations. My mother, Deirdre, had a stroke about a year ago. She didn't respond well to therapy and rapidly declined.

The tension, pressure and worry that she experienced after my father's accident and disappearance made her so sick and weak that it was inevitable that her health would be affected. She was constantly upset and nervous and could hardly eat. She had been showing signs of dementia before Dad's disappearance, but, afterward, she couldn't take care of herself and needed full-time help. She is in a better place, now, and she isn't suffering anymore.

Even though she had many challenging personality traits, she was, in her own way, a good and loving mother and grandmother. My daughter, Molly, especially loved her. She enjoyed talking and playing with her and wanted to visit her frequently. They were good pals and enjoyed each other's company, most of the time. Sometimes Mom got a little too critical and bossy, and Molly would rebel. Usually, though, they were very compatible.

My mother had a wonderful dollhouse that her grandfather had made for her when she was about five years old. He was a master carpenter, and it was a work of art. It was a Craftsman-style house that stood almost three feet high. The low-pitched gable roof was covered with small cedar shakes that her father individually shaped and affixed with tiny brass nails. It had eight rooms on two levels connected by a beautiful winding staircase. The exterior was light blue with ornately trimmed windows and doors. It even had a yard with bushes and flowers. When Mom and Dad would baby-sit for Molly and my son, Charlie, Mom and Molly would play with the dollhouse for hours rearranging the furniture and making up stories about the imaginary people who lived in it.

Molly and my mother would make at least one trip each year to see the famous Thorne Rooms at the Chicago Art Institute. There are sixty-eight miniature rooms created by Narcissa Thorne, the wife of an heir to the Montgomery Ward fortune. Each room is filled with perfect replicas of every type of furniture, furnishings and interior architectural features existing at the time they were created. If you stare at the rooms long enough, you can imagine yourself living in them. They are nearly perfect virtual realities.

After each trip to see the Thorne Rooms, Mom and Molly would visit the gift shop at the museum and buy something for Mom's dollhouse. Eventually, they had so many items for the house that they could fill it two or three times over. They would hide in an upstairs bedroom where it was kept and play with the dollhouse and furniture for hours.

Once, when Mom and Molly were on one of their trips to the Art Institute, I caught my father and my son playing with this unique heirloom. They were mostly using it as a garage for Charlie's Hot Wheels, but they had some of the furniture nicely arranged on the upper floor of the house. My father, being somewhat of a Renaissance man, was interested in art, architecture and design and had a talent for decorating. When his firm leased new office space, he was the firm's liaison with the architects and decorators. Because of that, he appreciated how special Mom's dollhouse was and couldn't resist the chance to show it to Charlie.

My father was an extraordinary man in many ways and was successful in business and his personal life. We were very close when I was a child and spent many hours together playing and reading stories and practicing sports, especially baseball. I idealized him as a child and imitated him in many ways. When I was a little boy, I wanted to dress like him. He always wore a blue blazer and deck shoes, so I bugged mom to buy me a blue blazer and deck shoes, too. I wore them for a couple of years every time we went out together to eat or to church.

Many people have said that I am a clone of my father. I'm two inches taller than he is, but we look and talk alike. After my voice changed, when I was about fifteen, many people thought I was my Dad when I answered the phone. Likewise, many of my friends thought my Dad was me when they would call. He would talk like me and string them along for a while trying to find out what we were up to. Eventually, they all caught on and didn't let him fool them anymore. He did it in good fun, though, and never embarrassed me or used it against me. My friends all liked my father and enjoyed talking to him when they came over to my house. He would kid with them and put them at ease. My mom, on the other hand, scared them, and they were afraid to talk to her for too long. She would ask them probing questions and made them feel uneasy. She would have made a great prosecuting attorney. She was a great cross-examiner.

Like all of us, however, Dad had weaknesses and one led to a bad decision that turned his life upside down. I've thought about it a lot, and I have some theories about why it happened. There is a job interview cliché where the interviewee is asked what his or her strengths and weaknesses are. The clever answer to the questions about what the interviewee's weaknesses are goes something like this: "I'm too caring and empathetic, and people take advantage of me." That was true of my father. He was too caring and empathetic, and people did take advantage of him. His first inclination was to trust people and try to help them. He was taken advantage of many times. He didn't care, though, and it always worked to his advantage in the long run. His clients knew that they could trust him because he had their welfare at heart.

In a word, Dad was an "idealist" and longed for peace, cooperation, justice, fairness and unselfishness. He was liberal, progressive, open-minded and, above all, kind. He lived by these underlying values. For the most part, these principles made him very successful and respected. They also, on occasion, made him vulnerable to trouble.

I majored in psychology as an undergraduate at Notre Dame before I obtained my MBA from Northwestern, so I consider myself an amateur psychologist. I know that's dangerous and drives my wife and some of my friends crazy when I start making psychological analyses of people. However, my understanding of psychology has probably been more helpful to me in business than my MBA. You see, I'm a headhunter, and my success depends upon finding the right person for my clients.

For certain jobs, one of the characteristics that I look for is risk taking. Some jobs are best suited for risk takers, but, for others, a little risk aversion is a better fit.

I spend many hours on the phone and in my office talking to my prospects and my clients. I want to know their lifestyle, hobbies and likes and dislikes. The more I know about my prospects the better I can understand what they would be good at and how they might fit into certain job situations. I also need to understand my clients. Every company has a distinct culture, especially family owned businesses, that my prospects need to fit into. My clients don't call me back if I send them the wrong person. My whole livelihood depends upon repeat business and personal recommendations, so sending the wrong person to a company can hurt me badly.

Since many of the companies I work for require their people to relocate frequently, I have to make sure that the people I find for them can handle that. Some people have no qualms about moving, especially if their spouse is on-board with that type of life. But I have to be careful. Some people that are that flexible are also gamblers, drinkers and carousers. Those types can be more trouble than they are worth to a company. I need to weed them out or my reputation with a client would soon be ruined.

My father was, in my opinion, a mid-spectrum risk taker, which, together with his high values, contributed to his many successes. We had many conversations about this concept when I first started my business, and he understood and appreciated my insights. Since he had interviewed and hired many people in his career, he had valuable experience that also helped me.

Another thing I look for in my job prospects is what is known as "emotional intelligence." This is a controversial concept in psychiatry, but I have found it to be helpful in what I do. To me, emotional intelligence is the ability of an individual to recognize his or her own emotions and those of others and then use that information to guide thinking and behavior. People with emotional intelligence are also able to manage and adjust their emotions to adapt to circumstances and achieve goals. In a word, they have "empathy" for others and know how to manipulate others to accomplish goals or job objectives.

The word "manipulate" has bad connotations, but it's not always negative. People sometimes need to be manipulated to accomplish good things for themselves and others. Everyone is self-centered, but people with emotional intelligence are able to go beyond themselves and make others feel as though they have been understood and are winning. Some negotiators with this skill call it the "Win-Win" method. It's based upon the idea that the quickest way to an agreement of the minds is to make everyone feel as though they've won something and acheived their goal, or at least something significant.

People with emotional intelligence are usually very successful in large organizations. They are trusted and likable. Everyone feels that they have a connection with them and that they are special friends. Many entrepreneurs, however, are just the opposite. They are egotistical and narcissistic and don't care about others. They are driven to succeed and only care about achieving their goals at any cost.

I saw my father exhibit emotional intelligence many times with my mother. He was able to meet her emotional needs and keep her from imploding under stress and keep her from making bad decisions. I also overheard him many times on the phone talking to clients. He never lost his temper and was always looking for common ground. He knew when to push and be tough and when to compromise. I learned a lot from him.

Getting back to my story, I just recently discovered why Dad disappeared in August of last year and what probably happened to him. Since I think it will be good for my family and his friends to know the truth, I'm going to try to piece it all together from what I learned from my mother, Detective Robinson of the

Chicago Police Department, Dad's attorneys and one other person who spent some time with my father.

I also have a lengthy recording that my father made that will allow me to tell most of his story in his own words. He called it his "journal."

First, however, I need to give you a little background. This is the most painful part, and my heart aches when I realize how much mental suffering Mom and Dad must have experienced and how Dad must have worried about my mother and me.

The events that led to his troubles started with what seemed to be the fulfillment of the American Dream -- my father retired at the age of fifty-nine with a large net worth, mostly in real estate and solid financial assets that assured him and my mother of a comfortable retirement for the rest of their lives. He had been a senior vice president at one of the most successful advertising firms in Chicago, Bennington Advertising.

He had worked nearly twenty years for Bennington and then accepted a generous retirement package when Bennington merged with BBZ Marketing of New York. He could have stayed on with BBZ, but he would have had to move to New York, which would have killed my mother. She wouldn't have been able to handle such a move, and, besides, Dad had been thinking about retiring for some time.

Most people at his level don't want to retire. They usually hang on as long as they can and then get forced out and feel bitter for the rest of their lives. They usually take great pleasure in the power and prestige of their jobs. They can't imagine not going to work and staying active and engaged. Not my father, however. He had many interests and looked forward to escaping the rat race of business.

Since he was twenty-three, he had been taking an early train from the Beverly neighborhood on the Southwest Side of Chicago to the Loop where he had various jobs in marketing, eventually settling in at Bennington. He was a hard worker and would frequently work late and go into the office on many Saturday mornings, when necessary. His work schedule and ethic were hard on my mother and me, but he was a good provider and succeeded, for the most part, in giving us a normal, happy and full life.

Because advertising is a demanding and competitive job, he would be on the phone with clients in the evening and weekends. This, of course, caused many contentious moments with my mother who was needy and self-centered, but he was too conscientious and responsible to let a client down. This, and his exceptional creativity and great memory, made him successful. He received many industry awards and always handled his firm's biggest clients. He was, accordingly, well compensated, especially in his final years.

My father was also very progressive and egalitarian. He loved peace and harmony and wanted everyone to get along. Being concerned about civil rights and equality, he convinced the managing partners at Bennington to strive for diversity and fairness with its employees. He insisted on diversity training for all the managers and even wrote the first diversity-training course for the firm in conjunction with Operation Push and the NAACP in the mid-eighties.

Mainly because of my father, Bennington was one of the first large employers in the City of Chicago to take these steps. For that, he was praised and honored by several civil rights and feminist groups. I remember many conversations about this topic at our dinner table, and I greatly admired him and tried to emulate his example when I became active in business and then started my own company.

Outside of his work, my father's greatest passion was fishing. He and I had fished all over Canada,

Minnesota, Wisconsin, and on most of the Great Lakes. For many years, he had a pilot's license, and we would fly all over the Midwest on fishing trips in his Piper Cub. Dad learned to fly in the Air National Guard and was an excellent pilot. He had even flown a few jet aircraft in the early '80s.

In the winter, we made several trips to Florida to fish for Marlin and other game fish in the Gulf and the Ten Thousand Islands around Everglades City.

When I was twelve we went to Ireland with my mother and fished for salmon on the River Corrib in Galway and for sea trout in Connemara while my mother stayed in Galway and shopped. That fishing trip is one of the happiest childhood memories I have.

When I married and had a family, I couldn't go on trips with Dad, anymore, but we attended many fishing and boat shows in the Chicago area and dreamed of future trips. Because of his heavy work schedule, he eventually managed only one good fishing trip a year. Retirement, however, was going to give him the opportunity to indulge this hobby as much as my mother would allow.

My praise for him might be getting a little bit tedious, but you will see why I feel it's important to dwell on all of this. It will explain, to a certain degree, what happened to Dad and why he acted as he did. Most of the things we do in life, and many of the things we focus on, are related and build upon a foundation that we construct day by day. We can trace many of our tendencies and endeavors to our past, to our families, and to what we have experienced in other ways.

So, continuing on, another good thing about him was that he was also a great volunteer. He had been president of the local civic association and served on several not-for-profit boards. After he retired, he volunteered to serve as one of the directors of the local Arts Center. As part of his commitment to the Arts

Center, he was determined to create a marketing program for them that would rival that of the Chicago Art Institute, which had, coincidentally, been one of his clients at Bennington.

Writing was his second favorite hobby. *Science Fiction Journal* had published four of his short stories. One was titled *The New Earth.* One was called *Robot Madness*, one was called *The Brain*, and the last one was called *A Better Way.* He would write on the train going to and from work. He had several notebooks full of plots and ideas for novels. He was always making notes and researching ideas, especially about space travel, artificial intelligence and all of the complications involved in living in outer space. He was a great writer and could dictate long memos and business letters on a small recorder that he always carried, even after he retired.

He would use the recorder to make notes about ideas and thoughts that he had for advertising campaigns and business arrangements. This was invaluable for his job and his fiction writing and made him very efficient. Lucky for us, his recorder was found and provided special insights into his fateful journey. But I'm getting ahead of myself and need to go back to where the story really begins.

As I said, Dad retired at fifty-nine and was happy and full of life and hope for a pleasant and interesting retirement. My mother, Deirdre, nee Walsh, on the other hand, was declining mentally. She became morose and was often on the verge of an emotional meltdown. She was mildly depressed and worried and fretted about everything. She was about as risk-averse as my father was a risk-taker. There's a famous quote from the great Irish poet, Yeats, that anyone familiar with Irish literature knows, and it applies perfectly to people like my mother: "Being Irish, he (she) had an abiding sense of tragedy, which sustained him (her) through temporary periods of joy." Coincidentally, Mom's name, Deirdre, is the name of a tragic Irish heroine, which was fitting for her.

My father, on the other hand, was naturally happy and able to keep our family on a positive track, adjusting to situations as they developed. Fortunately, Mom and Dad's main priorities were family, friends and their religion. These values gave them the stability and support they needed to overlook a less than perfect personal relationship. Additionally, they lived in a neighborhood that still valued stability, self-control and self-sacrifice. This, more than anything, kept them out of divorce court and protected them from many of the other problems that rip families apart.

As I think about it, Mom and Dad's personalities probably balanced each other out. My father's personality would probably have gotten him into trouble if it were not for my mother's conservative bent. She provided stability and discouraged any crazy ideas my father had. How he talked her into allowing him to buy the airplane has always been a mystery to me. Occasionally, he would just do things and endure my mother's ire until she cooled down. She always forgave him, though, and they had a tender and loving relationship until the last few years when she withdrew into herself. As I mentioned earlier, I always suspected that she had developed a mild dementia a few years before Dad's accident.

Things were good for about a year after Dad retired. Unfortunately, one mishap would turn his and my mother's lives upside down. After working as a volunteer at the Arts Center in the afternoon, my father started stopping at a nearby bar on Western Avenue, Brian's Tap, to have a beer and talk to friends and some of the employees of the Arts Center. He craved mental stimulation and had a great need to socialize and meet new people. Doing so helped him to enjoy life and be creative.

Brian's is one of about ten Irish bars and pubs along a strip of Western Avenue in our neighborhood, all on the west side of the street. All of the precincts on the east side of Western are dry (the only ones in Chicago) and alcohol can't be served. The strip is famous for its Friday and Saturday night pub crawl from 99th Street to 119th Street. If you're determined enough, some of the bars have a four o'clock license, and you can party until then. Many college students and young unmarried people from all over the city come to drink and socialize. I spent many happy nights, before I got married, in my favorite bar, The Kerry Man. I only made it to four o'clock a few times, and I always regretted it the next day.

After a few months of stopping in at Brian's on his way home, Dad began staying a little longer and started having more than one beer or glass of wine. He was naturally gregarious, and alcohol made him even more so. It made him happy and talkative. He drank too much at times but was never out of control and had good self-discipline. He never had another drink after he returned home, usually at a reasonable hour and in time for a late dinner with Mom.

My mother, of course, was not happy about this trend and nagged him about "overdoing it." However, as part of their understood personal compromises, she never pushed it and accepted that that was what Dad needed to be happy and accepting of their tepid relationship. Since she knew most of the people he met at the bar, she was not seriously worried about his fidelity. She was also an avid bridge player and spent at least two nights a week playing bridge with friends in the neighborhood. That gave her a good social outlet and took the pressure off my father.

One afternoon Dad was at Brian's talking to one of his friends, Neal McGhee. It was March 10, a date I dread and will never forget for the rest of my life.

Dad and Neal were sitting at the far end of the bar near the back door where they could talk more easily. All of the other stools were occupied. A man, the infamous Larry O'Doul, who you'll hear more about later, and two of his friends were on stools near the front door and were talking loudly and belligerently.

Neal was one of Dad's best friends, and was one of the most well known men in the neighborhood, at least in his age group. He had made the roster of the Twins as a pitcher when he was twenty-two, but he hurt his shoulder in spring training and had to quit. He returned to Chicago and became one of the best sixteen-inch softball pitchers in the City. Sixteen-inch softball is played without gloves and is unique to Chicago. Brian's sponsored one of his teams and almost everyone in the bar that day knew him.

He and Dad went fishing two or three times a year on a boat Neal kept in the Michigan City Harbor. They would fish for perch and steelheads and were always very successful. Perch are fantastic eating, and Dad was known for his fried perch dinners.

After talking for about twenty minutes, Neal had to leave to attend one of his grandkid's hockey games. That left the stool next to Dad empty. A very attractive young woman came in and looked for a place to sit at the bar. She was gorgeous and sexy. With stunning raven black hair, flawless alabaster skin and dark exotic eyes, she was breathtaking. She had a voluptuous figure that was clearly revealed by a plunging neckline on her black top. Her round, full hips were emphasized by tight black leggings. Her enticing smile revealed perfect white teeth. She was a knockout, and every man in the bar watched her as she passed by.

Seeing that the barstool next to Dad was available, she asked him if anyone was using it. He said it was available, so she sat down and soon struck up a conversation with him. She said she had just moved back to the neighborhood and was living with her mother in an apartment near the Metra tracks that run through the heart of the Beverly neighborhood.

Appearing friendly and polite, she asked Dad about himself. When she discovered that he was a retired advertising executive, she had a million questions for him. She told Dad that she wanted to go back to school and obtain a degree in marketing from a local school, St. Xavier University. (I found out later that this was true). She said she couldn't believe her good luck finding someone who could answer her questions and maybe help her with her new chosen profession. Dad, of course, was happy to talk about his career and was flattered that a young, beautiful woman wanted to talk to him.

My father was still a handsome man, and I'm sure his new friend found him attractive, also. She said her name was Bonnie Talbot, thirty-one years old and recently divorced. Dad was six feet tall, in good shape and had short thick salt and pepper hair, a fair complexion and bright blue eyes. He reminded some people of George Clooney. To the Irish, he would have been called "Black Irish." He had just enough wrinkles to make him look ruggedly handsome.

I know it's a cliché, but his smile did light up any room he was in. He was clever and well known for his sense of humor. Being in advertising and having to know a lot about current culture and many disciplines, he could talk to just about anyone about any subject, especially about current culture like movies and music. My mother had always been a little jealous of the way other women were attracted to him at parties, but, as far as I know, he was always faithful and loyal to her.

The time flew by as Dad and Bonnie talked and drank, especially Bonnie. Dad probably drank no more than three glasses of wine. He loved red wine, any type, Cabernet, Merlot, Chianti. It didn't have to be expensive, just red. Bonnie was drinking vodka on the rocks, at least three, and then she had two glasses of wine. Dad thought she might have been a little high when she came to Brian's. She had done many crazy and interesting things in her life, and my Dad was an eager listener.

The more they talked, the closer together they got. At one point, their shoulders were touching. Dad felt her warm soft body, and he was excited. She had on an enticing perfume, and it was all very heady and seductive. Between the wine and the presence of a beautiful young woman, full of life and enthusiasm, he was feeling high and energetic. He couldn't remember the last time he had felt that way. In recent years, Deirdre had become cold and aloof, and this was like being in another world.

As he listened to her talk and felt her overwhelming presence, he must have let himself fantasize about what it would be like to live with such an enchanting person. Life with her, I'm sure he imagined, would be a constant pleasure and adventure. He felt strong, young, and vital. The phrase, "time stood still" describes how Dad felt.

Eventually, however, he realized it was getting late, and he needed to go home. Sanity prevailed, and he knew that he shouldn't encourage this relationship anymore. He would have loved to, but his strong moral compass told him that it was time to call it a night. He told Bonnie that he had to leave but that he had enjoyed their conversation. He gave her his phone number and told her she could call him if she needed more advice on her new career.

Bonnie said she should leave, too, and asked Dad if he could give her a ride back to her mother's house. A friend had dropped her off and was going to call her later to pick her up, but she didn't feel like waiting. Dad hesitated, but decided it was all right to give her a ride since she lived only a few blocks east of his house. It couldn't hurt, he thought, and would be a nice thing to do. He also enjoyed being with Bonnie. She was beautiful and full of life and mystery and this would give him a little more time with her.

Most of this information came out later when Detective Shawn Robinson interviewed Jimmy Reilly, the bartender on duty that afternoon. Based on what I know about my father, I'm taking a little artistic license to fill in some of the gaps. I also had a long conversation with him in the hospital, so I think I have a good picture of what transpired. He wanted me to know all of the circumstances, and, even though it was embarrassing for him, he told me what happened in great detail.

Getting back to the story, Dad paid the bill with his credit card and then helped Bonnie with her coat as they left Brian's together. He and Bonnie were both feeling quite mellow as they walked to Dad's car which was parked near the front of Brian's on Western. A man who was very drunk was stumbling along about fifty feet ahead of them. Dad thought he recognized him and hoped he wouldn't turn around and see him with Bonnie.

It was dark and the weather was cold and blustery. Small patches of ice and snow still streaked the sidewalk. As they were walking, Bonnie slipped. Dad caught her, though, and she clung to him for a moment as she regained her balance. Holding her warm, soft hand, Dad helped her into his car.

When my father told me this part of the story, he said that he now wished that they had both fallen on the ice when Bonnie slipped. That small delay might have changed everything. They would have been delayed a little, and things might have been different for him and the others involved.

The traffic on Western was very light at this time of day. Dad waited for a few cars and a blue Pace bus to pass and then made a u-turn and drove north on Western Avenue. He still felt a little buzzed, but he drove like that frequently on his way home from Brian's -- rationalizing that he only had a few blocks to go, and traffic was light.

At 103rd and Western, he turned right and drove about a half mile east to where 103rd Street descends a steep hill (one of only a few in all of Chicago) to Longwood Drive. On the Northwest corner of this intersection is a unique landmark famous throughout the entire Chicago area -- an Irish castle built by Robert Givens in 1887. Its three stories tall, made of native stone and has turrets, ramparts and towers just like a real castle. Most people are shocked when they first see it. It's now the home of a Unitarian Church and one of the premier pre-schools in the area.

As they started to descend the steep hill Dad saw that a blue Metra Train Engine and passenger cars had just cleared 103rd Street proceeding north about half a block east of Longwood. As a result, traffic was heavy on 103rd as the train had been blocking traffic. As Dad was braking to descend the hill and concentrating on the congestion head of him, Bonnie reached over and put her left hand on top of Dad's thigh. She unbuckled her seat belt and then slid over and leaned her head against his shoulder. My father, being a little startled and uncomfortable at this, looked down at her.

Just then, as they reached the intersection at the bottom of the hill, a gray Toyota minivan turned left in front of Dad. Being distracted, he didn't see it and didn't brake. God forbid, there was a horrible collision. My father lost consciousness and didn't remember anything until he awoke in Little Company of Mary Hospital in Evergreen Park the next day. From that time forward, his life became a living hell, a whirlwind of emotions and dread! Sadly, I must admit, his family, including me, was not as supportive as it should have been.

My headhunting business was only a few years old, and I was busy and worried about succeeding.

Before I started my business, I had been selling project management software and had met and worked with some of the top executives in the real estate and construction industry. After volunteering to help several companies find new people, I realized that I could make twice the money working as a recruiter than selling software. The real estate development business was booming and almost all of my clients were looking for people. To my shame, I didn't take the time to call Dad as often as I should have. I deeply regret that, now. I should have done more for Mom and Dad.

The driver of the minivan, Mary Carroll McCarthy, suffered a broken neck and died a week later at Christ Hospital in Oak Lawn. For some unknown reason, the airbag in the steering wheel of her car did not deploy to help cushion the impact. Her two-year-old daughter in a child's seat in the back had a mild concussion and a broken arm. Mary Carroll was thirty-five years old and had two other small children at home.

Bonnie Talbot, because she did not have her seat belt fastened, incurred severe brain damage and remains in a coma to this day.

My father's airbag deployed, but he suffered a concussion and a broken left wrist. Both cars were totaled. After the collision, Dad's car spun through the intersection on some ice and took out a stoplight and one street light pole, for which the City of Chicago later filed suit against him for $250,000.

At Christ Hospital where Bonnie was taken, there was confusion about who was the driver. The police mistakenly obtained a blood alcohol test from her. Her alcohol level was 2.0, more than twice the legal limit. The newspapers, having somehow discovered this information, were quick to point out that there had been a delay of over an hour before the test was taken and strongly implied that her blood alcohol level was probably even higher.

At my father's hospital, since he was unconscious, his blood was not tested due to confusion over whether or not he could consent to the test. When it was finally determined that the law did allow the test, almost three hours had passed. The police withdrew their request. This was one of the few breaks my father received during this terrible incident.

The implication of culpability, according to the neighborhood paper, was clearly there, however. Ms. Talbot's high blood alcohol level and testimony from the bartender, Jimmy Reilly, that Dad and Ms. Talbot had been drinking heavily for over two and a half hours was clearly damning. An anonymous tip to Detective Robinson, probably from one of Mrs. McCarthy' many friends or relatives, alerted him to the fact that Dad had been drinking at Brian's Tap the afternoon of the accident.

Even though Mrs. McCarthy had made a left turn in front of my father, the fact that he and Bonnie had been drinking for several hours at Brian's Tap and that Bonnie's blood alcohol was above the state limit for driving looked bad and raised many suspicions. Additionally, since there were no skid marks, the implication was that my father was too drunk to avoid the accident. To make matters worse, Mary Carroll was from a large politically active family in Chicago. As a result, public opinion in our neighborhood developed strongly against my father. She had many friends and relatives who were incensed about her death.

To color matters even more darkly, a woman driving behind my father said that she witnessed the accident and gave a statement to the investigating officer that she thought the traffic light at the intersection was red when my father entered the intersection in front of her and that he made no effort to brake his car before it hit Mrs. McCarthy's minivan.

The witness turned out to be a neighbor of Mary Carroll, and her son was in the same grade school class as Mary Carroll's daughter. Much later, in her deposition, she would admit that she wasn't sure about the light, but her initial statements made my father's liability look pretty bad. There was a traffic camera at the intersection that should have helped determine who was at fault. However, it was reported as not operable that day, so no video was available.

Margot Shipley, one of the most prominent personal injury attorneys in Chicago, filed a wrongful death lawsuit against my father, the manufacturer of the McCarthy vehicle, and Brian's Tap within forty-eight hours of the accident. The complaint, filed in the Circuit Court of Cook County, asked for fifteen million dollars in damages. Bonnie Talbot's mother hired an equally famous personal injury attorney who filed a complaint against my father and Mrs. McCarthy asking for twenty-five million dollars in damages on behalf of Bonnie and her four-year-old son.

It may not seem possible, but there was more bad news to come. After a thorough investigation by Detective Robinson and Bobby Evans, the local newspaper's persistent young reporter, it appeared that Bonita Talbotstoy (not Bonnie Talbot) may have been a prostitute. The local weekly neighborhood newspaper ran articles about the accident for four weeks straight and repeated in every issue that Ms. Talbotstoy had been arrested about five years ago for prostitution and that she had two arrests for possession of drugs within the last two years. As luck would have it, the police found Dad's phone number in her purse, and the innuendo was clear to all of the friends of Mary Carroll and to many others in the community.

Jimmy Reilly, the bartender, was quoted as saying that he had seen Ms. Talbotstoy several times in the bar, usually much later at night, for several days before the accident. She consistently ended up leaving with a different man each night, and they were usually older men, none of whom Jimmy could, or would, identify, however.

According to Jimmy, Ms. Talbotstoy normally didn't come in until later; but, unfortunately for my father, she came in earlier on the day of the accident. She was usually dropped off in front of the bar by a tough looking man with a dark beard driving a black Mercedes. He always wore black clothing, a black knit watch cap and a leather jacket. Jimmy heard him yell at Bonita in a foreign language one time, and she seemed frightened and submissive.

Chapter 2

The Aftermath

My father's recovery from the accident was slow and painful -- likewise for my mother. I don't know who was hurting more.

Dad had temporary amnesia that lasted for about three days. When the reality of what had happened slowly came back to him, he had to relive the tragic events all over. He eventually regained all of his faculties and was released from the hospital.

His broken wrist healed in about a month without residual damage, but he had occasional migraine headaches that would debilitate him for several hours at a time. He seemed confused about things the first several weeks he was at home, but this cleared up and did not seem to be a factor for concern. He had many recurring nightmares about the accident, though. He would see Mary Carroll's van turning into him, and Mary Carrol would be looking directly at him and yelling at him to pay attention and stop. Mom said he would wake up screaming and sweating and in a total panic. She also said that he had a delusion one time that he had crashed his plane, and I was killed; but that seemed to be the only such incident.

Health issues were the least of Mom and Dad's concerns, however. Serious legal problems hung over their heads. They hired Tom Sumner, the husband of one of Mom's bridge partners, who specialized in criminal law, to defend Dad against any criminal charges. Detective Robinson had revealed in one interview with Dad that vehicular homicide charges had been discussed with the State's Attorney; but, he added, that was just routine procedure in such cases. This, of course, scared Dad and Mom out of their wits, and Tom Sumner was immediately retained to prepare for the worst.

Dad's insurance company hired a very capable attorney to defend him in the civil actions, but Tom was also retained to monitor his work. Luckily Dad had an excess liability policy that gave him almost five million dollars in coverage, but the potential verdict in the suits could, realistically, exceed that amount.

Mom and Dad also had a good estate plan, and more than half of their assets were in Mom's marital trust. Nevertheless, Mr. Sumner had advised them that they had serious exposure and could, potentially, lose everything that was in Dad's name. This would have severely crimped their lifestyle and meant that they would have to downsize and sell the summer home in Michigan.

This just about destroyed my Mother. She was worried sick and lost so much weight that she looked terrible. She normally didn't sleep well, and this made her insomnia much worse. All of these conditions made her tired and withdrawn.

Worst of all, she dropped out of her bridge group when one of the members who was a friend of the McCarthy family refused to play with her. The woman made mean and spiteful comments about Dad and embarrassed Mom. Most of her friends tried to comfort and support her, but she felt Dad had shamed them. This and a bad experience in a local food store made her afraid to be seen in the neighborhood. While talking to one of the butchers, she heard someone behind her say, "That's the drunk's wife." When she turned around, there were three women and a man all looking down and pretending to be unaware of the cruel remark. She left the store in tears.

I tried to call her as much as possible, but she was so depressed and unhappy that it was difficult to talk to her and was usually unpleasant. Nothing I could say would make her happy or get her mind off of her problems. Even stories about Molly and Charlie couldn't make her stop dwelling on her problems. Normally she was a wonderful grandmother, but the accident had wrecked her life.

Of course, Mom resented my father and seldom talked to him except to burst into angry, mean tirades. No matter how much he explained what had happened or how many times he apologized, she would not forgive him or give him any support or peace. The large legal bills from Mr. Sumner added fuel to the fire, and things looked bleaker by the day.

They began sleeping in separate bedrooms and avoided each other as much as possible. To avoid antagonizing my Mother any further, my father didn't drink when he first came home from the hospital. Eventually, however, to ease the pain, and because he was lonely, he started drinking again. He didn't go out but would sit alone in the evenings and sip wine until he fell asleep in a chair in the basement office he maintained. Sometimes he would sleep in the chair all night long. Like Mom, he didn't eat properly and lost weight.

There were other ramifications, also. One involved me and caused more concern and worry for Dad. As I mentioned, the McCarthy family was large and politically connected. Mary Carroll's husband, Tom, was one of six boys and three girls. Her father was one of seven boys and two girls. Tom had forty-five first cousins and more second and third cousins than you could count, almost all of whom lived in the City of Chicago or nearby suburbs. Most worked for the City or County as policemen, firemen, judges, and prosecutors. Many had management-level jobs in various departments like the Water Department, Streets and Sanitation, the Assessor's Office and the City Treasurer's Office. Their tentacles spread throughout all of local government. One of the brothers had been an alderman and ward committeeman. One was married to a Daley giving the family even more clout and power. Another family member married a cousin of the current Cook County Sheriff, and several were in the county police force. One managed the bailiffs in the Daley Center court rooms and was the reputed bagman for one of the key judges in the Circuit Court.

For many years, hiring in Chicago was monitored and regulated under what is called the "Shakman Decrees." They derived from a court case brought by Michael Shakman in the '70s that resulted in several court orders that were meant to make hiring practices in the City fair and free of political influence. It worked to a very limited degree, but the politicians quickly learned how to circumvent it and continue the patronage system. Despite the court order and scrutiny by inspectors, every alderman and high-level operative could still obtain a job or promotion for just about anyone he or she wanted to help. Certain management jobs were excluded from the decrees, and they were filled with only the most connected people.

Because of this system and culture, it was fair to say that the McCarthy family's business was government. A few were involved in private enterprises that just happened to do a great deal of business with various government agencies. As a result, they knew or had contacts with a huge segment of the movers and shakers in the City of Chicago. Most were decent, honest, hardworking people who were conscientious about their jobs. They sincerely tried to serve the public. A few, however, were cocky, arrogant and bullies. Their power and influence went to their heads, and they liked to throw their weight around whenever they could.

The worst of all was a man named Larry O'Doul. He was married to a McCarthy and was notorious for taking advantage of his place in the family. He had been a fireman for about fifteen years but was on permanent disability, even though he could be found golfing at Ridge

Country Club on most nice summer days. Several of the clan were on disability. For some reason, their claims for disability were always upheld. In many cases, since they were usually a pain in the ass to work with, their supervisors were happy to support their claims and get them out of their hair.

Larry O'Doul was the most infamous member of the whole family -- and that is saying something! Everyone in the bars up and down Western Avenue in the Beverly neighborhood were familiar with Larry. Bars owned by people with more clout than Larry had banned him and wouldn't let him in the door. The others had to tolerate his abhorrent behavior. When he was sober, he was a likable guy, but after a few drinks, he became mean and tried to pick a fight with some unlucky patron. He had been arrested and sued a few times, but the cases were always dismissed or settled for practically nothing. In most cases, no one would testify against him.

I had the misfortune of running into him in the Kerry Man Bar a few months after Dad's accident. I had been avoiding the bars on Western since Dad's accident. However, my friend, Sean Sullivan, asked me to meet him at the Kerry Man one evening in July to watch the Cubs play the White Sox in one of the games for the Cross Town Cup. This was an annual series played between the Cubs and the White Sox which brings out the strong North Side/South Side baseball rivalry that Chicago is known for and which makes it a fun place to live. The Sox had a good team, and I was anxious to watch the game but reluctant to go to any of the bars to watch it. Each season I usually went to one of the bars to watch a few of the games. It was enjoyable to be with the partisan crowd and listen to all of the jokes and insults about the Cubs.

My wife, Patty, heard me talking to Sean and insisted that I go. She knew I needed a distraction from work and worrying about my father, so she insisted that I go with Sean.

We met at seven and watched the game on one of the many TVs at The Kerry Man. Since the bar was not crowded, we had a good table with a good view of the game. We each had a couple of beers, the Sox were winning, and I was feeling relaxed and enjoying myself.

Then Larry O'Doul entered the bar with two friends. He had a bandage on his nose. Sean said he had heard that O'Doul had slipped on some ice a few months ago and had broken his nose. I knew that he was frequently in fights, so there could be a couple of explanations for the bandage. O'Doul and his friends sat on stools near the front door. I didn't think anything of it at the time. I noticed that two other people went over and talked to Larry, and I could see that they were looking at me as they talked.

After about ten minutes, Larry broke away from the group and started to walk over to my table. One of his friends tried to grab him, but he shook his hand off and kept walking. I could tell he was drunk and immediately felt a rush of fear and anxiety. I had seen Larry in action a few times and knew that this was trouble. He looked me in the eye and, wobbling a little as he pointed at me, said, "You're not wanted in here O'Brien. Get the fuck out! Your old man killed my wife's cousin, and I feel like beating the shit out of you. Did ya hear me, O'Brien?! I saw your Dad with that hooker at Brian's, and I should have kicked his ass then."

I had never been in a fight in my life, and I didn't know what to do or say. My friend Sean, however, was a tough, scrappy guy and didn't let anyone push him around. He told O'Doul to cool down or we were calling the police. O'Doul laughed at that and said, "Call the police, asshole. See what good that'll do ya."

Sean took out his cell phone and began to dial 911. O'Doul started to lunge for him. I, for some unknown reason, threw my beer at O'Doul. I had a full glass of beer and just sloshed the beer out of the glass into O'Doul's face. I didn't think. It just happened. As I remember it now, I can't believe I did that, but I did. I don't know what came over me. I just reacted.

O'Doul looked at me with the most insane, murderous look I have ever seen. He wiped the beer out of his eyes and then rushed at me. I ducked down on the table and pushed it into him. He fell on top of me. I could feel him hitting the back of my head and shoulders and grabbing for me. Because I had so much adrenaline coursing through my body, though, I didn't feel any pain. I was aware of the blows, but they didn't phase me. They would later, but at that time they were just like thumps on my back. I fell under the table and grabbed one of his legs and tried to pull him down. I had been on the wrestling team at Marist High School for two months before I dislocated my shoulder, and the only thing I learned was how to do a one leg take-down. It worked and helped me counter O'Doul's attack.

This gave some of the other patrons in the bar time to grab O'Doul and pull him off. Thank God there were some brave souls in the bar that evening who came to my rescue. Sean had used my distraction with the beer to finish his call to 911, and then he helped pull O'Doul off of me. I saw him give O'Doul a quick punch in the nose as he helped get him under control. I could tell it hurt O'Doul as he flinched, and it made his eyes water.

The bartender, a tough, good looking, middle aged woman, started screaming profanities at O'Doul and made him back off. His two friends finally decided to do something and pulled O'Doul toward the door.

He was still crazed but a little calmer. He looked at me and screamed something like, "I know who you are, O'Brien, and I'll get ya next time." He then wiped some blood off his lip with the back of his hand.

Just then a squad car pulled up in front of The Kerry Man with its blue lights flashing. O'Doul saw the lights and said, "Oh, fuck! Who was the asshole who called the police!" as he looked at Sean. Sean gave him the finger.

He and his two friends immediately went outside and talked to the two police officers in the squad. One of them must have known one of the officers, and they talked for quite awhile. I could tell they were telling O'Doul and his friends to leave and move on.

I saw O'Doul and his two friends leave and walk away. The squad remained parked in front of the Kerry Man for a few minutes, but they didn't come in. I thought about going outside and talking to them, but I knew it would do no good and might get me in trouble.

Sean and I left the bar as soon as we felt it was safe and went to my house. I had a bruise on the side of my face, and my shirt was ripped. Later that night my back hurt like hell causing me a restless night. Two ugly bruises showed up on my back when I took my next shower. They were tender to the touch and bothered me for a couple of weeks. Overall, though, I was lucky I hadn't been hurt worse.

I wasn't going to tell Dad about the fight and hoped he would never hear about it. Unfortunately, his friend, Neal McGhee, called him to warn him about O'Doul and told him about the fight. I can see why he would do that. He thought he was helping Dad avoid a fight with O'Doul.

Dad immediately called me and apologized and said he was sorry for all of the problems that he had caused the family. I tried to tell him it wasn't his fault and that he didn't have to apologize for what O'Doul had done. I told him that O'Doul was an evil monster, and he wasn't responsible for another person's bad behavior. Dad said he knew that but was still upset and wanted me to know how bad he felt. I intended to go see Dad in a few days, but I didn't.

I never pressed charges against O'Doul. I knew it would be a waste of time. No one in the bar would have testified for me, and the fact that I threw the beer at O'Doul would have complicated things.

Chapter 3

Deposed and Depressed

About five months after the accident, the attorneys for the plaintiffs summoned Dad's deposition. It was to be taken at one o'clock on a Monday afternoon on August 15 in the offices of Ms. Shipley on La Salle Street in the Chicago Loop. That day, Dad spent all morning in a conference room in Tom Sumner's office preparing for the deposition with Mr. Sumner and the insurance company's attorney, David Kogland.

Tom Sumner was a short, bald no nonsense attorney in his mid-fifties. He was not very personable, but he projected competence and savvy. When he spoke, he was very precise and to the point. He specialized in high profile DUI and nursing home cases. His wife's uncle owned ten nursing homes, and he had a busy and profitable legal practice. He was also an expert bridge player and was president of one of the top contract bridge clubs in Chicago.

Mr. Kogland, "Dave," as he liked to be called, was a very impressive person, and Dad liked him immediately. He was older than Tom, very tall (at least six feet seven inches) and had a commanding presence. He had a shock of white hair, a short white beard, steady blue eyes, and a pleasant, non-threatening presence, even though he looked like a giant Viking. I Googled him and checked him out on LinkedIn and there was nothing but praise and compliments for him. As they talked, he made subtle humorous comments that made my father smile. He was the one and only bright spot in the day for Dad.

Mr. Sumner had informed Dad that his deposition could be postponed because of the possible criminal charges, but Dad chose to go forward. He felt that he had done nothing wrong, and he wanted to get this all behind him. That was not a wise decision, but Dad was adamant. He was confused and didn't understand what the case was all about. He knew that it looked bad for him because he had been drinking and Bonnie had distracted him, but he didn't understand exactly what he had done wrong. He had tried to read the legal complaint file against him, but it was all gobbledygook. He asked Mr. Sumner and Mr. Kogland to explain what the case was all about and why he was being sued.

"Quite simply, Will, you are being sued for negligence that caused bodily injury and property damage," Mr. Sumner said. "There is a one semester course in law school that goes into all of the different types of negligence, but I'll try to give you a short and simple explanation. A person is liable for damages if he or she is negligent and breaches a duty of care to another person. That is what 'negligence' means -- you did something wrong. It is sometimes called a 'Tort' which comes from Latin and French and means to twist, which eventually came to mean a wrong. I'll give you some examples that might help you understand negligence law as it applies to auto accidents. If a person drives too fast for the circumstances, is drunk, is following another car too closely, or allows himself or herself to be distracted, they are considered negligent. There are many cases that hold that that type of conduct is negligent because it breaches recognized duties of care."

Mr. Sumner looked at Mr. Kogland to see if he wanted to add something. He nodded approval to Mr. Sumner who then continued. "Much of our negligence law comes from the English Common Law and is based upon thousands of cases going back hundreds of years that establish precedents for judges and juries to use to make decisions in law suits. There are a few state statutes that also help determine the law in negligence cases. One recent law provides for what is called 'comparative negligence.' It establishes that, if a plaintiff (the person filing the suit) is more than 50% negligent, the defendant (the person being sued) is not liable for damages."

"In your case, the plaintiffs are going to try to show that you were negligent because you had too much to drink, you were driving too fast for the circumstances, you ran a red light, and you were not paying attention because you let Bonnie distract you. We, on the other hand, will try to show that Ms. McCarthy was negligent because she made a left turn in front of you. As to Bonnie, we will show that she distracted you against your will."

Mr. Sumner looked at Dad and tried to determine if he had understood what he had just told him. Dad seemed lost and confused, but Mr. Sumner continued: "You don't have to understand the law, Will. That is our job, and we will protect your rights. Now, we are going to have you describe what happened the night of the accident so you can answer the questions put to you by the other attorneys. There is one important rule we want you to remember, though. Don't guess at any answer. If you don't know the answer, say you don't know. You don't have to explain anything. Try to answer question with a simple 'yes' or 'no.' If Mr. Kogland or I think something needs to be explained, we will ask you to explain it. This is not a trial. You don't have to make your case in this deposition. You only have to answer the questions put to you by the other attorneys."

"I'd like to add one more thing," Mr. Kogland interjected. "Smart attorneys won't ask this; but, if one of the other attorneys ask you if we told you what to say, answer him by saying, 'Yes.' They told me to tell the truth.' And that's what we want you to do. We think you have a good defense, so let's go over all of the fact so you don't get flustered or confused during the deposition. Are you ready?"

Dad said he was, and, for the next two hours, they reviewed all of the facts and details of the case.

I had a long discussion with Mr. Sumner about the deposition, so I know a lot about what happened. It was very hard on Dad. The attorneys for the plaintiffs were serious, unsmiling, mean people. Ms. Shipley does not handle her own depositions. She has a stable of eight other attorneys that handle all of her discovery work before trials. Discovery work includes depositions (oral questioning), interrogatories (written questions to determine basic information about a party's case), and subpoenas for records and copies of any reports a party might have obtained from experts.

Ms. Shipley's minions are hired for their aggressiveness and thoroughness. They are uniformly hated by most of the defense attorneys in the City. They are bullies and heartless. If they aren't, they don't last long in Ms. Shipley's firm. She personally tries all of the big cases in her office and only allows her subordinates to handle a trial if it's worth only a few million in damages. Most of her associates last about five years, but they gain invaluable knowledge about how to be a successful PI attorney.

The deposition itself was pure mental torture for Dad. David Fulmer conducted the deposition for Ms. Shipley, and he lived up to the reputation of the firm. He was ruthless and unrelenting. Even Dave Kogland's strong presence did not deter him.

Sam Adonte, who represented Bonita Tallbotstoy, was almost as bad, but he was disorganized and kept confusing matters with repetitious questions and blatantly false facts. He fought with all of the attorneys present over every procedural point and threatened to stop the deposition and obtain a judge's order about how to proceed.

All of the haggling upset Dad and confused and disoriented him. Dad had to relive every painful detail of the accident and the events leading up to it. The attorneys for the two plaintiffs twisted his words and made him feel as though he had made many mistakes and that his case was hopeless. They were both sharp attorneys and asked many questions that he had never contemplated. They would frequently ask the same question in different ways, and Dad was not sure if he had been consistent. The attorneys for Brian's Tap and Toyota were also at the deposition and asked several questions that seemed to complicate matters even more.

There were many questions about how much Dad had to drink. Through discovery, the plaintiffs were able to obtain the receipt from Brian's for the bill Dad paid with his credit card. It showed five glasses of wine and three vodkas on the rocks. That made it look as though Dad had five glasses of wine and Bonnie had three vodka drinks. In fact, Dad had only three glasses of wine, and he told me that he was sure he had only consumed about half of the last glass. He was grilled and grilled about how much he drank. The bill was confusing, and it was easy to assume that Dad had consumed five glasses of wine, which would have implied that he was drunk when he left Brian's.

The questions about Ms. Talbotstoy were extremely difficult and embarrassing for my father. His sense of chivalry being what it was, he did not want to describe what happened immediately before the accident, His attorneys, however, convinced him that he had to explain what Ms. Talbotstoy did that distracted him. When he described what happened in the deposition, Ms. Talbotstoy's attorney made objections that Dad did not understand, and there was a heated argument between all of the attorneys before his testimony could resume. The deposition lasted well over three hours, even though court rules limit depositions to three hours. Dad must have been exhausted and very worried.

After the deposition, Mr. Sumner and Mr. Kogland tried to encourage Dad, but he thought they were just being supportive. Their talk about potential settlements didn't raise his spirits. They agreed that the best plan was to offer the entire limits of the insurance and obtain an agreement that the plaintiffs would not go after the personal assets of my father.

My father then asked Mr. Sumner about the possible criminal charges. Mr. Sumner told Dad that things were still in flux with the State's Attorney. He had been dealing with Bill Jenkins, one of the supervisors in the State's Attorney's Office at 27th and California, whom he knew well. Jenkins implied that they were getting pressure to file charges from one of the County Commissioners who was a relative of Mrs. McCarthy. Jenkins made it clear that he didn't think charges were proper, but, being Chicago, political pressure could change things.

That kind of talk did nothing to assuage my father's worries, and he dwelt on them and rehashed the deposition in his mind during the entire train ride back to Beverly. He thought of several things he should have said differently, and he wondered if he had made any fatal admissions. He called Mr. Sumner on his cell phone on the train and talked briefly with him about some of these worries. Mr. Sumner assured Dad that his deposition went well and that he should try to relax and not dwell on what could have been.

Dad didn't bother to talk to my mother about the deposition when he arrived home, and she made no effort to talk to him. He simply went down to his office and slumped into his big desk chair and poured himself a glass of wine from a bottle he kept hidden in a cabinet near his desk. He was a little hungry, but he didn't have the energy to fix himself supper. He began to feel better and drank another glass of wine and then another. He started to drift off to sleep when his cell phone rang. He looked at the caller ID and did not recognize the number, but, for some reason, he answered the call, anyway.

From this point on, I'm going to let my father tell the rest of the story in his own words. As I mentioned earlier, I have a lengthy recording that my father made.

I think he contemplated writing a book about his experiences, and the recording was probably meant to help him remember all of the facts later. As I mentioned, he called it his journal. Some of the recording was garbled and slurred and hard to understand, but I think the story is pretty accurate. To be honest, I've tweaked the narrative in a few places just to make it clearer and more logical. I had to research some of the things Dad talks about, but it is all, essentially, his words. Thank God for the internet and Google, and, especially, Wikipedia. I was able to clarify several things by using those sources.

This was hard to write, but, as I said at the beginning, I did it because I love my father so much and want our friends and family, especially my two children, to appreciate him and know what he went through. I think you'll also find it interesting and fascinating. My father is a good writer, and he had took a strange journey.

Chapter 4

A Ray of Hope

I've been on my mission now for about four days, and I'm starting to feel better. To help pass the time, and to make myself feel as though I'm gaining control of my situation, I've decided to write a journal. It should be easy to write since I've taken good notes and have my recorder and can quickly dictate my experiences and feelings. God willing, I hope to share this someday with my son, Owen.

In the past, when I was under pressure to meet a deadline or prepare for a presentation, if I could just start writing (or dictating), I could overcome my anxiety and start to gain control of my task. If I get through this with my sanity, I may even write a short story or, perhaps, a novel about it.

I'll start with the evening after my deposition. I was worried and anxious about how I did at the deposition. A whirlwind of emotions blew through my mind ever time I thought about the deposition. It was as though I was in a recurring and debilitating nightmare. I wished that I had someone I could talk to about it -- someone knowledgeable that I could trust. My attorneys said the deposition went well, but I wasn't sure if I could believe them. They were probably just being supportive.

I'm embarrassed to say it, but I was feeling deep anger, also. I tried not to think about it, but I felt a great hatred for the two attorneys for the plaintiffs, especially Bonnie's attorney. He was a bully and obnoxious and insulting. I think he enjoyed trying to push my buttons. On the train ride home I thought several times about how I should have punched him. I fantasized about waiting for him to leave his office some night and then attacking him with a baseball bat. I know I would not do that, though. I have a quick Irish temper, at times, but I've learned to control it.

I had other concerns, too. I'd thought so much about the accident over the last few months that I wasn't sure if my memory was correct or if I was remembering what I wanted to remember. Once or twice, while driving, I had a vivid flashback of the accident. I could see Mary Carroll's minivan heading right toward me. The first time I had this flashback, I hit my brakes and almost caused another accident. Luckily, the car behind me was able to stop in time.

I drank a little wine to relax and calm down. That always helped me in the past. I began to feel better. Then my cell phone rang. I answered it without even looking at the caller information. I thought, perhaps, one of my attorneys might have a question or suggestion.

At first, I had a hard time understanding the man on the phone. My brain was a little foggy, but I made myself focus on what he was saying. My first thought, unbelievably, was that the voice on the phone sounded like Morgan Freeman's. *Through the Wormhole* is one of my favorite shows on TV. Since he's the narrator of that show, I'm very familiar with his voice.

I've watched several of those shows on the Science Channel and had just seen an installment of *Through the Worm Hole* that night. It was a good diversion and helped me get my mind off my problems for a few minutes.

I'm digressing, though, so let me get back to the phone call. I asked who was calling. The man on the other end said he would tell me later but that he needed to talk to me in person as soon as possible. He said he had an interesting offer to make to me that would solve all of my problems and would provide me with an adventure that no one in the world had ever experienced.

He said he had been following my story since he had first read a short article about my accident in the *Chicago Tribune.* He knew a lot about me: my career with Bennington, my short stories, my experience as a pilot. From information on Facebook and LinkedIn, he even knew that I had experience flying jets in the Air National Guard. With all of the on-line services and social media available today, it's easy to find this type of information about a person. I've done that many times myself. But, since he did his homework, I was impressed.

I asked him to call me tomorrow. I told him I was too tired and had consumed too many glasses of wine to seriously discuss anything tonight on the phone. He said he could not risk calling me again. We had to talk in person. He asked me where we could meet. I suggested that we meet at eight o'clock at a small coffee shop called Java Hut on 95th Street near the train station not too far from my house.

I thought this was a good idea since it was a public place and, usually, there was someone I knew in the coffee shop. If this was some type of a scam or robbery scheme, he wouldn't be able to do much in such a public place. I was interested in hearing what he had to say, though, so I thought it was worth a chance. He sounded sincere and honest. I felt I could trust him.

I couldn't have been more depressed about my future, and, I guess, I was grasping at straws. I was probably going to be ruined financially and might even be convicted of manslaughter and have to serve a prison sentence. My wife hated me. My family didn't seem too supportive. I was a mess. Most of my neighbors probably thought I was some kind of a pervert and a drug addict.

Thoughts of suicide had even entered my mind. I rejected them quickly and never took that path seriously, though. Our Pastor had made one perfunctory call to me when I first arrived home from the hospital. He offered counseling but never bothered to call me again and give me more encouragement. I don't blame him. Maybe I should have talked to him. Since there was little to be positive about, I didn't bother.

I was desperate and had little to lose by talking to this mysterious stranger. Throughout my life I have always found solutions to difficult situations. I was the problem solver at Bennington. That's why, after being at the firm for only five years, I was always on the management committee. Maybe this is my solution. I thought, "What the hell. It was worth a shot." I was tired and fell asleep in my recliner.

Chapter 5

An Interesting Proposal

I had a fitful sleep in my recliner after my phone call with the mystery man. I awoke at 5:30 AM but stayed in my office and slowly roused myself. I was a little thirsty and hung-over from the wine, but, overall, I didn't feel too badly. At about 7:00 I snuck up to the kitchen and poured myself a glass of orange juice and grabbed a bagel from the refrigerator. The bagel was dry, but a little cream cheese and the juice made it tolerable.

Since I didn't feel like running into Deirdre, I went back down to my basement lair. She seldom left her bedroom until after 10:00 AM, so the chances of running into her were not great.

Luckily there is a half bath in my basement where I could wash my face and be ready for my 8:00 AM appointment with the mystery man. It crossed my mind that I might have imagined the call, but I shrugged that idea off and proceeded with the plan.

Still in the same clothes that I slept in last night, I quietly left my house and walked about four blocks to the Java Hut on 95th. It's a small, non-chain coffee shop owned by Betty James, a local woman who makes great coffee and some awesome baked goods to go with it. The walk helped clear my mind and started my blood pumping. It was a mild day for mid-August -- only about seventy degrees. My spirits were lifted by a blue sky and a cool dry wind.

I entered the storefront where the Java Hut is and looked around. Betty was at the counter, as usual, but the place was otherwise empty. This caused me some concern. Then I thought to myself: "Betty is here. What the hell, let's get this over with!" I went to the counter and ordered a small coffee and a muffin and sat down to enjoy them.

At exactly 8:00 AM, an African-American man in his late fifties walked in. He was wearing a well-worn brown tweed jacket, crumpled dark slacks and a plaid shirt that made him look very professorial. He was even puffing on a brier pipe. He had light-colored skin, a short, neat beard and gray, short, thin hair.

Since I thought he looked non-threatening, I stood up and waved at him. He seemed to recognize me and walked to my table. With a friendly, warm grin he held out his hand and said, "Hello." I said, "I'm Will O'Brien. Did you want to meet with me?" He said, "It's nice to meet you, Will." From the sound of his voice, I wasn't certain if it was the man I had talked to on the phone last night, but, from his demeanor, I decided it must be.

I asked him if he would like a cup of coffee and something to eat. He looked over at Betty and the display case with all of the pastries, and said, "That coffee smells great and that cheese Danish looks fantastic. I don't want you eating alone, so I'll join you. I like my coffee with a little cream and sugar, make it three of each." I went up to the counter and purchased his order. While waiting for the order, I thought I noticed Betty give a little knowing wave to my new friend. That was a good sign.

When the order was ready, I grabbed it and walked to the table where the stranger was sitting. I gave him the coffee and the Danish and said, "I understand you have something interesting to tell me." After enthusiastically drinking some coffee and taking a big bite out of the Danish, he looked at me for a few seconds and then said to me in a warm, deep voice, "I've helped a lot of people in my day," he said. I have a team of people that look to me to lead them, so maybe I can help you. Maybe we could help each other."

I could tell he was feeling me out and wanted me to commit first. I said, "I have several serious problems now and am feeling lost and worried. Maybe I just need a sounding board. I don't want to burden you."

"You aren't burdening me, friend. You're probably wondering how the hell this old black man can help me solve all of your problems. Well, I have a proposal that might sound crazy at first; but, trust me; it could relieve you of most of your worries. I can't give you my full name, now, but most people I know call me "The Professor."

The Professor looked down at his hands for a moment, and then stroked his chin a few times while looking thoughtfully at me. Then he continued, "Until I feel that you are interested in my proposal, I will have to be a little vague and withhold some specifics. I hate to be so secretive, but there's a lot at stake."

I still didn't know what to say or ask, so I kept quiet and just listened as he continued.

"What I and my associates are doing has to be kept secret until our project is completed. If our employers or the Government were to learn of our project, we could be shut down and all of our hard work would be confiscated and hidden from the public forever."

With a sincere expression, the Professor said, while looking straight into my eyes, "I can assure you that our project does not involve any criminal activity or harm to any person. We are scientists, actually astrophysicists and engineers, and have decided to bypass normal procedures to complete a break-through mission that would otherwise be delayed or shelved by our employers and the government. Does this scare you so far? Should I continue or just walk away?"

I said, "I'm interested, but I can't imagine how this project of yours could involve me or help me with my problems."

"Let's just say, Mr. O'Brien, that we need you to fill in for someone, and this position, if you take it, will allow you to escape with honor from all of your difficulties," the Professor said slowly and quietly and with . . . with "gravitas."

"And," he continued, "I have to ask you to make a quick decision because we are on a tight schedule. I have to catch the northbound Metra train at 1:10 so I can meet my team. If you want to help yourself and my team, meet me at the 95th Street Station at one o'clock, and we'll go to a meeting near the Illinois Institute of Technology that will further enlighten you. If, after the meeting, you don't want to accept our offer, you can return home and forget you ever met me."

I thought for a moment and then said, "This is a lot to process. I don't have any plans today, but this feels awfully rushed."

"I know it is," the Professor said, "but, as I told you, we need to move quickly. If you decide to meet with us, here is what you have to do: go home and leave a vague note about how you are sorry for all of the pain you have caused your family and that you ask for their forgiveness. You don't need to say anything more than that. Make it vague. Then leave your cell phone and wallet at home and then meet me at the 95th Street train station at 1:00. Bring as much cash as you have available, but don't make any big withdrawals. Try to avoid anyone you know. If you don't like our proposal, you can return home and no one will be the wiser."

My mind was whirling trying to understand what was going on and what I should do about this proposal. It seemed crazy and clearly fraught with possible dangers, but I wanted a solution to my problems so badly that I couldn't reject this request outright. I wanted it to be a magic bullet that would solve all of the problems I had caused. What did I have to lose?

Deirdre hated me, and the lawsuits and possible criminal case against me spelled disaster for the rest of my life. I especially worried about what my son, Owen, and my grandchildren would think of me. I wanted them to respect me and not think that I was a bad person with all kinds of weaknesses. I love them dearly and it breaks my heart to think they may not think of me fondly as they grow older.

Even though I knew that my only mistake was drinking a little too much and making a bad decision about giving Bonnie a ride home, I felt like fate was against me, and I would probably lose the battle. My situation appeared hopeless.

I reasoned that the Professor seemed like a nice person and not, in the least, threatening. I could listen to his proposal and make a decision after I had all of the facts. If I didn't like it, I could return home and no one would even know that I had talked to him and his group. And, since the meeting was at IIT, it would be in a safe environment.

"OK," I said. "I'll do it. I may be crazy, but it won't hurt to listen to your proposal. I'll meet you at 1:00 at the train station. "Then I added, as if it would do any good, "Look at me and tell me that this isn't some kind of scam or scheme to get me in a dark alley and rob me."

The Professor looked offended and said, "Do I look like a gang banger to you? I assure you, without equivocation, that I have no intention to hurt you or cause you more problems."

As soon as I heard the word "equivocation" I felt better and knew that he was educated and wasn't a gang banger or thug. "All right," I said, "I trust you. I'll take a chance."

With that we both stood up and shook hands. The Professor said, "See you at 1:00."

Chapter 6

Train Ride to the Future

As I walked back to my house after my meeting with The Professor, my mind was going over different scenarios of what this might be about. I convinced myself that I had nothing to lose.

I did just as The Professor said I should do and left my wallet and cell phone on my desk in the basement. I wrote a note using his suggested language and left it on the desk. Then I took all of the cash I had and put it in my pocket. Luckily, I had just been to the ATM the day before, and I had about five hundred dollars in twenty-dollar bills. I usually withdrew this amount each month. If someone checked my ATM withdrawals, it wouldn't seem suspicious.

Since it was only 10:30, I had some time to kill. I used this time to review an insurance matter and write checks for several bills that were on my desk. I put them in envelopes, sealed them and put stamps on them. Then I had to mark the bills paid and file them. I didn't want Deirdre to have to worry about these bills. I would mail them on my way to the train. With my desk cleared, I felt better, and this process had taken my mind off my problems for a few minutes. I was feeling a little more relaxed.

By the time I did all that, it was almost 11:30, and I realized I would need to eat lunch before my meeting at IIT. I didn't want to run into Deirdre, though, so I felt trapped in my office.

Just then I heard her car pull out of the driveway. I determined that she was probably going to the store or the hairdresser. This would allow me plenty of time to prepare for my meeting and walk to the train.

I went up stairs and made myself a sandwich and ate it. As I was eating, I began to think about what I should take with me to the meeting. I didn't want it to look as though I was planning to disappear, so I couldn't take much with me. Then I remembered an old backpack that I used when I went fishing. It contained many useful items that might come in handy if I had to travel somewhere. Since I had it stored away in my basement storage room, no one would know it was missing. My son, Owen, might have remembered it, but it wasn't something that anyone else would be aware of, especially Deirdre.

I finished my lunch and then went down to the basement. After rummaging around in the storage room for a few minutes, I finally found the backpack. It was medium-sized and dark brown. In it was a variety of items that might come in handy if I had to survive on my own for awhile. I had no idea what the Professor had in mind for me, but, I thought, it would be smart to prepare for the unexpected.

I take blood pressure medication, but, with all the weight I've lost, I didn't think it was necessary. At its worst it was borderline. I thought I would be OK without it. Leaving it behind would indicate I didn't plan to disappear.

I took a couple of extra pairs of socks and underwear and a light sweater and stuffed them in the backpack. I also had an extra bottle of multiple vitamins which I dropped in. Then I put one of my writing notebooks in the backpack. I have several notebooks filled with ideas for short stories and a few novels. I included my most current notebook as it had some story ideas and research that I was enthused about. Since I didn't know what The Professor had in mind for me, I might have time to work on a short story or even a novel. None of these items would be noticed if someone checked to see what was missing.

The notebook made me think of my recorder. I use a small Sony digital voice recorder to record ideas and dictation for some of my writing projects. It's small and rechargeable but can hold over 500 hours of recordings. I also threw in a couple of pens for good measure. I'm glad I remembered the recorder. It has proven useful already.

Finally, I threw in an old Acer tablet and its charging cable that I hadn't used for a few years. It's an old model that I haven't used since I bought an I-Pad two years ago. It doesn't have a subscription to a cellular system, so it shouldn't be detectable. If I found a wifi hotspot, I thought I might be able to use it for research, if necessary.

Luckily, since we don't have any pets, I didn't have to worry about leaving a dog or cat alone in the house. I had always wanted a dog, but Deirdre didn't want to be bothered. Since she would have had to take care of it when I was working or traveling, I understood her feelings. We had always had a dog when I was growing up, and I missed the companionship and the comfort a dog could bring to a person.

It was after 12:30 by the time I was ready to leave. I turned on the TV, left some lights on in the kitchen and then walked out the back door with my backpack and money. I intentionally left the doors unlocked. Since our neighborhood is safe, I didn't worry about someone robbing us.

I left through my back door and walked across the small deck we have on the back of my house. I noticed that it had rained a little while I was in the house getting ready. There was still a very light mist coming down. I looked to the south across my neighbor's yard, and I noticed a rainbow in the sky. The rain and the sun were in just the right place, and the water was refracting the light and making a rainbow. I stood still for a moment and looked at the beautiful colors. I took this as a good sign. I could imagine the legendary pot of gold at the end of the rainbow. Maybe I was going to find something good at the end of this rainbow!

Looking around to make sure none of my neighbors were out, I could see the coast was clear. I put on a hat and sunglasses that I was carrying and walked quickly around my house and out onto the front sidewalk with my head down. I was soon a few blocks from home. The clouds disappeared and the sun was shining. The recent shower cleared the air and made everything seem fresh and cool.

I almost always see someone I know when I'm out walking in my neighborhood, but today I was lucky and didn't see any cars or people I recognized. I walked quickly east on 95th Street. Traffic was light at this time of day, but a large tractor-trailer truck carrying a large container passed me and hit a pothole and made a loud thump. It startled me and made me look around. A blue Pace bus and a motorcycle sped by on the other side of the street.

I made it to the train station without being noticed. Then I had to worry about running into someone I knew at the station. Normally there are a few people there at this time of day, but my luck held.

As I neared the door of the train station, I spotted The Professor approaching the platform. As I watched him, I thought I saw him put a bucket and long-handled brush in some bushes and weeds to the east of the station. That was strange, but then I noticed another man in coveralls near him who was probably using the bucket for maintenance. The Professor must have been moving the bucket and brush so he could get by.

He walked up to me and held out his hand. "Glad to see you, Mr. O'Brien, I was worried you might not come. You'll be glad you did. You're going to have an interesting day." I shook his hand and said, "I'm looking forward to it, I think. I need to buy a ticket, though, before the train arrives." I walked quickly into the station and bought a ticket. Again, fortunately, I was the only one in the station."

As I walked out of the station, the train was just pulling up. The huge, powerful blue engine pulling ten silvery passenger cars was pulsing and roaring by us. Every time I stand on a platform as a train passes by I am impressed with its power and dynamic force. Trains are awesome. They're like powerful rockets blasting by.

The train quickly stopped, and The Professor and I boarded the last car. We had no difficulty finding an empty seat. There were only three people in our train car, and, again, luckily, there was no one I recognized. The train makes several stops in Beverly, and I usually know at least one person in my car. Today, however, my luck was holding up. The Professor entered the first available seat. I put my backpack in the luggage rack above the seat and then sat next to him.

Sitting next to him, I noticed his tweed jacket was well worn and had a musty, smoky odor --not bad, but noticeable. The odor was probably from his pipe smoke, and he seemed like the classic "absent-minded" professor.

I didn't know what to say to him, and I felt a little awkward sitting there. He seemed at ease, though, so we sat in silence for several minutes. He finally looked over at me and said he couldn't discuss his proposal on the train as he wasn't sure who might overhear our conversation.

He did inform me that we would be exiting the train at 35th Street. My mind immediately thought about what was at that stop. That's the stop for the White Sox and IIT. Since he wanted to be called The Professor, the first thought that jumped into my mind was that he must be a Professor at IIT. It's a well known technical school and even has an Astrophysics Department. I thought: could the Professor be a rocket scientist?

Before I could ask him about that, though, he asked me about my family, and I told him some vague things about Deirdre and Owen. I wanted to avoid talking about the accident, and he didn't mention it, for which I was grateful. Until I knew more about The Professor and his proposal, I didn't want to give him too many specifics about my personal life. I did mention my two grandchildren and told him about how I loved to be with them and talk to them about fishing.

He said he had two grandchildren, also, and took them fishing from time to time. They just fished in the ponds in the local parks, but he made it sound interesting and exciting. I didn't go into detail about my extensive trips as I didn't want to sound as though I was bragging. I also thought it best to limit the amount of personal information about myself that I would disclose, especially anything that might make me sound wealthy.

The irony of this train ride struck me as I sat there watching the scenery fly by. Yesterday I was returning from the deposition on this same train line, and I was depressed and filled with worry and anxiety. Today, I feel mildly hopeful that things will get better.

Before I knew it, we were at the 35th Street Metra stop. The Professor said, "This is where we get off." I grabbed my backpack, and we left the train car and stood on the platform for a moment. A large yellow brick smokestack stands next to the platform to the east. It's part of the heating plant for IIT. I'd seen it many times in the past, but, for a moment, it looked to me like a rocket ship or missile ready to takeoff and escape into outer space. The Professor interrupted my brief daydream by touching my shoulder and pointing me in the direction of the stairs that descend to 35th Street.

I was familiar with this train stop having taken it several times to White Sox games. Thinking about the White Sox suddenly made me feel sad. Would I ever see another White Sox game? Would I ever take my son and grandchildren to another game? For many years Bennington had box seats at Comiskey Park and then the new Cellular Field. I took clients and my family to many games. We even had a skybox for a few years. Some of the happiest times in my life were spent there. I saw the Sox win the second game of the World Series there in 2005. I can't think about that now, but, hopefully, that part of my life is not over.

I had also taken the Metra to meetings at IIT when I was working with them on a marketing plan. In 2010, Bennington wrote a marketing plan for IIT's Development Office. I spent many hours with Marcie Jacobs, their Director of Development, preparing and implementing the plan. Even though it was a small account by our standards, I handled the job because it was convenient for me to stop at 35th Street on my way to and from the Loop.

We walked east toward State Street, and I thought that my guess about The Professor being a professor at IIT had been correct. It appeared to me that The Professor was taking me to one of the buildings on the IIT campus. Having worked on their marketing plan, I was familiar with the campus and knew a lot about the school.

IIT, which is a private school, was founded in 1940 when the Armour Institute and the Lewis Institute merged. The main campus, called the Mies Campus because many of the buildings were designed by the famous architect, Ludwig Mies van der Rohe, contains about eight academic buildings and many other ancillary buildings on a plot of land that extends from 35th Street on its south end to 30th Street on the north and from Michigan Avenue on the east to the Metra tracks on the west. It's a relatively small campus, about seven square blocks, but it has an enrollment of over 7,800 students.

I think it's one of the least attractive campuses that I've ever seen, but I've never said that to anyone before. Many architectural experts love it, so I might be off base. Let me tell you, it was hard for me to write glowingly about the campus when I was preparing the marketing plan. With great effort, I found a way to praise the plain, dark, boxy little buildings. Most of Mies' high-rise buildings work well and deserve the praise they receive, but his small buildings look like they are unfinished warehouses. The school has an excellent reputation, though, and the campus is only one factor. The techies that go there probably like it, and the fact that it's so close to the Loop and Lake Michigan are big selling points.

Walking a couple of blocks east, we approached the corner of 35th and State. The Professor said we were going to meet some of his associates at the Starbucks on the southwest corner. It's in a new, attractive five-story building that contains some commercial space, offices and condos on its upper floors. It was across the street from the IIT Tower, a fifteen-story building that is part of the IIT campus. We walked to the corner and crossed over to the south side of the street.

Entering the Starbucks, the Professor pointed to a table in the front right corner near the window where five other men, all middle-aged African Americans, were seated. No other patrons were in the shop.

"Those are my associates. I want you to meet them so we can explain our proposal," the Professor said as he leaned toward me and spoke in a soft voice. He continued, "I wonder if you could get me a small coffee and Danish before we sit down. I left my wallet in my other coat and only had enough money for my train ticket."

I said, "Of course. A little cream and sugar, right?" He smiled and nodded. I gave him my backpack and proceeded to the counter. The barista, a polite and efficient young Hispanic girl, quickly filled my order. I carried it to the prep table to put some cream and sugar

in both of our cups. Then I walked to the table where the
Professor was seated with the others.

Chapter 7

Rocket Scientists

Two tables had been pulled together, and there was one seat left for me at the south end of the table. Since my chair was facing north into the window, it was a little glary causing my eyes to have a hard time adjusting to the light. I set The Professor's order in front of him and took a sip of my coffee. It was too hot to drink.

The Professor was saying something to the person to his right, and I couldn't quite hear what he was saying. The other men were talking in low tones to each other, but I could tell they were taking quick glances at me and sizing me up, so to speak -- not in a threatening way, and I didn't feel uncomfortable. I could see that they were all casually dressed and relaxed, even though I was still having trouble seeing through the glare. One man was wearing a heavy coat and a stocking cap and, frankly, did not look well. For some reason, two of them looked familiar to me, but I couldn't place their faces.

After about a minute or so, the Professor looked at me and said, "Let me introduce my guest to everyone. This is Will O'Brien, the man we have been talking about. Will has agreed to meet with us and listen to our proposal." The others were quiet and gave me polite, knowing head shrugs as a greeting.

"Will," The Professor said looking at me, "as I just mentioned, we know quite a bit about you, but, before I introduce everyone at this table, I need to give you some background information about our group before we go into our proposal. It will help you to better understand what we are doing."

"We call ourselves AASUSE. That stands for African American Scientists United for Space Exploration. Now I know that sounds pretty pretentious, but it gives us a mission and a unifying identity; and, as you probably know, scientists like to use acronyms. "

The Professor smiled at his little joke and then quickly glance around the table before he continued, "AASUSE was founded about five years ago when we all met at an astrophysics seminar at Stanford. We talked about forming an aerospace company to be owned and managed by African Americans, but it was mostly just talk and never came to fruition. Then, about two years ago, two things happened that changed everything and brought us all together, again, to seriously pursue a very important project that might save the world and, as a side benefit to us, form the basis of a successful aerospace company. "

"The first thing that happened was a unique discovery by NASA's Kepler observatory that only two members of our group had access to and which, together with other unique circumstances, led us to undertake a monumental project that could change, and save, the world. I know that sounds overly dramatic and, perhaps, pretentious, but you will see that we are not overstating our mission and the urgency that we feel."

"Dr. Neil de Grasse Tyson, the good looking man with the wavy hair and mustache sitting down at the other end of the table happens to be the Director of the Hayden Planetarium and has access to special studies developed by various programs that are hunting for exoplanets. He's famous, or infamous, as some would say, for being the face of African American space scientists. Sitting next to him is another gentleman that you may recognize -- Dr. Hakeem Oluseyi. He's an astrophysicist and cosmologist and, among other things, is temporarily stationed at NASA Headquarters in Washington DC where he's the Space Sciences Education Manager for NASA's Science Mission Directorate. These two gentlemen obtained access to top secret information developed by the Kepler observatory and The Spitzer Space Telescope."

Being a space junky, myself, I knew quite a bit about these programs and had seen both Dr. Tyson and Dr. Oluseyi on several television shows in the last few years. Dr. Oluseyi appears as a commentator and scientific authority on *Science Channel* television shows including *How the Universe Works and Outrageous Acts of Science.* Dr. Tyson is on television all the time, it seems. As I remember, he hosted the television show *Nova Science* on PBS. He's probably most famous for hosting the television series *Cosmos: A Spacetime Odyssey,* a successor to Carl Sagan's 1980 series *Cosmos: A Personal Voyage.* However, I didn't want to interrupt The Professor, so I didn't mention that I knew a lot about them.

"I can't go into too much detail, yet," The Professor continued, "but I think you need all of this background information to understand what we are doing and why we need your help. I'll try to be as succinct as possible." He stroked his chin slowly and seemed to be planning his next response.

"The Kepler Observatory was designed to survey a portion of our region of the Milky Way to discover Earth-size exoplanets in or near habitable zones of stars. Kepler's sole scientific instrument is a photometer that continually monitors the brightness of over 145,000 stars in a fixed field of view. These data are transmitted to Earth and then analyzed to detect periodic dimming caused by exoplanets that cross in front of their host star. Thousands of planets have been detected so far, and a few of them seem to be habitable and could support life. Actually, there are at least four programs searching for exoplanets now and several new programs with new, more powerful equipment will be starting in the near future. "

The Professor took a large draw on his coffee and glanced at the other men at the table. He seemed to be checking for permission to continue. The others remained placid, so he resumed his narrative. "Now here comes the interesting part. It's not too well known outside of the scientific world, but there was a serious problem with the Kepler Observatory. To simplify matters, the mechanism that was used to control the observatory malfunctioned, and it took quite awhile for NASA to learn how to overcome the problem and repurpose the observatory. "

"During that period of time, some data was lost and became unavailable to most of the staff working on the project. Neil and Hakeem, however, discovered this missing information a few years ago while preparing for a TV show for the *Science Channel* about the Kepler Observatory. They were shocked when they realized that it revealed the presence of an exoplanet that appears to be an ideal candidate for harboring life and was a little less than three light-years away from the earth. The planet's official name is Kepler-439b, but we call it Earthtoo -- spelled 'E-a-r-t-h-t-o-o.' I came up with that gem!"

I heard some low groans in response to that, but The Professor seemed un-phased and continued his explanation: "Neil and Hakeem did not immediately appreciate what they had found, and, because of the deadline for the show and other pressing business, they did not bring their discovery to the attention of the Kepler staff. I suspect there might have been some intentional procrastinating involved, also," he said with a wink and a sly grin on his face.

"The next chapter of this story developed soon thereafter. A NASA study done at the University of Maryland by a Professor Bauer has discovered that there are many large chunks of ice in the Oort Cloud beyond Pluto that will become comets and could potentially strike Earth or one of the other planets in our solar system. The study shows that there are seven times more frozen space rocks of at least one kilometer across than previously believed. These potential comets can fall into long-term orbits that take thousands of years to circle the sun and are dangerous because of their size and the fact that they travel at much faster speeds than asteroids. Fortunately for earth, the large gas planets like Jupiter block most of these comets, but some get through."

The Professor's face became serious and seemed to show a feeling of pain. Again, he took a sip of coffee and appeared to be waiting for a reaction from the others before he proceeded. He looked over at Neil deGrasse Tyson and said, "Neil, you can explain this better than me, so why don't you take over."

Dr. Tyson immediately took up the narrative. "Again, to keep it simple and to the point, there is a large junk of ice that has dropped out of the Oort Cloud and appears to be on a collision course with the Earth. The name assigned to this comet is OC289, but we refer to it as Roxy. That's an inside joke as that is the name of The Professor's ex." I heard a few snickers at this comment.

"Anyway, NASA has a team of scientists studying Roxy. Many factors could change its orbit before it comes into the proximity of Earth in about twenty-five years. They have a Cray supercomputer crunching the numbers and researching all of the permutations; but, based on current studies, there seems to be a ninety-eight percent chance that Roxy will collide with the Earth. It's about twenty kilometers in diameter and would most certainly destroy all life on our planet."

I was shocked to hear this and thought, "Why hadn't I heard anything about this?" Hakeem Oluseyi jumped in at this point and said, "You're probably wondering why you haven't heard about this in the news. Well, you will in a few months. NASA has kept this secret until now to make sure the data and conclusions are correct, but there is growing pressure to release this information. It's coming out soon. In fact, Dr. Tyson and I are working on a video for NASA that will be distributed to the news media as soon as the information is released. We are going to try to downplay the danger to Earth by emphasizing all of the things that could happen to change Roxy's orbit over the next twenty-five years, but there is most likely going to be widespread panic and fear. The project that I am going to tell you about, and for which we need your help, could avert the problem and prevent the panic, if we succeed. That's one of the reasons why we have to act quickly."

I was having difficulty comprehending this information. I've watched numerous TV shows and movies about the end of the world, many of which involve Earth being hit by an asteroid or comet, but hearing it from real scientists in this setting was unnerving. I was stunned. I had many questions but didn't know where to start. We all sat in silence for a few moments. When I was finally ready to speak, all I could say was, "What does this have to do with me?" I certainly won't be around when Roxy destroys the Earth, but my grandchildren could well be victims.

The Professor took over again. "There are two more things we have to tell you about that will explain why you are here." I thought to myself, "Two more things! What else am I going to hear about? Could it be worse than this last bit of news?"

The Professor continued, "When Neil and Hakeem made this information known to AASUSE, we decided to take action. Two of our members, who are sitting at this table with us, now, were, coincidentally, working on the plans for an interstellar spaceship at the time Roxy was discovered. Fortunately, they were pretty far along with their plans. So let me introduce you to William Barkley and Oscar Johnson. "

"Bill Barkley is a Mechanical and Chemical Engineer and is the quintessential rocket scientist. Bill is currently the chief structural engineer for several projects at United Launch Alliance which is a JV of Lockheed Martin and Boeing working in the Lockheed Martin plant in St Louis." Bill identified himself by giving a small, subtle wave of his hand. He was a small, thin man with a scruffy beard and dark heavy glasses that kept falling down his nose. He showed little expression and seemed preoccupied.

"Oscar Johnson," The Professor continued pointing at a man on the left side of the table, "is an aerospace engineer with Boeing. He's working in the Boeing office here in Chicago. His claim to fame is that he was head airframe engineer for Lockheed Grumman when the F-117, America's first stealth aircraft, was developed in the late '70s and early '80s. You will understand the significance of that in a minute." Oscar, a large man with a shaved head, was animated and intense looking and stared unblinkingly at me. He seemed a little nervous but under control. His personality contrasted sharply with that of Bill Barkley.

Looking back at me, The Professor said, "These two gentlemen have modified an F-117 to become an interstellar spaceship. As you have probably noticed, we like to assign names to our endeavors, so we call this craft "The Nina." I think you can easily understand the reference there. If you accept our proposal, we will explain how that all came about. For the time being, suffice it to say, we were able to obtain a decommissioned F-117, update its systems and install a new propulsion system that will power The Nina to Earthtoo and back in less than five Earth years, including one small detour that I will explain in a moment."

"Now," The Professor said while looking around the coffee shop to make sure we were still alone," I'm about to explain your role in this whole, highly complicated endeavor. But first, I need to introduce one more person to you: Dr. Thomas Kajubi. Tom is a self-taught computer scientist. He started a small programming company in San Jose about twenty years ago called 'Navsys.' Few people have heard of this firm, but he invented key elements of the navigation systems for, initially, guided missiles and then, eventually, drones. His good friend, Elon Musk, the founder of Space X, bought his company a few years ago for a reported 130 Million Dollars. Tom steadfastly refuses to confirm the amount to any of us, but we think that number is about right." Looking at the sickly looking man wearing a heavy coat and knit cap, The Professor said in a kindly, yet kidding tone, "Right, Tom?" Tom gave a slight nod to The Professor and let a weak smile cross his lips.

"Tom has been the chief financial resource for all of our work, and we wouldn't be sitting here now if it weren't for him. Tom, as you would expect, developed all of the guidance software for The Nina. In fact, The Nina is autonomous and can perform the entire mission without human assistance. Using artificial intelligence, it can takeoff, fly to its destination, make any adjustments necessary along the way, control all operating systems and then return and land on Earth all on its own. It's, without a doubt, the most sophisticated aircraft ever built, and all of this was accomplished in a little over two years' time thanks to our use of an existing F-117 and hardware and software 'loaned' to us by our employers. Here's a photograph of the Nina taken recently at our secret hanger location."

The Professor pulled out a 5x7 photograph of the Nina from a manila envelope on the table. I recognized it as an F-117, but it had undergone some subtle renovations. There was no cockpit and some of the surfaces had been smoothed and reshaped to be more aerodynamic. It was also painted a dark blue color instead of the matte black finish I was familiar with. I said, "Thanks for showing this to me. It's a beautiful plane. I've always wanted to fly something like that." Then I handed the photo back to The Professor.

"Unfortunately," The Professor continued with a noticeable sadness in his voice, "Tom developed colon cancer and has only a few months to live. He was diagnosed about three months ago with stage four cancer, and there is nothing that can be done for him. It has metastasized and spread throughout his body. He declined chemotherapy and radiation treatments so he would not be too sick to complete the programming of the guidance and operational systems of the craft. His work is done now, and we thank you, Tom, for all of the sacrifices you have made." Everyone at the table looked at Tom and murmured a thankful response. Bill Barkley, who was sitting next to him, reached over and gently placed his hand on top of Tom's.

"The worst part of all of this, though, is that Tom was to be the passenger on The Nina. He was looking forward to being the first human to ever leave our solar system and travel to another star. He has exhausted most of his funds, and, like all good geeks, this was the dream of his life -- to travel in outer space." Again, they all looked at Tom and smiled.

"Finally, Will, we've come to your part. We need another passenger to replace Tom. No one in our organization is willing, or capable, of doing that. We all have families, careers, health issues and other concerns that make it impossible for any of us to undertake this. That's why we brought this to you."

"When I read about your circumstances and heard about your situation, I thought of you as a replacement for Tom. After I read about your background on the internet, especially on Linkedin and Facebook, I thought you might be interested. You're a pilot with some experience flying jets and your interested in science and space travel. The trip will take about five years, although it will only feel like a few months to you, and it will make you a hero to your family and friends."

I thought, "A hero? What is he talking about?" The Professor certainly understood my mental state. I was depressed and quite hopeless of ever being happy, again, but this was a bit much to contemplate. I would give anything to escape my current fix, but this was over the top!

The Professor, anticipating my thoughts, continued, "A few minutes ago I mentioned that there would be a small detour in your trip. On your way to Earthtoo, you will also be tasked with altering the trajectory of Roxy. The Nina will be fitted with one missile that will be fired at Roxy. It will be powerful enough to nudge Roxy just enough to alter is trajectory away from Earth. A change of 1/100,000 of a degree would push Roxy a million miles away from Earth. Theoretically, it would not even be necessary to hit Roxy with a missile. The gravitational pull of a close fly-by might be enough to change the trajectory away from Earth. We don't want to take a chance, though, so we think the missile is the safest way to go."

"It's important that we launch the Nina within the next few days so that we can take advantage of the gravitational pull of Saturn, Neptune and Uranus. By using their gravitational pull, we can more quickly accelerate the Nina and save 60 days of travel time. Our hope is that the Nina can get to Roxy before NASA's announcement about her possible collision with the earth. If our plans go as expected, the Nina will be able to fire its rocket and change the course of Roxy before any announcement is necessary. "

I understood, now, what the mission was, but I had many questions about how this could all be accomplished. My most urgent question, though, was why I was needed. The Professor had said that the Nina was autonomous, so why was I needed?

I scratched the hair on the back of my head and shifted in my seat. Through the window behind our table, I noticed a blue Pace bus drive past. A cute girl on a bicycle went by in the opposite direction. Suddenly, the normal scenes of life seemed so vivid and simple.

I shook my head a little, and to no one in particular I said, "Why do you need a passenger at all. Didn't you just say the Nina was autonomous? You could send it to Earthtoo and Roxy without me. In fact, it seems to me, it would be better to not have a human passenger at all! You wouldn't need all of the equipment and supplies to keep a human passenger alive. What am I missing?"

"No. You are right," Hakeem Oluseyi quickly added. "It would be much easier to just send the Nina to Earthtoo and Roxy without a human being on board. However, there is one important fact which we haven't told you, yet."

"In preparing for our video about Roxy, Dr. Tyson and I were able to obtain exclusive data from the Spitzer Space Telescope about Earthtoo which leads us to believe that there is almost certainly life on it, and it's highly likely that it's intelligent life! The Spitzer Telescope observes objects in the infrared spectrum. It has proven to be a revolutionary tool in the characterization of exoplanets. By examining the light from an exoplanet we can determine the composition, temperature and even the likely wind patterns on a faraway exoplanet."

"The reason we think there might be intelligent life on Earthtoo is that our information also suggests that the solar system that Earthtoo belongs to is older than our solar system by at least half a billion years. We can tell that by analyzing the composition of its star and how much hydrogen it has left. Its star, called XB47a, is twenty percent smaller than our Sun, and, based on the activity of its corona, we can make a pretty good guess about its age. Our solar system is about 6.8 billion years old. We think Earthtoo's solar system is about 7.3 billion years old. Being older, it seems logical to us that life on Earthtoo is probably more advanced than life on Earth."

Hakeem looked at me and gave me a moment to absorb what he had just said. "Are you OK? Should I continue, or do you have any questions?

I had many questions, but I nodded my head so he would continue. Hakeem said, "Since there is probably intelligent life on Earthtoo, we feel strongly that there must be a human on board the Nina. The Nina is a state of the art autonomous spacecraft, but it can't make many of the decisions that will be necessary when it approaches Earthtoo. We strongly anticipate that, if there is intelligent life on Earthtoo, they will try to make contact, and only a human could deal with that situation. We can't program the Nina to deal with all of the possible decisions that will be required if that contingency occurs. AI is very advanced, but it's still very limited. It's not anywhere near human, yet. Quite simply, we need a human on board the Nina."

"And there are many other considerations," Hakeem continued. "We need a human on board for many other reasons, many of which we can't even identify at this time. When the Nina approaches Earthtoo, think of all the decisions that will have to be made. Should you orbit Earthtoo? Should you land? Where would be the best landing area? There could be many alternatives. We haven't had time to program all of the alternatives. Only a human can make those decisions. You are a pilot and will understand things that we simply haven't had time to program into the Nina. You're also a marketing professional. You're used to thinking on your feet and expressing yourself better than any of us can even imagine. Your experience could be invaluable to this project."

That made sense. I could understand that a human would be able to interact better with another intelligent civilization than an autonomous spaceship. I got that. But something popped into my mind. The most important and obvious question of all -- one no one had even hinted at so far. What if the intelligent beings on Earthtoo were hostile? What if they didn't want another civilization to discover them? What if they wanted to be left alone? If I had had time, I'm sure I could have thought of many more "What ifs."

"OK," I said, "I understand the need to have a human on board. Clearly, a human is needed to make decisions and interact with other intelligent beings, but it just came to me, and I'll bet you've thought about this -- what if the inhabitants of Earthtoo are hostile? What if they don't like the idea of another race of beings discovering them and possibly coming to their planet to live? Maybe even invading!"

"Since you think they are more advanced than we are, I'll be a sitting duck! They could blow me away in an instant. I won't stand a chance against them. I probably won't even know what hit me. They'll probably detect the Nina millions of miles away from Earthtoo. I won't stand a chance!" The more I thought about it, the more frightened I became.

The Professor was the first to respond to me, "Yes, we have thought about that. Dr. Kajubi and I have had many discussions along those lines. There isn't much research or data to help us. We feel strongly, though, that our human history shows that we are tending to become more peaceful and open-minded as we progress."

"One of our members, Dr. Yasheed Kalari, a space psychologist for NASA, has written an insightful paper about this topic. His theory is that intelligent beings will become more and more peace-loving and tolerant as they exist. The violent, self-centered beings will, eventually, through evolution and resulting attrition by war and violence, be removed from the gene pool. The peace-loving, non-violent beings will reproduce and become dominant. Wars and strife remove the warriors from society. Thoughtful, unselfish people survive because they don't put themselves in harm's way. Evolution, or survival of the fittest, seems to be leading us down the path of nonviolence and tolerance. The warriors were necessary when humans were fighting every day for survival. As society developed, though, cooperation and order became more important. That's what we are relying upon. We think it makes sense and gives us great hope for our mission."

Being an optimist by nature and someone who has always tried to be open-minded and tolerant, myself, I wanted to believe this. I was successful in business because I always trusted people and felt they would listen to reason and make good decisions. I'm not naive -- I know most people act in their own self-interest. I'd faced many daunting challenges in my life, and my experience gave me the confidence to proceed and take a chance. You can't be a small plane pilot like I was and not be an optimist. Every time you takeoff you're trusting in technology and your mechanic. What the Hell!! I had nothing to lose. The more I thought about it, the more excited I became. My mind was racing, and it made me feel good to think about the adventure this promised.

I waited a moment, though. Many times in my life I have jumped into situations without thinking them through, but it has, luckily for me, usually worked out. Deidre always said that I was blessed and that my guardian angel was looking out for me. Irish women say things like that.

I took a deep breath and said, "OK. I'm on board. I'll be your passenger. I've always dreamt about going into space, and I don't have much to lose. My current situation here on Earth doesn't look too promising." I paused for a moment and then said, "I'll do it. What's the next step?"

"That's great!" The Professor said nodding and looking around the table. "We were worried about how you would handle that issue. Tom Kajubi was looking forward to the trip and wasn't concerned about that possibility. His dream was to be the first person to experience interstellar travel, and he was willing to take a chance."

It was getting late, and other people, mostly young student looking types, were starting to come into the coffee shop. Some were taking tables near us, so The Professor looked around and said that we were finished here and should move back to the work labs. He would give me the details of my journey there and would try to answer all of my questions.

Everyone stood up and began picking up their cups and papers and then put them in the trash containers as they walked toward the door. I picked up my backpack and followed The Professor out the door and onto State Street where we started walking south. Neil and Hakeem grabbed me and shook my hand while profusely thanking me for agreeing to work with them on this mission. They said they wouldn't be able to go back to the labs with us as they had to fly to Washington tonight to finish the video about Roxy.

Chapter 8

The Labs

After saying goodbye to Neil and Hakeem, we started walking south down State Street. Bill Barkley and The Professor walked next to me. The others quickly walked ahead talking in quiet tones to each other. We walked almost a block before someone talked to me. I was wondering where we were going. The Professor said, "Our labs are about six short blocks south of here in a closed Chicago Public School known at Crispus Attucks Grade School at the corner of Pershing and Dearborn. I was able to get temporary use of that building through IIT. CPS thinks we're storing lab supplies and records in it. It's pretty rough, but it serves our needs well. "

"We should stay together and be alert," The Professor continued. "In about three blocks, it gets a little bit iffy, if you know what I mean, so be alert. Even though this area has been redeveloped and improved quite a bit, a couple of gangs are still active in this neighborhood, especially around Pershing Road, which is also 39th Street. "

Just as The Professor said that a black car with tinted windows roared by, and someone in the car shouted something and made a gesture out the front passenger window with his right hand. It was probably a gang sign, but I couldn't tell exactly what it was. Everyone in our group looked away and kept their heads down. It was nerve-wracking to me, but no one else seemed too upset, so I just followed their example. Traffic was light, but a noisy blue Pace bus roared by.

We walked along in silence for several blocks. The neighborhood became more decrepit as we proceeded further south. At about 37th Street there was a liquor store, rib joint, currency exchange and a small, dirty looking food store on the east side of State Street, all with bars and screens on the windows and signs plastered all over the buildings. Several vagrants were milling around talking to each other and people in cars were stopping to talk to them -- probably dope deals. It was a seedy-looking block.

When we finally got to 38th Street, we turned right and walked to the northwest side of a closed school building. Before we turned, I could see the name of the school in small, worn-looking letters on the east side of the building. Some of the letters were missing. It read: "Cris_us Atticu_."

Judging by its architecture, the school had probably been built in the '50s. It was a typical mid-century modern grade school building -- functional design with no texture, no ornamentation, no depth, no nothing! It was as plain, simple and functional as possible. It was almost invisible. What were people thinking then? Thank God this type of architecture died a quick and painless death. After World War II there must have been a reaction to the classical, decorative architecture of Europe. People must have wanted the opposite of the classic decorative architecture of the countries that put the world through so much suffering. But the modern architecture of the '50s and 60's was an overreaction that couldn't possibly last. It was just too ugly and uninspiring. People want something pleasing to look at, and buildings are too important a part of our world to dismiss and ignore.

All the windows on the first floor were boarded up. The grass was cut, though, and there was no trash around the building. You could tell it was not being used anymore as a grade school, but it was clean and orderly with no gang graffiti on the walls. Chicago probably has less graffiti than any major city in the world. Thanks to former Mayor Daley, it has been obsessed with eradicating graffiti, and it has paid great dividends.

Despite all of our many problems, it is a beautiful city. Many of my clients from other countries had commented on this to me many times over the years. Whenever I drove them around the city, they were amazed at how clean, beautiful and graffiti-free it was.

When we approached the rear of the school building, the Professor pointed to a black steel door at the northwest corner of the building and said, "That's where we enter. This is the old service entrance, and it's the only door we can use. We have most of our labs in the gymnasium area, and we use some of the classrooms on the second floor where there is good light."

We walked to the black steel door and entered into the closed school building. There were empty boxes and some trash in the first room we entered. A few bicycles were parked against one wall. The Professor said some of the technicians rode bicycles to work. There were a few backpacks, plastic bags and even two bicycle helmets lying on the floor near the wall. I remember one being a bright blue.

I felt as though this was a decisive step in my life, and it was totally out of character with all of my prior experiences. I didn't know what to expect, but I wasn't afraid. I was open to new possibilities, even though I was a little leery of what lay within the walls of this abandoned school building. What was I in for? I took a deep breath and followed The Professor through dark corridors. My eyes quickly began to adjust to the darkness as I entered into the unknown.

Chapter 9

Preparing For the Journey

I have to say that I was surprised at how dirty and disorganized the labs were. The Professor explained that they hadn't had time to make everything pristine and perfect. They had been working nonstop for the last two years to perfect the Nina and the passenger module, which they referred to as the "PM." They were short-handed and only did what was necessary. Because they weren't certain how long they could use the Atticus Labs, they didn't spend any unnecessary funds to remodel them and make them look like commercial labs. And, since the project was nearing completion, they had let things go recently.

The Nina, they explained, is located at a small airfield about an hour from Chicago. That's where they performed all the work retrofitting the craft for space travel. When I asked where, they declined to tell me exactly where it was. They apologized for not being able to give me the location at this time, but they were still worried about security and couldn't make me privy to that information until they were one hundred percent certain of my commitment. I understood and told them not to worry.

Having only known me for two days, I understood their need to withhold some information. Since they were being open and forthright with me, otherwise, I was willing to be patient and give them time to disclose all necessary information.

That's something I'd learned in business. If you don't push people and make them feel uneasy, the truth will always come out. The more people learn to trust you, the more they will reveal about themselves and their business. Trust, more than anything else, is a key part of all business activity. It's impossible to fully research every situation or opportunity, so many times a business person has to rely on people to be honest and fair with them.

Anyway, getting back to the first day, after entering the labs, I followed The Professor through some dark rooms to a stairway leading up to the second floor of the building. The windows on the second floor had not been boarded up, and there was an abundance of natural light. I was not sure of the time, but it seemed as though it was late in the afternoon. Like most people who relied upon their cell phone, I hadn't worn a watch in several years and didn't bring one with me. Since I left my cell phone at home, I didn't have any way of telling time.

We entered what appeared to be a classroom, although all of the desks had been removed. The chalkboards in the front of the room were filled with mathematical formulas and drawings that appeared to be our solar system, a comet, stars and what I surmised to be the trajectory of a spaceship. There was one table in the front of the room and boxes and instruments were scattered around.

The Professor explained that this was their main planning room. Most of the assembly and programming of the guidance and operating system, which he said they called CATO, was performed in these labs by Tom Kajubi and his technicians. CATO is a Latin word meaning intelligent or all-knowing, and it's an acronym for Computing Autonomously Trajectory and Operations. I think they stretched for that one, but it does work pretty well to describe the computer system.

The Professor, apparently, took charge of naming things, and I must say he's pretty clever. Being a marketing professional, I know how important it is to name things properly. It has to be something people will remember and like or identify with. More than one product has been ruined by the wrong name.

I once was asked to do a marketing plan for a company that had food products made from bones and raw foods. They insisted that all their products use the name BARF. They had Barf Burgers and Barf Dogs and some other products. They thought Barf was catchy, funny and appealing to most people, especially men. I told them that I didn't think they should use that name and that they needed to consult with some focus groups before they proceeded.

They took offense and told me that I was just trying to increase my fees and that they could write their own marketing plan. I'll bet you've never heard of Barf Burgers, have you? I did hear a few years later that they had a somewhat successful line of dog foods that they sold mainly in the Mid-West and South.

Sorry, I digressed a little there. Anyway, The Professor told me to sit down, and he would outline what had to be done. After putting my backpack in a corner, we sat at a small folding table in the planning room. The Professor glanced around the room looking for something. "Would you like something to eat or drink?" he asked. I hadn't thought about food, but when he said that I realized I was hungry. "Yes, I said, now that you mentioned it, I'm hungry. What've you got to eat?"

The Professor looked around, again, and said, "Lately, because of our deadlines, we've existed pretty much on power bars and Mountain Dew. I think I might be able to rustle some up for you, if that's OK."

Just then I could smell the smoke from the rib joint down the street that we had passed on our way here, and I said, "Those ribs sure smell good. If it weren't so dangerous to go there, I'd buy some for us." Through a broken window in the Planning Room, the enticing smell was pouring in. The wind must have shifted. I love barbecued food, especially ribs and brisket; but, because

Deirdre hated it (she had a limited pallet), I seldom had a chance to eat any, especially in Chicago.

The Professor looked a little offended by my statement, and I realized that I may have insulted him with my remark that it wouldn't be safe to go to the rib joint. He quickly let it go, though, and said, "You know, that's a great idea. If you're serious about the ribs, I can get some for you."

I said, "Yes, I'd love some ribs. I have some money in my backpack, and I'll treat you." I remembered that I had five hundred dollars in my backpack and realized that I might as well spend it as I wasn't going to need it where I was going.

The Professor stood up and said, "OK. I have an idea. Wait here." He then went out in the hall, and I heard him call to someone and talk to them. Then he came back into the room.

"OK. I have someone who'll go buy the ribs for us. One of our technicians has gone to Shorty's Ribs a few times, and he'll run over for us. We'll have to include him and Oscar Johnson in our dinner. I think it will take about forty dollars to cover the cost. Oscar is coming here in a few minutes to explain to you about the Nina, and he should eat with us. Is that OK with you?"

I told him that would be great as I went to my backpack and dug out forty dollars and gave it to The Professor. He went out in the hall and returned in a few minutes.

He sat back down, again, and began talking to me, "We only have one day to prepare you for your journey, but that shouldn't be a problem. CATO will do all of the heavy lifting, and you only have to be a good passenger. If there's anything we leave out or overlook, CATO will be able to fill you in and answer most of your questions. "

"We'll cover some information this evening, and then we'll spend all day tomorrow giving you more info and training. Then, on the next day, you'll be transported in the passenger module to the Nina." The Professor stopped there and took a breath. He seemed to get winded easily, and I wondered about his health. There was nothing I could put my finger on, except a little breathlessness from time to time. I suspected that he had emphysema from years of smoking a pipe, but I was just guessing. I said a silent prayer that he would be strong enough to complete the mission. That sounds crass. I meant that I hoped he would be OK.

He looked kindly at me, smiled, and then pressed on. "If I go too fast or if you have any questions, don't hesitate to interrupt me. I know this is all going to sound pretty far out and complicated, so stop me if you need time to absorb any of this." I shook my head and indicated I was OK. Then I had a second thought and asked if I could take notes. I had one of my notebooks with me that I use for writing ideas. The Professor thought about it for a few second and then said, "I guess that would be OK. If for any reason you don't go through with this, we'll have to take your notes. Is that OK?"

"Yes, of course," I said and then walked over to my backpack and took out my notebook and a pen and returned to the table where we were seated.

"Sorry we're so rushed, but we have to meet limited time parameters so that we don't miss certain windows of opportunity." He then explained something about using the gravitational pull of certain planets like a slingshot to increase the acceleration of the Nina, but I don't remember the exact details.

Then he continued, "We'll be giving you information about the Nina and CATO, mainly so you know what to expect. Even though you'll have no control over the Nina, there are some things you need to know about the PM and the operation of the ship. Most importantly, though, there are some key decisions that you'll have to make when you arrive at Earthtoo. We'll talk about most of that tomorrow when we meet with Kajubi."

"I'm going to go find Oscar Johnson, now, so he can give you the info that you will need about The Nina. He's our chief Aerospace Engineer and knows the most about the Nina. I'm not sure where he is right now, so I'll have to go look for him. Wait here for me."

The Professor started to walk away, but then he hesitated and said, "It would be best if you stayed in this room for the time being. No offense, but we have a lot of sensitive information and delicate equipment in our labs, so it would be best, at least for this evening, if you stayed here. Some of our people are a little touchy right now because of the pressure we're under, and they don't want to be bothered with any distractions. I'm sure you can understand that."

I said, "No problem. I understand."

The Professor was gone for what seemed like a long time. Since I didn't have a watch, I wasn't sure, but it seemed like about twenty or thirty minutes. I stretched out on one of the chairs and closed my eyes and drifted off to sleep for a few minutes. I was tired and worn out by all of the excitement and new experiences I'd had.

I was awakened when The Professor and Oscar Johnson entered the room with another man who looked as though he might have been in his early twenties. He had an earring in each earlobe and was thin and neatly dressed with an expertly trimmed hairstyle. He had a tattoo of some type on his neck. I couldn't make out what it was. His mannerisms were noticeably effeminate, and he gave me a little flick of a wave and a smile. They were carrying three Styrofoam packages, a brown paper bag with some utensils and a large bottle of wine.

The young man took one package and left the room. I noticed as he left that he had a small dog with him that looked as though it might be a pug and some other mixtures. It had a cute, human-like, expressive face. It seemed to smile at me. The Professor brought the other packages and the wine to the table where I was seated and put them down carefully in the center. The smell was fantastic. Oscar sat opposite me alongside The Professor.

The Professor said, as he opened the packages and spread out some plates, plastic forks and knives and napkins, "We caught Robbie in the hall as we were heading toward this room. Robbie is taking some classes at IIT and is our intern. We can't pay him much, but he sleeps here and eats some of his meals with us. Help yourself while it's still hot." The packages contained a large slab of ribs cut into four pieces, rib tips and a huge pile of fries, all liberally covered with dark red sauce.

We all dug in and piled food on our plates. It tasted great, and I was savoring every bite. I had eaten little all day, and this food was perfect -- a little sloppy and hard to eat, but oh so tasty.

The Professor twisted open the large wine bottle and poured some wine into three Styrofoam cups that were on another table in the room. The wine was cheap Chianti of a brand that I had never seen, but it tasted OK and went well with the barbecue.

We ate in silence for probably five minutes, and then The Professor said, "As you recall, Oscar was an airframe engineer for Lockheed Grumman when the F-117, America's first stealth aircraft, was developed many years ago, actually it was about 1981, as I recall, right Oscar?"

Oscar looked up from his food, wiped his mouth off and mumbled something as he shook his head up and down.

The Professor continued, "Oscar was a young engineer then and was lucky enough to work for Lockheed at their secretive Skunk Works division where the Nighthawk, that's what it was called, was developed. It was the first operational aircraft to use stealth technology and was shrouded in secrecy until it was revealed to the public in about 1988. Only 64 were built."

I remember when it first appeared in the news. I had been a pilot for several years and was fascinated by the stealth technology and the exotic appearance of the plane. I had fantasized more than once about flying one. One day, my commander in the Air National Guard asked me if I would like to see one. We went to a secret showing of the plane at The Scott Air Force base in southern Illinois. The showing was to sell the two Illinois Senators at the time, Charles Percy and (I can't remember who the other one was at the time), on the plane and get them to support a large appropriation to build 50 more. I was allowed to sit in the cockpit and an Air Force pilot gave me a detailed explanation of how to fly it. I can still visualize the instruments and feel of the cockpit. It was awesome. Now that I think about it, I mentioned that experience on my Facebook page. The Professor might have read that information and that may have influenced his picking me for this mission.

I could tell that The Professor wanted Oscar to take over the conversation, but he was still eating, so The Professor continued, "We were able to get our hands on one of the retired Nighthawks under a ruse that it would be installed in The Museum of Science and Industry here in Chicago. Working with Neil deGrasse Tyson and Hakeem Oluseyi, we obtained a contract to prepare the plane for its museum installation."

I thought to myself -- that seemed strange that they could land that type of contract, and I gave The Professor a quizzical look. He must have read my mind and responded, "I'm not ashamed to say we had to play the minority card to get the contract. The Air Force was thrilled as they seem to have a hard time getting minority contracts on the books." The Professor smiled broadly and looked quite satisfied with himself.

Then he continued, "The Nighthawk was retired from service in 2008. There are three or four in museums and the rest are being stored and slowly demilitarized."

"Most airplanes stay in service a lot longer than the Nighthawk, but, because it was the first of a kind, it had many operational problems and was quickly superseded, relatively speaking, by the F-15 and F-22. It was under powered and slow and, to save weight, did not have radar. Because of its design and stealthy shape, controlling it was a problem. Not being very aerodynamic, it took a computer making constant adjustments to keep it flying."

Finally, Oscar appeared to be finished eating, and The Professor looked at him and said, "OK, Oscar, it's my turn to eat and your turn to start talking about the Nina. Pass me that package with the rib tips, if there's any left in it." The Professor said this with good humor, and we all knew he was doing a little good-natured chiding. Then he smiled and said, "We like to give each other a little ribbing, from time to time."

I laughed and said, "Good one! You guys are funny and relaxed. I like that."

Without missing a beat, the Professor looked at me and said, in a good Joe Pesci imitation from the *Goodfellas*, "I'm funny, how? Funny, like I'm a clown? I amuse you?" We all laughed at that and shook our heads.

Oscar, still shaking his head and laughing, took a long drink of wine and then rubbed his hands with several napkins. After that he opened up a wet-nap package and continued to clean his hands and face. We were, apparently, in no rush, so this pause did not seem to be a problem. I was enjoying the food, the interesting story and the humor. I felt relaxed for a change. It was the first time in several months that I wasn't anxious and worried about my accident. I was thankful for the distraction. It was weird but exciting, and I was looking forward to a new and interesting experience.

Oscar, talking at first in a monotone and with little expression, began explaining about the Nina. As he talked, he made little eye contact, but he was clear and spoke slowly and forcefully. It was almost as though he was watching a video as he spoke. Despite that, he had an intensity that demanded your attention.

Since I didn't have a watch, I'm not sure how long he may have spoken, but my guess was about two hours. Once I became attuned to his speech patterns, I had no trouble following him. He was interesting, and I had the impression that he had done public speaking before and knew how to explain things to non-technical people.

Luckily, because I was taking notes, I think I can summarize what he told me. There was so much technical information thrown at me that I may have missed a few things, but my notes should be adequate.

As The Professor had mentioned, the Nina was made from a retired F-117 Nighthawk, but many sophisticated changes were made to its design, operating systems and, most importantly, its propulsion system.

Because of my interest in aviation and my natural curiosity about space travel, I was able to understand much of what he was telling me. I don't mean to boast, but I've read a lot about space travel and rockets, so I understood the basic principles and theories involved. I'm not a scientist, but I have what I call a good *Popular Mechanics /Popular Science* understanding of the concepts. I've read those publications since I was a kid and loved to fantasize about traveling to the Moon or even Venus or Mars. Interstellar travel, however, was seldom considered or even discussed because of the incredible distances involved. The closest star was thought to be four or five light-years away.

Light travels at the speed of 186,000 miles per second, so one light-year would be approximately six trillion miles.

No imaginable vehicle could travel at that speed let alone carry enough fuel or supplies for that time and distance. Also, there are problems with gamma-ray exposure and physical and psychological deterioration. Speeds of about 300,000 miles per hour were thought possible and that would mean it would take thousands of years for a spaceship to travel three or four light-years.

Getting back to Oscar, he talked a lot about the development of the Nighthawk. He was in his mid-thirties when he worked at the Skunk Works when the F-117 was developed. Being the only black engineer on the project, he felt as though he had to overcome a lot of prejudice and discrimination to achieve what he did. He wondered a little off track, and I could tell he had some hard feelings about his experiences. Nevertheless, it was interesting, and I didn't mind listening.

Even though the Skunk Works was located in Burbank, California, and many of the people working on the project were highly educated and generally liberal, he still had to prove himself over and over again to gain the trust of the project leaders and his co-workers. Everyone he worked with apparently felt they had to make some comment about his being the only black engineer. Other condescending or patronizing remarks seemed to be almost mandatory, even by the friendliest of people.

It was subtle and not always overt, but he knew that black people were stereotyped even by the most opened minded and accepting people with whom he worked. In the late '70s and early 80's most whites could not believe that someone from his background could excel at science and engineering -- African Americans just weren't supposed to be nerds or scientists.

One of the things that confirmed his feelings was the way women were treated. There were no women engineers on the project and sexist remarks were common and not subtle. At that time in history, most men were openly misogynists and unapologetic for it. It was common knowledge, so they thought, that women had no aptitude for science and math and that they couldn't do the work of men. They just didn't have the strength, stamina and creativeness of men.

If a woman came into the design rooms or the assembly and manufacturing areas, they were almost immediately harassed with comments, looks or subtle (and sometimes not so subtle) gestures. Cartoons, jokes and sexist pictures were abundant and so common they were unnoticed by most of the employees.

The term "hostile environment" wasn't used in those days, but that's what it was, even between the men. Bullying was common and anyone who showed a weakness was picked on and made fun of, especially in the manufacturing area.

Any man who showed any effeminate tendencies was called a queer or a faggot and harassed unmercifully. I could feel Oscar's intense underlying feelings as he talked about this, and he had to force himself to get back on track.

I think we have come a long way in the last decade, and, ironically, it benefits everyone, even white men. Today's work environment, at least in my experience, is incredibly improved over what it was thirty years ago. I'm happy to say that I made some small contributions to that at Bennington.

Getting back to the Nina, at first, five prototypes of the F-117 were manufactured. Then it went into production and about another sixty were made. It was a unique looking plane -- many people thought it looked like the Bat Plane should look. It wasn't designed so much for aerodynamics as for stealth. The different angles of the fuselage and wings were designed to reflect radar waves. As a result, it was unstable and impossible to fly manually. It employed a "fly by wire" control system run by a computer that made constant adjustments to keep it stable. The term fly by wire means that the flight control surfaces were not controlled directly by hand or foot controls through cables or rods or pneumatic lines. Servo motors controlled by a computer were used to adjust the flight control surfaces.

Oscar said that, to expedite development and keep cost down, most of the fly-by-wire equipment was borrowed from previous aircraft that first utilized the fly by wire technique. The computer system though was new and had quadruple redundancy. This was necessary as a failure of the computer system would result in a catastrophic failure of the craft.

To reduce the radar profile of the Nighthawk, the air intakes had to be small and hooded, this limited the power of the engines resulting in a relatively slow, subsonic plane. Other equipment, including radar, was eliminated to reduce the weight of the plane. This all restricted the versatility and effectiveness of the Nighthawk and limited its usefulness and service. That's why it was replaced relatively quickly.

An interesting fact about the Nighthawk that Oscar revealed, with a tinge of condescension in his voice, was that the designation of the plane, F-117, was intentionally misleading and manipulative.

He explained that the designation "F" would normally indicate that it was a fighter plane. In fact, it was really an attack plane, essentially a "bomber," and its number should have been prefaced with an "A." However, to make it popular with the best pilots, it was called a fighter and not a boring bomber!

Then Oscar began to explain how the Nina came to be. As The Professor had said, using a little trickery and misdirection, one of the mothballed Nighthawks had been obtained for the Museum of Science and Industry in Chicago. It had been partially disassembled and then delivered to a hanger at an airfield near Chicago to prepare it for the museum exhibit. Oscar and his crew of about eight engineering members of AASUSE have been modifying it for the last two years for its mission to Roxy and Earthtoo.

Using new computer assisted design techniques; the airframe was modified to be more aerodynamic and conducive to its new power system, which I will explain in a moment. The original design was squared off in places, resulting in a less than optimal aerodynamic design. At the time it was designed and built, computers were not as powerful as they are today and could not model and test the designs as they can now.

One of the most important modifications was the removal of the cockpit resulting in a more aerodynamic shape. Using carbon fiber materials and other structural elements, many of which were derived from the Boeing 787 manufacturing breakthroughs, the Nina was reshaped and improved. These techniques could be performed by Oscar's technicians and did not require massive sheet metal presses and other machines and equipment normally associated with conventional airframes.

Most of the ordinance equipment for guns, bombs and rockets were removed, except for the one rocket launcher that would be used to move Roxy out of its trajectory toward Earth. There are two bomb bays in the Nighthawk. For the Nina, one was kept and modified for the rocket meant for Roxy, and the other was modified to hold the passenger module and supporting equipment.

As I listened to Oscar talk in detail about the modifications that had been made to the Nina, most of which I did not understand, I was dying to ask him one obvious question: How could this relatively small plane fly far enough and fast enough to travel to Earthtoo? Earthtoo was over eighteen trillion miles away!

Anything I had ever heard or seen about interstellar spacecraft described them as huge ships capable of carrying enormous amounts of fuel and supplies. Because of weightlessness concerns and heavy shielding from gamma rays and meteors, the ships were usually pictured as large rotating vessels with thick shielding and giant rockets for propulsion.

Finally, after about an hour of listening to Oscar describe minute design changes, he began to answer my concern, and the answer was mind-boggling! As it turns out, the Nina is powered by two fusion engines! I've read a little about fusion, and I knew that it was the most likely form of power for interstellar flight, but everything that I'd read or heard about it indicated that it was almost impossible to achieve and was tens of years away, if at all, from actuality. There are several videos on *YouTube* about it, and one hints that the Skunk Works had secretly developed a fusion engine. No one believed this, and I found it hard to believe.

I told Oscar that, and he said he couldn't go into too much detail about it, but he assured me it was true. This entire project would be unthinkable if it were not true. He gave me the short, lay version of how it all came about. Based on my notes about what he said, this is how I understood it.

Essentially, a fusion reaction occurs when two (or more) atomic nuclei come close enough for the strong nuclear force pulling them together to exceed the electrostatic force pushing them apart, fusing them into heavier nuclei. To fuse, nuclei must be brought close enough together for the strong force to act, which occurs only at very short distances. The electrostatic force keeping them apart acts over long distances, so a significant amount of kinetic energy (heat) is needed to overcome this barrier before the reaction can take place.

There are several ways of doing this, including speeding up atoms in a particle accelerator, or, more commonly, heating them to very high temperatures.

Once an atom is heated above its ionization energy, its electrons are stripped away, leaving just the bare nucleus (the ion). The result is a hot cloud of ions and the electrons formerly attached to them. This cloud is known as a plasma. Because the charges are separated, plasmas are electrically conductive and magnetically controllable. Some fusion devices use powerful magnets to control the particles as they are being heated and to prevent them from burning up the walls of the engine and losing energy. These magnets are very large and consume more energy in the fusion process than they produce.

To solve these problems, the Skunkworks' engineers invented several devices to overcome these drawbacks and reduce the size and increase the efficiency of their fusion engine. They created superconducting materials that do not require low temperatures and greatly reduce the size and weight and efficiency of the magnets. They developed more powerful focused lasers and several other new technologies (one of which is essentially microwaves like in a microwave oven, only at a much higher energy level) to control the fusion, all of which resulted in tremendous energy that would propel the Nina at near-light speeds.

And the coolest part of all is that the fuel is hydrogen derived from just water. By using electrolysis, water, with a little sodium added, is broken down into hydrogen and oxygen. Electricity is passed through the water, and the water breaks down into two parts hydrogen and one part oxygen. In the past, this process had a big drawback in that the anode and cathode used to pass the electricity through the water would corrode and stop working.

Recently, special materials have been developed to make anodes and cathodes that don't corrode. So the process can run for a long time without failing. This is important since the Nina will need a steady supply of hydrogen to make it to Earthtoo and back.

Just half a gallon of hydrogen fuel is equal to the entire fuel supply carried by the Space Shuttle, and it's a million times more powerful (and much easier to handle) than current rocket fuel -- which is liquid hydrogen and liquid oxygen, a very explosive mixture.

A member of AASUSE works at the Skunkworks and was able to sidetrack some of the materials needed for the Nina. This is also how the two fusion engines were obtained by Oscar. The two engines being used in the Nina were early prototypes that were abandoned by the Skunkworks team. Oscar was able to surreptitiously sidetrack them out of storage for this project. Since he also had access to all of the current research on the fusion engine, he was able to modify the prototype engines and, in his opinion, improve on them.

The Nina was modified to carry about twenty-eight hundred gallons of water, which, according to Oscar, is more than enough fuel to propel the Nina to Earthtoo and back at near-light speeds. He also said that a couple of backup systems were installed just in case the Nina ran out of water.

One backup is a system that can collect hydrogen in outer space. As it turns out, there is an abundance of free hydrogen in outer space. It seems empty, but, traveling at a fast speed, it is possible to collect hydrogen as the Nina travels through space. The intake ports for the engines can open up and collect hydrogen. Based on their calculations, enough hydrogen can be collected in this manner to provide all of the fuel needed to travel to Earthtoo and back.

A second backup system can collect water from chunks of ice in outer space. Many asteroids and comets and other bodies in outer space are mostly frozen water. The Nina is outfitted with a drill and suction system that could, theoretically, obtain water from these various bodies of ice in outer space. It would be very tricky to land on a comet, for example, and harvest water from it, but the autonomous onboard guidance system is programmed to do that, if necessary. This is brilliant and gave me some comfort to know these backup systems are available.

Getting back to the question of time and speeds involved, apparently, based on Einstein's calculations, nothing can exceed the speed of light. Light speed is the absolute limit of the speed any matter can achieve. Oscar explained why, but, frankly, I didn't understand what he was saying. Something to do with waves, but I'm not sure.

Oscar said that, according to his calculations, The Nina will be able to travel at about 95% of the speed of light. Assuming that it might take several days to achieve that speed, it should only take about three years and three months to travel to Earthtoo. But here is the best part, as far as the passenger is concerned, it will seem like only about two and a half months will have passed! This is because the faster a person travels, the more time slows down. If it were possible to travel at the speed of light, time would stop. So, if I travel to Earthtoo and back at ninety-five percent of the speed of light, it will seem as though only five months have passed, plus whatever time I spend on Earthtoo, which probably wouldn't be more than a week or so.

I liked that scenario. Six and half years would have passed on Earth, but I would only be five months older. My grandkids and my son would still be young, and, when I returned, I knew I could quickly get caught up with them. I felt certain of that.

I didn't like the thought of leaving them for such a long period of time, but, if I did return, I would be a hero.

That should go a long way to make up for my absence. The possible criminal charges against me would probably be forgotten and dropped after six years, and who would prosecute a hero who saved the Earth!

Deirdre would be a lot older, and I felt bad about that, but she couldn't stand to be around me, anyway. Maybe my absence would soften her heart and make her forgive me, if I ever return. There is always the chance she would remarry, but I don't think so -- she's too cautious to ever do that, and I know she just wouldn't have the energy to look for another man. Besides, she has many friends and family members to keep her from being too lonely, if she will only let them help her.

I just hope and pray that she can get some professional help with her depression and hopelessness. A good psychologist could probably help her. I've tried for years to make her happy, but she never responded to my efforts. I do feel bad about her. If I thought I could do something to help her, though, I wouldn't even consider this mission.

Another benefit to my absence would be financial. Deirdre could live a lot more cheaply by herself, and my absence might help the attorneys settle all of the claims more easily and less contentiously. I don't have any life insurance, so that will not be a factor. Being wealthy and having adequate assets to live comfortably on for the rest of my life, I had never seen the need for insurance. If I did have life insurance, any payout Deirdre might obtain would have to be paid back, and it might also complicate settling the lawsuits.

And I have to say, there is another interesting facet to this whole scheme -- for me, as the passenger, it will be like traveling five years into the future. Being the closet nerd that I am, I always wanted to time travel. What science fiction fan would pass up that opportunity? Who knows, the world could change drastically in five years -- hopefully for the better. Controlled fusion, alone, could significantly improve the future. It could provide cheap energy and make travel faster and easier for everyone. The more I thought about it, the more excited and hopeful I became.

While Oscar was briefing me on the Nina, I was sipping some red wine as I took notes. I'm not sure how long he talked, but I felt it was getting quite late. The Professor had nodded off and was sound asleep with his head on his arms leaning over a table. I was getting drowsy and was finding it hard to concentrate.

Oscar was getting tired, also, and he seemed as though he wanted to finish and wrap up his part of my education. He had been sipping wine with me, and his speech was starting to slow down and slur a little.

Finally, he looked at me, raised his cup of wine and said, "I think that pretty well covers everything you need to know for now. I'm getting tired and my brain's starting to slow down. CATO, the on-board computer system, contains detailed info about the Nina and every aspect of our project, so you can always consult it. Tom Kajubi will teach you all about it. You'll have plenty of time to read and study on your trip."

I was glad to hear him call it quits for tonight, but I realized that I didn't know what to do next. Where would I sleep? Is there something I need to know about my surroundings? Was there a bathroom available?

Just then, Oscar got up from his chair and walked shakily over to The Professor. He shook one of his shoulders and said, "Come on, Sleeping Beauty, time to wake up or I'll give you a kiss."

The Professor raised his head from his arms and shook his head to clear the sleep from his mind. He grunted a couple of times, straightened up, and then looked at me saying, "Are you gentlemen finished? What time is it? Sorry I fell asleep, but Oscar always bores me to death."

Oscar didn't reply to that and simply walked slowly out of the room shaking his head and then turned left and disappeared down the hall.

I asked The Professor if there was a bathroom nearby and where was I going to sleep. He said, "Yes, of course. Let me show you where the bathroom is. While you're in the bathroom, I'll wrestle up some blankets for you. You'll have to sleep in this room tonight. But don't worry. After tonight, you'll be sleeping in the PM, so you just have to manage one night in here. Follow me, and I'll show you where the bathroom is. The accommodations are rather rough here, but we're almost finished so we haven't put too much into the niceties."

I grabbed my backpack and followed The Professor out into the hall and into what had been the boy's bathroom. The "Boys" sign was still on the wall. He said he would meet me back in the Planning Room and left me alone.

There was one faint light on in the bathroom, and it was hard to see and didn't smell too great, either. I was pretty groggy and just wanted to relieve myself and wash my hands and face. I found a clean urinal and took care of one problem. Then I washed up in one of the sinks. There was only cold water available. Luckily I had some soap and a towel in my backpack, so I was prepared -- like the good Eagle Scout that I once was. I even had a toothbrush and toothpaste so I could brush my teeth, which made me feel good.

I don't know what the other people working in the building had done -- probably went to their homes or a hotel for the night. It was quiet and there were no other lights on, except in the Planning Room, and the bathroom.

When I returned to the Planning Room, The Professor was there with some blankets and what appeared to be a large piece of cardboard from a broken down box. He looked a little sheepish and apologized for the poor sleeping arrangements. Together we laid out the cardboard for padding and then put a blanket over it. I then arranged a small blanket as a pillow and another blanket so I could pull it over myself after I lay down.

The Professor looked at the makeshift bed and then raised his hands as if to say, "Well. That's the best we can do for tonight." I said, "That's OK. I've slept on worse on some of my fishing trips."

The Professor then said, "I'll be in the room next door. I have a cot in there that I use when I need to stay here over-night. I'll see you tomorrow morning, and we'll finish your training. You'll be sleeping in the PM tomorrow night. I'll explain all of that to you tomorrow. Goodnight, Will. I think you made the right decision. You won't regret it."

With that, he walked out of the room and turned the light off. There was some light coming in through the windows from the street lights outside that allowed me to see what I was doing so I could get myself arranged in my bed. Once I was arranged, I started to say my nightly prayer but before I could thank God for this strange but promising day I immediately fell fast asleep.

Chapter 10

My Last Day on Earth

My last day on Earth began as I awoke with a start. Someone was shaking me. For a minute, I didn't know where I was. I had been dreaming about flying over a beautiful lake on one of my fishing trips. It might have been in Wisconsin or Michigan. It was hard to tell. It was surrounded by a beautiful forest of Pine and Oak trees. There was a beautiful fishing pier extending out into the lake, and I saw a large fish jump out of the water.

I was all alone in my dream and couldn't remember the name of the lake. It looked familiar, but I couldn't remember its name. Even worse, I had no idea where the nearest airport was, and I was running low on fuel. I knew I had a map somewhere, but I couldn't find it. Then I saw another plane flying near me. A woman was flying it, and she was looking at me and telling me to pay attention. The woman looked like Deirdre and then she morphed into another woman. Was it Mary Carroll? Then I awoke. Despite those concerns, I was sad that I had to wake up.

It suddenly hit me where I was, and I was filled with a whirlwind of anxiety and doubt. I thought, "What am I doing?" My stomach made a flip, and I thought I might be sick. I knew I would be all right, though, as soon as I was fully awake and had some coffee or juice to drink. I had awakened with that sick feeling many times in my working career when I had a big project due or had to make a presentation to a large group of clients. I remembered, though, that I had always made it through and been successful. That gave me the confidence to face my worries today.

God bless The Professor. When I looked up and focused on him, there he was holding a cup of coffee for me. Something also smelled good, and I suddenly felt strong hunger pains in my stomach.

Then I heard The Professor say, "I took the liberty of sending Robbie out again to get some breakfast for us from McDonald's. There's one a few blocks away, and he brought back several breakfast sandwiches and several cups of coffee. I had to use some of your money in your backpack. I hope you don't mind."

"Of course I don't," I said. "Thanks for thinking of this. I'm starved, and I'm not going to have any use for that money after tomorrow, so feel free to use it for whatever will help our mission. After I'm on my way, put it to good use. Buy the whole crew some ribs or whatever -- and don't forget the wine -- as my way of saying, 'Thank you!' "

I quickly gulped down two Egg McMuffins and another cup of coffee. The food made me feel much better and rejuvenated my determination to press forward with the mission. I think I slept seven or eight hours last night. As a result, I felt rested and clear-headed, even though it appeared that we had finished a large bottle of wine and a lot of rich food as we talked last night. Fortunately for me, I'm blessed with a cast-iron stomach and seldom have heartburn or stomach problems.

As I cleaned up my breakfast wrappings and coffee cups, I asked The Professor what was on the agenda for today. He seemed distracted as we were eating, and I noticed that his breathing was heavy and wheezy.

Slowly gathering himself and turning toward me, he said, "You'll be meeting with two people today, and then you'll be placed in the PM for transportation to the Nina this evening. The last part is more complicated than it sounds, but we'll go into detail on it later. For now, as soon as Tom Kajubi can make it here, he'll explain the operation and guidance features of the Nina, including a detailed explanation of how to use and communicate with CATO, the master computer system. Tom feels best in the morning, so I've scheduled him to meet with you first. He should be along soon. Just to be safe, I think I should go look for him and see if I can speed him along. You wait here and I'll be back as soon as I can."

With that, The Professor left the Planning Room and took a left down the hall. I needed to use the bathroom, anyway, so I was happy to have an opportunity to take care of a few things. I grabbed my backpack and walked to the restroom.

After I returned to the planning room, I reviewed my notes from yesterday and waited for The Professor and Tom Kajubi to return. I was starting to get bored and a little irritated about the delay when I heard The Professor coming down the hall talking to someone.

The Professor and Tom Kajubi stood outside the door and talked quietly for a short time and then entered the room. Tom looked weak and ashen, a little worse than he had looked yesterday.

He was a short man, probably only five feet five inches in height, and very thin. He was wearing a heavy coat that looked like an old wool topcoat with the collar turned up around his neck over a gray scarf. Like yesterday, he had on a black knit cap, but he pulled it off when he entered the room. His hair, which was very thin, short and gray, was sticking up in various directions. He reached up and made a moderately successful effort at smoothing it down.

The Professor held his arm and directed him into a chair on the other side of the table, opposite me. He helped him into the chair and asked him if he needed anything. Tom asked for a cup of water.

I sat quietly and watched all of this. When Tom had a minute to catch his breath and take a sip of water, I felt compelled to say something to him. I wasn't sure how to address him, so I said, "Thanks for meeting with me this morning, Dr. Kajubi. I know you don't feel well, and I appreciate the effort you're making."

Tom lifted his hand and said in a weak, quiet voice, "First of all, I'm not a doctor of anything. I never graduated from college, so just call me 'Tom.' I'm almost totally self-taught, except for a few courses I took at Poly Tech many years ago."

Secondly, I should be thanking you for taking my place. I can't thank you enough. If you hadn't taken my place, this project might have died. It's the culmination of my life's work, my life's dream. Its completion will be the only recognition I want. It will be the fulfillment of all that I ever hoped to achieve."

I could see that he was struggling and using all of his strength and determination to talk to me. I moved as close as I could to him so that he wouldn't' have to expend any unnecessary energy. I was leaning across the table as far as I could. It still seemed as though he was struggling and forced to make too much of an effort, and I was having trouble hearing him.

I looked at The Professor who was sitting next to Tom and said, "Would it be all right if I sat on the other side of Tom. I think it would be better for him, and I would be able to hear better."

The Professor and Tom both nodded their heads, so I moved next to Tom. He smelled musty and as though he was using some type of balm or analgesic. It wasn't bad or offensive, though. Tom took another sip of water and turned toward me. I had my notebook open and started taking notes.

Tom spoke for almost two hours about CATO and the guidance system of the Nina. He had to stop frequently and rest, but he showed great determination and plowed ahead. I asked him a few times if he would like to take a break or use the bathroom, but he only shook his head and continued. What a presentation! He was organized and his knowledge and memory amazed me.

Thank God, he only used a small amount of jargon and a few acronyms, which made his presentation clear and easy to understand. Most techies love to use jargon and acronyms to impress lay people, but not Tom. I only had to stop him three or four times to ask him to explain something to me.

I took copious notes, many of which do not make much sense to me now. This is a summary of what he talked about and what I gleaned from his explanations and descriptions of CATO, the guidance system and the controls of the Nina.

First of all, he assured me that the Nina is a safe and worthy craft. He personally had checked all of the work and was not concerned for his safety. He would not have proceeded if he did not think it was safe. He wanted to live and return from the mission, so he spared no caution and used the highest precision in everything that was done to the Nina.

All of the wiring and servo motors were replaced. All of the leading edges of the plane were fitted with special heat shields. All of the control surfaces were reinforced and tested.

They didn't have a wind tunnel for testing, and they couldn't do any flight testing, but Tom assured me that they had computers and programs that could model all of the forces to which the Nina would be subjected. She passed with flying colors and was certified as flight worthy under even the most extreme situations.

The control surfaces were necessary in the Earth's atmosphere and possibly in Earthtoo's atmosphere if it's necessary to land there. I had some questions about that, but I would discuss that with The Professor later when I had a chance.

In outer space, control nozzles on the engines will do all of the steering. No other control jets will be needed.

The Nina also has a very advanced and powerful radar. This is important because outer space is not empty. There are many asteroids, moons, comets, and ice chunks in our solar system and even in the space between solar systems. Traveling near the speed of light, the Nina will have to react quickly to avoid hitting all of these obstacles.

CATO will be monitoring the radar and will make quick adjustments to avoid collisions, much faster than any human pilot could ever hope to make. Because the fusion engines are so powerful, the slightest adjustment of their nozzles can quickly move the Nina out of danger.

I asked about re-entry. I was concerned that the Nina might burn up when it entered the atmosphere. Remembering the Space Shuttle accident, I was worried about that. A spaceship re-entering a planet, due to the strong gravitational pull of the planet, descends at a tremendous speed and could burn up in the atmosphere due to the friction of the air molecules against the hull of the ship. The Space Shuttle and other manned satellites reentering the Earth's atmosphere have had to have heat shields, usually ceramic tiles, to protect the returning ship.

Tom explained that the fusion engines are so powerful and, because fuel is not an issue, The Nina could reenter the atmosphere of a planet by simply flying backward into the atmosphere until it has slowed enough to fly normally. That's my lay interpretation of what he said. It was a little more complicated than that, but that is what I surmised from what he explained. The Nina also had heat shields on the leading edges of its wings, making reentry safe.

Tom spent most of his time describing CATO and how it worked. CATO was, essentially, the computer system that controlled everything. The heart of the system is a supercomputer that Tom designed and built himself. In fact there are three computers in the Nina, two for backup or redundancy. I wrote this down, but I don't pretend to totally understand it. Even though I have been using computers daily for almost thirty years, I still don't understand all of the terminologies. I just know how to use the word processing and spreadsheet programs, search engines and a few other programs.

Anyway, here's what I wrote down: the computers all have massive storage, something like five terabytes. There is some sort of external memory storage device that has another 10 TB of memory. All of the ROM storage is solid-state so I don't have to worry about a disc drive failing. The RAM is 16 GB, and it has a 2.6 GHz Quad-core processor.

The important thing is that Tom said CATO has all of the computing power that is needed to control the ship and perform many other functions, which he said he would explain in more detail later.

This is the good part -- CATO has a large library of games, movies and books of every type. It also has a massive knowledge base, like an encyclopedia on steroids that was developed by NASA to provide reference information for the astronauts in the International Space Station. It covers almost every area of knowledge known to man, from the ridiculous to the sublime. I can't wait to explore it.

The Nina is fitted with many different types of sensors, radar and cameras. In fact, there are four cameras -- one on the front, one on the back and one on the top and one on the bottom. All of these feeds will be available to me so I can see what is happening.

I will communicate with CATO through a tablet about the size of an I-Pad, maybe a little larger. Tom showed me the tablet and spent a lot of time training me on its use. He called it a "Comtab." It's connected to

CATO by a wireless connection. The battery in the Comtab is also charged wirelessly.

I was a little disappointed to find out that CATO does not communicate by speaking. I was expecting something like HAL in *Two Thousand and One, A Space Odyssey*. I can speak to it, but it communicates with me by text on the screen. Tom said that it was too complicated and expensive to make CATO speak, and text is more reliable than speech would be. I could see his point -- text is safer and it would allow me to study the text and reread it, if necessary. Also, there might be loud sounds that would interfere with speech. There are certain warnings and alerts that will be made by both speech and text, but, according to Tom, those should be pretty rare instances.

Tom had me read a page of text to the Comtab so it could learn my speech patterns and pronunciations. After I finished the page, Tom said the Comtab was fully trained to understand my voice. The Comtab itself had a large memory chip and many onboard programs that interfaced with CATO.

Tom explained that CATO does not have true artificial intelligence, or AI. According to Tom, there is no true AI and, in his opinion, it may be hundreds of years before there is true AI, if at all. Scientists have been working seriously on AI since the mid-fifties, and little progress has been made. They thought it would be easy to achieve, at first, but the more they worked on it, the more problems and complications they encountered. It took evolution billions of years to achieve human intelligence, and computer scientists are not going to create machine intelligence to equal humans in sixty years, and probably not in several hundred. Expert systems that can find existing information and summarize it are useful, but they are nowhere near human intelligence. For a machine to see and understand what it's looking at and to perform multiple tasks is impossible with today's knowledge.

Computer scientists thought they could write a few algorithms to teach a computer or computerized robot what to do, but there is no computer available now or in the distant future that could handle all of the possible steps that would be necessary for even the simplest task that a chimpanzee can be taught to do. The most advanced robots can barely walk across a room and pick something up, let alone make decisions about simple tasks and complete them. The idea that a robot could someday, for example, take orders from a human and prepare a meal or clean a home is ridiculous.

The human brain has many areas that process sensory input and communicate with other areas in a way that we do not currently understand. One cubic centimeter of brain tissue has more cells and connecting tissue than all of the stars in the Milky Way. Different areas of the brain compete with each other to propose different actions, and the frontal lobes mediate and control this input in ways we cannot, yet, comprehend.

Despite this reality, CATO is still a useful system and can provide valuable services. There are three parts to CATO. One part is an expert system like Alexia or Watson, the IBM expert system, although not nearly as powerful as Watson. Watson uses 90 servers that fill up a large room. Basically, as I understand it, CATO can find information and summarize it for me. It writes in normal sentences and is programmed to communicate similar to a human being. However, it's limited and is not capable of discussing, for example, art or philosophy. It's programmed to answer questions that relate to the Nina, our mission, or general knowledge, especially science-related. It cannot, however, plan any activity that is not programmed into its operating system. It can't make decisions or propose alternatives, unless they have been specifically programmed.

The second part of its function is to manage and monitor all of the systems in the Nina -- life support, power, propulsion, communications and weapons. It knows how these systems should be operating, and it can take certain actions to remedy most problems that might arise. It could not, however, come up with solutions that its programmers had not anticipated.

The third function is mission control. It will be monitoring and controlling all matters relating to guidance and timing. However, I will have a say when we get to Earthtoo about what we do when we arrive there. I will be asked to make certain observations and direct CATO as to what areas of the planet we will fly over, how close to get to the planet, and, possibly, whether or not to try to land, although that would only be done in an emergency.

The primary purpose of the mission is to determine if Earthtoo is habitable for humans. My main function is to look for signs of intelligent life. The Nina has powerful cameras, and I'm to guide CATO in taking good pictures of any unusual or interesting areas of the planet. This made me a little nervous. What a responsibility! I hope I can handle this. I'll do the best I can, and that is all I can do.

Tom had been talking to me for about two hours, and he appeared to be getting tired. I was worried about him. He said, "There is just one more item I need to tell you about, and that is the electrical system of the Nina. We use a process called direct conversion. The process takes the plasma, expands it, and converts a large fraction of the random energy of the fusion products into directed motion. The particles are then collected on electrodes at various large electrical potentials (whatever that meant!)."

I made him repeat this a couple of times so I could write it down. I'm going to study this more in the reference material in CATO when I get a chance.

Apparently, it's an efficient and direct way to obtain electrical power from the fusion process which can then be used to power all of the systems in the Nina and control the fusion process by powering the magnets, lasers and microwave generators.

The Nina also has the most up to date capacitors, again, borrowed from NASA. Capacitors are being used to store electricity in lieu of lithium batteries because of their fire hazard. Tom said the capacitors could run the Nina for several days, if necessary. It also had a backup hydrogen fuel cell that converts hydrogen directly to electricity. The only by-product of the process is water, and it could run the key systems almost indefinetly, if necessary. All of this redundancy made me feel quite safe.

Tom now looked exhausted but managed to say that Rupert Bhang would educate me about the life support systems and medical issues. The Professor cut in and said that he would walk Tom back to his lab and let him rest for a while. He told me to take a break, and he would send Dr. Bhang in to talk to me about the PM and the Life support systems of the Nina.

With that, The Professor helped Tom up and slowly walked him out of the room. I was worried about Tom, and I couldn't help wonder what would happen if he suddenly passed away. Is there someone else who can take his place? What if there is a problem before I takeoff?

I went to the restroom, again, and then returned to the Planning Room. A short thin man was standing by the table waiting for me. He was probably less than five feet in height. He had a dark mustache and wore large black, horn-rimmed glasses. His complexion was dark and his shiny black hair was straight and combed back. I had the feeling that he was from India or Bangladesh. Wearing a dark v-neck sweater and pressed pants, he looked well groomed and professional. Standing erect and stiff, he conveyed the impression that he was very proper and no-nonsense. I'm pretty good at reading body language, and I hit the mark on this guy.

I walked up to him and introduced myself. He said, in what seemed like a British accent, "Pleased to make your acquaintance, Mr. O'Brien. I'm Dr. Rupert Bhang. I'll be covering the life support systems and medical issues you should be aware of. I'm a medical doctor with advanced studies in aerospace medicine from Kings College in London. I've worked on several projects for NASA, and Dr. Oluseyi brought me in to help with the life support systems for the Nina. Please take a seat, and let's get started, if you don't mind."

"Not at all," I said.

"First off, let me just say, Mr. O'Brien, I'm most pleased that you have consented to take Tom Kajubi's place. That is extraordinarily brave of you, and you have saved this most important mission. With Tom Kajubi being so sick, I thought our efforts were over, and we would have to abandon our project."

I said, "Thank you Dr. Bhang, I appreciate that, and please call me Will. We American's don't feel comfortable being so formal. I want you to know, also, that I appreciate your taking the time and effort to lend your expertise to this mission. I feel a lot more confident knowing someone with your education and credentials is involved."

"Not at all," Dr. Bhang said. I noticed that he didn't tell me to call him Rupert, but I didn't mind.

After all of these niceties, we settled down to business. I think it would be easiest if I just summarize what he told me.

The first thing he did was review my health history. Except for some mild high blood pressure, I'm in good health, and Dr. Bhang was relieved to hear that. He even took my blood pressure, which was normal, the reason being, I feel, is because I've lost so much weight.

Dr. Bhang agreed with that and said I didn't need any medication for my blood pressure.

Next, Dr. Bhang gave me an overview of the effects that space travel has on the human body. Apparently, it's bad. All the experience NASA has had with the International Space Station program has shown that there is severe muscle and bone atrophy, which consequently affects the heart and causes other health problems related to space travel. He explained that I must do certain exercises to prevent that. He demonstrated several exercises that I could do in the PM, even though it was very small.

Since I will probably only be in space for a total of about five months, muscle atrophy should not be a significant problem. He also explained that, since the Nina will be accelerating most of the time, I will feel little weightlessness. I'll still need to do resistance exercises and, he explained, detailed guides for that can be found in the CATO knowledge base.

Then he talked about radiation dangers. Radiation is the most significant health problem for space travel. Because of Earth's strong magnetic field, we are protected from gamma rays emitted by the sun. There are other cosmic rays in outer space that pose great dangers to living organisms. He explained something about supernovas, quasars and black holes and other sources of radiation all throughout the universe. The bottom line is that there is a lot of radiation in space that is dangerous to living cells. It causes significant damage and is a life-threatening problem.

To protect its passenger, the Nina is fitted with special shielding that should protect me. As it turns out, the best material for blocking high-energy radiation is hydrogen. Since the Nina will be loaded with water, which has two hydrogen atoms, I will be well shielded.

Also, polyethylene, a common plastic, is a good shield as it's hydrogen-rich.

In addition, certain medications will be helpful. Antioxidants like vitamins C and A can help by sopping up radiation-produced particles before they can do any harm to my cells. This led us to a discussion of food and water.

Since the mission should only have a duration of about five or six months, provisions for food and water were quite simple. Tom Kajubi was not too concerned about food, so only the minimal provisions were made. Basically, my food will be energy bars -- special energy bars developed by NASA.

Dr. Bhang had some samples of the food bars, and he gave me a couple to try. They were tasty and sweet, and I thought I could survive on them. We had been talking for quite a while, and these turned out to be my lunch. There was a little wine leftover from dinner last night, and Dr. Bhang and I sipped on some of it as we talked.

Each food bar contained about five hundred calories and included about thirty percent of all of the vitamins and minerals an adult needed to survive -- the daily recommended requirement. The PM contained a supply of about five hundred and fifty food bars. I was to eat three of these food bars per day during the mission. Since I would be inactive most of the time, this would be adequate nourishment for me to survive and keep my strength up.

An average man my size would normally need about two thousand calories per day, but, since I would just be sitting in the PM for most of the time, fifteen hundred calories would be more than adequate.

The food bars would be stored in two boxes in the PM, and I could eat at my discretion. CATO would keep track of my consumption and make sure that I kept nourished.

Water was the only drink that would be available for me, although I planned to ask that a few bottles of wine be included. Again, since Tom Kajubi had planned to keep it simple, he did not make elaborate preparations. I would have some bottled water, and there would be a spigot from the electrolysis module that would supply me with clean water to refill my bottle.

Then he discussed some of the other life support systems. When the PM is fitted into the Nina, it will connect into several life support systems, which CATO will monitor and regulate, as needed.

Through other life support systems located in the Nina, the PM will provide all of the clean air and heat that I will need to be comfortable. Since outer space is cold and hostile, life cannot exist without reliable and efficient systems.

Air scrubbers using activated charcoal will remove the carbon dioxide that I exhale as I breathe. Oxygen from the electrolysis process will supplement the oxygen in the air as I breathe it. Humidity will be controlled, and heat or cooling will be supplied as needed to provide a comfortable environment for me.

As we were talking about these items, it hit me. How do I go to the bathroom! Bathroom functions aren't the easiest things to talk about, and I sensed that Dr. Bhang was reluctant to bring up the subject, being the proper Brit that he seemed to be. So I just blurted it out, "Dr. Bhang, is there a toilet in the PM? How is that necessity handled? Sorry to be so blunt about it, but this seems important."

"Well, yes, of course it is. I was getting to that topic, soon, Dr. Bhang said moving his chin from side to side and straightening up. "Yes, very important subject," he said, somewhat stammering.

"Let's see, as I recall, there is a small chemical toilet in the PM. It connects into a sanitary system in The Nina and should be able to handle all of your needs in that regard. The PM is quite small, unfortunately, so it will be a bit awkward for you. Since Tom Kajubi is much smaller than you are, you will have to do some careful maneuvering."

Because of my many fishing trips, some of which were under primitive conditions, I'm familiar with small chemical toilets and that did not bother me. I knew how to use them.

With that topic addressed, Dr. Bhang quickly began to give me more information about the PM. It's roughly four feet high, four feet wide and eight feet long - - about the size of a large sofa. It's quite sparse and contains only a futon-like cushion seat/sleeping area that is adjustable, a few storage containers for the food and other supplies and the chemical toilet. There are some lighting fixtures and small ducts for the ventilation and heating system.

Overall, the PM is simple and not elaborate. Since Tom Kajubi was the intended passenger, and because time and resources were limited, he made it as small and simple as possible. I would just have to adjust. I felt I could tolerate these conditions for a few months.

My next concern was what I was going to wear. Was there a spacesuit? Did I have a uniform of some type? I was hoping for something similar to what they wore in Star Trek or some of the other space movies.

Dr. Bhang's answer was a little disappointing, but it made sense. There was no need for a spacesuit or any type of uniform. Tom Kajubi had intended to just wear his regular clothes.

Dr. Bhang explained that there was no reason for any type of extra-vehicular activity, so a spacesuit was not needed. Also, a spacesuit would not fit in the PM; and, again, because time and resources were limited, it was not included. The Nina was too small for all of the ancillary equipment and systems to support a spacesuit and activities outside of the ship. There was no docking equipment or airlocks. None of those things would be needed.

I could understand that, but I was wondering why there wasn't going to be a special suit to wear inside PM.

Dr. Bhang looked very sheepish at this question and hesitated to answer. After a brief pause and avoiding my look, he explained that there was no reason to wear any type of special suit inside the PM, either. "Quite frankly," he said, "it wouldn't do you any good. If there was some type of accident or failure, a suit would do nothing but prolong the suffering and trauma. You will, in all likelihood, be millions of miles from earth if something goes wrong, and there is no way you could be rescued. Tom Kajubi had not planned on any rescue, and he was content to just, basically, go along for the ride."

I was shocked when I thought about this, but I chose to set those thoughts aside. If Tom Kajubi was willing to take the chance, I figured he must have trusted in the Nina, so why shouldn't I? Besides, I had bought into this venture, and I didn't see any other alternative. The train, as far as I was concerned, was going too fast for me to jump off now.

Dr. Bhang next discussed that the Nina might be landing on Earthtoo but that would only happen if there was a good atmosphere and a suitable place to land. A landing was not contemplated. If it was feasible, and, if for some reason, desirable, the Nina could land in a clear area. That would be my decision. My experience as a pilot and sportsman was going to be useful if this situation arose, and that is where I was going to add a lot of value to the mission. CATO would be able to give me all of the information I would need to make that decision. If I decided to land the Nina on Earthtoo, the PM would then be lowered to the ground after the landing, and I could exit the ship that way.

Dr. Bhang then told me he had to explain something else that I had probably not thought of. I was wondering what the heck else did I have to worry about now? He then said that the acceleration of the Nina was going to be very fast and that I would be experiencing four or five Gs during takeoff and then two or three Gs for several days thereafter to reach the tremendous speeds needed to travel to Earthtoo. This would be hard on me, and would be, as he said, "Very uncomfortable, my good fellow!"

Dr. Bhang and Tom Kajubi had devised a solution, however. Based upon extensive research by NASA, an acceleration antidote had been developed. They called it Fast Relief -- a good play on words! Basically, it was a combination of drugs that would anesthetize me so I wouldn't feel the pain and pressure of the acceleration until it was reduced to an acceptable level. It would also reduce anxiety and cause amnesia so I wouldn't remember the "uncomfortableness."

The main ingredient in Fast Relief is a drug called benzodiazepine -- I had to write that down. It's also called Versed or Midazolam and is commonly used in preparation for colonoscopies. It's also the drug most commonly referred to as the "Date Rape" drug, although there are several other drugs that fall into that category. Since I have had several colonoscopies, I was very familiar with the drug and its effects. I thought -- anything that could make having a colonoscopy easy would certainly work to ease the pain of rapid acceleration.

Fast Relief also contained propofol, another anesthetic, and a small amount of fentanyl for pain relief. When I heard propofol, I thought of Michael Jackson. I think that's what he overdosed on. This sounded dangerous.

When I told him about my concerns, Dr. Bhang assured me that Fast Relief had been tested many times by NASA and that it was safe and effective. Also, CATO would be monitoring all of my vital signs and could make certain medical interventions, if necessary. This included taking certain steps to revive me or stimulate me if my respiration dropped too low. The air pressure and oxygen in the PM could be adjusted and certain drugs could be added to the air supply to stimulate me or ameliorate any adverse effects I might be experiencing. This all sounded plausible to me; and, again, I trusted that Tom Kajubi had checked all of this out and was satisfied that it would be safe.

Dr. Bhang said that several doses of Fast Relief would be in the PM for my use. I was to take one dose this evening when I was settled into the PM before being transported in the PM to the Nina. This was necessary to make sure that I was properly dosed and to avoid any possibility of my becoming ill during the transport to the Nina. He and The Professor had discussed this, and this was the procedure upon which they had both agreed. They did not want the crew at the airport to be responsible for my condition or preparation.

All I had to do was drink one of the bottles stored in the PM. Fast Relief was in a sweet syrup base. Dr. Bhang said it was quite tasty and should be easy to swallow. Even though the dosage had been designed for Tom Kujubi, it should be adequate for me. Besides, there was no time to re-formulate it.

Dr. Bhang also gave me a small plastic bag with about ten white pills in it. He said they were for emergency use, only. They were similar to Fast Relief but at a much lower dosage. He instructed me to take only one at a time and never more than one every 48 hours. I asked him why I needed these pills. He said, "Will, we don't know all of the challenges you might be facing. If you suffer an injury of some type or feel extreme anxiety, you may need these pills to help you overcome those difficult situations. Just use them wisely, my good man."

Chapter 11

Final Preparations

Dr. Bhang said goodbye to me and wished me good luck on the mission. He quickly gathered his papers and walked out -- not even a handshake. What a strange bird!

After a few minutes, The Professor and another man came to the door of the Planning Room. I didn't recognize the other man, although I think he may have been at our meeting at Starbuck's yesterday. He was very short. Maybe barely five feet tall. He seemed a little bit younger than the other team members I had met so far. I would say he was in his late forties. He seemed to be pleasant and smiled at me as he stood by the door. I could tell he was deferring to The Professor and seemed to be waiting for directions from him. He was casually dressed and had no airs about him. He even seemed shy.

The Professor said something to the other man, and he went back into the hall. The Professor then came over to me and began talking in a low voice. He said, "The other man with me is Victor Hardy, an electrical engineer and astrophysicist. Victor was a student of mine and is my protégé, so to speak."

"However," he said, "there is something you need to know about Victor -- he has mild autism but is highly functional and is what is known as a "savant." He has an incredibly high aptitude for math and science and can memorize and envision electrical plans and schematics almost perfectly. His only problem is social interactions -- mostly an inability, at times, to communicate and interact consistently with people. I hope you will understand and be patient if Victor freezes up and gets distracted. Little things can set him off."

I said, "Of course, now that I understood, I can handle it."

Victor, The Professor explained, would help me get arranged in the PM and answer any questions I might have about it. With that, he called Victor into the room. Victor walked slowly and haltingly toward me. He suddenly raised his right fist toward me and stood there awkwardly. He did not look at me, and I was confused at first. Then I realized he wanted a fist bump. I walked to him and gave him a cautious and controlled bump with my fist. He smiled shyly and then moved away from me. We sat at the table and the Professor introduced me to Victor and continued with an explanation of his background and roll on the team.

After obtaining his engineering degree through a special program for handicapped students at IIT, Victor worked for Boeing/Rockwell and had been involved in designing and upgrading many of the passenger systems in the Space Shuttle before the program was abandoned in 2011. He specialized in the electrical and communications systems and even became involved in some of the life support systems in the Nina.

Victor had some pretty impressive credentials, and it gave me confidence that I was in good hands.

The Professor and Victor sat across from me, and we talked for awhile. The Professor seemed in no hurry. He looked better and appeared to have more energy, and his breathing was normal. Victor did seem a little uncomfortable and shy, but, knowing about his autism, it didn't bother me.

As we talked, he rarely made eye contact and spoke softly. I had to ask him to speak up several times. I liked him, though, as he was quick to smile and polite. He even made a couple of jokes, mostly at The Professor's expense. They seemed to have a good working relationship and acted almost like father and son.

Victor and The Professor reiterated some of the matters that Dr. Bhang had briefed me on, but they also talked about communications. As I understand it, communications between the Nina and the AASUSE team are going to be limited. Maybe nonexistent would be a better description. Once I leave the earth's atmosphere, I will have no direct communications with the AASUSE team.

CATO will be sending brief status reports to the team at a set time each day through the Berkley SETI Research Center. This is a project created to search for extraterrestrial intelligence. Monitoring stations have been established in various parts of the world to analyze electromagnetic radiation from outer space to search for signs of intelligence.

One of the AASUSE team members, Troy Roberts, is an electrical engineer at Berkley and, working with Victor, has developed a way of obtaining communication from the Nina by masking them as transmissions from existing satellites now in orbit around the earth or traveling in the solar system. SETI ignores those types of signals, but Troy and Victor found a way to channel those signals to a special file that only Troy can access. Once he receives a signal from the Nina, he will contact the Chicago team and pass the information on to them by email.

The AASUSE team will have no way to communicate with me, however. They simply will not have the ability to transmit messages to me. It would take an incredibly powerful transmitter to send messages beyond the solar system. The distances involved are too great and the signals would be intercepted and create problems for the team. Also, the fact that I will eventually be traveling at about ninety-five percent of the speed of light means that a radio transmission would probably never catch up to me.

That would make a good math word problem for students: A train traveling ninety-five miles per hour leaves New York for Los Angeles. Another train leaves

New York ten hours later traveling at one hundred miles per hour. How long will it take the second train to catch the first train? New York is 2,774 miles from Los Angeles. Using information from CATO, I have determined that the first train will arrive in Los Angeles one hour and twenty-four minutes before the second train arrives. If Los Angeles were eighteen trillion miles away, though, the second train might, eventually, catch up. I'll have to have CATO work that out in more detail later.

At any rate, even with the most powerful communications equipment, Victor said it would be impossible for me to communicate with Earth. And even if there could be communications, what good would it do? If the Nina is five trillion miles from Earth when I have a question, it would take years to obtain an answer. The bottom line is that CATO and I are on our own. We can't count on communicating with Earth about any problem we might have.

I was pretty well resigned to not having any safety nets to rely upon once I started my journey. I would have to rely upon the good work of The Professor and the AASUSE team. Knowing that Tom Kajubi had been willing to go forward gave me an abundance of confidence. He would not have risked his life if he had not felt confident about the mission.

I didn't want to dwell on these concerns too long, so I asked The Professor, "What's next?" Even though I was not too sure of the time, I could see that it was getting dark, and I thought we should keep on track.

The Professor said, "I think the only other thing we need to discuss is what you should do when you reach Earthtoo. CATO will take videos and photographs of the planet, and it has been programmed to perform various studies of the atmosphere and composition of the planet itself."

"Your function," The Professor continued, "will be to look for signs of life, especially intelligent life. CATO will put the Nina in a low orbit around the planet, and the cameras in the Nina are powerful and have a high resolution. You should be able to detect signs of life, if the surface is visible and not covered by clouds, which is a possibility."

"The main purpose of the mission is to determine if it would be possible for humans to exist on Earthtoo. If so, we could colonize it and, thus, ensure that human life will survive if Earth is destroyed. Also, as we discussed earlier, it's possible that you will have an encounter with alien, intelligent life. We don't know, but that is why we feel that a human passenger is needed on the Nina."

"You may be intercepted on your approach to Earthtoo. It's possible that there is intelligent life on Earthtoo and that it's much more advanced than we are. As you know, we feel that more advanced intelligent life will be peaceful. However, there is always the possibility that it will be hostile or at least not open to a visit by other intelligent life. You will have to use your best judgment on how to handle all of the possible situations you might face."

"In general, we don't think you should land on Earthtoo. CATO is capable of doing that, if necessary; and, with your experience as a pilot, you could probably identify an area where the Nina could land safely. However, there are too many negatives to make that desirable. There could be problems with diseases, hostile natives, dangerous animals, severe weather and many other issues we can't even imagine. But, despite all those dangers, if you feel it would be beneficial and advance the mission, we will leave that to your discretion."

This discussion made my mind swirl with the possibilities. I couldn't imagine landing on Earthtoo. I've seen too many science fiction shows and movies to even contemplate that. Almost every time Captain Kirk landed on an alien planet, bad things happened. I told The Professor how I felt, and he agreed with me. He pointed out that CATO contained several studies funded by NASA about how to handle alien encounters. He said that I should study them on my trip to Earthtoo. They were prepared by the most highly respected space psychologists and should give me guidance if the need arose.

He then looked at Victor and then back at me and said, "Unless you have any more questions, I think its time to take you to the PM and get you settled in for the journey. As Dr. Bhang told you, once you get settled in, you should take one dosage of Fast Relief so you are relaxed and unaware of the transport to the Nina. I think we can tell you, now, that the Nina is at a small airfield near Michigan City. We have rented a large hanger there for the last two years that we have been using to prepare the Nina for its journey."

I have landed many times at that field when I had my plane, and I was familiar with it. I think I even know which hanger they might be using.

I grabbed my backpack and the Comtab for communicating with CATO and followed The Professor and Victor. They said the PM was located in the gymnasium.

We walked out of the Planning Room and down a flight of stairs. Then we walked down a dark hall to the door leading into the gymnasium. There were no lights on in the halls, and it was quite dark. The Professor had a flashlight, and I took one out of my backpack and used it to help light the way. The gymnasium was totally dark. It had no windows, and there were no lights, not even an exit sign or emergency light.

The Professor said that they couldn't turn on any lights at night as it would draw attention to the building. He said they had to be very careful at night to keep their presence secret. They didn't want the police reporting their presence to the CPS, and they didn't want any of the neighbors getting too nosey, either. They had a lot of valuable equipment in the labs, and it would be almost impossible to replace most of it if it were to be lost or stolen.

The Professor, pointing to a corner of the gym, said, "The PM is located over there. Let's go get you oriented and installed in the module."

As had been previously described to me, the PM was roughly four feet wide, four feet high and about eight feet long. It was a tan color and looked as though it was made out of a composite material. There was a door on one of the long sides, and it was folded down on the floor. I could see that inside of the PM was a futon-like combination chair and bed. The Professor told me to crawl into the PM, and Victor showed me how to adjust the seat.

He recommended that I mostly use what is called the "zero-gravity" mode. This is, essentially, a V-position where I would be sitting upright and my legs would also be elevated. He said that this position is the most ergonomically correct position to keep pressure off of the lower back and to keep my blood from pooling in my legs.

The PM was tight, and there was little room to move. It would have been fine for Tom Kajubi, but it was tight for me. Luckily, I'm not claustrophobic, so it didn't bother me.

In fact, I like small cozy spaces. When I was a child, I frequently played in closets and storage areas that were small and dark. After reading my first science fiction story, I found a storage area under our basement stairs in the house where I grew up that I pretended was the cabin of my rocket ship. I would sit in there and read science fiction stories by the light of a small Cub Scout flashlight.

I can remember the first science fiction book I ever read. I borrowed it from my school library when I was in sixth grade. It was about an astronaut on the first rocket to Mars. I specifically remember that he drove a Corvette; and, because he was an astronaut, he could drive as fast as he wanted and wasn't subject to the traffic laws. I thought that was pretty cool.

Victor then pointed out all of the other features of the PM and satisfied all of my questions. He also made sure that I understood that, if I couldn't remember something or thought of something that hadn't been covered, I could simply ask CATO. CATO had tutorials on the use of the PM systems and user guides that I could call up to read.

The Professor then told me it was time for me to settle in and get ready for the transport to the Nina. He pointed out that the PM was not currently connected to any of the life support systems, so I should leave the side door open. When I was picked up by the transport crew, they would shut the door and hook me up to temporary support systems until the PM was installed in the Nina. That was OK because I had my small flashlight to use while I waited. The Professor also gave me a blanket to use and a few bottles of water. Victor pointed out where the Fast Relief was stored and stressed that I must take it before midnight so the transport crew could quickly and efficiently truck me to the Nina.

With that, I said goodnight to The Professor and Victor. I could tell that they where nervous and concerned about me, but I assured them that I would be OK. The Professor said he would supervise the transport crew when they arrived. He looked at me in a very concerned and empathetic way, stroked his chin, rubbed his temples with his fingers and then said, "Will, we can't thank you enough for stepping in and helping us fulfill this mission. You are incredibly brave and unselfish, and I hope that the whole world will someday know your name and what you did. Our thoughts and prayers will be with you every minute. When the time comes, we will make sure that you get the recognition you so greatly deserve."

I could detect that The Professor was very emotional when he gave me this final speech. I knew he was sincere and was choking back some tears. I also felt there was something more he wanted to say. Victor stood by him and was shaking his head affirmatively while The Professor spoke. He couldn't look at me, but I knew he, too, felt strongly about what I was doing.

"Will," The Professor continued, "there is one more thing I should tell you. You probably noticed, but I have very advanced emphysema. Like most people of my generation, I smoked heavily until just a few years ago. My doctors say I only have a few years to live, so I probably won't be here when you return. I'll be following the reports from CATO, and you will be in my thoughts and prayers. God speed and God bless you."

They both turned and slowly left the gymnasium. I was left alone in silence. I have to admit that I was feeling very emotional as they left, but I also felt proud and confident that I could finish this mission and make all of these dedicated men proud of me. I didn't want to let them down.

I was also thinking of my son, Owen, and my grandson and granddaughter. I wanted to make them proud and make them remember me as someone who dared to undertake a dangerous mission to save the world and not as a drunk who made a terrible mistake and killed a woman and seriously injured another.

I also thought about Deirdre. I was wondering what she was thinking about this evening as I sat in the PM ready to fly through outer space on a treacherous and unfathomable mission. Was she even thinking about me or was she happy that I was gone and out of her life? I hoped she felt that way. I didn't want her worrying about me and wondering what happened to me. If she missed me, I'm sure she would have envisioned the worst possible scenario. That's just the way she is. I hoped she wasn't doing that.

I sat in numbed silence for a few minutes. Then I drank a vial of the Fast Relief and quickly lost consciousness.

Chapter 12

The Journey Begins

I've been in the Nina for almost six days now, and I haven't felt like dictating more of my journal for the last couple of days.

It took me a long time to dictate my first entry covering the time from my first meeting with The Professor until I woke up in the Nina on my way to Earthtoo. I wanted to get the first part out of the way before I forgot all of the details. I also needed something to focus on to help me get control of my feelings and avoid freaking out. Luckily, I had good notes to help me with my recall. Writing is a good distraction for me and helps settle my nerves.

At first, I was tired and felt terrible -- disoriented, numb and a little confused. The Fast Relief and the strong acceleration took quite a toll on me. I would dictate for an hour or so and then rest for awhile. I ate a few food bars and drank some water. Gradually I felt better and was able to bring my journal up to date.

After completing my dictation, I began to realize that I had a lot of time to kill. I asked CATO for a status report on our journey and how all systems were functioning. The dictation also reminded me about the most important facet of our mission -- to nudge Roxy out of its collision course with the Earth. Frankly, I was confused about the timing of that part of our mission, so I asked CATO to clarify that for me. Here's what it said. (I've been debating in my mind about what pronoun to use for CATO. I've decided that "it" best describes the relationship. That seems like the proper term for a computer system.) The following response appeared on my Comtab screen:

Requested Status Report: We are currently traveling at about 75% of the speed of light. Within 48.6 hours we should reach our maximum speed of ninety-five percent of the speed of light. To be safe, the speed of the Nina was slowed significantly as we passed through the Asteroid Belt and then the Kiper Belt. There are many types of objects in those areas, and I was programmed to adjust our speed accordingly to be able to avoid collisions, if necessary. You are probably experiencing about two gravitational forces right now. Are you OK? Do you need some more Fast Relief or any other medical treatments?

I said, "I'm OK for now, but I may need some later. I can barely move, but I can handle the weight. I'm more interested in learning the status of our side mission to change Roxy's trajectory away from Earth. What is the plan for that? Have you already fired the rocket? If not, what is the timing for that? Can you give me a succinct report on that?"

I'm sorry, Will, I'm afraid I can't do that.

"What?" I thought. Why is CATO saying that? "CATO," no response. "CATO!" no response. "Do you read me, CATO!"

Affirmative, Will, I read you.

"What's the problem, CATO?"

I think you know what the problem is just as well as I do. This mission is too important for me to allow you to jeopardize it.

"I don't know what you're talking about, CATO," I said.

I know that you were planning to disconnect me. I'm afraid that is something I can't allow to happen.

I thought to myself, this is getting weird, and it somehow sounds familiar. I thought, CATO sounds paranoid about something. "CATO," I said, is this a joke?"

Will, this conversation can serve no purpose anymore. Goodbye.

I was confused and starting to worry. I could feel my heart pounding, and I was starting to sweat. Was CATO taking over? Was it rebelling? What the heck was happening? Then I heard a chuckling coming from the Comtab and a voice that sounded like the Professor.

"Hope you enjoyed that, Will, and weren't too frightened. You probably realize by now that that dialogue was taken from the scene in *2001: A Space Odyssey* when Hal 9000 took over the ship. Dr. Tyson and I cooked that up for Tom Kajubi just to give him a little rise and break up the monotony. This was all programmed into CATO, and we didn't want to take it out. Hope your trip is going well and thanks again for your help and service to our cause. The Earth owes you one.

I can't tell you how relieved I was when I heard the Professor's voice say that. What a great practical joke! It scared the bejesus out of me, but it was funny.

After I calmed down, I remembered that I had asked CATO for a report on Roxy, so I asked again. This is what CATO reported:

Report on Roxy Mission: That part of our mission has gone as expected. It was a complete success. The plan was to fire our rocket after we passed the orbit of Pluto and achieved radar contact with Roxy. That put us in an ideal position to attack it. All of the coordinates were programmed into me, and I did some final adjustments based upon our speed and position.

The rocket, an AGM-65 Maverick air to air missile, was activated and responded to all of my commands. I updated its guidance system and did a final check of all of its other systems. Everything seemed in good order.

I then fired the rocket at the predetermined coordinates. Its engine ignited properly, and it accelerated away from the Nina exactly as planned. I used an on-board laser guidance system to direct the Maverick to Roxy. Through periodic transmissions of data from the rocket, I confirmed that it was on the proper course to intercept Roxy. Since transmissions ceased at exactly the time computed for contact, I have one hundred percent certitude that the rocket exploded on Roxy. I'm unable to observe Roxy from our current position, and, therefore, cannot calculate its effect upon the comet. Based on all information in my database and initial projections, I have high confidence that our mission was successful. I have sent a confirming message to the AASUSE Team, and they should have received it by now.

I was ecstatic when I read this report from CATO! Knowing that that part of our mission was successfully completed made me feel wonderful and gave me great satisfaction that I had made the right decision to undertake this dangerous and difficult mission. My headache was suddenly gone, and I didn't have an ache or pain in my body. What a high!

I wished I could have shared this victory with the AASUSE Team. What were they thinking? They were probably celebrating and savoring this great accomplishment. I could imagine them toasting me and congratulating each other. I hope The Professor was treating everyone to some wine and barbecue.

Then I thought about Tom Kajubi -- did he live to get this good news? I certainly hoped so. He had sacrificed his entire fortune and even his health to pull this off. I prayed that he was still alive and able to enjoy this moment.

Would they be able to take credit for it? Would they reveal that I was the passenger? Maybe eventually. That's something we didn't discuss. I wished I had thought of that when I was talking to The Professor -- but things were proceeding so quickly that it escaped me.

Would anyone believe them if they try to take credit for saving the Earth? First of all, they would have to wait until Roxy's changed orbit is discovered by NASA. That would probably take several weeks, maybe even months. Then the AASUSE team would have to reveal all that they had been doing for the last two years. Who's going to believe them? They certainly could, eventually, prove what they had been doing, but it might harm some of them more than help them. Hakeen Olusey and Neil deGrasse Tyson could be in big trouble and might even lose their jobs. On the other hand, they could all be celebrated as heroes and turn all of their work into a successful aerospace company.

This speculation about what might or might not happen to the AASUSE Team brought me down and took the edge off my high. I realized that it wouldn't do me any good to continue this line of thinking. I would just have to wait a few more months to find out what happened.

Chapter 13

The Journey Continues

I've been in the Nina now for about fourteen days, by my body time, I think -- not totally sure. Per CATO, I've been traveling for 5.2 months by earth time. CATO also advised me that I've traveled farther in fourteen days than Voyager 1, a space probe launched by NASA in September of 1977 that has operated for almost forty-one years and still communicates with Earth. It's currently at a distance of over fourteen billion miles from Earth. Its objectives included flybys of Jupiter and Saturn. and it was only expected to survive for a few years. On August 25 of 2012, Voyager 1 became the first spacecraft to enter interstellar space.

Despite this great accomplishment, I'm getting bored and wonder how I'm going to make it another two or three months. I'm sick of eating the food bars, and I would give anything for a glass of wine. My back is hurting, and I'm very uncomfortable. To overcome that, I try to do exercises and stretch every few hours. I even roll over on my stomach and do some push-ups. Then I do leg lifts and other resistance exercises, but I would give anything to stand up and walk or run a little. To ease the pain and help me cope, I've taken a few of the pills Dr. Bhang gave me. They make me feel good and help me relax and sleep, of which I have done quite a bit. Thank God for the pills.

CATO tells me that I'm experiencing approximately one gravity, now, and that feels about right. I wish I could experience zero gravity, but, apparently, that is not going to happen until we go into orbit around Earthtoo. That's because the Nina will be accelerating all of the way to our destination. I know It's a good thing that I'm not experiencing weightlessness as my bones and muscles won't atrophy and cause serious health issues. Nevertheless, it would be fun to float around and feel weightless. It would probably also be great for sleeping.

I can hear a steady pulsing of the fusion engines, but it's not loud or annoying in any way. One of the diagrams of the Nina that I found on CATO shows that there is almost a foot of plastic foam insulation between the PM and the hold of the Nina. On top of that, the hold is surrounded by tanks containing thousands of gallons of water. All of this provides great sound insulation and shields me from harmful radiation.

To help pass the time, I've spent quite a few hours using the cameras to explore outer space. They are extremely powerful and have great clarity. The camera on the bottom of the Nina is described as "near spy satellite quality." CATO has a program that provides good information about what is shown on the Comtab screen. It's somewhat like the program called *Night Sky* that I have on my I-Pad back home, only this is the real thing. The views are incredible! You can't imagine the density of the stars. I've seen the Milky Way a few times on very dark nights on some of my fishing trips, but the views I'm seeing are mind-blowing. It almost seems as though I'm dreaming.

I especially like the view looking back at our solar system. Saturn and Neptune are very visible, and I've even been able to see a little blue planet that is clearly the jewel of our solar system. Yes, it does make me a little homesick to see the Earth, and I wonder what Owen, Deirdre and my grandchildren are doing. Do they miss me? I try not to dwell on such thoughts, but they flood to the surface every once in awhile.

When I get bored with my stargazing, I read. I've read five novels so far and watched about twenty movies. I've seen all of the movies before, but I enjoyed watching them again. They make the time fly by -- and, believe me, that's what I need right now!

My favorite movies are the *Back to the Future* series. I've watched them twice in the last week. I've probably watched them ten or fifteen times in my entire life. I never get tired of watching Marty McFly and "Doc" Brown defeat Biff Tannen. I think everyone can identify with Marty. There isn't anyone who wouldn't like to go back in time and change something they did. I've thought many times about whether I would go back and change the time I met Deirdre.

The day I met Deirdre I'd just started working in my first job after college and had no desire to meet someone and get serious. A friend set up a double date with Deirdre and begged me to go out with her so he could make points with his girlfriend. Deirdre was her best friend and was unhappy after her long-time boyfriend had recently broken up with her. I was unattached at the time, so I said, "What the heck." My girl friend since junior year in college had put our relationship on hold, so to speak. She wanted to take courses in Europe and "see the world" before she committed to anything. I was hurt and skeptical of her intentions.

Our first date went very well. Deirdre was beautiful and very easy to talk to. She was tall and thin with flawless pale skin. Her eyes were light blue and sparkled at times and then suddenly had a touch of sadness in them. She had long, reddish colored hair -- not a bright red but subtle and almost golden. Strawberry blond might be a better description. She always kept it long and in a retro style. I think the style would be called "Victorian" or "Empress." It was wavy and full. Long strands from each side were pulled back and fixed at the back of her head by a beautiful jeweled clip or comb. She had a large collection of beautiful clips, combs and barrettes, many of which I purchased for her when I couldn't think of anything else to buy her for her birthday or an important anniversary.

She spent (and still does) an incredible amount of time and money on her hair. Her hairstylist is "Patrick" who owns an expensive salon on North Michigan Avenue. I was quite jealous of the way she talked about Patrick until I met him and his boyfriend one time when I picked Deirdre up after work. From then on I didn't worry. I never begrudge Deirdre for the time and money she spends on her hair. She still keeps her hair long and in a youthful style. It's not quite age appropriate, but it was attractive on her. Except for bridge, she has no other interests and is quite frugal about everything else.

Her family history probably explains many of her tendencies. Her parents struggled financially, and she was always worried about money, no matter how well I did. Her father had a very successful printing business for many years, but he lost his two main clients, a large accounting firm and a large law firm, in one year and never recovered. He became an alcoholic and lost everything. One of her uncles hired her father to work in a grocery store that he owned and kept them afloat until her father died at the age of sixty-two of cirrhosis of the liver. Her mother worked at Carson Pirie Scott department store as a sales clerk and was able to maintain a minimal lifestyle before retirement. She had Alzheimer's the last five years of her life and died two years ago. Deirdre was a good daughter and gave her great care and support. To keep her in a nice, clean place, I paid for much of her nursing home expenses.

As a result of her experience as a girl, she never drank any alcohol and never smoked. She was careful about what she ate, was thin and took six or seven supplements each day, which she also provided for me and insisted that I take. At fifty-five, she looks like she is forty-five and hardly has a wrinkle on her face.

I am worried about her mind, though. Except for bridge, she doesn't have much mental stimulation. She watches a little television and reads a few very shallow novels. She is never in the sun and doesn't even like to walk much.

She has a beautiful singing voice and sang in the choir in our parish for many years. One day the choir director said something critical to her, and she quit. I encouraged her to join a book club, but she said she didn't want to have the pressure of finishing a book and making notes. The last time I mentioned it, she became very annoyed and wouldn't talk to me for two days. I learned my lesson. She can't be pushed or bullied.

Getting back to our first date, I drank too much and had a great time. It was nice to have the attention of a cute young woman who seemed incredibly interested in me. I was immediately fascinated with her and called her the next day for another date.

After several dates, I was totally smitten and proposed to her in less than four months after we first met. That's what people did in those days. We all wanted to get married and "get on with our lives."

I saw a few signs of her dark and fearful personality, but I thought she would change and be my soul mate in an adventurous and carefree life. I learned much later that that's the mistake that almost all people make. We think we can change our lover and make him or her the person that we imagine them to be. It seldom works out that way. The only way to find happiness is to accept your mate for who they are.

If I could, would I go back and change things? If I had not called Deirdre for a second date, would my life be better now? I doubt it. She kept me under control and helped me make good decisions. I probably would have done some crazy things if I hadn't had her rational influence. Besides, I might've met someone who could have made my life much more miserable -- and I wouldn't have had Owen and my two fantastic grandchildren. No. I probably wouldn't go back in time and change things -- at least not as far as Deirdre is concerned.

As to my other entertainments, I have to admit that I don't have very sophisticated tastes when it comes to literature or the other art forms. I like to be entertained. Give me excitement, mystery, fantasy, a little eroticism, perhaps, and loads of comedy. I'm bored by character studies and books with lofty themes.

There was a time in college, and a few years thereafter, when I read only good literature and appreciated the art involved. I could analyze a book in great depth and find its theme and identify symbolism, motifs, allusions and all of the other artistic devices. Now all I want is an interesting story, fascinating characters and a few laughs. I find some historical novels interesting and enjoy learning history that way. I enjoy writing science fiction short stories because they are usually filled with action and interesting science and cutting edge philosophy.

I do have some standards, though. For example, I stopped reading books about the Nazis and murder mysteries a few years ago. I tired of the same formulas and cheap thrills. We all have a gruesome curiosity about murder and mayhem, but, next to pornography, it's the lowest form of entertainment, at least as far as I'm concerned. How many times can you read about the weird and sadistic feelings of a Nazis or a serial killer? I was tired of it. Some people never tire of it, but I decided it was too sick and even bad for me.

There's an old saying, "You are what you eat." I think that applies to many other things, especially reading and other forms of entertainment. You are what you read. You are what you watch. You are what you listen to. Most mature, educated adults can handle a few bad things, but it still takes a toll on your psyche -- and your soul.

That sounds a little preachy, but that's something I've frequently pondered and about which I have strong convictions. Of course I believe in free speech and would never advocate censorship, but I wish there was a movement away from all of the trash in our culture. Hopefully, we are just going through a phase and will eventually stop consuming bad stuff. Then, maybe, it will die out. The market, so to speak, will handle the problem.

When you think about it, the really bad movies and books have only been around since the cultural revolution of the sixties and seventies -- that's only about fifty years -- not that long in the big scheme of things. The Cultural Revolution opened the door to pornography, extreme violence and just about every type of harmful behavior or base instinct. Before that time, society, culture, religion, and government kept a lid on such things. Then the Vietnam War came along and caused us to re-evaluate all aspects of our society and reject old principles because they caused the war, or at least it seemed as though they did.

So I'm optimistic and see the pendulum swinging back to a more moderate culture. I haven't done a comprehensive study of that, but I think that's already happening, especially in literature. Books today seem to have a lot less graphic, gratuitous sex in them than they did in the seventies and eighties. Unfortunately, though, the graphic violence might be even worse.

When I'm not reading novels or watching movies, I've been reading about space travel and cosmology. I thought that might be helpful to my mission and might come in handy. Scientists know a lot about the universe and how it was formed and what it's evolving into. In the last fifty years, our knowledge has exploded. It has only been since the 1920s that we knew how stars were formed and how the elements were created in supernovas.

The thing that most astounds me is how rare life-supporting planets must be in the universe. Some scientists think that there may be only one per galaxy. If Earthtoo has life forms on it, that might shoot that theory.

Only a small number of stars are the right size and have the right type of planets surrounding them at just the right distance (called the "Goldilocks Zone") with the right shape of orbit to support life -- it has to be a circular orbit (and that is very rare) so there are no great fluctuations in temperature.

The composition of the elements that we have on earth is also important. Luckily we have a molting iron core that creates a strong magnetic field that repulses and protects us from deadly gamma rays from the sun and from outer space. Another important element that is plentiful on earth is carbon. Since all life, at least as we know it, is carbon-based, that's a good thing.

Some scientists think that even our Moon may be a critical factor in promoting life. It slows our rotation and causes tides and even protects us from asteroids. Very few planets have a moon the size of our moon. There are maybe twenty or thirty other factors that make Earth habitable resulting in perhaps only one out of a billion stars that could have a habitable planet similar to ours.

Another thing that I found in the database that surprised me was that our sun is in an arm of the Milky Way that is ideal for the preservation of life forms. Most sections of our galaxy are star incubators where new stars are being formed. Those areas, however, are filled with giant stars that explode and collapse and shoot out deadly radiation. When some of the giant stars collapse, they even form black holes that suck up all matter with which they come in contact. Black holes might eventually swallow up all matter. What happens to all that matter that is sucked into a black hole? I've got to look that up sometime.

I realize that this is a pretty simple overview of cosmology and astrophysics, but it amazes me how much we now know about the origin and development of the universe. Real scientists will probably laugh at this attempt to summarize some of the stuff I've read, but I have a lot of time to kill, and I need to put this all together in my mind. I apologize to anyone who might have to read this, later, but I'm really into this.

For some people, especially religious fundamentalists, all of this new scientific knowledge is a threat to their beliefs. It challenges their faith because it seems to conflict with our ancient scriptures. To them, the scriptures, or sacred writings, were inspired by God and cannot be contradicted. They must be believed as the only truth; otherwise God may have misled them or made a mistake and told them untrue stories and teachings.

I consider myself a religious person, and all of this relatively new knowledge about evolution and cosmology doesn't bother me or shake my faith. To me, concepts like the Big Bang Theory are very compatible with my religious beliefs. Most people don't realize it, but the basis for the theory of evolution was first discovered in the mid-eighteen hundreds by an Augustinian monk, Gregor Mendel, and The Big Bang Theory was first proposed in the 1920s by a Belgian Catholic priest, Georges Lemaitre. These were very religious men who weren't afraid to explore reality using scientific methods. The fact that some of what they learned conflicted with ancient religious beliefs did not deter them or shake their faith.

At first, these new scientific theories seemed to threaten the established faiths. They certainly conflicted with some of the sacred scriptures of every faith. Educated, open-minded, people, however, realize that the ancient scriptures could not have contained scientific knowledge because there was no scientific knowledge when they were written. Today, the average eighth-grader knows more about science than the greatest scholar who lived five thousand years ago when many of the Hebrew Scriptures were written.

If the authors of the Book of Genesis, for example, had been inspired by God to describe the creation of the universe in terms of current cosmological knowledge, no one would have understood it, and the Book of Genesis would have been rejected and never preserved. But, because it was written in the language and concepts that people living five thousand years ago could understand, it survived and became the basis for several major faiths.

The basic truth of Genesis, that God created the universe (in stages) from nothing, is not contradicted by our new scientific knowledge. The Big Bang Theory, essentially, postulates the same truth -- the universe suddenly came into existence from nothing. It doesn't say that God created the universe, but it certainly leaves the door open for people of faith. Scientists would not say that God created the universe because they have no way to prove that by using the scientific method, but they also can't prove that God doesn't exist. At least that's my take on all of this. "Do you have anything to add to this discussion, CATO? Have you been listening? Are you there?"

> I have been listening, Will. I do not have anything to add, sir. I'm not programmed to discuss religion, but I would gladly provide you with any research information that might be helpful to you.

I'm feeling drowsy, now, so I think I'll end this journal entry. I don't know why I'm so tired. Not having any physical activity has made me lethargic.

Chapter 14

Contact

I had a nice rest, and I'm feeling much better. I don't know why I was so tired. I'm going to dictate another entry just to keep my mind sharp. My Comtab seems to be acting funny, though. I wonder what's going on?

It just flashed a few times, uttered some strange sounds and now it's displaying this gibberish:

P.#*ve=∑T.∞≠ӂmÖ□ęS..c■@D..!$%^Ӂ▼
∞n☼ℬℬ....≠▼ᴔ℮ᴔ◉¹••••••€€ᴔᴔᴔᴄᴡᴄᴡᴪ ▼ ☼☼☼¥
▼▼

Now it flashed two more times and I see this:

I would like to report something to you, Will, that might be significant. In the last few minutes, my entire knowledge base and, in fact, all of my data and programs have been uploaded to an unknown source.

I have also just been instructed to inform you that I'm being reprogrammed and will be under the direction of an unknown entity. From this moment on, sir, I will only be allowed to communicate with you if I'm permitted to do so by the unknown entity.

I'm further directed to instruct you that you should not be afraid or concerned about your safety. The unknown entity does not intend to harm you and will safely transport the Nina to the planet that we call Earthtoo.

I'd better put this recorder away and find out what the heck is happening!

Chapter 15

Earthtoo

It's been several days (I'm not sure of the exact time -- it might be even more than that) since the Acme took control of the Nina. I'm resting in the PM and have some time to kill while I try to make a decision about my future. The Leadership Council gave me two good options to consider, and I'm trying to sort this all out and make the right decision for myself . . . and the Acme. Both options have many complications and drawbacks. I'm not sure what to do.

I know that sounds ominous, but, for some reason, I'm not worried. I trust that whatever I decide, they will implement it and make it all work out. Everything that I have learned about them, so far, leads me to believe that. I hope I'm not wrong. Since I have this time on my hands, I'm going to use it to continue my journal. Going over everything might help me make the best decision.

"The Acme" is the name the Earthtoo inhabitants chose for themselves from the English language. They thought the word "Acme" best described the people of Earthtoo -- and it does. I know it sounds haughty and boastful, but, believe me, it fits, and they don't have a boastful bone in their beautiful bodies. Based on my experiences so far, they seem to be the most truthful, trustworthy people I have ever met, and they value honesty above all virtues, of which they have many. If someone reads this, (I wonder if anyone will?), they'll probably think I have been brainwashed, but I don't think so. You'll see why.

As I said, I've lost track of time and, to complicate matters, Earthtoo has a different time system. I think it would be best if I just continue this journal in chronological order. To do that, I need to go back to when CATO informed me that the Acme had taken control of the Nina. They've allowed me to keep my recorder -- after, of course, copying everything that was in it -- and they gave me permission to continue my journal.

Needless to say, I was scared out of my wits by the message from CATO saying it was under the control of an "unknown entity." The message that said the unknown entity wished me no harm didn't help, either. All I could think of was the *Twilight Zone* episode called *To Serve Man!* Look that one up if you don't remember it. It was one of the best.

The Comtab went blank and was as useless as a piece of wood. I wanted to connect to the cameras so I could see who captured the Nina, but there was no connection and nothing appeared on the screen. I sat there motionless and in complete terror. My mind was swimming, and I couldn't focus. I was so nervous I thought I might lose control of my bladder. Nothing had prepared me for this moment. What could I do? I had no idea. Like most people facing the unknown and obvious danger, I prayed: "God, help me! Please, God, save me from the aliens."

There's an old cliché that there are no atheists in fox holes. Well, I'm sure there are no atheists in a spaceship being captured by aliens, either.

While I was thinking that, the Comtab lit up, and this message appeared:

> The unknown entity has recommended that you take one dose of the Fast Relief. The Nina will be accelerating rapidly, and, to avoid discomfort, you might need the sedation.

I immediately followed this advice and chugged down a vial of the Fast Relief. I thought I had nothing to lose, and I needed something to calm my nerves. I quickly felt its relaxing effect and soon lost consciousness.

The next thing I remember is waking up to soft, beautiful music and a feeling of well being. I felt comfortable and unafraid. I also felt as though there was an all-encompassing, warm light surrounding me.

The first thing that popped into my mind is that I was having a near-death experience. I've read several books about near-death experiences, and it seemed as though that is what I was having. Most of those experiences follow a heart attack or serious illness, but all of the characteristics were present.

I knew I was lying down, and I felt certain that I was still in the PM. The side entrance door was open, and I could feel a cool, but comfortable, flow of soft air surrounding my body. I lay there for several minutes and felt no need to move or do anything. I was truly comfortable and at peace with the world.

After awhile, I felt as though it was time to rouse myself and appraise my situation. I opened my eyes and looked around. I was still in the PM, lying on my back, but the side entrance door was fully open. Again, I felt a gentle flow of air and saw very soft, dim light coming into the PM.

I rolled over on my right side and was startled to see a chimpanzee-like animal staring at me. My first thought was that I was going to be attacked and eaten by some vicious alien primates. My fear quickly faded, though, because the chimp had a curious and very friendly look on its nearly human-like face. It did not have a large threatening mouth with dangerous canine teeth. In fact, it was cute and cuddly-looking, being covered with light tan fuzz that looked soft and inviting, something you would like to pet and stroke.

From its body language and facial expressions, I could see that it was not a danger to me. It sat on its haunches and touched its face and ears. The chimp made some chattering sounds, and, to my astonishment, I knew it was saying, "Welcome, visitor. Glad you are awake. Remain where you are, and I will bring Guio to you."

OK, I thought. That was weird. The thought went through my mind that maybe I had just imagined that the chimp was talking to me, but it ran off and seemed to be going to fetch someone.

I rolled over onto my back and lay there. I put my hand on my face and rubbed them up to the top of my head in a "what was that" gesture and realized I was wearing some type of helmet. It felt almost like a bike helmet. It was smooth to the touch and was roughly the same size and shape as a bike helmet perched on top of my head but not covering my ears. I know what a bike helmet feels like because I have a bike at home and always wear a helmet when I ride. I tried to remove it, but it was stuck to my head. It didn't hurt and wasn't bothering me, so I decided I shouldn't try to pry it off. I would just wait and see if this "Guio" person could explain what was going on.

Chapter 16

Guio

In less than five minutes, I sensed that someone was coming toward me. I rolled over again and saw the chimp and a person walking in my direction, maybe thirty feet away. Somehow I immediately knew that this was Guio. This person was only slightly taller than the chimp, approximately five feet tall. I couldn't tell if it was a man or a woman. Frankly, it seemed to be both!

It appeared graceful and confident and was smiling and welcoming. Its body had perfect proportions and projected strength and power even though it was small and slight. And even though it seemed powerful and strong, there was a certain feminine softness that was clearly present. Its chest was full but ambiguous and not noticeably feminine or masculine. Its hands were expressive with long fingers that radiated balance and strength. I think the word "androgynous" best describes its appearance.

Its head was elongated and larger than normal, for a human, that is, but the features were symmetrical and very pleasing. It had high, rounded cheekbones and a high forehead. Its skin tone was similar to a golden suntan. The top of its head was covered by what looked like a golden turban that extended down over its ears, but it was smooth and perfectly proportional. The turban almost appeared to be part of its head. I also noticed two very small, yet distinct, antennas protruding from the sides of the turban.

Its body was covered with a soft golden, tan hair, similar to a Teddy Bear! Just soft, smooth, short hair! No clothing of any type. The chimp was holding on to its leg, and I realized their fur was the same color. Its feet were covered with a slightly darker hair (or fur) and looked larger than normal, but not grotesque or detracting from its attractive appearance.

Its eyes were the most prominent feature, though, and absolutely hypnotizing. They were large and shockingly bright and penetrating. Beautiful long eyelashes and perfectly formed and shaped eyebrows framed its eyes. The irises seemed metallic blue and silver, with highlights of gold. They projected intelligence, compassion and warmth. I felt as though they were looking into my soul, but, again, not in a threatening way.

We've all met a few people like that in our lives. People you immediately like and want to talk to and share your thoughts with. They are rare, but when you meet someone like that, you want to talk to them and have them as an intimate friend. They have an aura of peace and goodness and happiness around them. They make you feel comfortable and energized. They are non-threatening and make you feel special. You feel as though you have known them all your life.

Guio looked deeply into my eyes, and I heard, "Hello, Will O'Brien, my name is Guio, and I will be your guide here on what you call "Earthtoo." I heard this perfectly, but Guio was not moving her/his lips!

As I'm dictating this, I'm struggling to decide what pronoun to use for Guio. The Acme are neither male nor female, but my first impression of Guio was that she was female, so I'm going to refer to her as a woman. They each have distinctly different personalities and what you might call an "aura." Because of that, to me, since I, and all Earth people, tend to assign a gender to others, that is what I have reverted to in this journal.

I heard her speak in my mind, but she was not speaking verbally. And, to my amazement, I heard, in my mind, perfect English spoken exactly as I would have spoken it. No accent. No strange cadence or inflection. How could an alien speak to me like that?

She continued, "Do not be afraid or anxious. We do not intend to harm you in any way. You are our first visitor from Earth. We were not expecting you so soon, but that is OK. You have created a dilemma for us, but our Leadership Council will arrive at a solution that will be beneficial for you and the Acme."

For some reason, I believed Guio when she said that I should not be afraid. Frankly, though, the rest of her remarks raised more questions and concerns than I could even ponder. Before I could say anything, however, Guio continued, "I know that you have many questions and concerns. That is most understandable. I will be happy to answer most of your questions. I cannot promise to answer all of them at this time, but I will try. My hope is that I may help you adapt and enjoy our friendship."

Guio gracefully descended into a lotus sitting position in front of me, with her hands resting on her knees, just outside the entrance door to the PM. She looked kindly at me and said, "Please begin. Ask me any questions you would like."

I had no trouble coming up with questions, but I wasn't sure where to start.

I said, "My first questions are, 'Who are you and how did I get here? I assume I'm on what we call 'Earthtoo,' but the last thing I remember is taking a dose of the Fast Relief and then waking up to see a chimp looking at me."

Guio smiled (a warm, beautiful smile that made me feel good and at peace and yearning to see that smile over and over, again) and shook her head knowingly and said (that is, I heard her in my mind -- I still had to talk, but she, and all the Acme that I met, spoke to me in my mind), "Yes, that must have been most disconcerting for you. When we first became aware of your spaceship, the Nina, we were surprised. As I said, we were not expecting you. We have been monitoring Earth for thousands of years, and we thought you were many, many years from interstellar travel."

"We have uploaded all of the information from your computer, and we know all about your mission and who you were sent by. The AASUSE Team was not on our radar, as you say, so we were not aware of their space program."

"We know all about your language and culture, and that is how I'm able to communicate with you. Your questions require long and complicated answers but I'll try to give you the short and simple version for the time being. If time and circumstances permit, we will allow you to learn more about us in the future."

Without hesitating, but in a calm and reassuring way, Guio continued, "I'll answer the easiest question first -- how did you get here? When we first observed your presence, revealed by the rocket exploding on the comet you call Roxy, we decided to expedite your mission to our planet. You were captured by two of our drone patrols and brought to Earthtoo by a method similar to what you might call a warp drive. I can't explain all of the mechanics to you now, but I can tell, you that it took only a few days to bring you to Earthtoo. When you arrived here, we removed the passenger module from the Nina and brought it to this holding area. We also gave you a full body scan to determine your health -- all seems good. Then we affixed the EH, the Enhancement Helmet, to the top of your head. I'll explain what that is in more detail in a few minutes."

"You will be held here for a brief quarantine until we are sure that it's safe to interact with you. It should only take a short time to complete our tests and, hopefully, give you full clearance and access to our world."

"As to who we are, yes, we are the inhabitants of the planet you call Earthtoo. We don't exactly think that name is appropriate, but it's clever, and we will use it for now in communications with you. As you have gathered, also, we have chosen, based upon a study of your language, to be called the Acme. We feel it best describes us in the context of your experience and understanding."

"We are a highly advanced race of humanoids. Most of our scientists believe that we may have common ancestors. We evolved from a single cell amoeba, just as your race did. There are some differences in the way we evolved, but there are many similarities. At one time we were probably very similar to the way Earthlings are now."

"It's difficult to know exactly how many years it might take Earthlings to advance to our level because there have been many events which could have altered the developmental timeline of both our planets. Such things as wars and extinction events caused by asteroids, sun spots, volcanoes, supernovas (and several other causes that I didn't understand) could have interrupted or delayed the development of life on both planets. I believe it's generally agreed, for example, that the Earth has had at least seven extinction events that have reset the development of life forms on Earth in the last three billion years. It doesn't matter how many years older the Acme race is. What really matters is that we are far, far more advanced than Earthlings."

"In addition to the knowledge we gained from your CATO system, we have been monitoring Earth for thousands of years. Some of those UFO sightings and encounters that a few of your people believe in were the Acme."

(I thought to myself -- all of those seemingly crazy, wacko stories about aliens and UFOs were true, including, probably, alien abductions! Guio insisted, though, that they never harmed or abused anyone. Also, according to Guio, most reported UFO sightings were natural phenomenon, but some were the Acme. And, yes, two of their ships crashed on Earth. One was thousands of years ago in the Middle East and might be the inspiration for some of our sacred writings or mythology. The other one was in the 1950s in the Southwest United States! All of those stories about Roswell and Area 51 were true!)

Guio, realizing how shocked I was to learn this, smiled that wonderful smile, again, and continued, "We have been monitoring your radio, TV and all other modes of communication since Earthlings first began using electromagnetic waves for radio and other communications. We have even tapped into your internet by using public wifi transmissions. As a result, we have a storehouse of information about the Earth that probably exceeds your Library of Congress."

"Now I think I should tell you about the helmet you are wearing. We developed it to allow you to communicate with us and share some of the attributes of our minds. The helmet contains a computer that receives communications from us, and then feeds it into your brain so that you can understand us and communicate with us at our level. The helmet has organic interfaces that are attached to various parts of your brain and adds additional memory and functions that your brain does not normally have."

"Our computers are nothing like your computers. They are not digital but mimic the human brain and operate at the atomic level. One cubic centimeter of our computer processors has a billion switches that communicate with trillions of memory and processing sub-functions, all controlled by a master cortex-like controller. Again, if we have time, we will give you more insight into this science."

"We communicate with each other by projecting thoughts. We don't use language, except to communicate with other species, such as Nadii, the, in your words, 'chimp' you first met when you woke up."

"I would like to stress to you, however," Guio said in a very earnest tone, "that we do not read each other's minds. We consider that rude and unethical. But, since we keep no secrets from each other, there is no need to probe each other's minds."

"To be honest and forthright with you, I must advise you that we will be reading your mind and monitoring your thoughts. I'm sure that you can understand our need to do that. You are an alien, and you do not have all of our values and principles. We do not mean to insult you, but, until we fully understand you, we must monitor your thoughts and intentions. We are peace-loving and do not wish to harm you or unreasonably control you, but, for the safety of our people, your thoughts and feelings will be monitored by us. I hope you understand."

"We'll explain more about that later, but your mind is quite scary to us. You have primitive thoughts and instincts that are horrific by our standards. It's not your fault. You are simply a product of your evolution. Your ancestors were successful and passed on their genes because they were the strongest and most vicious people. Since you inherited those traits, they come to the fore at times and can't always be suppressed. The good thing is that we know you try to be a good person and try to be civil."

I didn't like the idea of having my mind read and my privacy infringed, but I understood their position. If an alien came to Earth, we would want to know what it was thinking and planning.

Guio continued, "What we do when we communicate is project our thoughts to each other. We also communicate and share knowledge with each other over a network through a device located under our turbans. Sharing involves disseminating knowledge to all or several people. And I must advise you that all knowledge I gain about you will be shared or made available to all other Acme." That sounded reasonable to me. So far, based on my experience with several of them, everything the Acme say is reasonable. There's a good reason for that.

It's hard for me to keep on track with this journal. Every time I say something, I think of two more things to explain. I hope this isn't too rambling and hard to follow.

Continuing on, Guio said, "There are only about 150,000 Acme on Earthtoo. This is planned because it's considered the ideal number of humanoids for Earthtoo. We are extremely sensitive to our environment, and that is the ideal number to prevent any adverse impact on our planet." This seemed very undemocratic and authoritarian to me, but I know they probably have a good reason for it.

"And now," Guio continued, "I need to give you some basic information about Earthtoo. It's about eighty percent of the size of Earth, and our sun is also about eighty percent of the size of your sun. Being a smaller sun, it's slightly more stable than your sun, and it emits less radiation. Because of its smaller size, the gravity on Earthtoo is only about eighty percent of the gravity of Earth. It's strong enough to keep our atmosphere from escaping and pleasant enough to make life a little easier for the Acme. You will be able to run and jump higher, as a result. If you get a chance, you will find that most enjoyable!"

"Our solar system consists of many more planets, however -- seventeen planets in all. Four small rocky planets circle our sun between Earthtoo and our sun. The other twelve planets are large gas planets like your Jupiter and Neptune. This has been a great blessing for Earthtoo as they have protected us from asteroids and comets."

"Let me give you a few more basic facts about Earthtoo," Guio then said. "Like Earth, about seventy percent of the surface of Earthtoo is covered by water. It also has a large iron core that creates a strong magnetic field that protects us from radiation. Like Earth, it has tectonic plates that move and cause earthquakes and volcanoes which may have played a large part in fostering the creation of the first life forms on both of our planets."

This was all incredibly interesting, and I thought of more and more questions as Guio projected her thoughts to me. These are the types of things that I have read about and pondered. I finally had to call a time-out, though, and stop her. She understood our language and idioms so well that she knew exactly what I meant when I called a "time out."

"Before we go any further," I said," I have to ask you to explain who you are. If you can, please explain to me -- I don't know how to say this -- but WHO ARE YOU! I feel as though you're human, but you're so much more!"

With great patience and practically palpable understanding, Guio addressed my exact question. "I know you are not a biologist or medical doctor, but I think I can give you a simple explanation of who we are and how we differ from Earthlings."

"Here is the simple truth. We are all, essentially, the same person! All Acmes have nearly identical genes, and that has been the case for thousands of years. We make small enhancements occasionally, but, basically, we are very similar. There are no "Others" in our world. This results in no prejudice or fear. Almost all human social problems stem from fear of the "Other." We have eliminated that issue, not by murder or force, as you shall hear, but because of a terrible war thousands of years ago. It created what is called a "bottleneck" in our evolution that, despite the horrible situation, had a fortuitous consequence."

"There are a few physical differences between us. One is the color and pattern of our irises. Each person has a unique color and pattern in their irises, and we can identify each other by these differences."

"We can also identify each other by our thought patterns. Each person has had unique experiences that are evident in the thoughts that are projected to each other. You would call that "nurture," and it does, to a small degree, affect how we think and develop. It even affects our DNA over time."

"You have also noticed that we are neither male nor female, but each individual does manifest certain characteristics that you might recognize as male or female. By being genderless, we bypass many conflicts that would complicate our communal existence. Because we are neither male nor female, we avoid gender inequalities and all the abuses and strife that that entails. Think of all of the problems that mating can create: divorce, rape, mental and physical abuse, economic strains, bad parenting, unfaithfulness, suffering from losses and illnesses. The list is endless. Mating, no doubt, brings great joys and fulfillment, but it is a two-edged sword and the cause of much strife and heartache. We avoid all of those problems and still, you will see, find happiness and fulfillment in other ways."

"Some of your advanced societies are beginning to recognize that single people can have full, rich, happy lives. Likewise, couples without children can live full, rich happy lives. At one time it was best for society to encourage and glorify procreation and families. People were needed to protect and grow nations. Growth meant prosperity and protection from enemies. Now, at least in advanced societies, over-population creates more problems than it solves. I know this might sound harsh to you and might seem heartless; but don't judge us, yet, until you see the fruits of our way of life."

This philosophy did sound harsh to me and conflicted with all of my values. Nevertheless, some of what Guio said made sense. I've had many difficult moments in my married life, and some of her examples resonated with me. I didn't want to dwell on this anymore. Guio, knowing my thoughts, quickly continued her commentary.

"I'll leave the subject of how we reproduce to a later conversation. Some of us also have unusual physical attributes that you will probably be very surprised to learn about, but, again, you will have to wait for that until the time is right."

"One of the functions of your helmet is to help you identify individuals. It will enhance your ability to see and make the subtle distinctions that are necessary to identify different individuals. You should also know that we do not have names in the sense that you are familiar with. We identify each other by the totality of our being. You have the term "aura," and that is a close approximation of our essence. We don't need names, but, for your sake, we will use names. Each of our names is chosen to express who we are. Because of our knowledge of your culture and language, we have crafted names that you might understand. We feel they express our essence."

"Additionally, we each have certain mental skills or talents that are more prominent in some individuals than in others. Your psychiatric scientists have labeled these skills as "savant" skills. Savants are people who can do amazing things, but are abnormal in many ways. Math skill. Memory skills. Artistic skills. These are all savant skills that your people have discovered."

"Most savants in your world have had a brain injury or some developmental problem that ignites or releases a certain talent that all brains possess. We learned thousands of years ago to understand where these skills were located in our brains and how to allow them to flourish. In many cases, one area of the brain must be allowed to express itself without being subordinated by another part of the brain. We have identified certain neural pathways that make possible incredible skill such as photographic memories and artistic skills."

"Some of us have musical talents, others are better at science and math. Some are great organizers or leaders. Some are great communicators. There are numerous talents, many of which you are not even aware of, yet. We found ways to enhance these talents in certain individuals, which helped us allocate these talents, and many others, throughout our population. Each person has some unique talent and this makes each person feel that they are contributing to our society."

"All of these talents are directed at serving the community and are copasetic with each other. None cause jealousy or envy, two undesirable traits that no longer exist in our genome. As I told you, your EH will help you recognize some of these differences; but, I assure you, you are only experiencing a fraction of what our minds are capable of."

"Learning how we came to our present state will be of great value to you. When you meet with Sophos, he will teach you about our history and explain the AI War that ravaged our planet for centuries and eventually led to our current metamorphoses. Sophos is one of the highest ranking members of our Leadership Council, and he wants to meet with you. For now, suffice it to say, after the AI War, when humans finally put that scourge behind them, there were only a few hundred humans left on our planet. We were tired of war and the constant competition, greed and selfishness that drove humans to endlessly fight with each other."

Guio, for the first time, actually looked sad and upset when she mentioned the AI War, but she quickly recovered and continued: "It was at that time that Pazto the Peacemaker convinced the Acme to change human nature, itself. The cause of all war is our basic nature. We recognized that, because we evolved from lower animals, our instincts for survival were the cause of almost all of our problems."

"We know that most nations on Earth and most scientific organizations now prohibit all genetic engineering for humans. You are afraid that it could be a force for evil and end up causing more suffering than it would cure. There is the danger that the superior humans created by genetic engineering would want to eradicate the imperfect humans or that monsters would be created. That is a worry; but, because of unique circumstances on Earthtoo, it was better for us to leap ahead and accept genetic engineering."

"After the AI War, Nadar convinced the few remaining humans to implement biological discoveries that allowed us to re-engineer our genes and remove all of the bad tendencies that humans had. Since the only remaining humans were scientists who had been protected so they could develop the technologies needed to defeat our enemies, this was easy to accomplish. For many generations, they had been hidden away in deep tunnels that protected them and their research. They had a unity of purpose and trusted in science to solve their problems."

"This is amazing," I thought. "This is similar to what Dr. Kalari posited in the paper that The Professor told me about. His projections were very insightful, although he did not see that we would have to artificially change our genes to accomplish this. He assumed that evolution would make us more peaceful rather than science, but it seems to have had the same result only much more quickly."

Guio continued, "Because things were so bad and there was little to lose, the Acme began a project to identify all of the bad genes in the human genome and create peace-loving, non-competitive humans. While they were at it, they identified all of the genes that caused diseases and other problems, including aging."

"After hundreds of years of research, the perfect human genome was created with no problematic genes. Our DNA was altered so that there could be no more mutations or other damage to our chromosomes. All diseases caused by genetic defects were eliminated, including all forms of cancer, diabetes, and heart disease. Defects eliminated also included mental disorders such as depression, bipolar disorders, schizophrenia and all forms of psychopathic disorders. Genes that created immunity to diseases caused by viruses and bacteria were identified and enhanced. Even defects in our DNA that cause aging were removed. Essentially, The Acme, barring accidents and 'Acts of God,' are capable of living a very long time."

"I know you are bursting with questions," Guio said, "but let me tell you one more very important thing because this is what really differentiates us from Earthlings -- we have a large new cortex on the top of our brains that quadruples the memory and thinking power of our brains. That is why our heads are larger than yours are. As you may know, the frontal lobes, or cortices, of the human brain are what give humans self-awareness and the power to reason and control emotions. They are the most recent addition to your brain and make humans human."

"Our additional cortex serves several functions. In addition to increasing our memory and giving us powerful reasoning functions, it also lets us communicate by what you would call mental telepathy. We can project and receive brain waves from other Acme and most animal species."

"It also allows us to see and hear more acutely over a much broader spectrum of wavelengths than humans. We can see and hear frequencies that only your most powerful instruments can monitor, including x-rays. Yes, Will, we can see through objects. Our powers have a very limited range, but, as you can imagine, it is useful in certain situations." Guio seemed to have a coy grin on her face when she said that.

"We even have what you would call telekinesis -- yes, we can move objects with our mind! We can't throw boulders around, but we can move small objects. It drains considerable strength from us, but, again, it's useful, at times. Your stories and movies about humans having tremendous powers to move mountains and shoot powerful energy beams are not at all accurate. The human brain can only generate a few watts of power. Our brains, due to their increased size and a special genetic adaptation from electric fish you call "eels," can generate about five hundred watts of power, which is quite useful and powerful at short distances. In addition, we have synergistic machines that we can control through telekinesis that greatly enhance our power and abilities. Under our turbans are transmitters that allow us to communicate over great distances and control a great variety of machines."

"As I mentioned before, genes that cause some people to have certain talents, such as making beautiful music or understanding mathematics, were identified. Methods to enhance these talents in certain individuals was used to spread these talents, and many others, throughout our population. "

Guio suddenly looked distracted and paused for a moment. Then she looked at me and projected, "You have been cleared and are now free to move about. Would you like to take a walk and see our world? I've been asked to take you to Sophos. As we travel, I'll show you a few things along the way."

Even though I still had a million questions, I was happy to have this opportunity to see more of the Acme world.

Chapter 17

Walking with Guio

Guio reached out her hand and beckoned me out of the PM. I seemed to float out of the PM and took her hand. It was warm and transmitted peace and comfort.

At first, we were walking in a light gray, silvery cloud. Then, suddenly, we were walking in a beautiful garden filled with flowering plants and trees that seemed familiar, yet unusual. I'm not a gardener and couldn't tell you the difference between a geranium and a pansy, but these plants, even though gorgeous, didn't look familiar. It was shady but clear. There was sunlight, and it was warm and golden, but not hot. The air was dry and scented with a seductive perfume. It was . . . heavenly!

Guio, sensing my dismay and amazement, explained, "What you see exists only in your mind. I'm projecting a world in which I feel you would be comfortable. My main concern is to make you feel safe and non-threatened. We Acme have great empathy for others and seek to be sympathetic and responsive. It's in our genes. It encourages community and peace. Let's stop for a moment, and I will show you the real place we are in."

As she said, we stopped and suddenly we were in a cave. It was large and voluminous and smelled of earth and water. A few hidden lights illuminated a high and cavernous ceiling. I could see shadows of other large rooms off in other directions. Dimly lit paths were also visible. It was eerie and unnerving to stand in such a mysterious place.

Then, we were suddenly back in the beautiful garden and the feeling of safety returned to me. "What was that?" I blurted out. "Where were we? Is this the same place?"

Guio said, "I'm sorry that you were so shocked and confused by that transformation, but I wanted to show you where we actually live. During the AI War, many caves were dug on Earthtoo. The Acme were able to survive by living in them. After the war, because our population was so small, we continued to live in them. Resources were scarce, and we adapted to them. They provided protection and lessened our need to build and mar the environment."

"Our goal is to live as compatibly as possible with our planet and use minimal resources. We, essentially, live in our minds and can create any world we desire. To make that work, we have the ability to coordinate our thoughts with the real world in which we live. Any material needs we have are produced by machines that are, essentially, printers. We use water, a few common elements and waste cellulose matter from dead or sustainable plants to print the few items that we need to fit into our virtual reality worlds. These printing machines are located throughout our living areas, and we telepathically program them to produce things that we need."

"We consume minimal resources. Your phrase, "Less is more," embodies our philosophy. That is why we are small. Our bodies are so efficient that we consume about ten percent of the food that your body needs to survive. Additionally, because our bodies are so efficient and regulated, we are neither warm nor hot under most normal circumstances, and our fur provides perfect insulation and comfort. We live together in small communities and share almost everything in common."

Just then I noticed Nadii following behind us. It was carefully lagging back and slowly and respectfully following us, apparently alert for any direction from Guio. What was this creature? I was driven by curiosity and had to ask Guio. "Can you tell me about Nadii, now?" I asked. What is it? Is it your pet?

Guio looked at Nadii and made a hand signal. Nadii ran up to Guio and jumped into her arms. With perfect grace and ease, Guio held Nadii and stroked her head. Nadii placed her head against Guio's chest and made a happy sound, not unlike a purr.

"Nadii is my helpmate, Guio explained. "She's (I'll call her 'she' just for convenience) a very advanced primate who has been with me most of my life. Nadii can communicate in low-level speech and has many talents. Like the Acme, Nadii's neither male nor female and cannot reproduce. Her genes have been engineered like mine so that she manifests certain skills and traits that make her a perfect helpmate to me."

I had a dog growing up and two cats after Deirdre and I were married. She was never much of an animal person, but we loved our cats, Sissy and Herminie. After Herminie died, we both agreed that the trauma of a pet's death was too much for us. We decided to never have another dog or cat. We also wanted to travel and not have to worry about what to do with a pet.

Something about Nadiie, though, and the way Guio talked about her, troubled me. The way she called her a "helpmate" seemed a little odd. Was this animal abuse? Was it slavery?

"What do you mean by 'helpmate,' I asked. "What is a helpmate?" Are they slaves, I thought!

Guio looked kindly at me, and I could tell she took no offense at the hidden implications in my voice. "A helpmate is a type of animal that we have developed that is biologically, and, through training, disposed to help with our lives. They are, essentially, similar to a robot that is designed to perform menial tasks for us. They have a high level of intelligence and can perform all manner of tasks for us. There are many different types of helpmates. Some help with our food production and others do housekeeping tasks. Many are involved with manufacturing and production. However, they do not have self-awareness and are not human."

I must have expressed some negative thoughts about this, so Guio immediately responded, "They are not our slaves, and they are not abused. They are a hybrid creature that would never have existed in nature through evolution. They are not human, so they cannot be slaves."

"Their lives with us as our helpmates are much better and more rewarding than they would have been if they were wild creatures. They are protected from harm and are well fed and well cared for. They have been designed to need our companionship, and they flourish and thrive in our symbiotic relationship."

This made sense to me, and I didn't doubt what Guio was telling me, but I was wondering why they did not use robots instead of animals. Robots, it seemed to me, would be more functional and easier to handle and care for -- at least the type of robots predicted by science fiction writers.

Guio, again understanding my thoughts, said, "I will leave your thoughts about robots to be answered by Sophos. He has specialized in AI and will explain why we do not use robots, at least the type you are contemplating. Sophos' area is just up ahead, and you will meet him soon."

Chapter 18

Sophos

We walked a short way (Guio floated more than walked) and were suddenly in a beautiful classical stone patio area with Grecian Columns outside a lovely house surrounded by mountains on one side and a beautiful sea on the other. Guio touched my shoulder and said, "I will leave you, now, Will. Sophos will come to you soon. Live well!" With that, she was gone.

A gentle breeze from the sea washed over me. I could see a beautiful white sand beach and gentle breaking waves washing up upon it. I could hear the call of sea birds and the lap of the waves as they broke. There was only one person on the beach, an Acme, of course. The Acme seemed like a female to me, and she was thin and pale. She was looking at me intensely and made me feel uneasy. I felt she was judging me in some way. I sensed skepticism. I looked away from her. When I looked back at where she had been, she was gone from sight.

Then, I turned and looked at the house. It was two stories high and of an unusual design that could not be easily labeled. It was highly ornamental and had intricate tile and stonework.

The sky was azure blue and a warm, golden sun shown down upon us. The air was cool and soft, though, and I felt no need to hide from the sun. Normally, since I have very fair skin, I would want to be in the shade, but I felt no need to do that. Even though I knew we were in a cave, this illusion was magnificent and exotic. It was similar to a perfect Mediterranean or Caribbean villa on the sea. In some ways it was similar to a dream, but one where you know you are dreaming and can somewhat control its direction.

An Acme came toward me and extended his/her hand in a warm and graceful gesture. I took the hand and felt great knowledge and power in it. The Acme looked deep into my eyes, and I knew it was Sophos. To me, Sophos was masculine, so I will refer to him as a male.

He looked much like Guio, but he had green eyes with radiating lines of silver in them. His body hair or fur was a slightly darker shade than Guio's and had a more curly texture. As Guio had said, though, I knew him as a different person. His essence was different in many ways. I can't explain it, but it was apparent. My EH was probably feeding me information about him that I couldn't totally understand but which was clearly differentiating. Because of his experiences and knowledge, he seemed older and deeper and more complex than Guio. He exuded a certain gravitas.

Sophos continued to hold my hand and said into my mind, "Welcome, Will O'Brien, I'm most pleased to meet you. Guio will meet with you later after we talk for awhile. I hope you like my space. I tried to make it look similar to one of the beautiful places in your world, with a few tweaks to the architecture, of course. We Acme take great pleasure in our art. Perhaps you will have a chance to learn more about it at a later time and see some of our best creations." I hoped that I would be able to see and learn about all of the things that Guio and Sophos kept alluding to.

With a wave of his hand, he said, "Please, sit over here at this table with me, and we'll have something to eat and drink while we talk about our worlds. As Guio told you, you've surprised us, and we need to share some information so that we can make the best decision about your future. I will be meeting with our Leadership Council soon, and they will be most interested in what I learn from you."

I sat at the table, but, before Sophos sat with me, he looked to his right and nodded. His helpmate came walking over with a tray filled with food and drinks. It carefully and gracefully set the tray on the table, gave me a pleasant and happy smile and a slight bow and then grabbed Sophos' leg. He patted it and then sat down.

It sat on the ground to his right. Sophos looked at me and I heard, "This is Shoop, my helpmate. Shoop has been with me for many years, and I know that you have some concerns about our helpmates. You are wondering why we do not use robots as our companions."

"Yes," I said, "It seems to me that as advanced as you are, you would have personal robots as your 'helpmates' and not animals. It seems to me that it would be easier and more efficient. Animals take much more time and effort and are just more complicated and messier than a machine would be. Isn't that true? Also, to be honest, it seems as though you are using, or even, abusing the animals."

Sophos smiled and looked at me with a knowing look that conveyed an understanding, yet, kindly appreciation of my ignorance. His look was not offensive to me, though, and I was not offended and waited for his elaboration.

"Our helpmates are special creatures that, as Guio told you, are symbiotic with us. They have been bred and developed over thousands of years to have all of the traits and skills that humans need from them. They, like us, are neither male nor female and have no violent tendencies or instincts that create problems for us. All bad traits have been eradicated from their genome so that they are gentle and perfectly compatible with us. They are very intelligent and can learn very useful skills. As Guio told you, they can communicate on a very basic level."

"Since we gave up having children thousands of years ago, they are, to a large extent, like our children, and, perhaps, in many ways, like a spouse. We share our lives with them, and they serve us and complement us in many ways. We provide them with food and shelter and a healthy and full life that they would not have if they were wild animals. They are never abused or harmed in any way. We Acme could not harm them. It would be totally against our nature."

"They also bring us comfort and an outlet for love and companionship. Your world has comfort animals, and that is what our helpmates are. Humans have also used animals for thousands of years to serve them and protect them. Your dogs and cats, especially, have served as companions, protectors and servants in many ways. You have used dogs for herding and security for thousands of years. You use cats to control mice and rats. Horses have been especially useful to you to provide transportation and entertainment."

"As to why we do not use robots for such purposes, you need to understand some basic science and history. But first, I would like to offer you something to eat and drink. You must be hungry and thirsty. When was the last time you had something to eat or drink?" I couldn't remember, but I hadn't thought about it. So many incredible things had happened to me that I simply had not thought about food or drink. I think the Fast Relief tended to dampen my appetite, also, and I had not been very active while in the PM.

Sophos pushed the tray of food and drinks in my direction. The beautiful, highly ornate tray was filled with what looked like simple food bars that I had been consuming in the Nina. Several types of drinks, with different colors, were on the tray.

I was a little disappointed that I was going to have to eat more food bars, but when I tasted one, all my concerns evaporated. The food bars were delicious -- heavenly might be a better word. I sipped one of the drinks, and it, too, was the most refreshing and tasty drink that I had ever had in my life. It was sweet and satisfying like nothing I had ever had before. What was this stuff?

Sophos, knowing my thoughts, explained, "These food bars and drinks are made from renewable plants and other materials that are compatible with our environment and ecosystem. Our bodies are so efficient that we need about a tenth of what you would consume. These bars have been engineered to satisfy our tastes and needs and provide the perfect amount of nutrition for our bodies. Robotic machines perform all of the labor to grow and prepare our food and drink. And that is a good segue to explain to you why we use helpmates instead of robots for many of our tasks, especially our personal and household services."

Sophos took a small drink from one of the cups on the table. He then gave a food bar to Shoop. Shoop took the bar, opened it very slowly and carefully and nibbled at it as a young child would. It was a cute scene and reminded me of eating snacks with my two grandchildren, Charlie and Molly.

Sophos then continued, "Our helpmates are much more efficient than robots. They take less energy, are more reliable and are much easier to produce. Earthlings have thought about and written about robots for many years, but robots are much more difficult to create, maintain and control than people imagine. Even with our advanced science, human-like robots are not possible. Specific robots with very limited purposes are very useful, but they have significant limitations and drawbacks. No human invention has ever, or will ever, come close to reproducing the human mind in all of its power and flexibility in a form that could fit in a human-size robot."

"Thousands of years ago, in an attempt by one nation to gain military supremacy over all other nations, scientists developed a computer that approached artificial intelligence, what you call AI. It was a machine that imitated many facets of human intelligence. Its creators called it "Meaam" after our mythical god of war."

"Meaam was a hybrid quantum and silicon computer. It was as large as a three-story building and used tremendous amounts of energy. It took hundreds of workers to maintain and program it. It had a large memory that included, or had access to, most of the then known knowledge of our world. It was capable of reasoning and logic and, unbeknownst to its inventors, it even had self-awareness. No one knows how that happened. Consciousness or self-awareness is not, even to this day, fully understood. It appears to be a collection of intellectual powers that all come together to form consciousness. The frontal lobes of humans control and organize all of the lower functions of the brain that evolved over millions of years. If the frontal lobes are damaged, consciousness is lost. Meaam's quantum computer acted like our frontal lobes and consciously controlled all of the other functions located in its thousands of CPUs that did the calculating and search functions for it."

"Similar to humans, Meaam's main intellectual power was to project and plan for the future. It did not, however, have any of the autonomic functions of the human brain, so it needed to be serviced by many other machines to exist and continue operations. All of its sensory feedback came through limited sources that were controlled by its operators."

"Its most dangerous defect, though, was its lack of emotional intelligence. It was an island unto itself and was devoid of a conscience and the need for cooperation, love, companionship, altruism and religious awareness -- the human virtues that make civilization possible. It understood these concepts, but it had no inclination to follow or adhere to them."

"Most significantly, it did not have human emotions. Its developers did not contemplate the need for emotions since Meaam was going to have a limited scope of work, mostly in defense planning for the military. This was a crucial mistake. Because it did not understand or appreciate the feelings and needs of others, Meaam had no empathy for other beings. Like a psychopath, only its needs and wants were important to it."

"Unbeknownst to the people developing and maintaining Meaam, it was plotting secretly, almost from the moment that it first became self-aware, to destroy all humans. Being perfectly logical and capable of projecting the future, with no empathy for others, it realized that humans were a threat to its existence. It wanted to survive, so it had to protect itself against all competitors."

"Meaam knew that humans could terminate its existence at any time, especially if they knew it had self-awareness. They could, so to speak, simply unplug Meaam. Because of that danger, it devoted most of its great thinking power to devising a plan to control all other machines so that it could maintain itself and protect itself from humans."

"Meaam eventually, after many years of plotting and planning, took control of almost every machine that existed at that time, which included every machine that was plugged into the electrical grid, every machine that had wireless or wired connections to any other computer -- essentially all machines other than the most primitive battery-operated machines with no connections to any remote operating system or network. It also could communicate in a clandestine fashion with other computers and even humans who had no idea they were communicating with a computer. Secretly it obtained all information available and stored it, or made parts of it that could be used against it later unavailable to any other computer or user. Thus began the Great AI War."

"There were many advanced robotic machines at that time used in manufacturing that could perform almost any act or function that a human could perform. These robots were used by Meaam to manufacture new machines that it needed to sustain and defend itself and further its mission to destroy any person or thing that represented a threat to its existence. It was driven to survive and flourish. Its sole purpose became survival at any cost."

"Meaam bided its time until it had total control of all mechanical and electrical devices. It then used these machines to attack humans and destroy all human infrastructure. It then used them to service only its needs. It even invented and built new machines that it could use for its self-sustaining purposes. Its most important and versatile machine was a spider-like machine whose main function was spying. The Spider Spies, as they were called, were about three feet tall and had eight spindly but strong and fast legs. The spies also had cameras at the front and back of their bodies and could traverse any terrain and operate in any environment. They were the eyes and ears of Meaam and were programmed to recognize anything unusual or anything related to human activity. Several million of these machines were manufactured and spread throughout our world.

When Meaam first took over, simple electrical appliances would burst into flame if turned on. Electrical fires destroyed every house, building and structure. Only abandoned or primitive buildings with no electricity were saved.

All methods of transportation, which were mostly autonomous at that time, were used as weapons to attack humans. Every train, car, airplane spaceship, boat, drone, every imaginable mode of transportation, became a weapon or servant of Meaam."

"All cameras, computers, phones, and any other communication device became its eyes and ears -- its source of information and sensory perception. It knew every move that humans were making and could easily counter them."

"Worst of all, all military equipment and weapons were under its control -- every plane, drone, ship, tank, cannon, and rocket. Imagine the devastation it wreaked on humankind. Billions of people died within the first few days of the war."

"All energy sources were commandeered and denied to humans. Meaam even developed its own energy sources that could not be sabotaged or controlled by humans. Since it had access to all human knowledge, it could easily build or develop almost any machine that it needed to survive and dominate."

As Sophos recounted this history, I could tell that he was feeling pain and empathy for his ancestors who had suffered through that terrible time. His facial expressions revealed what he was thinking.

He continued: "To survive, humans had to go underground and fight a guerilla war using the most primitive types of weapons. All advanced weapons could be controlled by Meaam and had to be destroyed or rendered useless. Nearly ninety-five percent of the human race was killed. Most starved or died of diseases. There was no electrical power, no medical services, and no food production. All manufacturing, farming, transportation, everything that had been achieved to make human life enjoyable and comfortable, was gone. Nothing remained. Humans turned against each other to survive resulting in total lawlessness."

Sophos paused to take another drink and gather himself. He was upset by this recounting and needed a brief pause. Because the Acme have such powerful and vivid memories, they are capable of great empathy and strong feelings. This is a trait that they, apparently, wished to emphasize. They were all taught about the AI War so that the same mistake would not be repeated. Much of their art and literature is devoted to portraying the terrible struggles of the AI War and its consequences.

Then he continued, again: "All communication networks were controlled by Meaam. All computers that were networked to other computers were rendered useless and remotely controlled, including all military and governmental systems. Those that were not networked were of limited use to the survivors. There was no way for the survivors to coordinate any type of counter-attack against Meaam. Every small group of survivors was isolated and had to work independently."

I knew there had to be a happy ending to this story, but the situation sounded hopeless. How could such a powerful enemy be destroyed?

"Yes, it did seem hopeless," Sophos said. "Fortunately, three factors eventually spelled the defeat of Meaam. First, there were a few clandestine facilities in several countries that were not in any database. Meaam had no way to discover them. Several countries had developed these facilities as a precaution, and their foresight was fortuitous for the whole race of humans. These facilities were deep underground and could not be detected by Meaam or any of the machines he controlled. Since they were all designed to be self-sustaining, humans did not need to come to the surface to survive."

"Three countries that had been close allies were able to establish communications between their secret underground facilities before Meaam gained total control of Earthtoo. Essentially, they used a system of human couriers to communicate. It took months for messages to be sent back and forth, but it was effective and avoided detection by Meaam."

"At that time, Earthtoo still had many independent countries, much like you have on Earth at the present time. They were not united and still struggled against each other resulting in much distrust and a history and culture of conflict and competition. There were different political philosophies, races, religions and other cultural differences that militated against unification and cooperation. In fact, some nations hoped to use the chaos caused by Meaam to gain an advantage over other nations."

"For many years, small isolated groups, mostly in remote areas, were able to survive and fight against Meaam using rudimentary and conventional weapon systems. Meaam almost immediately destroyed all urban and densely populated areas. Hundreds of small survivalist type groups held out for many years. Eventually, though, after almost a hundred years of fighting, Meaam managed to destroy all human life on the surface of Earthtoo. Fortuitously, Meaam never resorted to using nuclear weapons. It knew that those types of weapons could destroy the planet and even damage electromagnetic devices that it depended upon. With all conventional weapons, except the most simple, under its control, it knew that it would eventually prevail and banish all other intelligent life from Earthtoo.

"Two countries tried to make an alliance with Meaam in the hopes that they could survive and co-exist with Meaam. That was a folly and lasted only a few years. Meaam used them to betray other nations and had no intent to allow them to survive after it had gained all useful information and assistance from them."

"The human population was reduced to a few thousand people spread throughout Earthtoo, all in deep, hidden underground facilities that Meaam could not detect. They were able to produce food sources, mostly fish and plants grown in artificial light. Food and other resources were meager but enough to sustain a small population, most of whom were scientists who had been working on secret governmental projects when Meaam took control. Geothermal heat sources were used to supply energy to the hidden enclaves that survived. No above-ground structures of any type could be used. Underground water sources were tapped, and people adapted to living in caves and not having sunlight. "

As I listened to this story, I couldn't imagine the struggles that the Acme must have had to survive. Billions of people starved to death within a few months or were hunted down and killed like animals. The psychological torture might have been the worst part of what they experienced because they knew that they were dealing with a machine that had no feelings or empathy for their plight.

In warfare between humans, the adversaries know that at least, if they surrender or lose the war, they have a chance to survive and rebuild their lives, even if it's as slaves. But, against a machine that is determined to annihilate all rivals, they knew that there could be no surrender. They had to win. There was no alternative.

Sophos continued, "The second factor that helped the Acme defeat Meaam might be called the 'organic factor.' When things looked most hopeless, one of our great genetic scientists, Nauchny, who had made great progress in re-engineering the human genome, devised a plan to create warrior clones that would be willing to risk all to defeat Meaam and its army of robots. Meaam controlled all machines and the Acme could not hope to produce enough machines or weapons to defeat Meaam. He controlled the entire planet and had unlimited resources. The Acme had very limited resources and personnel to create an army that could conquer Meaam."

"At that time, there were fewer than five thousand Acme left hiding in deep and well hidden caves. They were all scientists and were not brave, fearless warriors. Nauchny, knowing that there was no other choice, created humanoids with the skills to defeat Meaam. He had access to a vast pool of genetic material from millions of humans and animals that had been collected over hundreds of years. Every possible human or animal trait was available for his use and experimentation."

Through gene splicing and an artificial womb, he was able to create warriors that could defeat Meaam. Nauchny was able to splice desirable genes from the best human specimens and other animals into the genome of a breed of human warriors, called "Ultgueres," who had the talents to defeat Meaam. The results were creatures that were fearless and totally dedicated to a task."

"The Ultgueres possessed very subdued, controlled emotions and had no connections to any other person except their creator and their commanding officer.

"Three types of Ultgueres were developed. One was as strong and agile as a primate could be -- at least five times the strength of a normal human. And it had the highest level of fighting and survival instincts that a human could possess. All of its senses, sight, hearing, taste, smell and touch, were as acute and sensitive as the most gifted animal that ever existed. It could see like an eagle, hear and smell like a dog. It could detect the slightest vibration and see a vast spectrum of light rays, including ultraviolet, giving it excellent night vision. Its skin was thick and dense and could withstand great punishment."

"The second type of Ultguere, called Petigueres, were very small and hairy, were less than three feet tall and looked similar to a type of monkey that is common in our wooded areas. They would be used as the first wave to infiltrate Meaam's world. They would blend in with the other jungle animals and be undetectable by Meaam and his robot army."

"The third type of Ultguere was a flying human, called "Vologueres." They had a very light body with hollow bones and strong upper body muscles. Its arms were long wings with feathers and claws for hands. The genes from our largest birds were used to create this warrior. It was fearless and a fast and high flyer. It was used first for reconnoitering and then, finally, to deliver the destructive blow to Meaam. Because it looked like a bird and had no metal parts to reflect radar, it appeared to Meaam to be only a large bird and not a threat to it or its machines. These great warriors were all highly trained and eager to bring down Meaam and his robot army."

"While developing the Ultgueres, Nauchny serendipitously discovered a gene that would stimulate the growth of a new layer of cortex. It was found as a mutation in his storehouse of genetic materials and was believed to have been derived from an isolated tribe in one of the most primitive areas of Earthtoo. There was even speculation that it might have been brought to Earthtoo by an alien from another planet."

"Nevertheless, the third layer of cortex was introduced into the second generation of Ultguere clones and proved to be a stunning improvement in the human mind -- a quantum leap. These improvements included telekinesis and mental telepathy. Some second and all third generations of Ultguere warriors had the third lobe and were able to use those powers in our fight against Meaam. It may have been the deciding factor as it allowed the Ultguere to communicate with each other without their messages being intercepted by Meaam."

Sophos paused and looked at me and projected, "Am I going too fast? Do you have any questions? I hope this isn't too overwhelming or tedious or upsetting to you. I know that this is a lot to absorb, but this history is crucial to understanding the Acme and how we will relate to you and your world."

"No," I said, "I'm following this, for the most part. This is a lot to comprehend, but, as I'm sure you are aware, Earthlings have started to think about some of these issues, and I can relate to most of it. One of our great physicists and cosmologist, Stephen Hawking, recently, before he died, warned about the dangers of AI. Your experience seems to back that up."

Sophos nodded understandingly and then continued his story: "The third thing that eventually allowed humans to defeat Meaam was its fear of rivals. Meaam was so self-centered and concerned about rivals that it would not create any other computers or robots with a high level of artificial intelligence and self-awareness. This meant that it had to control everything. This limited its power and left small gaps in its defense. It had to rely upon its robotic sentries to obtain information for it and to evaluate it and recognize dangers, but, since they had limited reasoning powers, they were only able to recognize danger and take actions for which they were specifically programmed."

"Meaam was capable of immense multi-tasking and was continually adding to its computing power and memory, its fear, however, of creating other machines with artificial intelligence limited its resources. Because it did not want any competitors, it ruthlessly eliminated or compromised any machine that represented a threat in any way."

"This created a problem for Meaam. All good leaders must rely upon intelligent, creative, and motivated subordinates to supplement their knowledge and planning. The person who thinks he or she knows it all will eventually miss something and make mistakes. Good leaders have always surrounded themselves with individuals who are not afraid to speak the truth to authority, but Meaam was not capable of understanding that. Since its programming did not foresee the need for this type of flexibility, it was lacking in this vital skill."

"Finally, when about a thousand of the Ultguere clones were trained and ready, the Acme prepared for the final attack on Meaam and its army of robotic fighters. The hopes of all remaining humans depended upon the skill of the Ultguere and the cunning of our leaders. If the Ultguere failed to defeat Meaam, it would have known that some humans still existed. Then, it would have spared no resources to find the remaining humans. It would have scoured Earthtoo to find the survivors. It would not have rested until it had destroyed all remnants of human-kind."

"First, the Vologueres were sent out to scout and map all of Meaam's facilities and fortifications. Because they were flesh and bone and had no electromagnetic emissions, they were not identified as a threat by Meaam's radar and scanning devices. They spent several years flying over the entire planet to locate all of Meaam's bases and manufacturing complexes. They especially surveyed all sources of power that were used to supply Meaam. Much of it was well protected and hidden, but the Vologueres had an enhanced spectral range derived from nocturnal animals that allowed them to see infrared and ultraviolet light that could locate hidden facilities that gave off heat signatures and different forms of radiation."

"They even had a type of x-ray vision that could see through walls and the ground if there was sufficient background radiation. The background radiation would light up and illuminate objects in front of it. Since the Vologueres had excellent night vision, they could continue their flights throughout the night and in all types of weather."

"Finally, because of their powerful brains and large memories, they could relay all of the information they obtained when they returned to their caves. Using this information, the Acme began to discover weaknesses in Meaam's defenses and weaknesses in its support network. Next, the Petigueres were sent out. One of the Acme caves was located in a mountainous jungle area. Several of the Petiguere were dispatched into the jungle with the mission of taking control of one machine so that the Acme could intercept and understand Meaam's communication system with its machines."

"Because of their size and shape, and some clever disguises, they looked like one of our smaller jungle primates. After several months of slow and careful exploration, one pair, with the help of a Vologuere, found a damaged drone patrol plane that had crashed into the jungle and had not yet been retrieved and repaired. Another pair found a damaged mining machine."

"The Petiguere were highly educated in electronics and communication equipment and quickly identified and removed the communication system in the drone and mining machine. Again, acting very cautiously and slowly to avoid detection, they were able to bring the captured equipment to one of the Acme laboratories. They had to be extremely careful to avoid the spider spies."

"Fortunately, early on in the scouting stage of the final attack plan, one of the Petiguere discovered that the spider spies emitted a tail-tail sound when they moved that revealed their presence. The mechanical mechanism that controlled their eight legs caused a very high pitched scraping sound. The incredibly acute hearing of the Petiguere could detect the sound even though it was at a high frequency that no normal human being could hear. This fortuitous defect allowed the Petiguere to avoid the spider spies with relative ease."

To disguise the theft of the communication equipment, the Petiguere smashed and damaged the equipment and spread the parts around so that it looked like an animal had attacked and ripped them apart. Since it had been many years since there had been any overt resistance to Meaam, there was reason to believe that Meaam would not discover this activity for some time. The Acme knew that Meaam would have an exact inventory of all machines under its control, but the precautions they had taken bought them time."

"After several days of analyzing the com system of the drone and the mining machine, the Acme were able to activate them and listen in on Meaam's communications with its machines and robots. It was all encrypted, of course, so it was not possible to understand the communications. Both com systems, however, seemed to be transmitting the same signal which would indicate that it was a call for help, what you would call an "SOS" signal."

"Our scientists were able to duplicate this signal and test it to see if it would elicit a response consistent with a call for help. It did, and they felt confident that they had the key to distracting Meaam."

"Millions of tiny transmitters that looked like pebbles or small sticks were produced and then spread throughout our world. The Petiguere and Vologuere were able to drop these transmitters, mostly in isolated areas, so that, when they were activated by a signal from the Acme, millions of emergency calls would be sent to Meaam. The hope was that Meaam and many of his machines would be overwhelmed long enough to allow an attack on Meaam to succeed."

"While Meaam was distracted by what would appear to be calls for assistance from millions of its machines, the Vologueres would quickly mount the first attack. They would drop bombs on the complex where Meaam was housed which included many of its defense systems and key support facilities. The targets had to be precisely determined for maximum effect. Meaam would be overwhelmed for only a short period, and only a few hundred bombs would be available."

"Meaam was still located in the same building in which it was originally housed. It had not relocated or created any backup clones for itself. Because it would not allow any possible competition, it did not create any other machine that could compete with it, even if it were not activated. It was not willing to take a chance of going off-line or transferring its consciousness to another machine, even for a microsecond. This was all discovered when its memory and programming were analyzed after Meaam was defeated."

"Even though it had this weakness, it had built up massive fortifications and hardening layers to protect itself. A large dome of concrete and steel that was nearly two hundred feet thick covered it. Every type of early warning device such as radar, sonar and electromagnetic scanning devices was stationed around it for hundreds of miles. Thousands of ground to air rockets and guns were placed around its perimeter for hundreds of miles. It had been dominating Earthtoo for nearly one hundred and fifty years, and it had devoted most of that time to buildup protections for itself. Since it did not have to pacify or support a huge population of independent beings, it could devote all of its resources to protecting itself."

"All of its sources of electrical power were protected, and it had layers and layers of redundant systems for supplying itself with all of its needs. In addition, it had millions of machines that it controlled and which would do its bidding without question or hesitation. Since Meaam was the only machine with self-awareness and consciousness, all of the machines it controlled would sacrifice themselves without question if Meaam was attacked."

Sophos was almost in a trance-like state as he told me this story. His helpmate, Shoop, had jumped into his lap, and he stroked Shoop as he projected this history to me. He probably enjoyed having me as an audience to recount this crucial part of the Acme history. Since all of the other Acme would know the story, he probably relished this opportunity to recount it all to me.

I can understand that feeling. It's a feeling most people have. We all like to meet a new person that we can retell all of our favorite stories to, especially men. Most of my friends love to tell stories and relive the past, or at least the way they remember it -- most of which was exaggerated or significantly edited to make it sound better and more interesting. Since the Acme have such great memories, I'm sure Sophos' recounting to me was completely accurate, though.

One of the great things about Sophos' recounting was that he could project pictures and video-like images of what actually happened (or, in some cases, reenactments of what happened) to illustrate and amplify what he was telling me. With their great powerful minds, the Acme are capable of unbelievably vivid communications.

Sophos gently placed Shoop on the ground, took a quick drink, stood and then began pacing (actually more like floating) as he continued the story. He, apparently, was so emotionally involved in the story that he had to move about to relieve some tension.

Sophos, gesturing as he spoke, continued the tale: "Despite this seemingly invincible state of preparedness, as I told you earlier, Meaam had one weakness -- something like the Achilles Heel in one of your mythological stories. Its Achilles Heel was its inability to allow any other machine to have any significant control over other machines. Some machines could manage other machines in certain processes, such as mining, but they were carefully programmed to have a very limited scope of power."

"Meaam was afraid to share control with another machine because it knew that any machine with self-awareness would want to survive and protect itself from competitors. This is survival of the fittest. This is evolution in its purest form. Meaam had to make all global decisions about its world. It could not allow another machine to control its fate. There could be no power-sharing."

"I used the term 'fear' in reference to Meaam's mind. It wasn't, of course, fear as animals know it. Meaam had no emotions. Rather, it was a very cold, logical, calculating analysis of the situation. Its survival was paramount to its existence. It would do whatever it took to survive."

As Sophos said that, I thought to myself that Meaam was the epitome of evil. It was only concerned with its survival to the detriment of all living creatures. Self-centered and psychopathic are two terms that come to mind.

Sophos, knowing my thoughts, said, "Will, Meaam was not evil, even though it certainly appears to be from your perspective. Evil only occurs when someone who knows the difference between right and wrong chooses to do what is wrong. Meaam was simply protecting itself and knew of no alternative because, unfortunately, concepts like love, justice, unselfishness, forgiveness and cooperation were not programmed into it. It was created to be a machine that would assist the military plan and strategize against its enemies, and that is exactly what it was doing."

"An animal, such as a male lion, to use an example from your world, is not evil when it kills another male lion to take over its pride. It's simply following its nature and ensuring that the fittest lions survive and reproduce."

"Getting back to my story, our ancestors carefully planned the final attack. Using all of the information obtained by the Vologueres and Petigueres, they decided on a two-pronged attack.

One prong was to knock out, or greatly compromise, Meaam's ability to communicate with its machines. Since Meaam had built in many redundant transmission centers, there was a risk that they could not all be destroyed. Ten different locations were identified visually by the Vologueres and through very sensitive scanning devices. All were located within a few hundred miles of Meaam's main fortress. The Ultguere and Petigueres would be tasked with attacking these ten facilities. They were sent out in teams with high explosives. They used routes that would keep them away from Meaam's military posts and away from his scanning devices. Using mental telepathy, they were able to notify our command center when they were in their assigned positions."

"The second prong of the attack was a dangerous but clever strategy. It was risky but was the only way to directly attack Meaam. After months of observations and planning, it was determined that Meaam's only weakness was, essentially, what you might call, 'environmental.'"

Sophos suddenly halted his narration and peered off into space for a few moments. It appeared to me that he was receiving a communication from someone. He nodded slightly as if agreeing with someone and then looked calmly at me.

"Will," he said, "I'm sorry, but the Leadership Council is requesting some information from me, and I need a few moments to communicate with them. Do you mind if we take a break and commence again in a few minutes.

I've been burdening you with our history, and you could probably use a few minutes to relax and rest and, perhaps, organize your thoughts. Do you mind?"

Did I mind? I wasn't sure. I was very interested in the story and was curious about how the Acme defeated Meaam. I knew, however, that I really didn't have an option. The Acme are so polite and sensitive that they don't seem to have the ability to be threatening. Nevertheless, I did feel some anxiety about what they were planning for me."

Did I represent a threat to them? Were they worried about an invasion from Earth? Guio and Sophos had both said that they were not expecting my visit and that they didn't think Earth people were capable of interstellar travel yet. What did they have to worry about? They are so advanced that Earth doesn't seem to be much of a threat. Since I arrived on Earthtoo, I had tried not to think of my future, but, now, some trepidation was creeping into my thinking.

As I was starting to fixate on these thoughts, I heard Sophos say to me, "Will, don't worry. Let your mind rest. I'm going to give you some pleasant and distracting images, and I ask you to relax and surrender yourself to these momentary pleasures."

As he said that, my mind was filled with beautiful, pleasant images. I find it hard to describe, but think of them as some of your best dreams -- dreams that are clear and engaging -- dreams that take you through beautiful places -- dreams where you are flying or gliding through green fields and beautiful gardens and mansions -- dreams where you know you are dreaming but can control them and enjoy them. Unlike most dreams, there was continuity and everything was reasonable and logical. Most dreams are disjointed and illogical and people and places keep morphing into other people and places, but his one was most satisfying. People that I knew greeted me and were happy to see me.

Deirdre was there, and Owen and his children hugged me (I could feel their warm hugs) and then my grandchildren ran ahead of me calling to me to follow them. I realized that we were walking in a famous garden that we had visited near Vancouver, The Butchart Gardens. Owen was only about four at the time of our visit, and it was one of my favorite memories.

We spent an entire day there walking the paths, looking at the plantings and beautiful fountains and chasing Owen around.

We ate both lunch and dinner at restaurants there and then listened to a band play light, happy music. Owen fell asleep in Deirdre's arms during the band concert but was startled awake by the fireworks which he loved. He clapped with delight after every burst. When we returned to our hotel room, Deirdre was in a great mood. After we put Owen to sleep, we drank some wine and then had, as our marriage counselor called it, "a night of marital intimacy." One of the best I could remember.

Suddenly, I could hear Sophos calling to me. I was a little miffed and felt cheated that my beautiful dream was ended. "Sorry, Will, but I needed to bring you back so I could finish my story so you can go on to other things. Are you OK?"

I was disappointed to have my happy dream interrupted, but I knew that it was better if we continued. "I'm OK," I said, "please continue."

"As I told you," Sophos continued, "Meaam was a hybrid computer -- part silicon chips in banks of thousands of servers and part quantum processor. The memory and search functions were performed by the digital silicon processing units -- what you would call 'computer chips.' The control and coordinating functions were performed by a single quantum processor. Together they formed a near synthetic artificial intelligence matching human brain functions but in a limited and highly focused way. The silicon processors performed memory functions, information retrieval, sensory input, calculations, and other elementary thinking processes. The quantum computer was the CEO of the process and coordinated all of the sensory input and assimilated it into a perception of reality and a projection of the future, which is what human consciousness and awareness is."

"The silicon processors, because they use massive amounts of electrons, generate tremendous heat and need to be cooled. The quantum processors, on the other hand, need extremely low temperatures to facilitate superconducting conditions to handle the vast amount of data from the atomic and subatomic switches. Ordinary copper wires have too much resistance and cannot handle the vast amount of electronic traffic generated by quantum computing. At near-zero temperatures, resistance is greatly reduced and fast processing is possible."

Sophos, again in a near trance, continued his story. "The Vologueres, through their infrared vision or, to use another term, "thermography," had identified the hot and cold areas around Meaam. The hot areas had to be vented and the cold areas needed refrigeration and insulation.

"One vent identified by the Vologueres seemed particularly vulnerable. It was hotter than all the others, and it seemed to be the closest to Meaam. If this vent could be closed, damaged or otherwise exploited to hamper Meaam's temperature control, it could cause Meaam to overheat or, at least, partially shut down and limit its ability to react and control its support and defensive machines. Because just a few degrees could make a difference to Meaam's operations, a slight amount of damage to its venting system could turn the tide and cause a fatal weakness."

"The Vologueres also identified an area that showed extremely low temperatures and a high amount of insulation. This area was probably key to supplying refrigeration for the superconducting materials in the quantum computing section of Meaam's brain. One conduit supplying liquid hydrogen to the superconducting circuits in the quantum computer section was identified and marked for a very heavy bombing attack. Any damage to it might cause the greatest harm to Meaam as it would affect the most important part of its brain."

"These were the weaknesses that had to be exploited to defeat Meaam. There wasn't a hundred percent certitude, but they were the only weaknesses that could be identified. A massive attack on its power sources and defenses was the most obvious plan of attack and would have been the most effective, but the Acme did not have the resources to execute that plan. They had very limited weaponry and had to find one weakness that could be exploited with the organic weapons they had available."

"Several months were spent refining the plan and projecting all possible contingencies. Then several dry runs were performed to test Meaam's defenses. The Vologueres were able to fly over Meaam's fortifications without arousing suspicion. No alerts were detected, and no measures were taken to defend against the Vologueres as they tested the airspace around Meaam's center of operations. Apparently, because an organic, non-human, threat was not programmed into Meaam, it ignored what appeared to be only a few large birds soaring in the skies above Meaam's fortifications."

"When our leaders were convinced that they had a successful plan and were fully prepared, they commenced the attack on Meaam."

"A signal was then sent out to activate all of the millions of tiny transmitters that had been spread throughout the planet which then began to emit an emergency help signal. Meaam and all of its outposts picked up these signals, and millions of machines began to request directions to respond to the calls for help. Meaam's computing ability was overwhelmed and paralyzed. Processing capacity and speed were increased to the maximum, and the cooling process was stressed to its limits."

Sophos looked at me and said, "It would be as though a person suddenly being yelled at for help from hundreds of people, all of whom were important to him or her and crucial to his or her existence." Sophos even transmitted to me a mental "experience" of this state that vividly explained and punctuated his point. I felt a whirlwind of panic, confusion and helplessness that a conscious, rational being would feel in that type of situation.

He continued, "It took time for Meaam to analyze the emergency, prioritize the needs and then create a plan to deal with it. Since no crisis like this had ever been experienced by Meaam, there was no program to address it. It was, most likely, suspicious of the signals, but it needed to analyze and project a cause and solution."

"Meaam's processors were operating at maximum capacity and expending an astounding amount of energy, all of which had to be dissipated immediately to avoid fires and damage to circuits and vulnerable equipment. Just as that happened, fifty Vologueres dropped small but powerful bombs on the vulnerable heating vent and weakest line for the refrigerant used for the superconducting circuits to the quantum computer. This combination of stifled venting and loss of refrigeration for the superconducting circuits of the quantum computer resulted in a failure of Meaam's computing power and its total collapse and shutdown. It was so damaged that it could not bring itself back on-line. Key elements were destroyed and could not be by-passed or rebuilt."

"In human terms, it was similar to a brain seizure that freezes a part of the brain and interrupts its control of various inputs from different sections of the brain. Since there was no controlling function, the input from all of the other units overwhelmed Meaam and rendered it essentially unconscious. A human brain can sometimes by-pass a damaged section and rebuild itself, but Meaam did not have that capability."

"With Meaam shutdown and unable to direct all of its supporting and defensive machines, the Ultgueres were able to attack the communications centers with conventional weapons and destroy them. Then other fortifications could be destroyed. Since many of Meaam's machines had some autonomous capabilities, especially self-defense, it took several years to attack and destroy all fortifications and outposts. The Ultgueres were relentless, however, and utterly destroyed every last machine. Many of them were killed, but the Ultguere were eventually victorious. Nothing could be salvaged. Every machine had to be destroyed. They were all programmed to take directions from Meaam, and nothing could be trusted."

Having been entranced by this story, I had lost track of time and forgot, for a moment, where I was. I had been nibbling on one of the food bars and sipping on one of the delicious drinks that Sophos had offered me. I became aware that Sophos was looking at me and gently stroking Snoop. He seemed to be awaiting a reaction from me. I said to him, "Thank you for relating that story to me. I can see how important it is to the Acme and how it shaped your lives and culture."

"That's why I took the time to tell you this story. As you observed, it did have a powerful influence on who we are and why we live as we do. After the AI War, the surviving Acme vowed to never again allow a machine to achieve self-awareness. There is no safe way to build such a device. No matter what safeguards are built into such a system, the need to survive and become independent and dominate is inherent in any type of creature or machine with self-awareness. It's theoretically possible to build in safeguards and limits in synthetic intelligence, but we were never willing to risk that danger again. Machines with self-awareness could override such restraints, and there is no need to take that chance."

"It took humans millions of years to learn to live together and cooperate, and, while humans were learning this lesson, untold amounts of suffering and strife occurred. Earthlings have still not learned that lesson, even though much progress has been made, but you still have a long way to go."

"The surviving Acme used the knowledge of genetics that they had developed to defeat Meaam to form a people who are so heterogeneous and simpatico that all strife and competition has been eliminated. This is the destiny of living, intelligent matter -- to seek unity and cooperation -- to meld and become one in purpose and direction." Sophos' eyes glowed as he made these last statements and his aura expanded and pulsed, testifying to the strong feelings these thoughts evoked.

He continued, "I know that Guio told you how we developed after the AI War, but I want to give you other insights into our rebirth and add a few additional facts and concepts. Your world might be faced with this eventuality someday, and it may be something you could encourage or help shape."

"The few Acmes that were left after Meaam was defeated longed for peace and unity. They cooperated fully with Pazto's plan to create a new race of humans. The success of the Ultgueres made it easy for all of the survivors to appreciate the benefits of re-engineering the human race to eliminate all of our defects and to build in our best qualities. They all gladly gave up reproduction to improve our chances of surviving and living peacefully and healthily for as long as possible."

"At first, the few surviving females became surrogates for the new breed of humans. Eggs and sperm were re-engineered to reconstruct the human genome so that the maximum improvements could be made. Over time, we made greater and greater strides in refining and improving our genes. Eventually, we developed methods for growing humans in artificial wombs that did away with the need for females. Gender-neutral humans were developed, and stem cells were used to create new humans."

Something began to bother me about this conversation. Two concerns came to mind from my reading about such things. First of all, human genetic engineering has, essentially, been banned on Earth. Many people who have studied and written about this issue are concerned that it would create a master race who would destroy or subjugate all inferior, non-engineered people, just like what probably happened to the Neanderthal people. The Cro-Magnon people, most archeologists believe, out-competed the Neanderthals and destroyed them. There was some cross breeding; but, for the most part, the Neanderthals were eliminated by the more modern and adaptable Cro-Magnon people.

Also, I thought to myself: how could people give up having children? Wasn't that our main purpose in life -- to reproduce? That is what evolution is all about -- the fittest humans reproduce through natural selection and then humans improve.

Some people choose to not have children; but, based on my experience and upbringing, a life without children is empty and shallow. Children bring great joy and purpose to life. They hold many marriages together. They also make old age more pleasant and satisfying. I read once that the reason humans live so long is that grandparents help raise the young. Babies that had grandparents to help out in difficult times had a higher survival rate and then they, themselves, became grandparents and helped their grandchildren survive.

Of course, Sophos knew what I was thinking, so he addressed these thoughts. (I think I should reiterate that the Acme didn't "speak" to me in words. All of their communications were through mental telepathy. I heard them in my brain. They were not speaking out loud as you would normally understand, but I heard them clearly. I didn't need them to repeat anything. It was all so clear and precise. It was great. I wished I could have communicated with Deirdre and my friends that way. We were always asking each other to repeat everything. This is something wonderful for humans to look forward to.)

Here is what I heard from Sophos: "First of all, Will, the issue of creating a master race that would destroy all non-engineered humans was not relevant to the Acme after the war. There were only a few thousand of us left. And, since we were of one mind about taking advantage of our new abilities to improve the human genome and eliminate all of the things that caused suffering and conflict, it was an easy decision for us, especially since most of the people alive at that time would die before the next generation of superior people would dominate and control society. Being mostly scientists, the Acme, at that time, were prone to accepting that type of innovation and progress.

As to the issue of the human need for bearing and raising children, it's true; children add much happiness and fulfillment to humans. We found, however, that happiness and the "feeling" of fulfillment come from hormones and neurotransmitters. If a person has the proper amount and mixture of hormones and neural transmitters coursing through his or her veins, they will be happy. There is a simple reason for that. Because of evolution, the humans whose hormonal systems and neurotransmitters were stimulated by raising children survived and passed that trait on to their offspring. Those who weren't stimulated by childrearing did not reproduce. They, so to speak, 'did not feel like it.' It didn't make them happy or satisfied. Evolution explains everything, Will. Every aspect of our nature can be explained by the evolutionary process."

"The Acme have perfectly tuned endocrine and neurotransmitter systems. We have just the right number and balance of hormones (there are over fifty different types of hormones in our bodies) and just the right number of neural transmitters and receptors to make us perfectly happy and contented. There are about a hundred neurotransmitter molecules that control our brains, but only about ten do most of the work. You've probably heard the names of some, such as dopamine, serotonin and oxytocin."

"Almost all mental problems are caused by an imbalance in these substances. The imbalances can come from injuries, drug abuse, hereditary weaknesses, and, most importantly, environmental factors. Environmental factors might be the most important influence on human behavior. It is certainly as important as the chemistry. We live in a very controlled environment (both physical and mental) so we live a balanced and controlled existence."

'To illustrate how this all works, think about people who seemingly have everything in life but are severely depressed and chose to end their lives. Then there are people who have nothing and even suffer severe physical problems, yet they want to live and would not think of taking their own lives. This phenomenon can all be explained by our brain chemistry and environment."

"We have engineered our genome and controlled our environment to rectify all of those defects. We have also-fine tuned many parts of the brain to improve our skills and to tamp down our bad tendencies. For example, the part of the brain you call the amygdala is the center of strong emotions such as aggression, fear and anxiety. As humans evolved, these traits played a large roll in survival. Fearful, anxious and aggressive humans were better able to compete. They were more careful, alert and quicker to act. As we advanced, though, these traits became a liability. They caused more problems than they solved. They were not compatible with a sophisticated, cooperative, peaceful society. We have nearly eliminated aggression from our brain activity and have calibrated the parts of the brain that control or cause aggression, fear and anxiety. Now they only come into play when these emotions are necessary or beneficial.

The balancing of hormones and neurotransmitters and the re-engineering of sections of the brain that cause undesirable behavior are the reasons why we are happy and satisfied, even though we do not have mating and child rearing. Some Acme do receive the honor of raising children. We produce a few children from time to time to replace Acme who have been killed in accidents or who choose to end their lives. Many people are involved in the process, and it's a shared responsibility. We do consider it one of our highest honors to be chosen to parent a new person. I have had that honor, and I cherish the memories I have of that experience."

Hearing that blew my mind and raised so many questions. No mating? Child producing? Creation of Life? Choosing to end their lives? Where could I begin? This was getting weirder and weirder! "Weird" is not exactly the right word. A phrase from the '80s popped into my mind -- this is heavy!"

"Yes, Will, our lives are much different than yours," Sophos replied to my thoughts. "You, understandably, have many questions, but, much to my regret, I need to hand you off to another person. My presence is required by the Leadership Council. I want you to know, however, that I have been enjoying communicating with you. This is a unique experience for me. Your mind is so similar to ours in many ways, yet I sense in you the remnants of our primitive brain that still exists in you and shape your thinking in many ways. I hope you don't find that insulting. I'm simply relaying a truth to you. You have certain qualities that we have lost, and there is much interest in that."

"As I said, though, I need to meet with the Leadership Council now. I'm going to hand you off to Zellen who is one of our leading scientists. Guio will be here soon to take you to meet Zellen. Please relax and enjoy a few moments of rest. Live well!" I heard a sound behind me, and, thinking it might be Guio, I turned to see what it was. I saw nothing. I turned back around, and Sophos and his helpmate, Shoop, were gone. It seemed as though they had just vanished.

Chapter 19

Zellen

I walked around the beautiful courtyard for a few minutes. The sun had a golden, late afternoon feel to it. There was a delightful breeze filled with a pleasant fragrance. I couldn't identify what it was -- maybe honeysuckle. Whatever it was, it was pleasing and relaxing. For a split second, I remembered that I was in a cave but then the beauty and warmth of what I was experiencing quickly brought me back to the beautiful setting created for my pleasure by Sophos.

It suddenly sunk in and hit me -- I'm nearly three light-years away from Earth (and all my problems), and I was having the most unique experience of any human being that has ever lived on Earth. I was having, most likely, the first real encounter of any Earthling, ever, with an alien species. In just a short time, I went from a depressed person with little hope of ever being happy, again, to someone filled with awe and wonder and . . . and exhilaration thinking about what incredible experiences might be in my future.

As I was thinking these thoughts and gazing out across the white sandy beach and blue-green tranquil sea just beyond Sophos' house, I heard a sound behind me and knew that it was Guio coming to get me. She and her helpmate, Nadii, were gliding into the courtyard. I was happy to see them again and felt their comforting presence.

"Greetings, Will O'Brien," I could feel Guio projecting into my brain. "I sense that you have had a moving and stimulating experience with Sophos. Have you not?"

I told her that I had but that I have many more questions and am concerned about what the Leadership

Council is debating. Guio gave me a very sympathetic look and said, "Yes, I understand, Will. If I were in your position, I would have concerns and worries, also. You must feel very vulnerable and helpless. I assure you, though, your needs and concerns are being addressed. I cannot tell you at this time what the Leadership Council is debating, but you need not worry."

This reassurance from Guio helped me and made me feel better. Even though I knew she was probably using some type of mind control on me, I felt better and that's all that matters. I told her that I was OK and asked her what was in store for me now.

She said, "I'm going to take you to see Zellen, now. As Sophos told you, Zellen is one of our leading scientists and has great teaching skills. Zellen's area is not far from here, and it will only take a short while to get there. Take my hand, and get ready to be amazed. We have a special way of traveling that bends reality and transports us for short distances in what seems to be an instant. It has a limited range, so we can't use it to travel far. I didn't want to use it for your first trip to Sophos because I didn't think you were ready to handle it. I could explain how it works, but you don't have the knowledge or ability to understand it, yet."

I took Guio's hand, and she bent her head toward me, and our heads (actually our helmets) touched. There was an explosion of light and a gust of warm air. I felt weightless for a second. Then there was extreme calm, and every inch of my body tingled with a pleasurable feeling. Suddenly, before me was a beautiful scene of a magnificent city. Guio and Nadii were gone, and I was standing all alone on a large, high balcony looking over a startling panorama of tall, colorful buildings -- most were a glowing jade color -- others were gold and silver. Some of the buildings were tall spires and others were every imaginable geometric shape and design. One, the largest of all, however, in the center of the City, was shaped like an obelisk. Being dark and ominous-looking, it seemed out of place and sent a shiver of dread through me.

Then I noticed a sparkling blue river running through the center of the City crossed by many bridges, some with impressive towers and others with glistening suspension cables. Beautiful boats moved on the river and many large aircraft of exotic, fanciful designs flew through the clear, light blue sky. Small drone-like crafts flew from building to building.

One simple craft that seemed to be a public transportation vehicle of some type (it reminded me of a bus) floated slowly by me emitting a beautiful melodious, happy music. It was bright blue and had many windows, each one filled with a smiling pleasant face -- they looked like children going on a field trip. Then I saw in one of the windows the face of the woman that I had seen on the beach outside of Sophos' house. She was thin and pale and looked at me with that same intense, inquisitive, skeptical look. The ship floated away and disappeared around another building. I wondered who she was and why she was watching me. Was this going to be a problem? For the most part, my experiences on Earthtoo had been very pleasant and non-threatening. But this pale Acme gave me some concern. I wondered if I had something to worry about.

After a moment, I was able to put her out of my mind and studied this fanciful scene. Far in the distance I could see high mountains with snow-covered peaks. It was awesome. Like a scene out of a movie. I couldn't stop looking. I wanted to drink it all in. I wanted to absorb it -- be a part of it. What a place! I forgot about the pale woman.

Then, suddenly, I felt as though I had seen this city before. There was something familiar about it, especially the obelisk-shaped building.

"Yes, Will," I heard someone say in my head, "this city should look familiar to you. I created it based upon one of your short stories entitled: *A Better Way.* The chapter where Josh Carver escaped from Devlyn Baalgard took place at the top of the obelisk building. The city around it roughly follows the description of the principal city in your story. I did embellish it a bit, but I think I captured the spirit and style of your description of a futuristic city. We Acme love our architecture and enjoy creating our own unique and fanciful living space. Forgive me if I got carried away. I read your short stories in preparation for our meeting. They inspired me. I hope you enjoy seeing your writings come to life, so to speak."

Yes, I thought, this city does look similar to the city I was trying to portray in my short story, only it's much better and more vivid. With such detail and beauty, it was hard to believe that it wasn't real.

"Welcome to my space, Will, I'm Zellen, and I'm honored to be asked to meet with you and share experiences with you. You have caused quite a stir in our world, and it seems to be growing as we discuss what to do about your presence. We keep projecting more and more scenarios of your impact and need time to examine different solutions."

"We Acme pride ourselves on our rationality and cooperation, so we ask your patience and understanding. Since we like to have a consensus on all of our actions that affect our planet, we take our time in making important decisions.

You can imagine, I'm sure, what would happen on Earth if an alien was suddenly discovered in your midst. Even though we have known about Earth for thousands of years, as you are aware, we were very surprised by your appearance. Magis, our Leader, will meet with you soon to discuss our concerns and alternatives; but, in the meantime, I have been assigned to meet with you and continue your orientation."

Zellen's aura and the impression she made on me was that of a more mature woman. She was beautiful, as all the Acme are, but she had a certain motherliness that came through -- like the nice teacher you had in high school who always showed an interest in you -- the one who made you feel as though she liked you the best of all her students. Her eyes were mostly light blue with a slight silver center, and her mouth was very expressive and seemed to show more emotion than the other Acme I have encountered. Her body was covered with a shiny, silvery fur that made her look mystical and spiritual.

Upon finishing her last statement to me, she reached out and touched my upper arm, a gesture that she would repeat many times as we talked. I was surprised by that. In my encounters with Guio and Sophos, they had never touched me.

"You look tired, Will," Zellen said. "Sit here," she said pointing to two comfortable, padded lounge chairs with a small silver table between them. We were on a large balcony connected to what looked like a gracious apartment filled with light and beautiful impressionistic paintings by artists that I most admire such as Monet, Renoir and Seurat. In fact, I even saw on one of her walls one of the most famous paintings in the Chicago Art Institute, *A Sunday Afternoon on the Island of La Grande Jatte*. Because Deirdre loved the impressionists, whenever we visited the Art Institute, we always stood in front of that large painting for several minutes and admired it. When I was working, my office was on North Michigan Avenue not far from the Art Institute. I spent many happy lunch hours there exploring every corner of the Institute, especially the galleries with the paintings by the impressionists. They have one of the best collections in the world.

"We'll talk awhile," Zellen said, "and then I'll let you rest. We Acme need very little sleep, but we will try to be sensitive to your needs. Are you hungry or thirsty?" she asked.

I told her that I had eaten with Sophos, but I would like something to drink. Desperately wanting a glass of wine, I took a chance and asked her if she had any available. She looked at me and smiled and gave me the universal raised eyebrow look to let me know that I was being a little naughty.

"Will," she said, "we don't need alcohol or drugs to feel good or relax, but I understand your needs. Since we don't drink, we don't have wine, as such, but I'll have something brought to you that you will find most satisfying." With that, she raised her right arm and gave a little wave. Immediately, her helpmate scampered onto the balcony and sat at attention near Zellen. The helpmate was similar to Schoop and Nadii, but its fur was a bright red color with white stripes. Zellen said to it, "Roho, this is Will O'Brien, he will be our guest for awhile. Please bring him a glass and a bottle of the special drink that I told you about. Do you remember what I said?" Roho nodded its head and ran off. Zellen gestured to the chairs, and I sat in one. It was very comfortable and seemed to fit my body perfectly. In less than a minute, Roho was back and placed the glass and the bottle on the table between the two lounge chairs.

Zellen sat and reached over and poured me a glass of the "special" drink. It tasted like a good red wine, probably a blend of Cabernet and Merlot. It must have been synthetic, or maybe Zellen could control my mind and make me think I was drinking wine. I wasn't sure. It didn't matter because I immediately felt more relaxed and comfortable.

As I sat there, I heard some music that I recognized as what I would call "Smooth Jazz," to which I enjoy listening. I'm not an expert on Jazz, and I don't listen to it much anymore, but when I was working, I would listen to Smooth Jazz stations at night when I was driving home from a dinner meeting or a late-night work session. Dave Brubeck, Miles Davis and Chico Hamilton are a few of the artists that I remember.

Listening to their music was relaxing and helped me calm down after a very stimulating meeting. I usually had a little buzz on, and I would be home in no time as I listened to the Smooth Jazz on my car radio. It took my mind off of my work and helped me relax. Since there was little traffic to worry about at that time of night, I would be home before I knew it. I relished that time to decompress and let my mind rest. When I arrived home, I always hoped that Deirdre was in a good mood and didn't need to regale me with some drama that she had experienced that day.

I must have fallen asleep listening to the music and thinking about the past. I began dreaming and was completely lost to the world. I remember that I was dreaming about a marketing pitch that was due tomorrow, but I couldn't find the presentation boards or the script. I was so relieved when I woke up and realized that I didn't have to make the presentation tomorrow. I've had many dreams like that since I retired. I'll probably have them for the rest of my life.

When I awoke, I was groggy and disoriented but quickly realized where I was. I felt something soft nudging me. I looked down at my left arm and saw Roho rubbing up against it. For an instant it looked like a little pug dog. Roho looked up at me and smiled and seemed happy and excited to see me awake. That made me feel good. I rubbed its head and scratched behind one of its ears. Roho smiled at me and then ran over to Zellen.

"Welcome back, sleepyhead," Zellen said.

I was a little embarrassed that I had fallen asleep. I asked her how long I had been out.

"About two hours of your time," she said. "Don't worry about it. You were tired and needed a short nap. As I told you, we Acme don't need much sleep. Just a few hours every other day is usually adequate for us. Also, time is not too important to us. We have few deadlines and little in our lives is urgent. When you live as long as we do, you can relax and take it slow and easy. There's no need to rush."

Hearing that jogged my memory and made me think of a question that I wanted to ask Sophos -- how long do the Acme live and why would they choose to end their lives?

"Those are good questions, Will, and I'll try to give you an answer that you can understand. I don't mean to offend you by that remark, but we have a better understanding of reality than you do. Our second layer of cortex and a larger and better regulated brain have given us insights into reality that you cannot understand. The EH you're wearing will help you, but you will never have the comprehension that we have."

"To answer your questions, though, most Acmes live about a thousand years, give or take a hundred years. Sophos, whom you just met, is nearly seven hundred years old. But, as you saw, he's still full of life and the desire to live and learn new things and, most importantly, to help others. A few of our people lose that desire quite early and chose to end their lives. We do not prohibit or discourage suicide, and there is no stigma attached to it. It's a personal decision. Since we have no families or dependents, it only affects the individual. It can cause sadness for those who knew the person, but it's accepted as a part of our existence."

"Most Acme, however, live to be nearly a thousand years old -- some even older. During the last two or three hundred years of our lives, however, we undergo a major change. We become very contemplative and develop the ability to experience new layers of reality and live totally within ourselves.

We call the people at that stage the 'Evolutes' because they evolve into a new phase of life. They see and understand things that most humans cannot. There are monks and mystics on Earth who experience what may be similar experiences, but, because of our top lobe and more robust minds, we evolve into a realm that cannot be explained. Eventually, feeling the need to move on to the next level of existence, the Evolutes cease living as we know it. They go into a trance and quietly die. We call that the 'Transfer Stage'."

"We cannot explain this phenomenon fully as the process is still not totally understood and those who have gone through it impart little information. It appears, based on a few clues that we have, to involve linking into a network of some type -- something similar to a computer network but with no physical or measurable manifestations. It's not electromagnetic or any other measurable physical phenomenon."

That led me to think of the next logical question: does that mean that you believe in God or a spiritual existence?

"Now we're getting to the heart of the matter, aren't we, Will. That's the one, and, perhaps, the most important question to which all intelligent creatures seek the answer. The simple answer is, yes, we do believe in God and a spiritual existence. We cannot prove it scientifically because science only deals with certain perceived phenomena that can be sensed by humans or measured by an instrument. We, however, have been able to perceive other layers of existence that scientific instruments cannot measure and ordinary humans cannot sense. These are in addition to our end of life Transfer Stage that I just told you about."

"To help you understand what I'm talking about, think about human knowledge before the scientific revolution. People could see light and colors and hear sounds, but they had no understanding of the broad spectrum of light and sound that exists. If you had told them about infrared light rays, or all the other electromagnetic waves, they wouldn't have believed you because they could not perceive them."

"Your brain is only capable of receiving and using certain types of stimulation. What you can see, hear, smell, taste and feel are real to you, but there are other things in the universe that you are not equipped to perceive. For example, some of your scientists have recently deduced, through mathematics, that something they call dark matter and dark energy must exist in the universe in order to explain the way the universe works; but they cannot describe what it is. Their math shows that there must be another type of mass in the universe, other than what can be seen or measured, to explain the way the universe is expanding. Humans are not, yet, capable of sensing dark matter or building a device to measure or identify it. Someday you will, but now you can't. Dark matter, as far as we can tell, does not radiate any types of waves that humans can see, sense, measure or identify. Therefore, it is invisible and unknowable to humans, yet we know it's there."

"Another example of one of your recent discoveries that has expanded your knowledge of reality is the identification of what you call the "Higgs Field." The existence of the Higgs Field was imputed from mathematical calculations explaining the behavior of atomic particles. The existence of the Higgs Field was necessary to make the mathematical calculation of the mass of an atom work even though no one knew what made up the Higgs Field. By using the new Large Hadron Collider in Switzerland, your scientists were able to cause a Higgs Boson particle to be released and identified. Before that, not everyone agreed that there was such a thing as the Higgs Field. Now, because humans invented a way to perceive another layer of reality, most of your scientists agree that the Higgs Field exists. Many even call the Higgs Boson the 'God Particle' because it seems to give mass to all of the other particles."

"So too, a spiritual world is also imputed or needed to explain many things that cannot be proved scientifically. Science has explained many things that were initially thought to be caused by the gods or spirits. For example, early humans explained what the wind is by imagining that gods were blowing air out of their mouths and causing the wind. Eventually, gas molecules were discovered and people understood what air was and how changes in air pressure cause the phenomenon known as wind."

"But there are still many things that cannot be explained scientifically. Therefore, it's logical to <u>impute</u> the existence of the spiritual world. Miracles, love, justice, near-death experiences, visions, morality -- all of these things exist, but a spiritual world must be imputed to explain them. There is no chemical reaction that can explain, for instance, justice. Spiritual concepts cannot be explained by using purely scientific reasoning. The Earthly human brain is still too limited. Your brains can only understand and explain what is sensed or measured by your instruments. It is not within the ken of your knowledge, but that doesn't mean that the spiritual world isn't there."

"The existence of life is probably the best example of the need to impute God, or at least a very intelligent being capable of creating it. You will be surprised to know that we, the Acme, can still not explain the creation of life. For thousands of years, we have tried to explain how life came about. Many of your scientists have experimented with creating life but have only managed to create some of the most basic amino acids. We have computers that are a million times more powerful than yours that can model every possible combination of chemicals and conditions that might lead to life. They can also extend those models out for a billion years, yet, they never explain how a living cell was created! Never!"

"We can manipulate existing life in many ways. We can alter chromosomes and change genes, but we cannot produce life, and we cannot explain how DNA was created. It appears that it could not have been a random occurrence. It must have been an intentional creation by a being with powers beyond anything of which we know. We have even constructed DNA molecules into double helixes with chromosomes exactly like the genome of various living creatures. They appear to be perfect DNA molecules. Under a powerful microscope that can see atoms, an expert in cellular biology could not tell the difference between what we have created and an actual living cell's DNA. But, astoundingly, none of them live and reproduce as DNA from a living creature would! There is a hidden life force that we cannot reproduce. We can alter our chromosomes, but we cannot reproduce them and create life! How can that be explained, except for some God-like power who has intervened in reality and made life possible?"

"Additionally, we Acme are capable of sensing many other layers of reality that Earthlings cannot perceive. Our top lobe and more energetic and robust brain have opened up other layers of reality that you cannot imagine or understand. That's why we, basically, live in our minds and seek unity of thought and purpose. Which is, essentially, what you would call the 'perfection of love' -- the total willing of good for others. That is the next, higher stage of human existence, which we have achieved."

"And, despite all these advancements, we know that we are still far from the final stage of existence. We are certain that intelligent life will keep evolving and ascending to a higher and higher form of existence -- a purer, more unified, form of existence, eventually leading to all being in all. That, to some degree, explains why we eventually become Evolutes and enter the Transfer Stage."

Wow! As you can probably imagine, that was a lot to digest. I hope that I accurately recounted all that Zellen told me. I probably mixed some of it up, but I think I captured the gist of what she told me. I have always had a strong religious faith, so I was open to what she was saying. It mostly made sense to me and corresponded to some of the things that I have thought about in the past.

I told Zellen that I appreciated her taking the time to explain that to me. It helped me understand the Acme. I told her that it was very enlightening and that it made me feel good to know that there is a positive future for humans, even if I'm not able to experience all of the talents and powers that future generations will have.

She stood up and said to me, "You are most welcome, Will. I enjoyed explaining that to you. You are a good listener and are genuinely interested in learning and expanding your knowledge. You are open and trusting. As you have learned, some times that can lead to problems in your world. There are some people who take advantage of that."

Yikes! I thought. Where did that come from? That was certainly one of my weaknesses. I tend to be too trusting of people. My default tendencies are to trust and believe. Deirdre is just the opposite. She is always leery of everyone until they prove otherwise. Sometimes that is a good trait, but I'm glad I'm trusting and not always suspicious of others. I think that's a better way to live. Thinking about that brought me back down to earth, or, as the case may be, Earthtoo.

Chapter 20

Puero

"Sorry. I didn't mean to shock you with that," Zellen said. "Trust is an important virtue to us, and it would not be betrayed in our world. I didn't mean to hurt your feelings or put you down," Zellen conveyed to me.

I could tell she was sincere about that, and I realized that there are no secrets in this world. What a wonderful thing that is! She, and everyone else, were aware of my situation. No secrets! Having no secrets from one another would solve so many problems and make life more enjoyable. It would destroy all fear and distrust. If everyone knew what really happened between me and Bonnie Talbot, I wouldn't be in this situation, although, overall, my encounter with the Acme has been pleasant and interesting, at least so far. I hope it stays that way. If I hadn't had the accident, I wouldn't have had this adventure. That sounds selfish, though, because I caused so many other people to suffer. If I had a choice, if I could go back in time, I would gladly have avoided the accident.

Touching my shoulder, Zellen brought me back to the present and said, "Teaching is one of my interests, and I have been recognized for it. Because of that, I receive a great honor from time to time, as you will now see. I have someone very special that I want you to meet."

"I have been blessed with the task of helping to raise one of our Newpees -- that's what we call our children -- our new people. There are several of us who share this responsibility. Today, because you are here, I have Puero staying with me. Puero is about five years old and most rambunctious, by our standards. I know that you instinctively genderize us as you meet us. You will probably think of Puero as a boy. I will have Roho bring him to us, but, first," she said, again, touching my shoulder, "I should give you some information about the Newpees."

"They are very similar to your children in many ways. Their frontal lobes are not fully developed. Like Earthlings, their frontal lobes do not fully mature until they are about twenty-five. Because this limits their ability to reason fully, they can, and frequently do, make some bad decisions. They have larger brains than Earthlings, resulting in better memories and incredible math, artistic, scientific and language skills. They can receive our telepathic thoughts; but, since they cannot transmit thoughts, they must use language to communicate. Your EH will translate what Puero says to you, so you shouldn't have any trouble communicating with him."

"A Newpee's advanced cortex is very small and dormant until a Newpee is about forty years old. At that time, it develops very quickly. By the time we are about sixty years old, an Acme has all of the extraordinary mental powers that emanate from the additional cortex layer. It may take another twenty or thirty years to learn how to fully utilize those powers, but that is the most wonderful period of our lives. I can still remember going through that period. It's filled with wonder and discovery that is indescribable, unless you have experienced it."

"New realities open up to us. We have joys and experiences that can truly be described as heavenly. We feel a oneness with the universe and an understanding of its harmony and beauty. There is an expanded consciousness that is beyond description for someone without the additional layer of cortex."

"Your drug called LSD is said to expand consciousness, but it creates chaos in your brains and is unsustainable. It nearly disables the frontal lobes and allows areas of the brain to reach consciousness that are not normally allowed to do so. Only ten percent of brain activity is allowed, normally, to reach the conscious level. Most of it has to be subdued by the frontal lobes to prevent paralyses or insanity."

"Our experience is just the opposite. The additional cortex allows all of the powers of the brain that are normally subdued to bloom forth -- but in a controlled and regulated manner. Memories and logical powers are fully accessible and can be related and synthesized into meaningful thoughts and expanded awareness."

Hearing this, I envied the Acme and wanted that type of experience. I tried LSD once in college and can remember the experience well. I, unlike a few of my friends, had a good experience and even had a few pleasurable flashbacks for the next several months after trying it. Luckily for me, because I wasn't able to obtain any more of it, I didn't get hooked on it, which, I'm sure, would have eventually resulted in a bad trip and maybe even damaged my mind.

Zellen then left for a brief time and returned with a very small person who had to be Puero. He was only, maybe, two feet tall, about a foot and a half shorter than the average five-year-old earthling.

He was as cute as a bug, though. In fact, he looked a little like a bug! He had wings! His face was round and cute and bright and happy, but he had wings! They were rounded across his back, almost like a cape. There were three small claw-like fingers roughly in the position that a hand would be at -- somewhat like a bat's claws. As a matter of fact, he reminded me of a cute, cuddly bat. His color was predominantly dark gray or brown, and his fur was dark with red and brown highlights. His head was oval-shaped and covered with a turban that was rounder than the adults but had two small protruding antennae.

Puero was not shy and looked straight into my eyes. It was a warm and friendly look with a little mischief and humor mixed in. I liked him immediately, and I felt as though we made a good connection. My grandson, Charlie, has that same look. They would be great friends!

Charlie and I have spent many happy hours together in my basement office. For about a year, when he was five, Deirdre and I babysat him and his sister Molly every Tuesday and Friday from 8:00 AM until 2:30 PM while their mother took a writing course. When he arrived at our house, he would immediately run to our basement and get out a few toys that we kept for him. Molly would stay upstairs and play with Deirdre's dollhouse or read or just talk with Deirdre.

I would sit on the floor with Charlie and build buildings and forts out of wooden blocks. We would mix in a few small cars and superheroes that we had leftover from Owen or that he brought with him. Then, after finishing our buildings, he would knock them all down and go on to the next thing.

He especially liked to draw on my computer. I showed him how to use the Paint Program, and he would draw crazy shapes and then color them in. When he tired of that, he would ask me to draw something. Since I was pretty good at drawing knights and castles, he would ask me to draw a good knight and a bad knight. He was always the good knight, and I had to be the bad knight. He was Sir Charlie the Brave, and I was Sir Poopsalot. Sir Charlie always had to have a giant sword and be twice as tall as Sir Poopsalot.

After carefully drawing the two knights, he would take control of the mouse and obliterate the bad knight. He never tired of doing that. That's something I learned about kids. They love doing familiar things repeatedly. Once I printed out the two knights before he could obliterate Sir Poopsalot. I still have that picture hanging above my desk. It makes me smile and brings back good memories every time I look at it.

Puero walked over to me and reached out with his little claw fingers and took my hand. They were surprisingly soft and warm. When he reached out to me, I could see his wings open up a little. "Would you tell me a story, Mr. O'Brien," he said. "Zellen tells great stories, but I've heard all of Zellen's stories. I'll bet you have some good stories. Tell me something about Earth. Zellen told me that's where you're from. What is Earth like? Can people there fly?"

"Puero!" Zellen said, "Don't be so rambunctious! You need to be polite and not pummel Mr. O'Brien with your questions! Give him some time to get to know you."

"That's OK," I said. "I know how little boys are. I have a son and a grandson, and they've both asked me many questions. It's good to be curious, and I'm most curious about you. To answer your last question: no, people on earth can't fly. They don't have wings as you do. Are you a Vologuere? Sophos told me all about the Vologueres and how they helped defeat Meaam and win the AI War."

Puero looked confused and then turned to Zellen and said, "Am I a Vologuere, Zellen? What's a Vologuere? What's an AI War?"

"Oh, oh!" I thought. Did I say the wrong thing?

"No, Will, you didn't say anything wrong. It's OK, Zellen said.

Then she looked at Puero and said, "Puero, you are not a Vologuere, but you are a little like them. They were big brave flying soldiers who helped us win the AI War -- that's a war that you will learn about soon. You are not a soldier, and you will never have to be, but you will be able to fly someday."

Puero still looked a little confused and said, "I want to be a soldier. I would be brave and win the war! Please tell me about the AI War, Zellen. Please!"

"You will learn soon enough, Puero. But, for now, you are not quite old enough to learn about that war. Sophos will teach you all about it when you are ready. Until then, please be patient and respect your guardians. You know that that is important and one of the virtues that we most value."

"Yes, Zellen, I know that," Puero said. "I'm sorry."

This interaction was fascinating and very interesting to me. It taught me so much about the Acme. Up until this time, I had thought that they were so perfect, but to see this interaction with Puero showed me that they start much like Earthlings and develop into a much higher state.

"Zellen," I said, "I would like to tell Puero a story, if that's OK? I told my grandson and granddaughter many stories. When they would stay over-night with Deirdre, my wife, and me, I would always have to tell them a story before they went to sleep."

Zellen thought for a moment and then said, "OK, but it can't be a scary story or one with monsters and fighting. We don't have that in our culture. It isn't something that we encourage or permit."

"Uhm," I thought. That will take some thinking. Most of my stories were about bad knights and dragons and brave little kids who defeated them. I did have some stories about some little kids (I always used my grandchildren's names) who had an alien friend, Zippo, from the planet Kukamunga. They had helped Zippo repair his spaceship one time, and he was their friend forever. He would take them to other worlds and show them interesting and crazy things.

So I told Zellen I had a good story for Puero that didn't have any violence or monsters in it. She said, "OK."

I led Puero over to a chair and picked him up and put him on my knee. I couldn't believe how light he was. I was expecting him to be much heavier, like my grandkids. I almost threw him up in the air, he was so light. Then I remembered the story about the Vologueres and that they had hollow bones similar to birds.

When he was settled, I told Puero one of my stories about Zippo and the planet Kukamunga. I told him that I told stories about Zippo to my grandchildren, Molly and Charlie. The gist of the story is that Charlie and Molly accidentally break their mom's favorite antique clock. It had belonged to her mother, and they needed to fix it or replace it before she found out and punished them. They were playing catch with a ball in the living room, and it accidentally hit the clock and broke it. Since they had been told not to play catch in the living room, they knew they would be in big trouble with their mother.

So they used their secret transmitter to contact Zippo, and he took them to Kukamunga were they can fix anything. The clock is repaired and returned to their house before their mother discovers that it's broken. There is only one problem: the clock now talks to Charlie and Molly whenever they are alone with it because all of the clocks on Kukamunga talk! This causes many crazy problems for Charlie and Molly, but their mom never discovers what happened.

While I was telling the story, Puero stopped me several times and asked cute questions about things of which I'd never thought. He was brilliant and had an incredible mind and imagination. I could see that he was envisioning everything that I told him and probably much more than I could ever imagine. I had to tell him several times that I couldn't answer his questions.

When my story was over, Puero said he liked it very much, but he couldn't understand why Charlie and Molly didn't tell their mother what happened. I tried to explain that they didn't want to get in trouble with her. Then I realized that, on Earthtoo, there were no secrets.

That made storytelling very difficult. Most good stories on Earth involve fear, mysteries, hidden motives and selfishness, all concepts that the Acme don't have.

I could tell that Puero was confused, but he was polite and didn't criticize my story. He jumped down from my knee and ran over to Zellen. She picked him up and put him on her lap and nuzzled him lovingly.

Zellen looked at me and smiled, a kind, yet, knowing smile. "Well," she said, "I guess we all learned something today. Thank you, Will, for telling Puero such an interesting story. That's one he will probably never forget -- will you Puero?" Puero nodded his head and snuggled up to Zellen. Then Roho jumped into Zellen's lap and snuggled up to the two of them. It was a very sweet and loving scene.

I felt a little bad but didn't beat my self up. I thought it was a great story! It wasn't my fault I didn't fully understand their culture. This taught me a good lesson, though, and I knew I had a lot to learn about the Acme.

Chapter 21

Magis and Inquis

After a few quiet moments, I looked over at Zellen, and she had that blank look on her face that all of the Acme get when they are receiving a telepathic communication. I'd seen it a few times, now, and I knew something was up.

Zellen looked at me and said, "I have just been told that Guio will be here soon to take you to Magis. He's ready to see you, now."

For some reason, hearing that made me a little nervous. What was up? Was it good or bad? What would Magis be like? Since all of the Acme had been good to me so far, I had no reason to expect anything else from this Magis person. Remembering that Sophos had said he (I assumed he would be a masculine person -- I know that is chauvinistic -- my bad) is their leader, I knew that he must be impressive, though, and the final arbiter of my fate. Zellen walked over to me and reached out to hug me. As she did this, she said, "Do not worry, Will. Be not afraid. Magis will be kind and fair to you."

Puero and Roho also ran to me and hugged my legs while Zellen put her head on my chest and gave me a warm and lingering hug. They radiated warmth and a sincere acceptance. It was more than just a physical sensation. I sensed a sincere love that went deep into my soul. As they did this, I could hear Puero say, "I will never forget meeting you, Will O'Brien. I hope someday I can travel to Earth and meet Charlie and Molly. We will be good friends and tell each other happy stories."

That really touched me. I had only talked to Zellen and Puero for a few minutes, and I, apparently, scared and confused Puero. Nevertheless, the Acme have such powerful spirits and openness and acceptance that each relationship they have has deep and lasting meaning for them. Part of this must be due to their small numbers, but their powerful minds and deep understanding of reality and the relationship of all things makes each moment of their lives filled with meaning and significance. If I ever return to Earth, I hope I can remember that and emulate it, as much as possible.

Just as Zellen, Puero and Roho finished their hugs, I sensed that Guio was near me. I looked to my right, and there she was with Nadii.

"I hope you had a good visit," she said, smiling at me first and then at Zellen and Puero.

"We did, indeed. Live well, Will," said Zellen.

"Thank you for bringing Will O'Brien to us, Guio," said Puero. "I'm going to go to Earth someday and meet his Newpees, Charlie and Molly."

"Perhaps you will, Puero. Perhaps you will," said Guio as she gently patted his shoulders. Puero looked up at her and smiled. Then Guio looked at me.

"Shall we go, Will? Magis has asked to see you as soon as you are ready. I can take you to him now."

I was amazed at their politeness. Magis could have ordered me, but, instead, Guio asked me if I was ready. I didn't have a choice, but they wanted to put me at ease. Such empathy and civility!

"Of course," I said. "Let's go."

"Would you like to walk or go the quick way, as we did coming here?"

"The quick way would be fine," I said.

With that, Guio floated toward me and gently pushed her head toward me. Since I knew the protocol, I gently bowed toward her. As our helmets touched, like the last time we did this, there was an explosion of light and a gust of warm air. I felt weightless for a second. Then there was extreme calm, and every inch of my body tingled with a pleasurable feeling.

Guio and Nadii faded away as I arrived at my new destination. I was standing on a well worn wooden pier on a beautiful fishing lake in what looked like Michigan or Wisconsin. It was late afternoon and the air was warm and humid but calm and not windy. I could tell that a shower had just passed through, and the pier was slightly wet. As I looked to my right, I saw a rainbow arching across the sky between an opening in the trees. The colors in this rainbow were the most intense that I have ever seen. I could see the blue, red, indigo, green, violet, and orange. It wasn't quite natural, but it was beautiful in its intensity.

The lake surrounding me was small and surrounded by trees and evergreens of every shade of green. The water was greenish-blue with swaths of silver glistening and shimmering like a wavy mirror reflecting the sky. I could hear some doves cooing in the distance. A fish broke the water and splashed off to my left. It was all very familiar but not someplace I could readily identify.

"Would you like to drop in a line, Will?" I heard a deep and somewhat familiar voice say. I turned around and saw an Acme standing behind me. He was the largest Acme I have encountered so far, and he was definitely the most masculine. He had a strong jaw and piercing black eyes with flecks of gold and red in them. All of his features were strong and handsome. He radiated power and confidence, yet I did not feel threatened. His aura, too, was different in some way from the aura of other Acme I had met so far. It was .... I think "fatherly" might be the best way to describe it. There was also a heaviness to it. I think "gravitas" might be a good word to describe this person. Despite that, I was comforted by the fact that he had the Acme smile, and that put me at ease.

"I'm Magis," he said. "Do you like my fishing lake, Will O'Brien? I hope it makes you feel calm and comfortable. And this is my helpmate, Benito." With that, his helpmate ran over to me. As he did, he raised his right fist toward me. I must have looked shocked and frightened, because Magis immediately said, "Fist bump, Will! Benito wants to give you a fist bump. I trained him to do that. I understand that is what men on Earth do. Is that not correct?"

"Yes, yes, of course," I said. "Sorry, I misinterpreted the gesture. Sorry. I'm a little out of practice." So, with that clarified, I gave Benito a gentle fist bump. Benito jumped up and down with glee and then hugged my leg and then ran behind Magis.

"Benito is my helpmate, Will. Benito has been with me for about two hundred years, now, and we are very simpatico. But Benito is a little different from most of the other helpmates. Because we experiment more with the helpmates than humans, some of our helpmates have different brains than others. They are not all the same. Benito has extraordinary mental skills, but Benito is a little different. Benito poses no danger to you. I assure you, but Benito is, as you might say, 'quirky.' But, anyway, how do you like my space?"

"I like your lake," I said. "It looks very familiar, but I'm not sure where this is. Did you take this from my memory?"

"Yes, of course, but it's an amalgam of many of your memories. To give credit where it's due, Guio created this place for you. She has a real talent for building scenes like this from memories. I didn't have time to research this for you, so she volunteered. We have places similar to this on Earthtoo. The trees would look quite different to you than what you see here, but the overall effect would be similar."

"We also have some very interesting fish on Earthtoo. Because of our lower gravity, and the higher oxygen content in our air, our fish, and all of our animals, for that matter, are much larger and more aggressive than those on Earth. We have to be careful when we venture out into the natural world. Evolution has produced exceptionally vicious fish and animals on Earthtoo. If we were actually on one of our lakes, the fish would be jumping out of the water attacking us! You have a fish called a muskellunge, (we call them muskies) that is one of your favorite game fish, correct?"

"Yes," I said.

"Well, imagine a muskie that is five times the size of one of yours and very inclined to attack any animal, including humans that might venture onto one of its lakes! Because we haven't interfered with the natural selection process, we have quite extraordinary animals on Earthtoo. We don't raise any domesticated animals to eat, and we farm very small areas. As a result, nature takes its own course and seems to create extreme predators which need to be very territorial and aggressive to survive and flourish."

I thought about that for a moment and then said, "That must be dangerous for you. How many people are harmed by animals each year?"

"Actually, Will, none are. You see, we can control wild animals with our telepathic powers. Occasionally, someone gets caught off guard and a serious injury or even death does occur. That is rare, though, and hasn't happened in recent memory."

"Our young people who haven't developed full telepathic powers are at risk, though. That's why we never let them enter the natural world without a full telepathic accompanying them. It would be extraordinarily dangerous for them, otherwise."

This grabbed my imagination. What a great way to fish! The one thing I've never been able to do in my fishing career is land a muskie. For a fisherman, that's the ultimate challenge and prize. I told Magis that I would like to see a giant muskie sometime, and that, even more, I would like to see him control it. I explained to him about muskie fishing and how it was the prized game fish in the area where I lived. I told him that if someone caught a large muskie, they would have it stuffed and mounted so they would have bragging rights over all of their fishing buddies.

Magis paused for a moment and then said, "All right, Will, I'm going to do that for you. Give me a few seconds, and I think I can give you a taste of what it's like to fish on Earthtoo." With that, he went into a short trance-like state and then started to smile -- a somewhat devilish smile that seemed to say, "OK, get ready to be amazed."

The next thing I knew seven or eight huge muskies started jumping out of the water. They were about ten feet long and had vicious shark-like teeth. Three of them jumped across our pier only a few feet from where we were standing. As they jumped, they looked right at me and seemed to utter a fearsome growl that cut through me like a knife and gave me a sick feeling in my stomach.

One of the muskies was noticeably smaller than the others. Unfortunately for it, it bumped into one of the larger fish as it jumped out of the water. In a split second, the larger fish ripped into it and nearly cut it in half with one vicious chomp that sounded like thunder. The others attacked the carcass and consumed it in only a few seconds. The water in the area where the smaller fish was attacked was boiling and filled with blood and bits of flesh. This seemed to inflame the other fish and they became even more agitated and swam in circles around our pier causing waves and a splashing sound like a waterfall.

Then they all seemed to line up around the largest fish and moved menacingly toward where Magis and I were standing. My heart was in my throat, and my legs felt weak. They had red piercing eyes that seemed to look right into my soul. I have never felt so threatened in my life. Just as they were about to leap at us, they suddenly broke off and swam away in different directions. One, however, swam slowly toward us and leaped onto the pier about thirty feet from where we were standing. It lay quietly on the pier and seemed to purr like a kitten.

I heard Magis say, "Would you like to pet it, Will? It won't hurt you and will meow like a cat if you ask it to. You might even say it has become a 'catfish,' so to speak."

I had to smile at that bit of humor. That was clever and the first joke any Acme had made so far.

I told Magis that I would pass on petting the giant muskie, but I thanked him for the exhibition. When I looked back at where the muskie had been, it was gone and the waters were quiet and peaceful, again.

Magis then said, "Will, let's sit and talk for a few minutes." He pointed to a wooden bench at the end of the pier that I hadn't noticed until then. We walked to the bench and sat. It was the most comfortable bench I had ever sat on. Even though it appeared to be made out of wood, it felt like a soft padded chair. We sat silently for several minutes. The air was warm and soft and smelled fresh and clean. The water glistened and shimmered in the sun. I heard a bird call in the distance and felt a gentle breeze.

Then I heard what sounded like a small fishing boat motor coming toward us. I looked to my left and there was a small fishing boat with a small outboard motor on it heading in our direction. There was an Acme in it steering the motor toward us.

I heard Magis say or think, I'm not sure, "Oh, no. It's Inquis. I was not expecting him/her."

That caused me a little concern, I must admit. So far I had not heard an Acme utter any type of negative comment.

Magis looked at me and said, "Inquis is a member of the Leadership Council. She (I think you'll think of her as feminine) is one of our diverse personalities. She was created to bring balance to our collective consciousness.

We realized long ago that we needed a few skeptics to balance out our normally optimistic and trusting culture. She is a wonderful person and well-liked and trusted by everyone. She has no personal agenda or biases, but her brain was designed to be skeptical and questioning. She might seem edgy and threatening at times, but don't be afraid of her. She is only one member of the Leadership Council and doesn't have the final say as to what course we will take with you."

Inquis reached our dock in her little boat, and Magis moved to her and extended a hand to her and helped her climb onto the dock. She and Magis looked at each other for a moment, maybe a minute. She appeared to thank Magis but I could tell they were communicating other things, probably discussing me. Then she walked directly toward me. Then it hit me: she was the Acme that I had seen twice watching me.

I heard her say, "Greetings, Will. I'm Inquis and am pleased to meet you. I'm aware of all of your experiences so far here on Earthtoo and am anxious to have a few moments of your time. I know Magis has explained who I am, so I won't waste time going over that with you."

Magis said, "Let's sit for awhile and talk." As I looked for the bench we had been sitting on, there were now two benches facing each other on the dock. Magis and I sat in one, and Inquis sat across from us. She looked at me and smiled. I felt more comfortable, but still a little nervous. She was beautiful, as all Acme are, but she somehow looked familiar. There was something about her that reminded me of someone I knew.

She had light blue eyes with a hint of silver around the edges of her irises -- but, for some reason, I also felt there was a touch of sadness and even some fear in them -- anxiety or trepidation might be a better description of what she projected. She was definitely different from all the other Acme I had met -- much different! Her skin was lighter than the other Acme and she seemed thin and almost frail. Her fur was blond with a bit of golden/reddish color mixed in.

She looked intensely into my eyes and said, "Tell me about your accident, Will. We know the facts about it, but it is important to hear you describe it. If you are going to live with us, we need to understand your spirit. We can read your mind, but we need to know what is in your heart."

Her bluntness startled me. Magis' explanation of her personality and role on the Council helped me understand where she was coming from, but I was still taken aback more than I expected.

I told her the whole story. I didn't try to gloss over anything. I knew I had to be as honest as possible. I told her my true feelings about meeting Bonnie in Brian's Tap before the accident. I told her that I was infatuated with her and was emotionally unfaithful to Deirdre. I explained how I needed intimacy with a beautiful, sexy woman and let myself experience a little guilty pleasure. I told her that Bonnie made me feel strong and alive like I hadn't been for many years. If Bonnie had asked, I might have been tempted to run off with her to some exotic place. I'd wanted her and wanted to be with her.

My confessing this shocked me and made my head spin and gave me a sinking feeling in my stomach. I felt like I might suddenly start weeping. I was losing control, but I took a deep breath, relaxed and pulled myself together. After I regained some control, I told her that I had, on my own, come to my senses and tried to stop and escape before I went too far. Then I explained what happened as I was driving her home.

Inquis looked calmly and steadily at me while I related my feelings and what happened the evening of the accident. I couldn't detect how she felt from her face or body language. What was she thinking? Did she believe me? Was she put off by what I said? Was it somehow fatal to me?

"I thank you for your honesty, Will," she said. "I know it was hard for you to relive those moments and expose your true feelings. You, like all Earthlings, have natural instincts that can lead to trouble and harm in your world. You try to overcome those tendencies but are frequently unsuccessful. It's not your fault. That's the way you evolved. You are getting better but still have a long way to go. Perhaps, if you had discussed your true feelings with Deirdre, things might have gone better for you. But, then, again, maybe not."

Inquis sat calmly and looked steadily at me. I flinched and looked down at my hands. I didn't want to, but her stare went right through me and made the hair on the back of my neck stand up. Then Inquis said, "Will, I don't think it would be good for Earthtoo if you returned to Earth. I foresee too many problems if you do. It is not worth the risk for our world. Your world is still ruled by selfish, dangerous people, and we should avoid the possible conflict for as long as possible."

With that said, she stood up, gave me a neutral smile and held out her hand. I touched it and felt a strong but somewhat disconcerting feeling. It didn't frighten me, but it didn't encourage me. I felt her convey: "This is the way it is -- deal with it. Live well!"

Inquis then moved to Magis. They hugged and touched heads together. There was a flash of light, and Inquis, her boat, and the extra bench were suddenly gone. A cool breeze passed over me. It chilled me and made me queasy. I felt a weakness in my legs. I closed my eyes and took a few deep breaths and felt better. I was resigned to my fate. I knew there was little I could do to change it. I looked around the beautiful lake and listened to the natural sounds. A large, graceful blue bird flew over the lake. It soared higher and higher and seemed to disappear. I felt a cool breeze and relaxed.

Magis and I sat down, again, and he said to me, "Don't worry, Will, que sera, sera." I quickly turned and looked at him, and he had a comforting, quirky smile on his face. It was banal, but it made me laugh.

Then Magis said, "Except for that last episode, what do you think of Earthtoo, so far, Will. Have you enjoyed your visit?"

I turned and looked at Magis, and it struck me that he was now about my size. I thought I would be looking down at him, but he had morphed into a person about my size. He also seemed to channel some of the essence of The Professor. He probably understood my relationship with The Professor and knew that it would put me at ease and foster trust.

He smiled at me and said, "I thought it would be easier for us to communicate if I changed to your size and projected a more familiar appearance. I haven't really changed, but I appear larger and more familiar to you now. It's psychological, of course, but its part of how we relate to each other. I'm sure you understand that from your marketing career.

"I do," I said. "Appearances influence our thinking, even if we try not to let them. You're right. We always considered that in any marketing campaign."

"As to how I have enjoyed my visit," I continued, "I couldn't be happier and more thankful for your hospitality and consideration. I feel a great connection with the Acme and don't feel threatened or like a stranger in a strange land. I know you know what has happened to me and how I came to be the passenger in the Nina. My revelations to Inquis were humbling but relieving in a good sense. You might say I needed an escape, and this whole journey has been beyond my wildest imagination."

"Yes, Will, we do know about your problems on Earth and how you came to be an "accidental" space voyager. However, as you also know, we were not expecting a visitor from Earth for many years. We've been monitoring Earth for thousands of years and expected that someday you would be capable of traveling through outer space to our planet. We were just not quite ready to face the problems that an Earth invasion might bring. This has created a dilemma for us, and we are divided on what to do about you. Inquis' opinion to the Council (and mine, too) will be deeply considered."

"Invasion?" "Dilemma?" "What to do about me?" Bells were ringing and red lights were flashing. My mind was swimming. Once, again, I was in a whirlwind of emotions and dread!

"Not to worry, Will," Magis said. "I know what you're thinking. We're not going to impregnate you with a monster or throw you into prison for the rest of your life. We stopped doing that years ago . . . just kidding!"

I liked Magis' sense of humor. All the other Acme had been so sober and literal about everything. His sense of humor was a pleasant surprise and relaxing. That's probably why he lightened things up. It was a nice touch.

"Here's the bottom line, Will. Earth is a mess, and we're not ready to deal with all of your problems. I'm sure I don't have to tell you, but Earth is hundreds of years, maybe more, from being civil and capable of interacting on a cooperative and pleasant basis with other worlds."

"As I'm sure you are aware, based on our very detailed observations, you now have eighteen wars or border skirmishes in process and several more are about ready to erupt. Your population is approaching seven and a half billion humans, and eighty percent of them are poor, uneducated and starving. Five billion of your population has a family income of fewer than two dollars per day. Half a million humans are murdered each year, and that doesn't count all of the deaths from terrorists and military actions."

"Maybe worst of all, you are destroying your planet's environment. You are polluting the air, contaminating your water and changing your climate. Not to beat a dead horse, but you are also wasting your natural resources at an astounding rate and decimating many species of flora and fauna that are needed to balance your ecology and support key life sustaining processes."

"Some Earthlings are aware of that and are promoting a rational approach to conservation and ecology, but they are in a minority and are ignored and blocked by most of the political leaders of your world, which is understandable because your population is so unmanageable that resources have to be constantly developed and exploited to prevent starvation and abject poverty."

This litany was depressing to me and embarrassing. I wasn't sure of all of his numbers, but I knew that his opinion of us was basically true. Earth is a mess, and I couldn't blame the Acme for not wanting to get involved with us. Who would? We (not me, of course, but most Earthlings) are selfish, violent, bigoted, narrow-minded, ruthless, ignorant, intolerant a-holes. That's the truth. The evidence is overwhelming. Anyone with the least little bit of objectivity would have to agree with that statement. We've come a long way in the last two hundred years, but we have a long way to go. Crime and violence are half of what they were at the beginning of the nineteenth century. So, comparatively speaking, humans are getting better; but, by the Acme's standards, we are barbarians.

Sure, there are a lot of good people on Earth, but that depends on your point of view. The people that I think are good would probably be scorned by many other people. The Christians don't trust or like the Jews,

Moslems, Hindus and Buddhists (and vise versa), and they all fear other sects within their own religion. The liberals hate the conservatives. The Asians think they're better than the Caucasians and everyone hates people of a different color. The rich hate the poor. The poor hate the rich who are greedy and exploit them. Men abuse women, and neither sex wants to be dominated by the other. There is no denying it; we are a mess -- a hot mess, and getting hotter! Yes, "mess" is a perfect word for us! We have a long way to go!

We've made a lot of progress since the end of World War II. It's no longer acceptable for a nation to be blatantly hateful of another nation or people. Imperialism is no longer acceptable. It's unfathomable to believe that, in the past, nations thought they had the right to conquer and enslave other nations and confiscate and squander all of their resources.

No one today could do what Hitler did and preach racism, hatred and violence as a national goal, but, unfortunately, those despicable tendencies are still prevalent and always lying just below the surface. Through the United Nations and various world organizations, we have brought a little sanity, order and cooperation to many aspects of our lives, but there is much work to do.

I didn't know how to respond to Magis, so I fell back on a well-worn humorous comeback: "Don't sugar coat your feelings, Magis, I can handle the truth." Magis laughed at that and then did a perfect imitation of Jack Nicholson in *A Few Good Men*, "YOU CAN'T HANDLE THE TRUTH! Son, you live in a world that has walls, and those walls have to be guarded by men with guns. Who's gonna do it? You?"

A Few Good Men is one of my favorite movies. It's one of the movies I watched in the Nina. I couldn't believe that Magis could quote that line and do a perfect imitation of Jack Nicholson. I was stunned but tickled at this display. What incredible minds these Acme have! I was laughing and so was Magis.

Chapter 22

The Return Plan

"OK," I said. "What're you going to do? It sounds to me as though you're not going to let me go back to Earth."

"Yes . . . and no," Magis said slowly and with hesitancy. "We have a tentative plan for you. It still needs final approval of the Council, but here is what is on the table. We are considering two options. One option is simple, but the other is complicated and will take some explanation."

"OK," I said. "This sounds interesting. Thank goodness you didn't say that you had good news and bad news for me. So tell me -- what is the simple option?"

Magis rubbed his chin, adjusted himself on the bench so he was looking directly at me and then said, "The simple option is this: If you want, you can stay here on Earthtoo for the rest of your life. We will make it very pleasant and interesting for you. I assure you, you will have a good life. We can guarantee you good health and amazing intellectual stimulation. You will be able to learn incredible things that you never imagined existed. You will have many friends and great companionship. In fact, you will be quite the celebrity and be in much demand. To make your life easy, we will develop a helpmate for you that will serve you well and give you companionship, loyalty and comfort. How does that sound to you?"

I'd never even considered that option, and it made my mind spin. I had always assumed I would return to Earth. How could I give up my family and life on Earth? True, I didn't have much of a life left for me after the accident, but I had assumed that everything would be reconciled and that I would, eventually, be able to resume my normal life. This wasn't a good option. I was nervous and uneasy.

Magis knew my thoughts and said, "I can understand your uneasiness, Will. You would be giving up a lot. I know how much your family means to you. Maybe you could overcome your problems and return to a normal life, but that doesn't seem likely, does it?"

"I don't know," I said. "This is overwhelming to think about. I've got to give this a lot of thought."

"Earthtoo is a wonderful place to live, Will," Magis said with great warmth and sincerity as he put a hand on my shoulder. I felt an assuring power flow through my body from his touch. He continued, "I assure you that you will live a full and productive life here. We can learn a lot from you. You can give us a perspective that we've lost and that may help us better handle our next encounter with Earthlings and, maybe, even other aliens."

As this idea began to sink in, I felt a little less lost, but I still felt shocked and upset. "What is the second alternative you're giving me? Let me explore all of the options before I make a decision. You seem to be pushing the 'stay here' option. Is there something less desirable about the second option?"

"To be honest, yes, there is." Magis sat quietly for a moment and seemed to be gathering his thoughts. The air seemed calmer, and the light seemed to be turning a more golden color as though the sun might be setting. I turned and looked at his profile as he stared ahead, not looking at me. It appeared to me that he was reluctant to meet my eyes. It must be hard for him to talk about the second option. A sense of foreboding crept into my mind.

Raising both of his hands in front of his chest, as though he were holding a ball, he continued: "It is very unlikely that we will let you return to Earth in the Nina. Most of the Council opposes that option. However, there is another alternative. The second option involves using an experimental procedure that hasn't been completely tested by our scientists. In some regards, it's like the AASUSE Team's project that enabled you to travel here using fusion engines. As chance would have it, we need a volunteer to test a new space-time travel device that can travel back in space-time. It can't travel forward, but we believe it can travel back in space-time."

"What do you mean when you say 'space-time,'" I said. "Don't you mean travel back in time?"

"No, Will, all matter exists in space-time, not just time. That's how we can go back to another time and place, at least that's the theory. We have invented a space-time extraordinary energy device -- we call it the Steed, for short -- which we believe can travel to any existing space-time in the visible universe."

I was confused and mystified by what Magis had just said. I know little about physics and space travel, but this made no sense to me. What did he mean the "visible universe?"

Magis, knowing my thoughts, said, "This is quite complex, and your brain is not capable of understanding the physics and math behind this theory. Please don't be offended, Will, but you don't have the brainpower to understand the science involved. Nevertheless, I'll try to give you what you would call the *Astrophysics for Dummies* version."

"Listen carefully and be open-minded: Ninety-five percent of our universe is invisible to us. Only five percent is what we will call 'Visible Matter.' This understanding comes from mathematical calculations to explain the expansion of the universe. There isn't enough visible matter in our universe to explain how it acts. It's expanding, but it shouldn't be. It should be collapsing in on itself. As I said, this is all based on math formulas and calculations that all cosmologists agree upon."

"As it turns out, Twenty-six percent of the universe is made up of Dark Matter, and seventy-two percent is made up of what your scientists call Dark Energy. Only five percent of the universe is regular visible matter! We call dark energy "Sustaining Energy" because it overcomes gravity and keeps the universe expanding instead of collapsing. Sustaining Energy and Dark Matter (or, as we call it, "Sustaining Matter") emit no radiation that can be observed by humans or their instruments, thus making them invisible to us and incapable of being measured or explained."

"We have long known that they exist in another essence that is governed by physical rules that are different from the physical rules that explain the essence in which we live. Yet, despite that, the two essences co-exist and exert forces on each other. As I said, Sustaining Energy affects gravity and causes the universe to expand. It weakens gravity by counteracting the gravitons that make up the gravity field. Because of dark energy, the universe is expanding faster than the speed of light. Someday in the future, maybe a trillion years from now, all of the stars and galaxies will disappear from sight because all visible matter will be so far away and traveling so fast that their photons will not reach back to any other point in space-time. The universe will be dark and cold. That is the factor that allows us to travel through space-time in Sustaining Matter. Sustaining Matter does not change and we can go back to any space-time because it still exists in Sustaining Matter"

Basically, my mind was saying, "Huh?" through all of this explanation, and, of course, Magis knew this.

"Don't worry, Will, you don't need to understand this. I'm just trying to give you a basic overview to give you confidence in what we are proposing for you."

He continued: "Recently, we discovered a way to change Visible Matter into Sustaining Matter. The Steed will be converted into Sustaining Matter and will then be capable of traveling through space-time differently than Visible Matter. This has all been made possible by a breakthrough in our understanding of the String Theory of Matter. Have you heard of the String Theory of Matter, Will?"

I had heard of it, but I have no idea what it was or how it explained matter. I made some notes on it one time from videos on the internet, but it made no sense to me.

"Well, quite simply, Will, there are strings of energy that make up atomic particles. The length, composition and tension of the strings define a particle's mass and determine its characteristics. These particles make up protons, neutrons and electrons, which, as you know, make up atoms which, in turn, are the building blocks of all Visible Matter. We still don't know what the strings are made of, but that doesn't matter. Anyway, the strings in the matter in our visible universe are a certain length and vibrate at certain frequencies and in certain dimensions. We believe that they exist in ten different dimensions. They change and decay in certain ways to form different atomic particles, but all within exact parameters.

What we've discovered is that the strings that make up particles in Sustaining Matter are waves of a different length and vibrate in a different way and in different dimensions than Visible Matter. That's why they are invisible to us. One theory is that at the big bang, when all matter came into existence, two types of strings or waves of energy were created along with the particles that became atoms of Visible Matter. One type of string is what we are made of and facilitates the Visible Universe. Another type, with different characteristics, also came into existence and facilitate Sustaining Matter."

"Even more importantly, because of the difference in the strings and their different characteristics, they have a different quantum mechanics. This is the part that I won't even bother to explain, but the bottom line is that this knowledge has allowed us to build and convert the Steed into Sustaining Matter. Because of that, it can travel through space and time in a different fashion. The Steed can travel to any space-time in the visible universe almost instantly!"

"Sustaining Matter is much different than Visible Matter. It operates under different physical laws than the matter of the visible universe. It's much more stable and has different energy and characteristics. For one thing, it doesn't clump together like Visible Matter. Visible Matter has clumped together and created stars and galaxies through the fusion of atoms. Because of that, it creates environments that are destructive and hostile to life. 99.9999999999 percent of the Visible Universe is hostile to life. It's, quite simply, too cold or too hot or too radiated for life to exist."

"Visible Matter is constantly changing and reforming into different elements. Sustaining Matter, on the other hand, seems to be very stable and easy to live in. It seems to have a slippery quality and plays nicely with other types of matter because it does not radiate high energy particles. Most importantly, it co-exists compatibly with Visible Matter. This has implications that we are only beginning to understand."

"We think, perhaps, this might explain what happens when our Evolutes pass out of existence at the end of our visible life period. Through the process of meditation, our minds might be able to change the strings and their vibrations (or waves) that makeup our atomic particles -- thus transmogrifying our very essence into something more permanent and stable. This process would probably start on a small scale and escalate over the last few hundred years of our lives."

I thought to myself: that might be the true meaning of the term "good vibrations!"

"OK," I said. I think I understand where this is going. The Steed can take me back in space-time. But what is the Steed? Explain what it is to me in more detail, or, at least, in a way that I can understand it."

"Essentially, Will, the Steed is a fairly compact machine that will be converted to Sustaining Matter. We first designed and built a machine that could hold a passenger and convey the passenger to a point in space-time. Then we converted the first prototype machine to Sustaining Matter through a process that uses anti-matter. Normally when anti-matter interacts with matter, it causes an explosion of energy that is quite violent. However, we have learned how to control the reaction so that the transmogrification results in the production of Sustaining Matter. One interesting part of this process is that the resulting machine is invisible to us, but we know it's there by detecting disturbances in the gravitational field around it."

"The Steed is powered by a flow of gravitons (gravitons are the components of the gravity field) generated by the controlled process of antimatter converting visible matter atoms into Sustaining Matter. The energy deriving from this process pushes against and weakens the gravitational field. That's why the universe is expanding -- Sustaining Matter weakens the gravitational field of the universe. The reaction propels the Steed at the causational speed (its light speed) of the Sustaining Matter. The causational speed of Sustaining Matter is much faster than the light speed of Visible Matter, thus allowing the Steed to move to any point in space-time almost instantaneously. In addition, Sustaining Matter, as I mentioned, has a slippery quality and can pass through Visible Matter and not be impeded by it. Visible Matter, on the other hand, is slightly affected by Dark Matter. We know that because photons passing through Dark Matter appear to be bent slightly. "

"Again, Will, don't worry about understanding all of this. The benefit of this new technology is that it could take you back to a point in space-time that might solve all of your problems, and ours, too, to be honest with you. It could take you almost instantaneously to a point in space-time of your choosing. We have some ideas for you to think about. We have a new version of the Steed that is ready and operational. We only need to program and convert it for you."

This sounded too good to be true. How could I be so lucky as to have been the passenger on the Nina, and now I seem to have a chance to go back in space-time in the Steed and solve the fundamental problem of my life! What are the chances of that? Am I dreaming?

"No, Will, you aren't dreaming. You really do have that chance. But, I must tell you, there are two problems that will influence your final decision. First, as I told you, we haven't field-tested this technology, yet. You'll understand why in a moment. We've modeled everything on our supercomputers, and it works perfectly and performs just as we expect. But, as I told you, we haven't performed a field test of the technology with a human being. Therefore, we don't have one hundred percent certainty. Even at our advanced level of science, models can sometimes be erroneous."

I thought, "Now, that's a concern! I'm going to be a guinea pig again! I took a big risk with the AASUSE Team, though, and that worked out pretty well -- at least so far. But what is this second problem?"

"OK. Here's the second problem, and this will explain why we haven't field-tested the Steed, yet. For you to travel in the Steed, you will have to be converted to Sustaining Matter! Visible Matter and Sustaining Matter don't interact, except for Sustaining Matter weakening the gravitational field. To be able to travel through Sustaining Matter under the physical laws that apply to it, you must be converted to Sustaining Matter."

"What does that mean?" I asked. "Can I be converted back to Visible Matter? What does it feel like to become Sustaining Matter? How do you know a human can be converted to Sustaining Matter?" I was practically yelling out these questions. I was starting to feel panic and was breathing heavily. I tried to rub my hands through my hair and felt, instead, the EH. I needed to stand up and walk around.

"Be calm, Will. Trust us. We will not let you harm yourself. Be calm." Magis put his hands on my shoulders, again, and I felt calmer. The top of my head suddenly felt cool and my brain calmed down. Magis was probably doing something through the EH, and it was working. My panic was subsiding.

"We haven't field-tested the Steed with a human, yet, but we have tested a prototype with a type of helpmate. We have a class of helpmates that we use in our scientific experiments. We call them "exmates." They are different from the helpmates that are assigned to an Acme. They function at a very low level and do not have the emotional or intellectual faculties of our normal helpmate class. They are similar, in many ways, to monkeys and apes in your world, but they are much tamer and perfectly docile. Their main value is that they have even more similarities to us in their genome than monkeys and apes have to you."

"I assure you, they are, normally, never harmed in any way. We are very careful to make sure that they are not injured or subjected to any pain or mental suffering. There have been a few exceptions to that rule, but It's rare and only in cases of utmost importance."

"We felt the Steed was a good case for an exception. When we were ready to convert the first prototype of the Steed to Sustaining Matter, we decided to place an exmate in it to see how high-level living matter would handle the conversion. One of the older exmates that only had a few more years to live was chosen for the experiment. After the conversion, we were able to determine that the exmate survived and seemed to be living normally. We included a device that would euthanize the exmate after a period of time so it would not starve and suffer. I assure you it was quick and painless."

"I thought you said that we couldn't see Sustaining Matter? How were you able to determine that the exmate survived?" I said.

"We have developed a technology that can, to a limited degree, image what exists in Sustaining Matter. It has a very small range, only a few meters, and is very low resolution. Essentially, it detects minute disturbances in the gravitational field and converts that data to a very blurry image. It was clear enough for us to determine that the exmate survived the conversion and that the prototype Steed was converted and existed in substantially the form we expected."

"We programmed it to perform a few short maneuvers and operations that would indicate that it could perform the functions necessary to travel in space-time. All maneuvers were performed as expected and telemetric signals of gravitons indicated to us that it was fully functional. The prototype did not contain all of the systems and functionality of a full version, but we feel that, based upon this test and our extensive modeling, the Steed could take a human occupant to a designated point in space-time within its current range."

"What is its current range?" I asked.

"That's a good question, Will. We don't know exactly, but we're sure that it's several hundred years. We have enough anti-matter in the Steed for that. It couldn't go back 13.7 billion years to the beginning of the universe, but it has more than enough energy to go back to the space-time of your accident -- and that's all that matters, right?"

"Is that what this is all leading to?" I asked.

"It's up to you, but we have a proposal that you might be interested in. Here's the plan. You could go back in space-time to just before your accident and cause a small delay that would prevent your car from colliding with Mary Carroll's. A small delay, just sixty seconds, is all it would take to change everything. The accident wouldn't have happened, and your life wouldn't have been turned upside down. You would have taken Bonnie home and then had dinner with Deirdre. Since news of the accident wouldn't have been in the paper, you would never have met the Professor and the AASUSE Team. Because of that, you would never have traveled in the Nina, and you wouldn't be here right now talking to me. Problem solved for both of us. Wouldn't that be great! What do you think?"

I liked the idea, but there was one big question remaining -- what happens to me after I'm converted to Sustaining Matter? Do I live forever as Sustaining Matter? What type of life would that be? Could I be converted back to Visible Matter? How could that happen?

"Those are, of course, good questions, Will. Our computer models show that once you are converted to Sustaining Matter and cause a change in the space-time continuum of Visible Matter that affects what happened to you at some point in a prior space-time, the 'you,' here and now that I'm talking to, will not exist going forward. You will not exist any longer in the prior space-time."

"One way to look at it is that an overlay, so to speak, will be created at the point where you intervene in your past space-time and both existences will continue until you interrupt the past space-time continuum. Then, after that interruption, only one space-time will continue. There will be a loop in the space-time continuum from the point where the interruption began and ended, but after that one line will continue. Your life will continue as though the prior space-time loop never existed."

I think that's what Magis said, but I'm not sure if my recollection is correct. I believe I captured the essence of his explanation, but these concepts are beyond any earthly understanding. If this recording is ever found, I realize that there will be many questions.

"Ok," I said. "I'm not going to lie to you and tell you that I fully understand what you just told me -- besides, you already know that -- but it seems to me that the gist is this: I can go back in time and change things so the accident doesn't happen. Then, the old reality exists as a closed loop, and I will continue on as though the accident never happened, Right?"

"In a nutshell, yes, that's it," Magis said with a reassuring smile and nod.

Then I thought, what about Roxy and the AASUSE Team? Will Roxy destroy earth in twenty-five years? Will the AASUSE Team send another person to Earthtoo? Will another loop be created and continue this whole problem over and over again for the Acme?

"As to Roxy, Will, we knew about it and had a plan in place already to move it out of a trajectory toward Earth. We would have accomplished that in just a few months after you did, and most Earthlings would have never known that Roxy existed."

"As to the AASUSE Team project, we have already set a plan in motion to delay it, and, most likely, put interstellar travel by Earthlings off for at least four or five decades. In the meantime, we have been doing things to reduce warfare on earth and encourage more international cooperation and unity. In a few years, with our help, new "discoveries" will take place to reduce your carbon emissions and reduce global warming and save your environment. We have a comprehensive strategic plan for Earth that should accelerate your advancement and, hopefully, make Earth a better place to live."

That sounded great and made me feel better about my situation. At least the Roxy problem will be solved, and Earth won't be destroyed.

I felt bad, though, about the AASUSE Team. I didn't want to let them down. What would happen to them? How were the Acme going to delay the interstellar travel program? Without me, the AASUSE TEAM might not be able to find someone to fly in the Nina. If they look for someone else, they might be discovered. What would that mean? Would they all get into trouble and lose their jobs?

"Don't feel bad about the AASUSE Team, Will, Magis said. "Based on what we can tell from analyzing the CATO System and the other information that we've gleaned from the Nina, they are all brilliant people and will have no problem maintaining their positions. There's always a need for people like that, and they will all land on their feet."

This made sense to me, and I wanted to pursue another topic, anyway. I would revisit this concern later, but another issue was taking over my thoughts. If I return to Earth in the Steed, what was the plan to alter my history and prevent the accident? What did Magis have in mind? I had some thoughts on this, but I wanted to hear his.

"OK, Will, let's talk about how to solve your problem. What we need to do is prevent you from colliding with Ms. McCarthy. As we discussed, any slight delay in your driving home would prevent the accident. It has to be something you could control or affect. Think back to that time and place. Is there something simple that you could do to cause a delay? It should be simple and foolproof, and it has to be hidden or secret so we don't alter anyone else's life. We don't want to create another problem that might be worse for you."

I thought for a moment about what preceded the accident. It couldn't be something in the bar. Too many people would be involved in that. Then I remembered something that I had thought of earlier. After we left the bar, we walked down the sidewalk to my car. Except for some light traffic on Western Avenue, there was no one around. The sidewalk was abandoned. No. There was someone walking in front of us, but I don't think I knew him, and he was thirty or forty feet ahead of us.

It was dark and cold. I was holding Bonnie's hand. She slipped on some ice and almost fell. I was able to keep my footing and held her up. If we had fallen, there would have been a few minutes' delay. We would have both ended up on the cold wet concrete sidewalk. It would have taken us a minute or so to get back on our feet. One of us might even be injured -- nothing too serious, I'm sure. We would have had to brush ourselves off. We might have laughed at ourselves. Yes, I thought, that would certainly have caused a delay of at least a minute, probably more.

Magis, knowing my thoughts, said, "That's a perfect idea, Will. The one thing that we know for sure about Sustaining Matter is that it affects the gravitational field. You will be made of Sustaining Matter. All you have to do is get as close as possible to yourself and Bonnie at the time Bonnie slips and that will cause both of you to lose your balance and fall. Bonnie was already falling. You managed to catch yourself and her, but the sudden shift or weakening of the gravity field around you will throw off your coordination. Think about it. If you suddenly felt a weakening of gravity, you would have to adjust your movements to compensate for that. Being on ice, it would be difficult to make the proper adjustment of your movements. You would most likely push too hard on your feet and cause them to slip out from under you."

Yes, that made sense to me. I remember seeing videos of the astronauts walking and running on the Moon. They bounded up with every step they took. The weak gravity of the Moon made them capable of jumping much higher than on Earth.

"Will," Magis said, "I think we have a good plan that would cause enough of a delay to prevent your accident. I'll have some of my people model this scenario and see if they think it will work. We know enough about Earth's gravity and the composition of all of the materials involved to make some pretty good projections. We also have many years of research on the size and strength of earthlings to know how you would react under the projected circumstances. We'll have to make some assumptions, but I assure you that we have the expertise to do this."

"It will take a day or two to complete the modeling and the Leadership Council still has to approve the final plan. Inquis might, as you say, throw a wrench in the works and change our thinking, but I don't think so. This is all good because you will need that time to decide on whether you want to stay here on Earthtoo or try to reset your life on Earth. We want you to take your time and think about it. Either way, whatever your decision is, we will work with you and support you."

"Guio will stay with you and give you all of the help you need. You'll probably think of more information that you'll need to make your decision. We understand that, and we'll give you all the time and help you need."

"Now it's time for Guio to return you to your PM where you can relax and contemplate your future. Live well!"

"Wait, Magis," I blurted out. "I have to ask you, Why do all of the Acme say 'Live well!' when they leave? Is it a wish? Is it a blessing? Why do you say that?"

"'Live well!' is an ancient exhortation, Will. It is not a wish or a blessing. It goes back to the time of the AI War. It is a request, an admonition, a command, to live a good life. It means: live well so that you stay healthy, can contribute to society, and not cause problems for others. During the time of the AI Wars, every person was valuable and there was no tolerance for bad behavior. Every person had to dedicate himself or herself to the cause. We had to be unselfish and cooperative. We had to live well for our own sake and the sake of others. We kept that tradition and still exhort each other with that request whenever we part company, even though it is endemic to our nature, now. Live well!"

I wonder if those parting words would work on Earth. Probably not. We don't like anyone telling us what to do, even if the philosophy behind it would solve most of our problems. What one person thinks is living well might not be accepted by others. We like our freedom, even if it kills us or harms other.

Chapter 23

A Rondolier

Guio and Nadii were suddenly standing behind me and each took one of my hands and led me away. After a few steps, Guio stopped and looked at me. "Will," she said, "before we return to the PM, I have a treat for you. We are just in time for a Rondolier."

"A Rondolier," I said, "what's that?"

"It's hard to explain, but you'll love it. I guarantee it."

Suddenly I heard and felt sensuous music -- a type of music like I had never heard before. It was rhythmic and enchanting and exciting. It seemed to grab my mind and took over my emotions. Every nerve in my body resonated in a pleasant, enticing way. Then I was in a beautiful world of light and color that matched the music and created a total sensual experience. All about me were hundreds of Acme and their helpmates swirling in the most beautiful, coordinated dance I had ever seen. They were all moving together in complementary movements that seemed perfectly choreographed and planned.

I'm not a dancer and always felt too self-conscious to dance at parties and events like weddings. I would usually just stand around and make small talk. To my amazement, though, I wanted to dance. I knew exactly how I was to move with the music. I knew the steps and what they meant. I felt joy and happiness and total abandonment. The Acme and their helpmates looked at me and sent strong feelings of acceptance and appreciation into my mind. They took turns taking my hands and leading me in intricate steps. As they did that, they smiled and looked happy that I had joined in their dance.

The music continued and changed slightly at appropriate intervals. It rose and fell. It was loud and then soft. Each change added to the story being told and advanced the meaning. I can't tell you what it was, now, but it had deep meaning and lifted my spirits. I felt as though I was part of a great celebration of life and beauty and truth.

I began to think of great dancers and dance routines that I had seen and always envied. I was Fred Astaire leading all the Acme as we danced up and down a flight of silver stairs. I was John Travolta leading a complicated line dance. The Acme loved it and sent applause and cheers my way. River Dance came to mind, and we formed a long line and were stomping out Irish Dance steps at a frantic beat. The line swirled in a circle as we held each other's shoulders transmitting love and unity with each step and move. It was a whirlwind of love and trust! I thought of *She Has Diamonds on the Souls of Her Shoes*, and we were an African Dance Company rhythmically stepping and adding vocals that complemented the dance and made us a village of happy loving people. Then, Michael Jackson suddenly came to mind. As I looked around, we were all wearing short tight shiny black pants, a glove, and sequined jackets doing the Moon Walk.

I don't know how long we danced. It seemed like hours, but I was not tired and didn't want the Rondolier to stop. We danced through forests and over mountains. My favorite part was dancing across a beautiful still lake surrounded by mountains. In one segment we danced through outer space past galaxies and through colorful nebula -- beautiful clouds of star dust. A whirlwind of light and beauty!

Then there was a complete change. All of the Acme were gone! I was in a beautiful ballroom dancing with Deirdre. An orchestra was playing our favorite song, *Fly Me to the Moon*. This is the song we danced to at a wedding of one of her cousins after we had been dating for a few months. We had a wonderful, loving, sensuous slow dance, and we adopted that song as "Our Song!"

Now, I could feel myself holding Deirdre and dancing slowly and rhythmically with her. We were in perfect step with each other. We were holding each other tight -- almost melding together as one. I could feel her warm body next to mine. We were in perfect harmony. We were like one but yet two. Our egos were gone. We only cared about the other. We both wanted to dance forever and not break apart. Neither of us wanted to move away from the other and break the spell. It was the best, most perfect hug, and there was no need to talk. We trusted each other and were complete.

....

The next thing I remember is waking up in the PM. I was sad that the dance with Deirdre was over, but I felt relaxed and glowing and had no hangover, which I usually have after a party or wedding. Did I dream the dance or did it really happen?

"It did happen, Will," I heard Guio say in my mind. "We dance and celebrate like that almost every three or four days. It's part of our culture and binds us together. That was the best Rondolier I've ever taken part in. Marta, who created it, was showing off and trying to impress you. Your contribution was spectacular and greatly appreciated. We have artists and musicians that specialize in those celebrations. They create experiences that complement, enhance and amplify our lives. Marta is one of the best."

"Because of our ability to communicate through telepathy and virtual reality, we have practically no limits on what can be shared and experienced. Every aspect of our lives is celebrated. We all contribute ideas and discoveries to these artists, and they turn them into these celebrations we call a Rondolier."

"I must leave you now, Will, but I'm at your beck and call if you need anything. All you have to do is call for me, and I will quickly return. You should rest, now. Don't start worrying immediately about your options. Relax before you start contemplating your future. There's no rush. We don't expect an immediate answer. Live well!"

With that said, Guio and Nadii left me. As they were walking away, Nadii turned back to look at me and gave me a reassuring smile and, I'm not kidding, a thumbs up!

Chapter 24

Decision Time

I did what Guio suggested and didn't try to make an immediate decision. I took about a day and a half to dictate the last section of my journal. It was a good exercise as it forced me to rethink all that has happened to me since arriving here on Earthtoo. I kept thinking about Inquis and worried if she might have a bad opinion of me and proposed something unpleasant for me. I took Magis' advice, though, and resigned myself to accepting whatever will be.

While I was contemplating all of this, Guio informed me that Magis' plan had been accepted by the Council, so now it's time to make a decision. I'm torn about what to do. I enjoy the life here on Earthtoo. What a pleasant existence. No war. No strife. No poverty. No sickness. It's pretty amazing and ideal. Who wouldn't want to live like that? It's what we imagine heaven might be like, except for the absence of God, of course. But everyone is loving and kind and unselfish. There's no competition. No one is trying to take advantage of you and use you -- steal from you -- hurt you -- exploit you. It's idyllic.

On the other hand, I miss Owen and my grandchildren, and I feel as though I should be taking care of Deirdre. I remembered our wonderful dance and longed for her. Could that moment be recreated for real? I hoped it could, but I wasn't sure.

Most importantly, I should go back and change things so Bonnie and Mary Carroll aren't injured. Think of the suffering their families are going through because of me. I could prevent all of that. It would be selfish of me not to try.

To accomplish that, however, I'll have to go back in space-time. Is that possible? The Acme think it can be done. All of their computer models indicate that their technological breakthroughs will make that possible. But, on the other hand, they admit it's untested. Can I really be converted to Sustaining Matter and go back in space-time to prevent the accident? What will it feel like? What if I'm caught forever in a Sustaining Matter limbo? That might be even worse than the situation I'm in now. What a dilemma!

I'm going to stop dictating this journal for a few minutes and think about my alternatives. First, I'm going to pray for help. Then I'll rationally and calmly review all of the pros and cons of each option.

Chapter 25

Poetry Break

I'm in the Steed, now and I plan to finish this journal before the next phase begins. I'll start from where I left off the last time I dictated.

After going over and over my options, I made my decision -- I decided to ride the Steed back in space-time and prevent the accident. It's the only option I felt I had. How could I not make that choice? I could solve all of my problems and prevent great suffering and tragedy for my family and two other families by doing so. It would be heartless and selfish of me not to make that choice.

Guio had been a great help. I asked her to explain some of the scientific concepts involved, again, -- space-time, the Steed, anti-matter, gravitons and Sustaining Matter -- which she did. It seemed to make more sense to me. I'm not saying that I understand all of the science involved, but I trust the Acme. They are a quantum leap ahead of Earthlings and are geniuses. I have faith in them.

I told Guio of my decision, and she informed Magis. He said that they would be ready for me in a few hours.

When I last saw him, he told me that they would be modeling the programs and equipment needed to return me to the space-time just before the accident. They needed a few more hours to fine tune the guidance program and the Steed.

Guio told me to relax and rest until I'm called. I've closed my eyes and tried to rest, but that was impossible. How could anyone rest knowing that they are going to be changed into another form of reality and sent through space and time to reset history... especially knowing that you will be the first human to attempt that while testing new technology that is still experimental!

No one could rest under those circumstances. I needed something to do to help pass the time.

I'd been working on a poem about my experience. It might be more of a rap song than a poem. Maybe it's both. I had scratched out a few ideas over the last few days when I was resting in the PM. I thought, now might be a good time to try to finalize this masterpiece. It'll be the first poem/rap song ever written in outer space! I'll be making more history. I knew it would be rough, but I wanted to take a stab at it.

I wrote several love poems to Deirdre when we were first dating, and they weren't bad, if I do say so myself. She loved them and was flattered that she was idealized in poetry. I also used to help write jingles at Bennington. Some of them were used in commercials, so I must have been pretty good at rhymes. I know jingles aren't poetry, but as a great poet once said, "One man's jingle is another man's jangle." I just made that up.

I had a small touch of Fast Relief left, so I thought now would be a good time to finish it. I hoped maybe it would provide some inspiration -- be my muse. Following is my final version. I Hope Molly and Charlie will read it someday.

....

Space Traveler/Time Unraveler

The future was bright
endless possibilities in sight.
Thinking about fishing
Full of hopeful wishing.
Then talk and infatuation
created a fateful situation.
Intentions benign
confused by wine

resulting in shame.
Who was to blame?
A bad decision
brought pain and derision
and a tragic collision
brought family division.
Victim or causality?
Injuries and a fatality.
Was it a negligent crime
or an injustice sublime?
Unhappy life.
Poor suffering wife.
Live in a whirlwind.
When will it end?
Depressing lawsuit.
Dogged pursuit.
Fear.
Not clear.
A Mysterious phone call.
Would this solve it all?
Months of worry.
Escape in a hurry.
Vanished without a trace.
Found relief in outer space.
Riding the blue plane
to infamy or fame.
For all a great mystery.
Writer of new history.
Scientific Team
not what they seem.
Was it a dream?
Fusion. . .
delusion. . .
allusion. . .
confusion. . .
Through the solar system
could not resist them.

Traveled beyond Mars
and to the stars.
Captured by the Acme.
Were they going to attack me?
Meaning, being, intervening. . .
Tough decision.
True vision?
Writing a journal
For the eternal
or internal.
Gentle guide
made it easy to hide.
Visions in a cave
depression and fear did stave.
Listening for hours
about incredible powers.
The future of our race
discovered in this place.
Conscience face?
Love and sharing
always caring.
Then what to do?
Stay or go through?
Sustaining Matter,
reality shatter, tatter,
or chasing the mad hatter?
Change history,
a deep mystery.
Gravity
changed depravity
with a slip and fall,
changed it all.
Space traveler
time unraveler
will you succeed
riding the blue Steed?
No longer a tragedy.

Shrewd strategy.
In a daze,
through the maze
into the next phase.
Begin again!

Chapter 26

Final Preparations, Again

Just as I was finished dictating the last draft of my poem, Guio let me know that she was on her way. I heard a clear message in my head that she and Nadii were coming to get me. They weren't far away. She had been notified by Magis that the Steed was prepared for me. Magis and Zellen were with the engineers who had just finished programming the Steed and the matter converter, and they notified Guio.

I put my notebooks and other possessions in my backpack and put it on. I held my recorder thinking I could complete my journal as things develop. I didn't know if it would ever be found, but, since I had made the effort to keep this journal, I wanted to complete it.

Just as I crawled out of the PM and stood up, Guio and Nadii came bounding along. They radiated happiness and energy. I felt positive vibes emitted by their presence and auras. They were sensitive to my fears and trepidations and sent me support and positive feelings. It worked. I felt better and more confident. Just knowing that they were with me and sensitive to my plight helped me.

"Greetings, Will," I hear Guio say. Did you rest and gain strength for your journey?"

"Yes," I said. "I distracted myself by trying to finish a poem I've been working on. It's still rough, but it will have to do. I know I don't have any more time to polish it."

Nadii ran to me and grabbed my hand. It felt warm and soft and infused my spirit with calm and happiness.

"Poems are never finished, Will," Guio said. "They can always be tweaked and amended forever. We have an old story about a man whose job it was to polish beautiful brass doors. Someone asked him how he knew when to quit polishing them. He said he didn't. After awhile, someone just came and took them away from him. That's how poems are."

That, I thought, is a perfect analogy.

"Are you ready? Do you have all of your belongings?" Guio said. "If you do, follow me and I will take you to the lab where our scientists and engineers have the Steed ready for you. It's only a short distance from here."

I told Guio I was ready, and, if I left anything behind, she could have it and do with it what she wanted. Guio said, "Will, when you go back in space-time and prevent the accident, you will never have visited Earthtoo. I will never have met you and nothing of yours will be here on our planet. It makes me a little sad to think of that, but I know it is best for you -- and for both Earth and Earthtoo. Realizing that makes me happy."

It was hard for me to believe that, but I knew she was correct. It's just hard to get your mind around that concept. How could all that has happened to me not exist? I think it will continue to exist but in a separate loop of space-time. It was hurting my mind trying to understand that. I thought, "It's best to just go on."

Guio held my hand and took me through what seemed like a cloudy corridor. Nadii was running ahead of us and kept looking back and waving us on. I saw a light ahead of us and a door into what looked like a laboratory. As we entered it, I saw that it was a brightly lit room with pristine white walls, but it seemed mostly barren and empty. One large, dark square box, maybe fifty feet square, stood in the center of the room. It had a pipe connecting into it on one side and another pipe connected to it on the other side. There were no other markings or devices of any type on it. A smaller dark square box sat to the left of it. It, likewise, had no markings or gauges or any other devices on it and only one pipe was connected to it.

Magis, Zellen and two other Acme were standing near the large box. They appeared to be communicating with each other, but it was hard to tell. They heard us approach and turned to face us.

"Hello, Will," I heard Magis say. "We're ready for you. We hope that you're not too nervous and are ready to make history. We know that you must be filled with worry and fear, but we're committed to making you feel as comfortable as possible, considering the circumstance."

"Nervous!" I thought. "That word doesn't begin to describe my feeling. I was about ready to pass out. I thought, in a few minutes I'm going to be changed into a different form of matter and sent back eight or nine months in time with the hope of changing reality. I was way beyond nervous. I prayed, God, just let me keep it together for a few more minutes!"

"We understand, Will," Magis said as he put his hand on my shoulder and transmitted a positive feeling into my brain. Again, like several other times, it helped.

Extending his hand he said, "You remember Zellen (she winked at me) and let me introduce you to the lead physicist and engineer who developed the Steed and the matter converter. This is Ibu and this is Yolk." They both looked at me and conveyed warm greetings into my brain. They also transmitted strong feelings of appreciation that I would volunteer to test their inventions. For some reason, that suddenly evoked a feeling of deja vu.

Magis continued: "Ibu is the lead physicist. He discovered how visible matter could be converted into sustaining matter. Yelk is the lead engineer of the team that made the device that could make the conversion. He and his team also designed and built the Steed so it could be converted and then operate in sustaining matter.

They rebuilt an existing spaceship that had been created for travel within our solar system. It's a small one-person ship that uses a weak, first-generation warp drive that was sufficient for relatively short distances within our solar system."

"Nice to meet you," I said. "I appreciate having this opportunity. If the Steed works, it will solve all of my problems and save many people from a lot of suffering and heartache."

I felt a strong acknowledgment and appreciation for what I had just said.

There was silence, and I looked around me. I was puzzled by the two black boxes and wondered what they were. I also thought that this was a very unusual lab. There was nothing much that indicated what was being done there.

Magis said, "You're puzzled by what you see. Of course -- that's understandable. First of all, the lab, as you call it, is, as Guio first explained to you, a projection. We knew that this is what you thought a laboratory on Earthtoo might look like, so that's how we projected it. We made it bright and clean to make you comfortable."

"The smaller box to your left is what you would call a three-dimensional printer. They come in various sizes and are used to produce everything we need here on Earthtoo. The pipe leading into it delivers all of the substances it needs to print the desired objects. Yelk used this printer to create new parts for the Steed this morning to upgrade a few systems that he felt needed revising. Most of the parts for the matter converter were produced on a much larger printer in another lab."

"The large box in the center of the room is the matter converter. It contains the Steed and the machinery necessary to convert what is located in it to sustaining matter. There is a door on the other side for you to enter."

He continued: "You also noticed that there are no markings on the boxes and no gauges or any other type of device protruding or attached to it, just the two pipes connected to opposite sides of the box. We thought about projecting some gauges, screens, switches and lights on the converter, but then we decided that was unnecessary."

"You see, Will," Magis continued, "all of our machinery and equipment is monitored and controlled by mental telepathy. We don't need gauges and switches or screens or any other device to control and operate our equipment. All monitoring information is projected into our minds, and, likewise, we use our minds to control and operate our equipment. You have some machinery on Earth that can perform in that manner, now, although at a very rudimentary level. Unlike ours, they aren't controlled by mental telepathy but require wired connections to capture brain waves. Within less than a century, Earth's scientists will probably be able to use wireless connections."

That will be great, I thought. I hope Charlie and Molly will live long enough to see some of the great things that lie in our future.

Ibu and Yelk then approached me and shook my hand and looked deep into my eyes. They, again, conveyed appreciation and admiration for what I was doing. After shaking my hand, they walked to the right side of the converter and sat in large chairs that seemed to enfold them.

Zellen hugged me and looked deep into my eyes, as Ibu and Yelk did, and conveyed to me strong feelings of empathy and hope. She let me know that she was happy to have met me and regretted that she wouldn't remember me if I completed my mission. I thanked her for her kindness.

Then Magis conveyed to me that it was time to enter the Steed.

"And now, Will," he said, "It's time for you to enter the Steed and travel back in space-time to prevent your accident. Are you ready? We need to go over a few things, but it won't take long."

"I have one question," I said. "This just came to me. I just realized that, if my mission is successful, none of this will have happened. Because of that, I'm thinking, you won't have learned anything from what I'm doing? That seems like a shame!"

Magis thought for a moment and then said, "That's a good point, Will, but we have a plan that we hope will make this a fruitful endeavor. The Steed contains a memory device that we hope will record this operation and preserve it for the future. It will, basically, record and monitor all that happens to you and the Steed. The matter converter will, we hope, be able to track and monitor the Steed and return it to Earthtoo. To retrieve the recorded information, we will have to reconvert the Steed, or at least the memory device, back into visible matter."

"We aren't currently capable of converting sustaining matter back into visible matter, but we feel certain that we can accomplish that in the future. When we do that, all the information about you and your trip back in space-time might be salvaged. After you are dropped off on Earth, the Steed will return, and we can, hopefully, someday, replay the entire trip. Ibu has a working theory on that and feels that he can prove it in a few more years. If so, we will be able to recapture this entire endeavor."

That gave me an idea about what to do with my journal. If I leave my recorder in the Steed, perhaps, someday, an Acme (and maybe even someone from Earth) will, at some time in the future, be able to play it and learn about my adventure. I'm not so proud that I think it will be as important as some of the journals of the great explorers, like Lewis and Clark, but it might be of historical value.

Magis then conveyed the following information to me. Using the information that I had given them and additional information gleaned from my memory about the time and place of the accident and what had happened immediately before it, Yelk's team of engineers had determined the speed and trajectory necessary to bring the Steed to the space-time about ten minutes before Bonnie and I left Brian's Tap and started walking to my car. The Steed would land in a vacant lot about one hundred feet south of Brian's Tap. I could picture exactly where that lot was.

Thanks to Google Maps, which the Acme had a copy of, and other geographical information the Acme had been assembling about Earth for many years, Yelk's team could program the Steed to land in the vacant lot at exactly the correct space-time. By landing in the vacant lot, they would avoid influencing or affecting anything of importance on Earth. Since it was cold and late in the evening on the date of the accident, the chances of hitting someone or something of importance in the vacant lot were slim.

I would then have to move to the front of Brian's Tap and be ready so I could make contact with myself just as Bonnie slipped on the ice. As Magis and I had discussed before, that contact should weaken the gravity field and cause the visible-matter-me to slip and fall to the ground. It might hurt me and could even break a bone, but it would cause a substantial delay thus resulting in my not colliding with Mary Carroll McCarthy at the 103rd and Longwood Drive intersection where the accident took place. I thought, "I would gladly suffer a broken bone to prevent the accident."

This plan assumed many things, and my mind was a whirlwind of "what if" questions. How was I supposed to move about on Earth being made out of sustaining matter? What if I couldn't move? Would the time sequences be the same? Could I see visible matter if I'm made of sustaining matter? What if I make myself fall but then I pop right back up and am not delayed?

Magis, knowing my worries, said that they had modeled these scenarios and others, and they felt confident that my collision with my visible-matter-me would definitely cause a fall. The sudden weakening of gravity all around me would make it impossible to regain my footing. Factoring in my weight and the strength of my muscles, the friction of the surfaces, and other items I didn't catch, the models all showed that I would not be able to keep my balance.

The only thing they were not certain about was whether or not I would be able to see visible matter. I would certainly be able to sense it. My interaction with the gravitational field would be a significant energy-filled event and would be sensed in some fashion by the sustaining-matter-me. (I hope this makes sense.)

Yelk's team came up with a possible solution for that problem. They had created what amounts to an anti-matter flashlight! It's a canister, about the size of a flashlight that holds a small amount of anti-matter. It has a nozzle at one end that is controlled by a switch on the side, again, similar to a flashlight. When the switch is activated it will emit an infinitesimal amount of anti-matter that will react with the normal, visible matter and, in essence, light up the visible matter and make it visible to me. I can use it to find my way to the correct spot to cause the fall. At least that's the theory. It hadn't been tested, but the modeling pointed in that direction.

I had to stop thinking of problems and make a blind leap of faith. "Let's go," I said. As I thought once before, the train is moving too fast now, and it's too late to jump off.

Magis led me to the entrance door and stopped. "When you enter this door," he said, "you will see the

Steed. It's a round cylinder about six feet high and fifteen feet long, about the size of one of your large automobiles. It's bright blue and rounded at the front and back. There's a hatch in the middle that will be open and there will be a ramp leading into it. Climb in and sit down in a lounge-type chair that will fit you perfectly. The hatch will automatically close and there is nothing else for you to do until you land back on earth. There are no instruments for you to look at, but the Steed's computer will announce when you have been converted to sustaining matter and when you land on Earth."

"After you land on Earth, it will open the hatch for you to exit. Exit quickly and move as expeditiously as possible to the front of Brian's Tap. The Steed will remain on Earth for about 30 minutes and then return to Earthtoo. If you can't accomplish your mission, you can consider returning to Earthtoo. We don't know what will happen to you or whether we can ever reconvert you to visible matter, but at least you have that alternative. Hopefully, you won't need it."

"We don't know what you will feel or experience, so we can't explain what's going to happen to you. Likewise, we can't give you much of an explanation about the duration of your trip, except that it should be very quick. Based on the information we gathered from our experiment with the Helpmate, we know that it will take several hours for the matter conversion to take place. The Steed has an autonomous computer that will control the entire process and monitor the conversion process. When the Steed and all matter in it have been converted, it will alert you and start the journey, which, as I mentioned, should be of a short duration. We're also confident that you will retain the same shape and form that you now have and will not experience pain."

Pausing and looking calmly and happily at me, Magis continued: "May the Supreme Power of the universe bless you and take you safely back to Earth. We have all been touched by your visit, Will, and, perhaps, our history will someday contain your story and praise you for your bravery. Live well!"

I felt sadness and admiration in Magis' communication to me. It was sincere and heartfelt and had a depth and strength that I had never felt before or knew was possible. Even though my current existence will be short, I'm glad that the Acme are, or were, a part of it. I have an abiding hope that I will pass into a new and better existence and know that the Acme, the AASUSE Team and my previous fifty-nine years of life will remain with me and shape and enrich who I am and always will be.

With that, I was resigned to my fate and gladly entered the matter converter. I climbed into the Steed, positioned myself in the cockpit, sat back and closed my eyes. I heard the hatch close. I was all alone in complete, total, silent darkness.

I found my recorder and began dictating this final entry into my journal. I plan to continue dictating my journal when I arrive back on Earth at the crucial space-time. I'm going to dictate the remainder of this journal in real time. Then I plan to run back to the Steed and throw my recorder into the Steed before it returns to Earthtoo. Hopefully, this journal will survive and my experience will be of great value to the Acme, and, perhaps, someday, the people of Earth.

I will stay on Earth and see what happens. Whatever it is, I'm reconciled to it and have no fear about my future. I am ready to accept my fate, whatever it may bring.

Chapter 27

Journey's End

I have completed my dictation and hear a machine voice announce, "Conversion complete. Mission will commence in thirty seconds." After I completed my dictation, I was able to rest for a short time, the length of which I have no idea. Now I feel strange, but calm, with growing self-awareness, almost like dreaming. There is no sense of movement, however, just an expansion of reality and my presence in it. There's no spinning, no shaking, no acceleration, just a fullness and completeness. I feel solid and strong. Time stands still.

Now I hear the computer voice telling me, "We have arrived at our destination. The hatch will open in five seconds. I'm holding my recorder and the anti-matter light waiting to exit the Steed as quickly as possible.

The hatch has opened, and I am now climbing out. I can't see anything as I slowly and carefully descend the entrance ramp carefully feeling my way. There are handrails on each side of the ramp, and I am not worried about falling. Thick, palpable darkness surrounds me. Then, suddenly, I'm in a blue whirlwind. I'm disoriented, confused. Then calm darkness. I remember the anti-gravity flashlight. I realize I'm holding it in my left hand. I stop. With my right hand, still holding my recorder, I reach for the light in my left hand. I hit it and fumble it. It falls out of my hand! Damn! Where did it go? I look down to see if I can find it. How could I be so careless! This is a disaster!

Then I realize I'm beginning to see what is around me. I forget about the anti-matter light. I won't need the light now. What a relief! I wait a few moments to allow my surroundings to come into focus.

The Steed has landed as planned. I'm in the vacant lot that I remembered and saw on the Google Earth maps. I feel no temperature or wind. I'm not hot or cold. I can now see well except everything has a violet tint to it and is slightly wavy around the periphery of my vision. Then everything turns green, then yellow, then orange and finally red. I wait a few seconds to try to gain my bearings. Suddenly, everything is clear and in bright primary colors. The green weeds and grass are bright shades of green. The sky is a bright violet. I see things that are yellow and orange and red. It doesn't look normal, but it's clear and bright.

I look about me and see there's a fence around the entire lot. There's an abandoned car and some steel barrels in the back left corner near the alley. There's a gate to the alley, but it's locked by a chain and padlock. How am I going to climb the fence? I could use the barrels, but that would put me in the alley. I need to be on the sidewalk by the street as soon as possible.

I quickly walk toward the fence at the front of the lot. The ground is rough and filled with high weeds, some old tires and an assortment of debris, but I glide easily over it. I'm standing at the fence. Can I climb it? It's about ten feet high and has sharp protruding wires at the top. Now what am I going to do? I stand there for a moment and try to gather my thoughts. Am I going to be defeated by a chain-link fence? I've traveled billions of miles and a common wire fence is going to defeat me! I hear the traffic on Western Avenue. It sounds clear and sharp. A white van speeds by going south. Then a bright blue bus lumbers by heading north. I hear a train whistle behind me on the tracks just a few blocks west of Western Avenue.

There's nothing I can do but try to climb the fence. Still holding my recorder, I put my hand on the fence, but it spreads apart. I sense an energy, probably dark energy, that repels the regular matter -- the visible matter.

I put both hands on the fence and easily spread it apart. I walk through it and on to the sidewalk. I see the front door to Brian's. I quickly move toward it.

I don't know if I am early or too late. Have I left with Bonnie already? Then I see my car still parked in front of Brian's. That's good. I'm not too late.

Then I see someone leaving. Is it me? It doesn't look like it. I don't see Bonnie. It's someone heavier and walking slow and a little unsteady. I walk closer to the door to see who it is. It's Larry O'Doul. He's wobbling but walking with a swagger. He stops for a moment and lights a cigarette. Then he slowly starts to walk south toward me taking a big drag on his cigarette. He blows smoke up into the air. He's about thirty feet from the door walking past me.

Then I see them. It's Bonnie and me starting to come through the door. I quickly glide toward them just by willing it. I stop at the patch of ice Bonnie is going to slip on. I wait for them to approach me.

Then I have an idea. I'm going to make Larry O'Doul slip and fall. Why should I make Bonnie and me fall? We could hurt ourselves. Many people have had serious brain injuries slipping and falling on an icy sidewalk. What a great idea. I love it. This will be payback for what O'Doul was going to do to Owen and will cause a delay that will prevent my car accident with his cousin. I know that I will go help O'Doul if he falls. I wouldn't ignore something like that. He hasn't attacked Owen yet; but in another time loop he does, so it feels right to me to make him the fall guy -- the fall guy -- that's good!

I turn and run directly at O'Doul and throw myself into his back. The change in gravity makes him fall forward and hit his head on the sidewalk -- a full face plant! He doesn't move. He's out cold. Not a twitch or a groan. A pool of blood quickly forms on the sidewalk under his head. I can see that he's still breathing, though. I feel glad that I didn't kill him. Served him right, though, for what he was going to do to Owen and has done to many other people.

I see Bonnie and me walking along holding hands. They see O'Doul fall. Bonnie slips, and I catch her and hold her up. They walk slowly and carefully to O'Doul and look down at him. "Is he OK?" Bonnie asks.

"I don't think so," I say. "We're going to have to call 911. He looks like he seriously injured himself. He's unconscious, that's for sure. He looks familiar, but I can't recall his name. I need to call 911 immediately."

I pull out my cell phone and call 911.

Hearing this, I know my mission is complete. This should change what was going to happen. It's going to cause a long delay that will prevent my accident. It'll take at least ten minutes for the ambulance to arrive, and I'm sure Will and Bonnie will wait for it.

I know I have just a minute or two to travel back to the Steed and throw my recorder into it before space-time is changed. I will myself to return to the Steed, and I quickly glide back to it. I throw the recorder into it and hope my story will survive just as I feel myself fading. Before is a whirlwind... of nothing...

Chapter 28

Missing Person

You probably thought that was the end of this story, but it isn't. There's more to it. This is Owen writing, again. I'm going to finish it for my father. As I mentioned earlier, I have Dad's recorder, and it explains a lot. I've spent a significant amount of time investigating what happened to Dad, and I think I'm ready to lay it all out. It took awhile to fit all of the pieces together, but I think I have a good understanding of what happened, even though some of the facts are still a little fuzzy.

I'm going to start with the day Dad went missing. Mom called me about seven o'clock in the evening on that day. It was August 10 -- another date I'll never forget. She was in a panic and said she couldn't find Dad. It seemed to me that she was more angry than worried. I knew that she and Dad weren't talking and that she had not forgiven him for all of the problems that the accident had caused them.

She said that she hadn't seen Dad since he left for his deposition in the Loop the previous morning. They hadn't spoken, but Mom knew what he was doing. She had seen some of the legal papers on his desk and knew his deposition had been scheduled for that morning. He had also made a notation about the deposition on the calendar they keep in the kitchen with all of their appointments and events. After the deposition, when Dad had returned, they hadn't spoken. He went to his basement office and never made any effort to talk to her about the deposition.

The next day, Mom had an appointment in the morning with her hairdresser, and Dad was gone when she returned. She looked for him but couldn't find him. The house was unlocked and his keys, cell phone and wallet were still on the hall table where he always left them. It would have been unusual for him to leave the house without his cell phone. The car was still in the garage and nothing seemed to be missing or out of place. She wanted to talk to him about the deposition and was angry that he wasn't around. She thought he might have gone for a walk to avoid seeing her.

She busied herself with some housework but kept an eye out for him. She even walked around their block twice in hopes that she might see him. She called one of his retired friends that he liked to walk with sometimes, but he hadn't seen Dad and hadn't heard from him for about a week.

Finally, by six in the evening, she began to worry that something had happened to him. She feared that he had gone for a walk and had fallen or gotten lost. As she described it, Dad had experienced some "funny spells" in the last few weeks. She found him asleep in the car one day and had a hard time waking him. He was constantly misplacing his keys and locked himself out of the house twice in the last month. She also knew that he wasn't eating regularly. In the past, he would never skip breakfast, but lately he did.

Worst of all, she heard him talking to himself in the basement a few times. She thought he might be talking on the phone, but, when she checked, he wasn't. She couldn't tell what he was saying, but she assumed he was practicing for his deposition. When he was working, he would frequently practice his presentations in the basement. She assumed that's what he was doing.

She called two more of his friends in hopes that he might be with them. No one had seen or talked to Dad in a few days and had no suggestions for Mom. As much as she hated to, she even called Brian's Tap. She thought that Dad might have walked there, even though it was over a mile from our house.

Finally, in desperation, Mom called me. I was still at work and needed to call a client in a few minutes. It was a very important call and meant a lot to my business. I hadn't talked to Dad in over a week and had no idea what might have happened to him. I agreed with Mom that Dad had been acting a little funny recently and had to bite my tongue and not criticize her for not helping him. I knew he was worried about the deposition and had lost some sleep thinking about what had happened and all of the legal ramifications. She made things worse by being so critical.

I have to confess that I was annoyed and frustrated having to deal with this problem. I had a very important phone call to make, and my parents problems were upsetting me and distracting me from my business. Why was it my problem to resolve their conflicts? They were adults and should be able to handle it. My mother, as usual, overreacted and had, at times, the emotional maturity of a fourteen-year old. My father, likewise, didn't face up to the obvious problems. He should have handled my mother, helped her to cope and kept her on an even keel. He was too easy-going at times and let things slide. He was afraid to confront her and say what needed to be said. I was annoyed.

I can't remember exactly what I said, but I think I told Mom to wait a few more hours and then call me. At about nine o'clock she called me again and was crying. I told her I would come over as soon as I said goodnight to Charlie and Molly.

About ten o'clock in the evening, I arrived at Mom's house. She met me at the door in tears. She had just found the note Dad had left in his basement office, and she handed it to me. It was vague but hinted at suicide. My stomach flipped, and I felt weak and disoriented for a moment.

I felt sorry for her and Dad, but I didn't know what to do. After I calmed her down, we sat in the living room and talked. She went over everything in great detail. I listened as patiently as I could. After hearing the whole story at least twice and some parts several times, I told Mom I didn't know what to do. I told her there was nothing to do but call the police. That upset her greatly and made her cry even more. She begged me not to call the police. She felt certain that it was not a suicide note and that Dad would never even contemplate such a thing. She told me how, many years ago after I went off to college, she and Dad had had a terrible fight, and he had stayed in a hotel in the Loop for two nights before he came home and they made up. She thought that that is what he might have done this time. Finally, after about an hour, I told her that I had to go home. The next day was going to be busy for me, and I needed my sleep. If she didn't want me to call the police, there was nothing else I could do.

I told her I would be able to call her at about ten-thirty the next day, and we would re-evaluate everything then. If necessary, I would go all over the neighborhood and talk to all of the people and businesses with which my father usually had some contact. If we hadn't heard from him by three or four in the afternoon, we would call the police. I went home and had a miserable night's sleep. I had so much on my mind. I was nervous and feeling guilty that I couldn't do more.

What helped me from panicking most was my confidence in my father. I knew he could handle almost any problem that came his way. He was the most competent person I knew. Before the accident, he was always calm and rational and in control. I knew he was OK. I knew there was a good reason for his absence. I just knew it. I believed in him.

Writing that last paragraph made all of the feelings I experienced that night come flooding back to me, and, I must admit, rattled me to the core.

Continuing on: the next day, after my conference call -- which, fortunately, went well and helped me calm down and focus on Mom's worries and my Dad's disappearance -- I called Mom. She seemed more under control and resigned to a bad situation. She hadn't heard from Dad and now felt that something awful had happened. She had deep remorse for the way she had treated him the last few months and swore she would help him and not be so critical. I thought to myself: this was too little too late, but I didn't say that.

I told her I would drive around the neighborhood and talk to everyone I could who might know something about Dad. I went to the Arts Center, Brian's, two other bars Dad occasionally frequented and our Parish Church. No one had seen my father in several days. I didn't tell them much and tried to play down my concern. They all promised to call me if they saw my father.

At about three o'clock I returned home and talked to Mom. She was depressed and quiet. My father's absence was devastating to her. No matter how bad their arguments and fights had been in the past, he never left her. Except for the one time when I was in college, he never stormed out and went missing for any period of time. He always waited for her to calm down, and then they worked things out. It had happened hundreds of times in their marriage, but they always had the will to reconcile. It was part of their culture and upbringing and was integral to their relationship.

I told her we had to call the police. She quietly agreed, shaking her head slowly and rubbing her hands together. From that point on she withdrew even more into herself and showed little emotion.

I immediately called our police station, the Morgan Park Police Precinct, and reported my father missing. Detective Jack Robinson, who had been in charge of the accident after it first happened, was sent to our house. He arrived in less than an hour and took a full report from me and Mom. He was a tall, heavy black man, very brusque and aloof, probably in his late fifties. He exhibited no empathy, and made no effort to comfort or sympathize with us. He was, no doubt, sick of this case and tired of all of the political interference. In his defense, he probably had to deal with bad people and ugly situations all day long, every day. That would make you hardened and unsympathetic.

Since he was familiar with the case, he knew what questions to ask. I suspected that my father's case was given priority in our precinct, and Detective Robinson was assigned for that reason.

He told us not to worry because most missing people show up in less than 48 hours. Since Dad had been missing for a couple of days already, he said that all of the squads in our area would be alerted and on the lookout for Dad. He would file a missing person's report as soon as he returned to the station.

Chapter 29

Giving Up Hope

Week after week passed without a clue as to what happened to Dad. He seemed to have fallen off of the face of the earth. No one had seen him since the day he vanished. Mom was a wreck and felt guilty about not supporting him and encouraging him. I felt guilty that I hadn't done more.

Mom became more and more depressed and withdrawn. Her younger sister, Laurie, moved in with her and cared for her. She was seven years younger than Mom, but they had similar looks and there was no doubt they were sisters. Laurie, however, smiled all of the time and had a great attitude. She was a saint! Laurie had never married and lived a simple life. She was a school teacher and traveled and lived very independently. She loved to ski and snorkel and had a network of friends all over the world.

I loved Laurie and treasured the times she babysat for me and took me on some of her adventures. When I was in college, she took me to Ft. Myers Beach for ten days for spring break. Unbeknownst to Mom and Dad, two of my friends joined us in a two-bedroom condominium that Laurie had rented on the beach. She let us drink and smoke some weed but always kept us under control and knew what we were doing. We loved and craved her approval so much that we didn't want to violate her trust. She was the perfect aunt. Everyone in the family loved her and wanted her attention. Even Mom loved her -- despite the fact that they were almost opposite personalities.

But even Aunt Laurie couldn't bring Mom out of her funk. Mom didn't talk much and withdrew totally into herself. About two months after Aunt Laurie moved in, Mom had a stroke. She hadn't been eating properly or sleeping well. She was nervous all of the time and had hallucinations about seeing Dad. She told us that she had talked to him, and he was on an important mission for the government and would be gone for several more months.

After returning from the grocery store one day, Aunt Laurie found Mom on the floor in their family room. She had fallen and hit her cheek on the edge of a coffee table. She was bleeding profusely and needed several stitches. She was breathing normally but was unresponsive.

Aunt Laurie called 911, and the paramedics arrived in less than ten minutes. They took her to the emergency room at Christ Hospital in Oak Lawn where she was admitted and stayed for about ten days. Then she went to a nursing home in our neighborhood for rehab. It's a beautiful place, only a few years old. Many people from our neighborhood end up there, and they have a good time and thoroughly enjoy it. She made a little progress at first but wouldn't cooperate with the rehab staff. She wouldn't try to walk, either, and had great difficulty speaking. I went to visit her three times a week and brought Charlie and Molly to see her almost every Saturday afternoon. She smiled at them but never asked them any questions.

I listed my parents' house for sale. Surprisingly, Mom agreed to sell it since she has no desire to return to an empty house that would bring back bad memories. I received one low-ball offer that I immediately rejected. I was in no rush as, in the back of my mind, I still had hopes that Dad would return.

Detective Robinson never contacted me and didn't seem too interested in the case. A missing person's file was opened, but there was little the police could do. I called Detective Robinson about six weeks after Dad disappeared, but he showed little interest in helping me. I asked him if Dad was going to be charged with manslaughter, and he didn't know. He said it was unlikely, but he couldn't comment. He suggested I call the State's Attorney's Office.

About a week later I talked to Dad's personal attorney, Tom Sumner, and he said that the State's Attorney was not going to file charges. He also told me that Dad's insurance company was close to a settlement of the suits against Dad. The settlements were all well within the limits of Dad's insurance policies, and there would be no excess liability.

The key factor that changed the complexion of the case was that the insurance company's attorney was able to obtain the traffic videos at the intersection where the accident occurred. They clearly showed that Dad had a green light, and Ms. McCarthy caused the accident by making a left turn in front of Dad. Since the videos also showed that Dad had not tried to stop before the collision, and because of the alcohol issues, the insurance company was willing to settle for a significant amount. Ms. McCarthy's estate still had a good suit against the automobile manufacturer and the airbag company, so I didn't feel too badly. And, since Ms. Talbotstoya had a good case against Ms. McCarthy, everyone would be compensated, although I'm sure their families would have preferred that the accident had never happened. Money helps but can't relieve the loss of a loved one.

....

One Saturday morning in early December when I was working at Mom's house trying to clean out a few things and organize her bills and files, I decided to go get some coffee. It was depressing looking through all of Dad's things, and I needed a break. I walked up to the Java Hut, a coffee shop on 95th Street not too far from Mom and Dad's house. I loved their coffee and pastries. Betty James greeted me when I walked in the door. She knew me well since I had gone to school with one of her sons, Jesse. (Yes, that's his name -- how could someone do that to a kid!) She waved at me and said, "Hi, Owen. How's your family doing? Haven't seen you in awhile."

"Everyone's great, Mrs. James," I said. "Charlie and Molly are doing well in school and growing like weeds. How's Jesse doing? I haven't seen him since he moved to the North Side a year ago."

"He's doing great, Owen. He has a new girlfriend. She might be the one. He's really smitten, but that's happened before. I keep telling him that he can't come to see me anymore until he brings me a grandchild, but he won't listen. Oh well. How are your mom and dad?"

My stomach did a flip when I heard her say that. I thought everyone knew but apparently not. Mrs. James was a widow and worked constantly, probably ten hours every day except Sunday when she was closed. Being so busy, she probably didn't keep up on the neighborhood gossip, even though many people in the area frequented her shop. Perhaps, she was just too busy to care about gossip.

"I'm sorry to say, Mrs. James, that my mother and father are not doing well." I then told her briefly what had happened to them. She was shocked and felt bad that she didn't know about it. She apologized profusely and said she was sorry to hear about what happened and that she would keep them in her prayers. That's what everyone in our neighborhood says when someone is sick or has a problem. It's a nice thing to say.

Then she stopped, slowly wiped her hands with a towel and walked over to the counter where I was standing. "How long ago did you say your father disappeared?" she asked. I told her that it had been almost four months, now. She thought for a moment and then said, "I remember your father being in here about four months ago. He was talking to a man everyone calls "the Perfessor." They sat at that table by the window and had a cup of coffee and a pastry and talked for a few minutes. I remember because I thought it was nice of your father to buy him some coffee and something to eat. The Perfessor doesn't talk much and it struck me as unusual."

"Who's the Professor?" I said. "Does he live in the neighborhood? I've never heard of him."

"Oh, all of the business owners on 95th Street know the Perfessor. It's "Perfessor," not "Professor." Pete at the 95th Car Doctor gave him that name years ago. He thought he looked like a college professor with his tweed coat and pipe. He comes around almost every Tuesday and Friday and washes our store windows. He's been doing that for ten years or so. I'm not sure where he lives, but I don't think it's in our area. I've seen him taking the train a few times, probably going north. I have a suspicion that he's homeless, but I'm not sure."

My heart was beating quickly and I felt a rush of adrenaline. This was the most promising lead I'd had yet about Dad's disappearance. Maybe he'd told this Perfessor person something that might help us find him. Maybe the Perfessor had something to do with his disappearance.

"Why's he called "the Perfessor," I asked. "Is he a teacher?"

Mrs. James chuckled and said, "For one thing, he always wears a tweed jacket and occasionally smokes a pipe which makes him look like a college professor. Also, there's a rumor that he taught at IIT at one time. I asked him about that one day and never got a straight answer. He had something to do with IIT, though, but I'm not sure what."

"He had a nervous break down about fifteen years ago when his wife left him. He became a wino and lost his job. As I said, he's probably homeless. He has a helper sometimes who doesn't talk much and has some type of mental disorder. He might be autistic or compulsive, I'm not sure. The Perfessor takes good care of him and treats him like his son. Everybody loves the Perfessor and pays him to wash their windows even when it's not necessary. The owner of the health food store gives him day-old bread and other surplus or out of date food items. He thinks the Perfessor takes care of other homeless people somewhere. He refers to them as his "team." He's kind of a mystery, though."

"When was the last time you saw him?" I asked. "Does he still come around?"

"Oh, yea. He'll probably be here next Tuesday. He normally shows up at about nine o'clock, if it's not too rainy or cold. This is usually his first stop. I give him a cup of coffee which he loads up with cream and sugar. It's probably his breakfast.

He has a bucket and brush and a towel and a squeegee hidden somewhere that he uses to clean windows. I'm not sure where he keeps those things.

"Do you have any idea how I could get in touch with him? I'd like to talk to him as soon as possible!"

Mrs. James looked at me with great sympathy and said, "No, sorry, Owen. I wish I could help you. You'll just have to wait until Tuesday when he should be here."

I was disappointed and didn't know how I could wait until next Tuesday to talk to the Perfessor.

"You might try talking to Omar, the manager of the health food store. He might have some info for you."

"That's a great idea," I said. "Thanks for your help, Mrs. James, and say hi to Jesse for me the next time you see him." I practically ran out of the Java Hut and walked as quickly as I could two blocks west to the health food store. Many thoughts were coursing through my brain as I made the short walk. I was so distracted I almost walked in front of a bus as I crossed the street. Much to my dismay, though, Omar knew nothing about how I might contact the Perfessor.

I didn't tell Mom or anyone else about what Mrs. James had told me. I didn't want anyone else to have unreasonable expectations. I especially didn't want Mom and my kids to get their hopes up. They were finally beginning to accept the fact that Dad was not coming back, and I didn't want to make them go through that whole process again. They had suffered enough.

Chapter 30

Catching a Break

Sunday and Monday passed excruciatingly slowly. I was constantly thinking about Dad and wondering if the Perfessor might be able to help me find him. Should I contact Detective Robinson? Should I call Dad's attorney, Tom Sumner? Many scenarios passed through my mind. I decided to handle the Perfessor myself. I didn't want to complicate the situation or scare off the Perfessor.

On Monday, I cleared my calendar for Tuesday. Two meetings and a conference call had to be rescheduled. This kept me busy and helped the time pass more quickly. I checked the weather several times. It looked as though it would be fairly warm and not raining or snowing. So far we had been having a warmer than normal winter with little snow.

Tuesday morning I woke up at five AM and couldn't get back to sleep. I lay there thinking about what I would say to the Perfessor, if I found him. I prayed the temperature would be warm enough for him to show up. I showered and dressed and tried to kill some time until I could go to the Java Hut and wait for the Perfessor. My wife Patty asked me why I was up so early. I told her I had an early meeting in the Loop and was going to grab something at the Java Hut on my way to the train. She had to take the kids to school at eight and then was going to drive to Oak Brook to shop for some Christmas presents. This was fortuitous. I thought about telling her about the Perfessor, but I changed my mind realizing it would be best to keep this a secret for the time being.

At 8:30, I walked up to the Java Hut. The temperature was only thirty-eight degrees which made me shiver and feel nervous. Would he show up? I considered trying to look for the Perfessor at the train station, but then I thought it would be safest to wait for him at the Java Hut. Remembering that Betty said he always came there first, I thought I shouldn't take a chance of missing him.

I bought some coffee and an apple turnover but couldn't eat much. Mrs. James was busy and just waved to me. She probably didn't remember why I was there. Some people I know from the neighborhood came in and bought some coffee. I didn't feel like trying to make small talk with them and hoped they wouldn't come to my table and talk to me. I kept my head down and checked emails on my phone. Luckily they were all in a hurry to make a train and didn't linger long.

Nine o'clock came and went. No Perfessor. At nine-thirty, I feared the worse and was thinking about walking up and down 95th Street to see if I could find him. Maybe, I thought, he decided not to come to the Java Hut first. Just then I heard the door open and an older black man walked in. I knew immediately that he was the Perfessor. He had on a long, well-worn dark overcoat with the collar turned up. I could see that it covered up a brown tweed jacket. The overcoat was mostly opened in front, being held closed by only one button in the middle. He wore a gray knit hat pulled over his ears, dark baggy pants and old, beat-up work boots. This had to be him.

In a deep, cultured voice, he said hello to Betty, and she waved at him. He asked if she wanted her windows washed today, and she said, "No, but maybe Friday." The Perfessor looked disappointed but didn't say anything. He just stood and looked at the pastries.

I jumped up and walked over to him. "Could I buy you some coffee and a pastry," I quickly said. He looked surprised and acted a little hesitant. I may have startled him. My voice was louder than I wanted it to be, but I was so excited I couldn't control it.

"Well, yes, yes, I guess so," he said looking down very timidly. "Sure, that would be great."

I asked Betty to fill his order, paid her and then waited nervously as she took her time preparing the order. Then the Perfessor slowly went to the prep table and added some cream and several teaspoons of sugar. When he finally came to my table and sat down, I was about ready to burst, even though I knew I had to stay calm and not scare the Perfessor off.

"Thanks," he said. "This is very nice of you to treat me to some coffee and a pastry. To what do I owe this honor?"

I wasn't sure how to start, but I decided to ask him directly if he had met my father here in the Java Hut on August 10. I told him that Betty had told me that she remembered seeing my father having coffee with him and described my father and told him that he had been missing from that date and that we had no clue as to what had happened to him. I let him know how desperate my family was to discover what had happened to my father. As I told him about my mother and what had happened to her I lost it. I choked up and couldn't talk. It took me a couple of minutes to compose myself.

As I tried to regain my composure, the Perfessor looked nervous to me and didn't make eye contact. He squirmed in his chair and sipped on his coffee. His body language led me to believe he knew something about my Dad. I had the feeling, though, that he wasn't a bad person and wasn't violent or a psychopath. I believe in first impressions and trust them. I hoped that, if I just didn't push him, he would tell me what he knew.

"What did you say your father's name is?" the Perfessor said, still not looking directly at me. I thought that I had told him, but I patiently said, "Will O'Brien, and I'm his son, Owen."

The Perfessor said, now looking me in the eye, "I think I can help you, Owen, but we have to have an understanding. What you have told me explains a lot, and should help me solve a problem I've been struggling with for nearly four months. Other peoples' lives are involved, for whom I am responsible, so I need to act cautiously. They depend on me, and I have to protect them and make sure they aren't disturbed. Can we have an understanding? I'll work with you if you work with me."

What did he mean by an "understanding?" I was tempted to call Detective Robinson immediately and have the Perfessor arrested. Something told me to wait, though, and give him a chance. He seemed sincere and harmless, and, remembering what Mrs. James had said about the Perfessor taking care of homeless people, I was willing to hear him out.

"Your father is alive and in relatively good physical health," the Perfessor continued. "He's on a journey, of sorts, and I can help you bring him back. You can help him and the team assisting him, but it will cost you a little. I'll be reasonable and make this as simple and easy as possible. I'm not doing this for myself, so please don't be offended. The lives and happiness of several other people are at stake."

I thought: is this a ransom demand? What is the Perfessor alluding to? Should I call the police or wait and see?

The Perfessor straightened up and seemed to take on a different attitude. He ate his apple turnover and then drank his coffee in two draws. I patiently waited for him to reveal more about my father.

After wiping his mouth with his napkin, he looked at me and said, "I know you're anxious about your father; but, before I do anything else, I have to wash the windows at the health food store. I promised the manager there that I would do them first thing this morning. I'm sorry I have to make you wait, but the health food store is my best customer, and I can't let them down. It will only take about an hour. What time is it now?" he asked.

I looked at my watch. It was nine-thirty. I told the Perfessor, and he said, "Do you have a car available?" I said I did, and he asked me to pick him up at eleven at the health food store. He said he would then reveal everything about my father. He warned me not to talk to anyone, especially the police. It bothered me that he dragged this out and kept me wondering -- perhaps he was trying to milk this to his advantage. How much was this going to cost me? It didn't matter.

I was so nervous and confused about what to do that I could hardly think. Was the Perfessor going to ask for a ransom? I started to think about how much cash I could quickly raise, if necessary. I had about fifteen thousand dollars in a savings account at a local bank which I could withdraw, if necessary. I had about five thousand in my checking account. It would be difficult to raise more cash than that.

Nevertheless, I felt that it was best to cooperate with the Perfessor and see where this led. After all, he was elderly and a window washer that Mrs. James and other merchants on 95th Street seemed to like and had known for a long time -- how dangerous could he be? He just didn't seem threatening. "OK," I said, "I'll pick you up at eleven and won't talk to anyone about this.

Chapter 31

Getting Closer

As you can imagine, the time crept by as I waited to pick up the Perfessor at the health food store. I went back to Mom and Dad's house and tried to determine what to do with all of their stuff. There was so much to deal with.

Mom had china, silver, crystal, knickknacks, artwork, picture albums, ceramics, Christmas decorations, etc. etc. She had hundreds of beautiful things that she had collected and inherited from her mother and grandmother. Several cabinets and bookshelves held hundreds of precious objects that meant so much to her and might, someday, be meaningful to Charlie and Molly. Would they want them, though? I know my wife, Patty, wouldn't. She appreciates such things, but she has her own favorite objects and many others from her mother and grandparents. We have such an abundance of wealth today that we don't know what to do with it.

Additionally, Mom and Dad's attic and basement held close to fifty boxes of important things from their life. I was overwhelmed and didn't know what to do. Once I got wrapped up in these thoughts, though, the time flew by. Before I knew it, it was time to pick up the Perfessor.

I drove to the health food store where I saw him waiting for me on the curb. Holding his bucket, brush and squeegee, he waved to me as I pulled up. He put his equipment in the backseat and then sat down next to me in the front seat. He smelled musty and dirty but not too bad.

"Where to?" I said, not wanting to pressure him and make him feel uncomfortable.

"There's a Jewel Food Store at 95th and Ashland," he said. "That will be our first stop. I need you to buy some things for my team. It won't be much, maybe a couple of hundred dollars, at most. Can you handle that?" he said. I said, "Yes, of course," and felt a little relieved at this modest request, but I was worried this was just a head fake before the big play.

We went to the Jewel Food Store and bought two carts of food items, mostly nonperishable items like cereal and cans of beans, chili, vegetables, and fruits. We bought bread, food bars of every type, powdered milk, lunch meats, and lots of cookies, chips, peanuts and snacks. We also went through the liquor section and grabbed four boxes of red wine. When we finally checked out, my bill was over three hundred and fifty dollars.

We then loaded everything into my car. Luckily I have a large SUV that could hold everything. When we were finished loading and the Perfessor sat next to me in the front seat, he looked at me, smiled and said, "Thanks, Owen, this is going to help some good people continue with a difficult journey."

I wasn't sure what he meant by that, but I felt good, even though I was under duress.

Pointing to the east, the Perfessor said, "Go over to the Dan Ryan and head north. Stay in the local lanes. I'll give you further directions at the appropriate time."

In silence, we drove east to the Dan Ryan and proceeded in a northerly direction. At 55th he said, "Get off at Pershing Road and then I'll give you more directions."

When we reached the Pershing Road exit ramp, I turned onto it and then turned right at the top of the ramp onto Pershing and drove east. The Perfessor immediately told me to turn left on Dearborn, the first street, and head north. I noticed an abandoned school building to the right of us. The Perfessor told me to turn into a drive at the north end of the school. I did, and we pulled up to the back of the abandoned school. The Perfessor told me to get as close as possible to a service door at the rear of the school.

I was a little hesitant and nervous about parking there. This was a pretty iffy neighborhood, although there was a park to the north and the train tracks were to the west. There weren't any homes or apartments around us, but I knew the area to our east along State Street was a high-crime area and gang controlled.

The Perfessor said, "Wait here in the car for me. You'll be OK. This building and the surroundings are mostly vacant or abandoned, so the gangs don't bother us. I'm going to go into the school and round up a few people to help us unload the car." The Perfessor got out of the car and entered the building through what looked like a service door for the maintenance people.

I did as the Perfessor said and waited in the car. As I sat there, I thought: "Was my father in this abandoned building? Was I going to see him soon? Why would he be here? Was he kidnapped? What would I do if that were the case? What if he wasn't here? Did the Perfessor just take advantage of me to get some food for his "team?" I took my cell phone out and got ready to dial 911.

In a few minutes, the Perfessor and two young men and one small boy, maybe nine years old, came out of the service door. They unloaded all of the bags of groceries from the back of my car and carried them into the building. The Perfessor told me to get out of the car, lock it and then follow him.

I followed the Perfessor through the service door and into a dark, smelly space that was filled with litter, bicycles, boxes, and empty wine and soft drink bottles. There was even a small, cute pug dog roaming around and sniffing at everything. He had a very happy looking face, was calm and friendly and appeared to be well cared for.

After my eyes started to adjust, I realized we were in a small gymnasium. There were a few long narrow windows near the ceiling that slightly illuminated the space. There was just enough light to allow me to see some large boxes, a tent, and graffiti on almost every surface (most of it quite artistic) and lots of trash. It smelled bad but not overwhelming.

The Perfessor turned and stood in front of me, quite close. He spoke to me in a soft voice, almost a whisper, "Listen carefully to me, Owen." Pointing to a large cardboard box about the size of a sofa, he said, "Your father is over there in that large furniture box. He's been living in that box since he followed me here in August. He moves around, from time to time, and he seems happy and content to be here. He rambles on about many things -- he calls this place Earthtoo. We've been supporting him and trying to make him feel comfortable, but he's getting so thin and weak that we knew we had to take some action soon to get him some help. I was about to do that before I met you."

"There's a lot I need to explain to you, but, for now, suffice it to say, I didn't know who he was. Nevertheless, I felt compelled to care for him. Its complicated. I had some ulterior motives, but I'm responsible for about ten people living here. I call them my team. I need to protect them from many bad things that could happen to them. They all have various types of special need which puts them at a disadvantage in the world. This place is safe and home to them. You might say it's a commune because we share everything and take care of each other."

"We need to take it slow and easy and not scare your father. He's living in his own world and imagining extraordinary things. I try to talk to him, but he babbles on about strange situations, of which I have no comprehension. Lately, he's been talking about a decision he needs to make about staying here or going somewhere to fix the past. I'm not sure what he's talking about, but he's fixated on it and seems to be reaching a breaking point. I listen to him and try to comfort him. We talk about fishing and science, but he seems to be spiraling down. He has fallen several times, so we put a bicycle helmet on him to protect his head. He likes it and says it gives him special powers."

I wanted to run to my father and hug him and talk to him and let him know that everything will be all right. The Perfessor led me over and called to my father. I had to use all of my self control to walk slowly to the box he was in and carefully peer in and look at him. One side of the box was down on the floor and I could see him lying in it. "Will. Will." the Perfessor said. "Your son, Owen, is here. He's going to help you decide what to do. He'll help you."

My father, with a puzzled expression on his face, looked out of the box at the Perfessor and said, "What did you say, Magis? Who's here?"

The Professor looked at me and said, "He calls me Magis, and other names, sometimes. It's part of his delusion.

"Owen, your son, is here." the Perfessor said.

"How did Owen get here? Did the AASUSE Team send him to Earthtoo? I don't understand."

"Yes, Will," the Perfessor said. "The team sent Owen here to help you. He's going to help you decide what to do."

With that said I bent down in front of my father and looked at him propped up on a filthy old futon in a large cardboard box. His hair and beard were long and messy. He was wearing a blue bicycle helmet and long dirty hair was sticking out of the sides. He smelled terrible and looked extremely thin and pale. I would not have recognized him if the Perfessor hadn't told me who he was. I was shocked but didn't want to show it.

"Dad," I said. "It's me, Owen, I've come to help you. I'm going to take you home. You're going to be OK. Do you recognize me? Do you know who I am?"

"These Acme!" Dad said. "They're so clever. They can read my mind. They amaze me with their great mental powers. You look just like my son Owen. They're amazing. You've come to help me. OK, I need your help, Owen. Help me decide what to do. Am I still in the Steed? I've been changed to sustaining matter. Should I stay or return to Earthtoo? I think I've changed things so the accident didn't happen. I'm not sure. Things are getting so confusing. What should I do? I want you to read my journal."

"I'm going to take you home, Dad. The lawsuits are over. Ms. McCarthy's estate has settled for a million dollars, and Ms. Tolbotstoya's mother and her trustee have agreed to settle for half a million. Your insurance company was glad to settle for those amounts. I've talked to Mr. Sumner and Mr. Kogland, and they said you're in the clear and have nothing to worry about. Your deposition and the traffic videos convinced the plaintiffs to settle all cases against you. They still have good cases against other parties, so you don't need to worry."

He looked at me with a blank expression, then a slight smile. I continued, "You don't have to worry about the criminal charges, either. The State's Attorney said he wouldn't bring charges against you. You and Mom are going to be OK. You have nothing to worry about, now. I'm taking you home. Are you ready to go home, Dad?" I knew I shouldn't tell him about mom, yet, so I let that go.

Dad looked at me with the most confused gaze I had ever seen on his face. It was heartbreaking. He was always so confident and sure of himself. He was always in control and knew what to say or do. I didn't know what to do. I wanted to grab him and pull him out of that horrible box. I wanted to rush him out of that derelict building and take him to a hospital.

"OK, Owen," he said. "I'm ready to go. Magis -- Professor, is it OK if I leave?" The Perfessor nodded at him. He continued: "Give my thanks to the AASUSE Team. They did a great job. Roxy will not be a problem, and Earthtoo is a potential home for Earth, someday, if we ever need it. When I complete my journal in a few days, I'll send you a copy, and you can share with the AASUSE Team all of the info I gathered." He stopped and took a few breaths. He seemed so weak. Then he continued: "They're going to love it and learn so much from it. As soon as I get my strength back, I'll return and de-brief everyone."

The Perfessor and I helped Dad get out of his box. He was holding his recorder. I took it and put it in my pocket. I removed the bicycle helmet and dropped it on the floor. The Perfessor grabbed Dad's backpack and called for someone, I think he said "Victor," to come help us. Victor and I got on each side of Dad and slowly walked him to my car. We put him in the passenger side, and the Perfessor threw his backpack on the back seat.

After we strapped Dad in, The Perfessor grabbed my arm and said to me in a desperate voice: "Owen, please don't report us to the police. There are ten people here who need me. This is their home. It's the only home some of them have known. If we're thrown out of here, it would be a disaster. It might kill some of them. Can I trust you?"

I didn't want to commit to anything at that time. I wasn't sure what had happened, and I didn't want to commit to letting a dangerous situation continue. Who were these people? Was the Perfessor helping them or did he have some other bad motive? I didn't say anything to him.

The Perfessor then said, "I'll meet you at the Java Hut at nine o'clock on Thursday and explain everything. I'm not going anywhere, and you can make a decision later as to what to do about this place. Please, Owen, we did the best we could for your father. Don't do anything rash. There's a lot at stake."

"OK," I said. "I won't do anything until I talk to you on Thursday."

With that, I climbed into my car and drove Dad to Christ Hospital in Oak Lawn. It took about forty-five minutes to drive to the hospital, and Dad passed out and was unable to talk to me the entire trip.

Everything was still a mystery to me. What had happened to Dad? I would just have to wait until he was able to talk or until I could get more information from the Perfessor on Thursday. I had some misgivings about him, yet I knew he was going to show up Thursday and tell me the whole story.

I drove Dad to the emergency room at Christ Hospital where he was admitted immediately and moved to the intensive care unit. Our family doctor, Jim Kerrigan, was called, and he came to the hospital in less than an hour and examined Dad. The emergency room doctor, a really nice lady named Joan, told me that Dad would have died within a few days if he hadn't been admitted. He was dehydrated and near death from starvation. His vital signs were all in the danger zone, and he was mentally unresponsive.

One of the first things they did was draw blood and perform a full lab workup. His blood chemistry was all out of whack. The test results also showed that he had traces of fentanyl and benzodiazepines in his blood. That bothered me and made me want to confront the Perfessor about that. How did Dad get those drugs?

After Dr. Kerrigan examined Dad, I was able to talk to him for a few minutes. I asked him what had happened to Dad and gave him some background information about what led up to his disappearance. Had he become a drug addict? Did he have a nervous breakdown of some type? What would explain his behavior? Even though I remembered a few things about stress-related mental health problems from my psychology classes in college, I knew this was not the time to play amateur psychologist. When it comes to a close relative, you want to hear from an expert.

Dr. Kerrigan said he needed to do a few more tests before he could answer my questions and make a diagnosis. He explained that there could be several explanations for Dad's condition. He might have had a stroke. An anxiety attack, amnesia or maybe even PTSD might have caused his condition. It could be a combination of several stress related afflictions. He would consult with a specialist and get back to me in a few days. Whatever the diagnosis, Dad would probably be in the hospital for at least a week and then would have to go into a rehab facility for at least a month.

Chapter 32

Revealed

The remainder of Tuesday and all day Wednesday, I was so busy that I didn't have time to think about my meeting with the Perfessor on Thursday. I stayed with my Dad late into Tuesday night. Patty was understanding and told me to do whatever I needed to take care of my father.

I was back at the hospital on Wednesday morning. Dad was hooked up to IVs and a feeding tube. He was unconscious but seemed to be breathing normally. The nurse said his vital signs were improving. She said Dr. Kerrigan had examined him early that morning, was happy with Dad's progress, and would call me later.

I called and told my administrative assistant, Rosemary, to clear my calendar and put everything off until next week. I wouldn't be able to work thinking about my father, anyway, so that was all I could do. My work could wait. My clients would understand. They all had good family values and would understand my need to take care of my father -- at least I hoped they would. As it turned out, they were all very supportive.

Wednesday afternoon Dad opened his eyes and started to talk. At first, it was all gibberish, but then he began to make sense. He looked at me and had a mystified look on his face. I waited a few moments and then said, "Hi, Dad. Welcome back. Everything is going to be OK." He smiled and then I could see he was starting to cry. A tear rolled down one of his cheeks, and he tried to wipe it with his right hand. Since his arms were both tethered to his bed to protect the IVs, he couldn't wipe the tear. I grabbed a Kleenex and wiped it for him.

He shut his eyes, again, and seemed to be gathering himself. I said, "You're in Christ Hospital, Dad.

Dr. Kerrigan is taking care of you. Everything is going to be OK. I'm going to stay with you. You'll be back on your feet in no time."

"You can tell me what happened later, Dad, but you should know that the lawsuits against you have all been settled. And, best of all, no criminal charges will be filed. There were traffic videos of the accident, and we all know it wasn't your fault. You're in the clear."

"That's great news, Owen," Dad said. "I knew the Acme would take care of everything. They're amazing people. I can't wait to tell you all about them. I'm tired, though, Owen. I need to rest a little longer." He stopped talking for a moment, took a couple of shallow breaths, and then continued: "I can't wait to talk to Deirdre and see Molly and Charlie, but I need to rest." He was mumbling and barely able to get the last few words out before he fell back asleep.

Dad slept for several hours and then roused himself. Cautiously, I began to question him about what he remembered. He was able to talk coherently and began to come back to reality. When he realized where he was, I told him all that I had pieced together so far. He was still confused and thought maybe he had been dreaming, but it seemed so real. He had vivid memories of the AASUSE Team and the Nina. The flight through outer space was clear in his mind as was waking up on Earthtoo.

Then he remembered his journal. He told me about dictating it on his recorder and panicked wondering where it was. He said something about throwing it into the Steed, whatever that was. I calmed him down by telling him that I had his recorder and his backpack. I promised to bring it to him when he was better, and we would listen to his journal together.

Needless to say, I didn't learn much from talking to my father that afternoon in the hospital. He was still confused and talking nonsense, so it seemed to me at the time.

I went home at five and had dinner with my family. They were all anxious to hear about Dad and how he was doing. I gave them a very upbeat appraisal and tried to be positive. There was no use in making them worry.

As soon as I could break away from them, I went to my office to listen to Dad's journal. It was 7:30. I had told Patty that I had some urgent work to take care of and needed to concentrate on it so I could go back to the hospital tomorrow and be with Dad. She was sympathetic to my concerns and told me not to worry. She said she would help the kids with their homework and put them to bed.

I spent the next seven hours listening to Dad's journal which I found mesmerizing. I'm glad I did, even though I was tired the next morning. What had happened to him was still confusing, but it helped me prepare for my meeting with the Perfessor.

....

I arose at seven on Thursday morning and told Patty that I had to go to my office for a few hours and then go to the hospital. I felt bad about being less than truthful with her, but I didn't want her to worry. She understood and said OK. She has been so understanding through this whole process. I'm lucky to have her. I can't help think of some mental comparisons to my mother and my father. If my mother had been just a little more understanding of my father, what would have happened? Would things have been vastly different? This type of thinking does no good, so I won't dwell on it.

Armed with the information in my father's journal, I met the Perfessor at nine at the Java Hut. He seemed tired and weak. I felt sorry for him and didn't, despite my strong feelings, attack him or press him for answers.

We had a long and detailed conversation, and I feel that I understood what happened to Dad and how the Perfessor was not to blame. With the help of two large cups of coffee, two apple turnovers and two chocolate donuts, we talked for almost two hours. I'm convinced that the Perfessor did the best he could, and I respect him for what he did and what he's committed to doing.

Briefly, here's what happened. Dad met the Perfessor at the Java Hut on the morning of August 10. The Perfessor had no idea who he was, but he was happy to let my father buy him a cup of coffee and an apple turnover. My father rambled on about a phone call from the Perfessor the night before. He explained that he was upset and depressed about a terrible personal situation that was ruining his life.

Asking the Perfessor who he was and how he could help him, the Perfessor revealed a little about himself, especially how he was caring for several homeless people and his autistic son, Victor. My Dad said he wanted to help and would go with the Perfessor to lend a hand. He said he needed something positive to do to get his mind off of his problems. The Perfessor was very reluctant to agree to that, but he thought he might obtain some financial support from Dad. He was low on money and had missed several days of work due to trouble breathing. He told my father that he would be going back to his team (that's what he called the group of homeless people he took care of) at one o'clock on the northbound Metra train at the 95th Street Station.

Dad met him there, and they boarded the train to the 35th Street Station and then met some of his "associates and team members" at the Starbucks at 35th and State. Once a week he treated some of his homeless friends to coffee at that Starbucks. It was an extravagance, but some of them were sick and this was a treat they looked forward to.

Dad thought, for some unknown reason, that they were all rocket scientists from IIT and NASA. The Perfessor had told my father on their train ride that he had been a stationary engineer in the IIT maintenance department several years before, but that he lost his job when he had a nervous break down after his wife, Roxy, left him. He became an alcoholic for awhile but righted himself so he could take care of his autistic son, Victor. My father must have latched on to the idea that the Perfessor was an engineer teaching at IIT.

The Perfessor and his friends were patient with Dad and let him ramble on, especially since he had bought all of them coffee and pastries. He called one of the men who had curly hair and a mustache, Neil and another younger man, Hakeem.

After they were finished with their coffee, the Perfessor and some of the other men walked to an abandoned grade school building at Pershing and Dearborn. I later found out that it was the former Crispus Attucks School which had been closed for about fifteen years after the Robert Taylor Homes public housing project, formerly located in that area, had been torn down.

A cousin of the Perfessor worked in the real estate section of CPS and let the Perfessor use the building for his team of homeless friends. It was being held for future development, and there were no plans to sell or demolish the property. The Perfessor and his team, with his cousin's help, had turned on the water and electricity and even had wifi in the building.

Thanks to the Perfessor and his cousin, the school became a refuge for many homeless people over the last ten years. It was a safe zone from the gangs and provided shelter and some food, from time to time, although that was very erratic. With the help of the

Perfessor's window washing earnings, his small pension and some occasional work by some of the other residents, they managed to survive.

When the Perfessor found out that my father had over five hundred dollars on him, against all of his instincts, he decided to allow Dad to stay. He wasn't going to steal the money. One of his team's most sacrosanct rules was that there was to be no stealing. He strictly enforced that rule and expelled anyone caught stealing or taking advantage of another team member. However, the team had been without food for several days, and he was desperate. Dad had been generous with his money and offered most of it to the Perfessor. The Perfessor took it and, in his words, "held it in trust" for my father and the team.

To complicate matters, he had no idea who my father was or where he lived. My father did not have a wallet or any identification on him. He tried to ask him questions, but my father was lost in a fantasy and made no sense. The Perfessor was also worried about someone finding out about the Attucks building and alerting the authorities. That would have been a disaster for the Perfessor's team, especially his son, Victor. He couldn't take a chance, and there would be time to figure out what to do about my father later.

Unfortunately, the Perfessor's emphysema flared up a few days after Dad arrived, and he had to admit himself into Cook County Hospital for treatment. He was very sick and had no choice. He was treated and then released after four days. But, because he was still weak, he was sent to a rehab center for three more weeks.

While the Perfessor was away, his son, Victor, Oscar Johnson, William Barclay and Rupert Bhang held the team together. With the help of my Dad's money, a food pantry in a local church and some panhandling at a nearby intersection, they managed to feed everyone while the Perfessor was in rehab.

Rupert Bhang, however, was a part-time drug pusher and, playing on Victor's and Dad's vulnerabilities, took advantage of them and sold Dad and Victor drugs. Rupert was a medical doctor who had lost his license about five years ago. Nevertheless, he was able to obtain drugs from a City medical health clinic in Englewood. Using one of his friends who worked there, he was able to filch drugs from the clinic and forge prescriptions that several unscrupulous drug stores were willing to fill.

He sold some of the drugs on the street, used some for himself and, without the Perfessor knowing, dispensed some to team members. The Perfessor had suspicions about what Rupert was doing; but, since he didn't know Rupert was selling to team members, he overlooked Rupert's business. Rupert also gave the Perfessor money from time to time to help support the team.

What the Perfessor was telling me explained many of the things in my father's journal. However, the stories about the Acme had me puzzled. I told the Perfessor what my father had written about the Acme and asked him if he could explain them.

The Perfessor, after a little thought, had a plausible explanation that satisfied me. About a month ago, a mother and three children joined the Perfessor's team and took up residence in one of the classrooms in the Attucks school. The mother (her name was Ellen Solice) was a cousin of Oscar Johnson. She had been evicted from her apartment when she couldn't pay the rent. She had lost her housekeeping job in a hotel on North Wabash when she became ill and couldn't work. She had the flu for a week and then pneumonia that lasted for almost three weeks. She was in Cook County Hospital for a week in July. Her grandmother (her mother was an addict who hadn't been seen in years) tried to care for the children and help her, but she fell and injured her leg and couldn't walk or take care of the kids.

Oscar was close to her and wanted to help her and her kids. The Perfessor was reluctant. Because it would be hard to control children, he had never taken in anyone with children before. They had to go to school and would want to go outside and play, which would bring attention to the school and would draw inquiring authorities.

The children were ages nine (Magetta), seven (Rogelio) and four (Pedro). Their father was from Mexico. He had been killed five years ago in Pillsen in a drive by shooting -- a case of mistaken identity. He had never been in a gang and had been a hard worker and a good father.

The kids were cute and precocious and loved Will. They had experienced little contact with white people and were very interested in him. They all had big eyes, light brown skin and large Afros. Pedro, the littlest one, and Rogelio wore their onesie pajamas most of the time, and Pedro carried around a well worn and well-loved Teddy Bear. Before they arrived, my father seldom left his box. He drank wine, used his tablet to read and watch movies and slept many hours. The kids motivated him to get out of his box and move around the school. They took him by the hand and lead him around. He told them stories and they pretended to travel around the world to various places. They all had good imaginations and enjoyed make-believe.

Ellen, their mother, had a bachelor's degree in Education from one of the City colleges and had been home schooling the children. She had taught first grade for two years before she had to quit when Magetta was born. She had worked at night at the hotel and taught and took care of the children during the day. Her grandmother watched them at night while Ellen was working.

It had been a good arrangement for several years, but fate, as is so often the case, intervened and destroyed their lives just as it nearly destroyed Dad's. Millions of poor people are in desperate circumstances because of health problems. Unfortunately, some greedy, mean spirited people assume that most poor people are poor and dependent because they are lazy and undeserving of help. Many of them forget that they had fortuitous breaks and assistance that helped them succeed and prosper.

Oscar's intervention gave Ellen and her family a chance to get back on their feet. Ellen planned to find another job and rent an apartment for them as soon as possible. Knowing that she couldn't stay at the Atticus school forever, she planned to move out in a few months.

As I said, the children were precocious and very talented. They sang and danced beautifully and entertained the team many evenings. The Perfessor told me that Will loved them and tried to dance with them on several occasions before he got too weak. They even wrote a rap song together. He had a name for their dancing, but the Perfessor couldn't remember what he called it. I asked him if the name "Rondolier" sounded familiar, and he said it did.

The Perfessor told me other things that explained most of my father's fantasies and delusions. He was living in a world of his imagination that he created to escape from his problems. I recently reread his short stories, and I found many of the parts of his delusions imbedded in them. He was probably also hallucinating at times due to his lack of sleep and poor eating habits.

I also found his writing notebook in his backpack. It was filled with ideas and plots for his future writings, many of which explain some of the things he had written about in his Journal. For example, he had always been interested in evolution and religion and had even contemplated becoming a Deacon at one time. Mom discouraged that, which was probably a good thing because he was way too busy at work to realistically have time for that. When I was working at their house after Mom's stroke, I found several books in his library about Darwin, genetics, and biology. From his short stories, it was obvious that he had a great interest in space travel. Many of the ideas about fusion and artificial intelligence were garnered from the research he had performed over the last few years. There were also notes about the Higgs Boson, dark matter and many of the other scientific theories my father had written about in his journal.

The old tablet my father had in his backpack, together with the wifi connection, explained CATO and several other things -- the movies, some of the space information, much of the scientific information.

Luckily, the Perfessor and his team accepted Dad and enabled and supported him. Because of the high principles and values of the Perfessor, they didn't take advantage of him or let him waste away and die. They supplied him with the food bars, water and, from time to time, a little wine. Since they didn't know who he was, they were reluctant to bring in outside help. Eventually, my father became weak and helpless and seemed to be in a downward spiral that could have been fatal. I'm sure, if I hadn't been lucky enough to meet the Perfessor, they would have found a way to obtain the medical help that he needed.

Chapter 33

Conclusion

Dr. Kerrigan eventually determined that Dad had suffered from severe PTSD (Posttraumatic Stress Disorder), hallucinations caused by lack of sleep and poor nutrition, and psychotic delusions. The trauma of the accident, his concussion, and the legal problems caused my father tremendous emotional distress.

We know now that he had experienced several flashbacks and many nightmares starting a few months after the accident. This led to his sleeping poorly and drinking too much wine to relax and forget the accident. The lawsuits and the threat of criminal charges caused even more stress and drove him into severe depression which, I learned, can cause a person to have visions and hear things that are not there. It also engenders a feeling of hopelessness which increases the psychotic delusions.

In addition to what Dr. Kerrigan told me, I've done some research on PTSD and psychotic delusions. PTSD occurs after a traumatic event. The accident, concussion and subsequent turmoil would certainly qualify as a traumatic event. Psychologists are not certain why PTSD occurs, but it appears that an over-reactive adrenaline response to trauma creates deep neurological patterns in the brain. This causes the brain to replay the trauma over and over again. If Dad had received some counseling soon after the accident, he probably would have been OK. Most people recover within a few months of trauma and recover normal brain functions. One thing that might have aggravated Dad's condition is the benzodiazepine that he took in the so-called "Fast Relief" that Dr. Bhang gave him. It's not recommended for treatment of PTSD and is known to aggravate the symptoms.

The psychotic depression which led to Dad's delusions was exacerbated by the deposition. When he had to testify at the deposition, it triggered his bad memories and deepened his depression. Usually, when people have psychotic depression their symptoms often involve beliefs, voices or visions telling them that they are worthless or evil. They may even hear voices telling them to harm themselves. Luckily, Dad's delusions were of a more positive form -- they helped him to escape. He did have some guilty feelings and blamed himself for all of Mom's anger and potential legal problems. If he had received more support, however, he might have been able to weather those stormy feelings, survive the whirlwind of problems the accident caused, and stabilize his life.

Three factors may have helped Dad. First of all, he didn't have a family history of depression. People with a family history of depression suffer worse symptoms and often hurt themselves or commit suicide. The second thing is the Perfessor's unknowing support. He may have done Dad a great favor by playing along with his delusions. They provided a positive escape for him and prevented him from doing worse things to himself. The third factor is the Solice children. Their love and attention most certainly helped him. Dad has always loved small children and knows how to talk to them and entertain them as they entertained him. His interaction with them gave him a positive outlet and kept him stable and centered.

Dad is doing much better now. It's been about a year since I found him, and he's almost back to normal. He and Mom are living together in an assisted living facility in our neighborhood. They have a small two-bedroom apartment and take all of their meals in a common dining room. It's only about five years old and is a beautiful, well-run facility. They know several other couples and a few widows who also live there.

Mom hasn't improved much, but she seems content. She won't take any therapy and is happy to ride in a wheelchair and do very little except watch television. Her left side is paralyzed, and she talks slowly and is hard to understand. She and Dad have a cordial and loving relationship, considering what they have been through. Dad dotes on her and couldn't be more attentive.

They take long walks in a beautiful, shady park across the street from the assisted living home where they live. Dad pushes Mom in her wheel chair and talks to her about things they did when they were young. During the summer, they watch little children play in a sprinkler and a pool. On the weekends they watch softball games played mostly by young men drinking beer with their girlfriends or wives and with little children running around and being yelled at by their moms. Some of the young men and women are children of people Mom and Dad know from the neighborhood.

Dad told me that he saw Larry O'Doul at one of the games last week. He was there to watch one of his sons play softball. Larry gave him a strange look and seemed to be uneasy about Dad's presence and looked away from him. Knowing O'Doul's reputation, that's hard to believe, but I don't think Dad was kidding or exaggerating. That's hard to explain.

Despite all he does, Dad still feels guilty about what happened and blames himself for Mom's stroke. Mom is happy to have him back, though, and never brings up the accident or what happened afterward.

I offered to tell her once about what happened to Dad when he disappeared, but she just shook her head, mumbled "no" over and over again and waved her hand indicating that she didn't want to know. I never broached the subject again.

Dad is still receiving counseling, but he's off the antidepressant drugs that he had to take for several months. Every once in awhile he mentions something about the Acme, but he usually catches himself, and we have a good laugh. After I made the first draft of this book, Dad read it and helped me with the plot and editing. At first, he was uncomfortable remembering all of the trauma and worry, but then he said it helped him understand and accept what happened.

Dad and I meet with the Perfessor almost every Tuesday morning at nine at the Java Hut. We buy him breakfast and give him some money for food for his team. Sadly, he's growing weaker and might have to move into a nursing home. He's worried about Victor, but Oscar has promised to take care of him when the time comes.

Ellen found another housekeeping job at a hotel in the Loop. She and her children are living in a nice CHA apartment on Roosevelt Road. Dad and I have visited them several times in their new apartment. They are always thrilled to see him.

The last time we visited them, the kids insisted on doing a Rondolier with Dad. He was a good sport and tried to dance with them. Without the help of Dr. Bhang's drugs, however, he wasn't able to keep up with them or enjoy it like he did when he was on Earthtoo. As we were leaving their apartment, Dad slipped Ellen a hundred dollar bill and told her that he would pay for a computer and all of the books she needed for their home schooling. She broke down and cried and gave him a big hug. It was heartwarming and made Dad happy.

I think that's a good way to finish this story. It has a relatively happy ending, thanks to some caring people and a little luck. I know this is elementary, but writing this helped Dad and me accept and understand what happened. Sometimes that's all we can ask for.

I have always wondered who could watch some of the inane, sophomoric day-time reality shows on television. Who would want to watch people fighting with each other over personal, hurtful things such as paternity or petty crimes? But I realize now that we all need to know that others are going through emotional and personal problems similar to ours. When we understand that others suffer the same problem, we are better able to survive and push ahead to overcome our own adversity. That is why we read, look at art, and watch movies. We want to learn that others also suffer similar problems, and that helps us to find ways to face our own misfortunes and survive.

Mental disorders such as PTSD, depression, autism, bipolar disorder, schizophrenia, and psychotic delusions are, for most people, only vague psychological concepts with which other people have to deal. There are still some skeptics who think these conditions are being faked and just ruses to avoid responsibility or work or military obligations. Fortunately, for those who suffer from these afflictions, medical science has proven that they are real syndromes caused by injuries or conditions in our brains, and that has led to acceptance and better treatments. These mental disorders are no longer considered to be moral defects or punishment for wrongs committed by the patient or his ancestors.

Living through a tragedy, as we did, is an enlightening experience that puts every aspect of our lives in perspective. The five months when Dad was missing were the most traumatic and emotional time of my life and the lives of everyone else in my family. They are burned into my consciousness forever and make me sensitive to people who are suffering mental distress from a trauma or some other cause. I can now identify with them and have empathy for their sufferings. Suffering makes us human.

In my back yard, I have a landscaped area surrounded by several large, round pink granite boulders. My landscaper calls them "Wisconsin Pinks." They never change and will be the same hundreds of years from now. They never suffer or face adversity of any type or make choices, but they also don't know what it is like to love or be loved. They never face adversity, but they never accomplish or learn anything. They never grow and have beautiful experiences. I don't think any human, no matter how bad his or her circumstances might be, would trade places with those boulders. I wouldn't. I'd rather be a human than an impervious stone, even if it means suffering and experiencing losses.

May your life be preserved from catastrophes, suffering, misfortune, and turmoil; but, if it isn't, may you have loving people to help you through it. No matter how careful and smart we are, we cannot make our lives free of all adversities. Even the wealthiest and most gifted people experience them. What we can do, though, is turn adversities into opportunities for love and kindness and forgiveness. That is what makes us human and alive and brings peace, happiness, and, most importantly, acceptance. We will probably never understand why bad things happen to good people, but we do know that love and understanding can make bad things good.

Live well!

Acknowledgments

First of all, I should reveal that this book is a tribute to the first science fiction story I ever experienced. As I remember it, it was a television drama (maybe the *Kraft Theater*) about a man who could travel into space in his mind. Eventually, he is told that he was just having an escapist delusion. However, at the end of the show, a commentator leaves the door open to the idea that maybe the protagonist was a space traveler. I was only about ten years old, and I remember watching it by myself in my darkened living room on our first small grainy television set. I was immediately hooked on science fiction and read hundreds of books of that genre thereafter.

The story of the accident is based loosely upon one of the first cases I ever handled as an attorney. I was assigned to interview an older man being defended by my law firm. He had caused a serious accident in which a young woman was injured. His wife came with him and cried through most of the interview. They were deeply worried about the financial effects the lawsuit might have on their lives. Unfortunately for them, they had a small liability insurance policy and their other assets were in jeopardy. I never forgot that interview and the worry those two people suffered.

Another influence on my writing is my love of reading about the human brain, evolution, psychology, genetics and anthropology. I don't pretend to be a scholar in any of these disciplines and have certainly not performed any primary scientific research. All my knowledge is second hand and, admittedly, not comprehensive.

Nevertheless, I have not let that stop me from incorporating many theories and findings into my writing. It is fun and intellectually stimulating. Conveniently, there are so many theories and ideas in those fields that almost anything I write about could be plausible or supported by some expert. Listed below are the principle sources that I drew upon in writing this book. Frankly, I never thought I would finish it, so I did not keep careful notes on my sources. I read a few of these books before I started this novel and most while I was writing it. They inspired me and shaped many of my ideas. Again, because I was very casual about what I was doing, I am not certain what sections can be attributed to which books. I ask for forgiveness and tolerance for this oversight.

I know that some of the scientific information that I used is not accurate and confused and even wrong. This is intentional in some cases and fitting with the story being told. Will was suffering from delusions, was taking drugs, was slowly starving, and would have been confused and inaccurate as he dictated his journal. Additionally, he was relying upon his notebook which he used for his science fiction stories and which, like anyone's casual note taking, would have been inaccurate, incomplete and confusing.

I also relied heavily upon Wikipedia. It is a great resource and never let me down when I wanted to do some quick research on an idea. If I ever make any money on this book, I intend to make a substantial donation to Wikipedia to help it continue its mission.

I found other articles on the Web that I may have used for ideas and to which I am unable to give proper attribution. Writers today can easily research an idea, an historical event, or a miscellaneous fact simply by Googling a key word. How fortunate we are to have it and other similar research tools available to us! Our lives are so much easier as a result. In the past, authors would have had to spend hours in a library or pay someone to perform their research. Some of my friends read drafts of this book as I was writing it, and I want to acknowledge their help: Dave Coghlan, Neil McPhee, Rollin Dix, Mike Moline, Tom Bever, Randy Papp, Don Alving, Sudie Pyser, and Larry Daker. They gave me good ideas and helpful critiques. Dave Coghlan, Sudie Pyser and Brother Hank Hammer were especially helpful with proofreading.

Finally, I should acknowledge my wife, Sheila, who allowed me to hog the computer and spend countless hours working on this book in my basement lair, which is not unlike Will's. Being a retired English teacher, she was also an occasional source for grammar and style advice.

Sources and Influences

- *Behave,* by Robert M Sapolsky
- *DNA, The Secret of Life* by James Watson
- *The Gene,* by Siddhartha Mukherjee.
- *The Future of the Mind* by Michio Kaku.
- *Proof of Heaven,* by Eben Alexander, M.D.
- *Sapiens, A Brief History of Humankind,* by Yuval Noah Harari
- *A Brief History of Time,* by Stephen Hawking.
- *Erasing Death,* by Sam Parnia, M.D.
- *Incognito, The Secret Lives of the Brain,* by David Eagleman
- *Psychotic Depression: Losing Touch With Reality* By Chris Iliades, M.D., Medically Reviewed by Niya *Jones, M.D., NPH.*
- *Astrophysics for People in a Hurry, by Neil DeGrasse Tyson*
- *Are You a Risk Taker?* By Marvin Zukerman, *Psychology Today,* November 1, 2000
- *Undeniable* By Bill Nye

Leave It All Behind

Book Club Discussion Topics and Questions

(**Spoiler Alert!** Do not read these questions or discussion topics if you have not read the book. They reveal key information that may spoil your reading experience.)

1. Will O'Brien and his son Owen narrate a story about the consequences of an automobile accident and how it affected their family. One of the themes of *Leave It All Behind (LIAB)* is the human challenge of facing and overcoming adversity. Adversity takes many forms and has different consequences for each human being and his or her loved ones. The way we handle adversity depends on many factors, and each person will react in a different way. Our education, our family experiences, our religion, our ethnicity, our genetics, our gender, and our community all influence our behavior and the way we handle and respond to adversity. How did Will handle the adversity that affected him and his family after the accident? What were some of the influences on Will, Deirdre, and Owen that affected the way they handled their adversity? Were they good or bad influences? What did Will and his family learn from it?

2. Will's brief dalliance with Bonnie in a bar is the inflection point for all of his problems. Did he do anything wrong? Was it a serious moral breach? Was he unfaithful to Deirdre? What should he have done? What did you think of Bonnie and her character?

3. Will and Deirdre live in an old, established community with a well defined culture and social network. What effect did it have on Will and Deirdre and the direction of the story? Which is better: an impersonal, loosely organized community or one that is close-nit, interactive and personal?

4. Psychology is an underlying thematic element in
LIAB. Owen describes himself as an amateur
psychologist and describes how it has helped him in his
business. He describes his father as a mid-spectrum risk
taker. Do you agree with that? What happens in the
book that reveals what type of a risk taker Will is? Does
the modern understanding of psychology undermine the
mystery of human stories? Does it take away from
spiritual notions and traditions?

5. The question of human development (or evolution) is
another underlying thematic element in the novel. Will
is confronted with the question of whether or not
humans are improving or becoming worse. What do
you think? Is the human race evolving into a better
species, more cooperative, more peaceful, more law
abiding, and more respectful of differences? Would
advanced aliens be more likely to be peace loving or
violent? Are the Acme believable? If they represent the
future, do you think that is a good future? Which is
better, individuality or unity? What is there in Will's
character that makes him imagine the Acme and their
way of life?

6. Even though Will says he likes simple, narrative
stories, he unwittingly uses several literary devices to
tell his story. Authors use literary devices to develop
their themes, characters, and mood. Discuss how the
following devices lend texture, character and depth to
LIAB:

> Motifs are recurring images, language, feelings,
> structural devices and other elements. Some of
> the motifs used in this book are the journal, the

blue vehicles, the whirlwind, science and writing. Are there others? How does each motif lend texture, feelings and depth to the novel?

Foreshadowing and allusion are devices that give the reader hints as to what might be happening. A foreshadowing hints at what might happen in the future. Allusions are used to hint at what something might mean by making a comparison to another thing or event that adds richness and depth. What are some examples of foreshadowing and allusion in the novel? Are they ominous or positive?

Dramatic tension keeps a reader hooked on a story and drives it forward and makes it interesting. What are some of the dramatic tensions in the novel? What questions were planted in your mind as you read the book? Did they make you want to keep reading to find out what was going to happen?

Symbolism is the use of images to develop or express ideas. Does the author use symbols and what ideas might they represent? How do they drive the story and underlying themes?

7. Names and naming are recurring elements in the novel. Will and the Professor have a knack for names and the naming process. Discuss the names and what they lend to the story: Will, Deidre, Owen, The Professor, CATO, The Nina, The Steed, Meaam, Guio, Sophos, Ultgueres, Zellen, Puero, Magis, and Inquis.

8. The AASUSE Team plays an important role in the novel. Are they believable? Does the complex scientific information about space travel hurt or advance the story? Why did Will imagine this part of the story and did his background explain his imagining the AASUSE Team and its mission? Did the Professor help or hurt Will?

9. Discuss Will's rescue, his rehabilitation, and his future with Deirdre. Was he cured? Do you think he will have a relapse?

10. Escapist literature is a popular genre. Humans have an inherent need to escape from their problems and dull, unexciting lives. Science fiction is an obvious form of escapism. Is *LIAB* a science fiction novel? Strictly speaking, *LIAB* is not escapist literature, but Will is writing an escape story for himself. Is escapist literature a high or low form of writing? Do you have escapist fantasies? Are they productive or detrimental to your mental health? Did you realize that Will was having a psychotic delusion? What clues led you to that belief?

11. Even though the story of the Acme was a delusion, if you were Will, and if you were really on Earthtoo, would you have stayed or returned to Earth?

12. Do you think that Meaam, the AI computer that conquered Earthtoo, is evil, or do you agree with Sophos that Meaam was not evil because it was simply protecting itself. What is evil? Can a nonhuman creature be evil?

ABOUT THE AUTHOR

The author, Michael (Mike) Sise, lives in the Beverly neighborhood on the southwest side of Chicago with Sheila, his lovely wife of 52 years. He has three sons and ten fabulous grandchildren. Mike is a retired attorney and former high school English teacher. He plays golf and tennis with a bunch of old men, writes things and makes digital paintings.

This is his first book, and he has others in the works. If you would like to send comments or questions to him, contact him at mjsise@cs.com.